ORCSLAYER

THE ADVENTURES OF dwarf Slayer Gotrek Gurnisson and his human companion, Felix Jaeger, continue in the eighth installment in the classic Warhammer fantasy series!

Honouring an ancient pledge, Gotrek & Felix help a dwarf prince reclaim his hold from savage greenskin invaders who have overrun it. But the intrepid heroes find more than they bargain for as they journey into the cold depths of the mountains.

A WARHAMMER NOVEL

Gotrek and Felix

ORCSLAYER

Nathan Long

To William King

A BLACK LIBRARY PUBLICATION

First published in Great Britain in 2006 by
BL Publishing,
Games Workshop Ltd.,
Willow Road, Nottingham,
NG7 2WS, UK

10 9 8 7 6 5 4 3 2 1

Cover illustration by Geoff Taylor,
Map by Nuala Kennedy.

A CIP record for this book is available from the British Library.

ISBN 13: 978 1 84416 391 5
ISBN 10: 1 84416 391 1

Distributed in the US by Simon & Schuster
1230 Avenue of the Americas, New York, NY 10020, US.

Printed and bound in Great Britain by
Bookmarque, Surrey, UK.

See the Black Library on the Internet at
www.blacklibrary.com

Find out more about Games Workshop
and the world of Warhammer at
www.games-workshop.com

THIS IS A DARK age, a bloody age, an age of daemons and of sorcery. It is an age of battle and death, and of the world's ending. Amidst all of the fire, flame and fury it is a time, too, of mighty heroes, of bold deeds and great courage.

AT THE HEART of the Old World sprawls the Empire, the largest and most powerful of the human realms. Known for its engineers, sorcerers, traders and soldiers, it is a land of great mountains, mighty rivers, dark forests and vast cities. And from his throne in Altdorf reigns the Emperor Karl-Franz, sacred descendant of the founder of these lands, Sigmar, and wielder of his magical warhammer.

BUT THESE ARE far from civilised times. Across the length and breadth of the Old World, from the knightly palaces of Bretonnia to ice-bound Kislev in the far north, come rumblings of war. In the towering World's Edge Mountains, the orc tribes are gathering for another assault. Bandits and renegades harry the wild southern lands of the Border Princes. There are rumours of rat-things, the skaven, emerging from the sewers and swamps across the land. And from the northern wildernesses there is the ever-present threat of Chaos, of daemons and beastmen corrupted by the foul powers of the Dark Gods. As the time of battle draws ever near, the Empire needs heroes like never before.

Nuln.

The Moot.

Grey Mountains.

Averheim.

rey
rest

Karak
Norn.

Black r

The
Vaults

Border Princes.

Ba
Va

Bac

To The land of
Go Not Ye This

Karak Kadrin.

Sylvania.

Dracken
-hof.

Zhufbar.

Black
Water.

fire Pass.

tains.

Silve

Karaz-a-
Karak.

mad dog Pass.

nds

Dead,
ay...

'At long last we were sailing home. After nearly two decades following the Slayer as he chased his doom east and south and east again, through Araby, Ind and Cathay, I was returning with him to the Old World and the lands of our birth. Years had I longed for this day, but when it came, it was not to bring either of us the joy or peace we hoped it would. Instead, we found terror and strife waiting for us the moment our feet touched land. My companion met an old friend, and was asked to honour an old oath; little knowing what horror and bloodshed would come of these things.

Before the nightmare came to its bitter, bloody end, I saw the Slayer happier than I had ever known him to be, but also more miserable. It was a strange time, and it is with great reluctance that I stir those sad memories in order to record them here.'

— From *My Travels With Gotrek*, Vol VII, by Herr Felix Jaeger (Altdorf Press, 2527)

ONE

'ORCS?' GOTREK SHRUGGED. 'I've fought enough orcs.'

Felix peered at the Slayer in the gloom of the merchant ship's cramped forward cabin. The thick-muscled dwarf sat on a bench, his flame-bearded chin sunk to his chest, an immense stein of ale in one massive fist, and a broached half-keg at his side. The only illumination came from a small porthole – a rippling, sea-sick-green reflection from the waves outside.

'But they've blockaded Barak Varr,' said Felix. 'We won't be able to dock. You want to get to Barak Varr, don't you? You want to walk on dry land again?' Felix wanted to dock, that was for certain. Two months in this seagoing coffin where even the dwarf had to duck his head below decks had driven him stir-crazy.

'I don't know what I want,' rumbled Gotrek, 'except another drink.'

He took another drink.

Felix scowled. 'Fair enough. If I live, I will write in the grand epic poem of your death that you drowned heroically below decks, drunk as a halfling on harvest day, while your comrades fought and died above you.'

Gotrek slowly raised his head and fixed Felix with his single glittering eye. After a long moment where Felix thought the Slayer might leap across the cabin and rip his throat out with his bare hands, Gotrek grunted. 'You've a way with words, manling.'

He put down his stein and picked up his axe.

BARAK VARR WAS a dwarf port built inside a towering cliff at the easternmost end of the Black Gulf, a curving talon of water that cut deeply into the lawless badlands south of the Black Mountains and the Empire. Both the harbour and the city were tucked into a cave so high that the tallest warship could sail under its roof and dock at its teeming wharves. The entrance was flanked by fifty-foot statues of dwarf warriors standing in massive stone ship prows. A squat, sturdy lighthouse sat at the end of a stone spit to their right, the flame of which, it was said, could be seen for twenty leagues.

Felix could see almost none of this architectural wonder, however, for a boat-borne horde of orcs floated between him and Barak Varr's wide, shadowed entrance, and a thicket of patched sails, masts, crude banners and strung-up corpses blocked his view. The line looked impenetrable, a floating barricade of captured and lashed-together warships, merchantmen, rafts, barges and galleys that stretched for nearly a mile in a curving arc before the port. Smoke from cooking fires rose from many of the decks, and the water

around them bobbed with bloated corpses and floating garbage.

'You see?' said Captain Doucette, an extravagantly
moustachioed Bretonnian trader from whom Gotrek
and Felix had caught a ride in Tilea. 'Look like they
build from every prize and warship that try to pass;
and I must land. I have to sell a hold full of Ind spices
here, and pick up dwarf steel for Bretonnia. If no, the
trip will make a loss.'

'Is there some place you can break through?' asked
Felix, his long blond hair and his red Sudenland cloak
whipping about in the blustery summer wind. 'Will
the ship take it?'

'Oh, oui,' said Doucette. 'She is strong, the *Reine
Celeste*. We fight off many pirates, smash little boats in
our way. Trading is not easy life, no? But… orcs?'

'Don't worry about the orcs,' said Gotrek.

Doucette turned and looked Gotrek from bristling
crimson crest, to leather eye-patch, to sturdy boots and
back again. 'Forgive me, my friend. I do not doubt you
are very formidable. The arms like trunks of the trees,
yes? The chest like the bull, but you are only one man
– er, dwarf.'

'One *Slayer*,' growled Gotrek. 'Now fill your sails and
get on. I've a keg to finish.'

Doucette cast a pleading look at Felix.

Felix shrugged. 'I've followed him through worse.'

'Captain!' a lookout called from the crow's-nest.
'More ships behind us!'

Doucette, Gotrek and Felix turned and looked over
the stern rail. Two small cutters and a Tilean warship
were angling out of a small cove and racing towards
them, sails fat with wind. All the fancy woodwork had

been stripped from them, replaced with rams, catapults and trebuchets. The head of the beautiful,
bare-breasted figurehead on the warship's prow had
been replaced with a troll's skull, and rotting corpses
dangled by their necks from its bowsprit. Orcs stood
along the rail, bellowing guttural war cries. Goblins
capered and screeched all around them.

Doucette hissed through his teeth. 'They make the
trap, no? Pinch like the crayfish. Now we have no
choice.' He turned and scanned the floating barrier,
and then pointed, shouting to his pilot. 'Two points
starboard, Luque. At the rafts! Feruzzi! Clap on all
sail!'

Felix followed Doucette's gaze as the steersman
turned the wheel and the mate sent the waisters up
the shrouds to unfurl more canvas. Four ramshackle
rafts, piled with looted barrels and crates, were
lashed loosely together between a battered Empire
man-o'-war and a half-charred Estalian galley. Both
of the ships were alive with orcs and goblins, hoot-
ing and waving their weapons at Doucette's trader.

The merchantman's sails cracked like pistols as they
filled with wind, and it picked up speed.

'Battle stations!' called Doucette. 'Prepare to receive
boarders! 'Ware the grapnels!'

Greenskins large and small were pouring over the
sides of the man-o'-war and the galley, and running
across the rafts towards the point where the merchantman meant to break through. True to the captain's
warning, half of them swung hooks and grapnels
above their heads.

Felix looked back. The cutters and the warship were
gaining. If the merchantman made it through the

blockade it might outrun the pursuers, but if it were caught...

'By the Lady, no!' gasped Doucette suddenly.

Felix turned. All along the raft-bound man-o'-war, black cannon muzzles were pushing out of square-cut ports.

'We will be blown to pieces,' said Doucette.

'But... but they're orcs,' said Felix. 'Orcs can't aim to save their lives.'

Doucette shrugged. 'At such a range, do they need to aim?'

Felix looked around, desperate. 'Well, can you blow them up? Shoot them before they shoot us?'

'You joke, mon ami,' laughed Doucette. He pointed to the few catapults that were the merchantman's only artillery. 'These will do little against Empire oak.'

They were rapidly approaching the blockade. It was too late to attempt to turn aside. Felix could smell the greenskins, a filthy animal smell, mixed with the stink of garbage, offal and death. He could see the earrings glinting in their tattered ears and make out the crude insignia painted on their shields and ragged armour.

'Throw me at it,' said Gotrek.

Felix and Doucette looked at him. The dwarf had a mad gleam in his eye.

'What?' asked Doucette. 'Throw you?'

'Put me in one of your rock lobbers and cut the cord. I'll deal with these floating filth.'

'You... you want me to catapult you?' asked Doucette, incredulous. 'Like the bomb?'

'The grobi do it. Anything a goblin can do, a dwarf can do, better.'

'But, Gotrek, you might...' said Felix.

Gotrek raised an eyebrow. 'What?'

'Er, nothing, never mind.' Felix had been about to say that Gotrek might get himself killed, but that was, after all, the point, wasn't it?

Gotrek crossed to one of the catapults and climbed onto the bucket. He looked like a particularly ugly bulldog sitting on a serving ladle. 'Just make sure you put me over the rail, not into the side.'

'We will try, master dwarf,' said the chief of the catapult's crew. 'Er, you will not kill us if you die?'

'I'll kill you if you don't start shooting!' growled Gotrek. 'Fire!'

'Oui, oui.'

The crew angled the gun around, huffing at Gotrek's extra weight, until it faced the man-o'-war, and then cranked the firing arm a little tighter.

'Hold onto your axe, master dwarf,' said the crew chief.

'Perhaps a helmet,' said Felix. 'Or a... '

The crew chief dropped his hand. 'Fire!'

A crewman pulled a lever and the catapult's arm shot up and out. Gotrek flew through the air in a long high arc, straight for the man-o'-war, bellowing a bull-throated battle cry.

Felix stared blankly as Gotrek flattened against the patched canvas of the man-o'-war's mainsail and slid down to the deck into a seething swarm of orcs. 'The real question,' he said to no one in particular, 'is how I'm going to make it all rhyme.'

He and the catapult's crew craned their necks, trying to find Gotrek in the chaos, but all they could see was a swirl of hulking green bodies and the rise and fall of enormous black-iron cleavers. At least they're not stopping, Felix thought. If they were still fighting, then Gotrek was still alive.

Then the orcs stopped fighting, and instead began running to and fro.

'Is he...?' asked Doucette.

'I don't know,' said Felix, biting his lip. After all the dragons, daemons and trolls Gotrek had fought, would he really die facing mere orcs?

The lookout's voice boomed down from above. 'Impact coming!'

With a jarring crunch, the merchantman crashed into the line of rafts, smashing timber, snapping cord, and sending barrels and crates and over-enthusiastic orcs flying into the cold, choppy water. The side of the man-o'-war rose like a castle wall directly to their right, her cannon ports level with Doucette's deck.

Grapnels whistled through the air to the left and right, and Felix ducked just in time to miss getting hooked through the shoulder. They bit into the rail and the deck and the sails, their ropes thrumming tight as the ship continued forwards. The *Reine Celeste*'s crew chopped at them with hatchets and cutlasses, but two more caught for each one they cut.

A thunderous boom went off in Felix's right ear, and one of the man-o'-war's cannon, not fifteen feet away, was obscured in white smoke. A cannonball whooshed by at head level and parted a ratline.

Felix swallowed. It looked like Gotrek had failed.

'Boarders!' came Doucette's voice.

The merchant ship had broken through the orc line and was inside the blockade, but was slowing sharply, towing the grapnel-hooked rafts and the rest of the ships with it. The man-o'-war was turning as it was pulled, and its guns remained trained on Doucette's ship as waves of roaring green monsters climbed up the lines and the sides and clambered over the rail. Felix drew his dragon-hilted sword and joined the others as they raced to hold them off – men of every colour and land stabbing, hacking and shooting at the age-old enemy of humanity – Tileans in stocking caps and baggy trousers, Bretonnians in striped pantaloons, men of Araby, Ind and further places, all fighting with the crazed desperation of fear.

There was no retreat, and surrender meant an orc stew-pot. Felix sidestepped a cleaver-blow that would have halved him had it connected, and ran his towering opponent through the neck. Two goblins attacked his flanks. He killed one and kicked the other back. Another orc surged up in front of him.

Felix was no longer the willowy young poet he had been when, during a night of drunken camaraderie, he had pledged to record Gotrek's doom in an epic poem. Decades of fighting at the Slayer's side had hardened him and filled him out, and made a seasoned swordsman of him. Even so, he was no match – physically at least – for the seven-foot monster he faced. The beast was more than twice his weight, with arms thicker than Felix's legs, and an underslung jaw from which jutted up cracked tusks. It stank like the back end of a pig.

Its mad red eyes blazed with fury as it roared and swung a black iron cleaver. Felix ducked and slashed back, but the orc was quick, and knocked his sword aside. There was another boom and a cannonball punched through the rail ten feet to Felix's left, cutting a swath through the melee that killed both merchants and orcs alike. Red blood and black mixed on the slippery deck. Felix deflected a swipe from the orc that shivered his arm to the shoulder. The catapult's crew chief fell back in two pieces beside him.

Another series of booms rocked the ship, and Felix thought the orcs had somehow got off a disciplined salvo. He glanced past his orc to the man-o'-war. Smoke poured from the cannon ports but, strangely, no cannonballs. The orc slashed at him. Felix hopped back and tripped over the crew chief's torso. He landed flat on his back in a puddle of blood.

The orc guffawed and raised his cleaver over his head.

With a massive *ka-rump* the man-o'-war exploded into a billowing ball of flame, bits of timber and rope and orc parts spinning past. The fighters on the deck of the merchantman were blown off their feet by a hammer of air. Felix felt as if his eardrums had been stabbed with spikes. The orc above him staggered and looked down at his chest, surprised. A cannon's cleaning rod was sticking out from between his ribs, the bristly head dripping with gore. It toppled forwards.

Felix rolled out of the way and sprang to his feet, looking towards the flame-enveloped man-o'-war. So Gotrek had done it after all. But at what cost? Surely there was no way the dwarf could have survived?

Out of the boiling fireball toppled the man-o'-war's mainmast, crashing towards the merchantman's deck like a felled tree – and racing out across it, half climbing, half running, was a broad, compact figure, face and skin as black as iron, red crest and beard smouldering and singed. The top of the mast smashed down through the merchantman's rail and pulverised a knot of goblins that was just climbing over. With a wild roar, Gotrek leapt from this makeshift bridge into the merchantman's waist, right in the middle of the crowd of orcs that was pushing Doucette's crew back towards the sterncastle with heavy losses.

The Slayer spun as he landed, axe outstretched, and a dozen orcs and goblins went down at once, spines and legs and necks severed. Their companions turned to face him, and seven more went down. Heartened, the merchant crew pressed forwards, attacking the confused orcs. Unfortunately, more were running across the rafts, and the merchantman was still caught in a net of grapnels, and pinned in place by the fallen mast.

Felix leapt the forecastle rail, yelling to Doucette as he plunged into the circle of orcs and goblins towards Gotrek. 'Cut the lines and clear the mast! Forget the orcs!'

Doucette hesitated, then nodded. He screamed at his crew in four languages and they fell back, chopping at the remaining ropes and heaving together to push the man-o'-war's mast off their starboard rail, while the greenskins pressed in to take down the crazed Slayer.

Felix took up his accustomed position, behind, and slightly to the left of Gotrek, just far enough away to be clear of the sweep of his axe, but close enough to protect his back and flanks.

The orcs were frightened, and showed it by trying desperately to kill the object of their fear. But the harder they tried, the faster they died, getting in each other's way in their eagerness, forgetting Felix until he had run them through the kidneys, fighting each other for the chance to kill Gotrek. The deck under the dwarf's feet was slick with black blood, and orc and goblin bodies were piled higher than his chest.

Gotrek caught Felix's eye as he bifurcated an orc, top-knot to groin. 'Not a bad little scrap, eh, manling?'

'Thought you'd died at last,' said Felix, ducking a cutlass.

Gotrek snorted as he gutted another orc. 'Not likely. Stupid orcs had all the powder up on the gun deck. I cut some ugly greenskin's head off and stuck it in a cook fire until it caught.' He barked a sharp laugh as he decapitated two goblins. 'Then bowled it down the gun-line like I was playing ninepins. That did it!'

With a screeching and snapping of rending timbers, the merchantman's crew finally pushed the man-o'-war's mainmast clear of the rail. Grapnel lines parted with twangs like a loosed bow's as the *Reine Celeste* surged forwards, straightening out before the wind.

The crew cheered and turned to fight the last few orcs. It was over in seconds. Felix and the others wiped their blades and looked back just in time to see the three orc pursuit ships smash together as they all tried to shoot the gap through the blockade at once. Roars of fury rose from them, and the three crews began to hack at each other while their boats became inextricably fouled in the mess of rafts, ropes and floating debris.

Next to the three-ship squabble, the remains of the burning man-o'-war sank slowly into the gulf under a towering plume of black smoke. Orcs from further along the line were hastily cutting it free so it didn't pull anything else down with it.

Captain Doucette stepped up to Gotrek and bowed low before him. He had a deep gash on his forearm. 'Master dwarf, we owe you our lives. You have saved us and our cargo from certain destruction.'

Gotrek shrugged. 'Only orcs.'

'None-the-less, we are extremely grateful. If there is anything we may do to repay you, you have only to name it.'

'Hrmm,' said Gotrek, stroking his still smouldering beard. 'You can get me another keg of beer. I've nearly finished the one I left below.'

IT WAS A tense twenty minutes, sailing into the harbour from the blockade, the crew warily watching the rafts and rowboats of orcs that chased after them from the floating barricade until they at last gave up and fell behind. As the *Reine Celeste* got closer to Barak Varr's cavernous opening, they had to pick their way through a litter of wrecked orc ships half-sunk around the sea wall. Signals flew from the lighthouse, which Captain Doucette answered speedily. Grim-faced dwarf cannon crews watched them from fortified emplacements below it. Dwarf masons were at work on the lighthouse itself, repairing a great hole blasted in its side.

Felix gazed in wonder as the *Reine Celeste* sailed between the two statues and into the shadow of the harbour cavern, staggered by the beauty and immense proportions of the place. The cave was so wide and so deep that he could not see the walls.

Hundreds of thick chains hung down from the darkness of the roof. At the end of each was an octagonal lantern the size of a nobleman's carriage, which provided an even yellow light that allowed ships to find their way to the docks.

The harbour filled the front half of the cave, a wide, curving frontage from which the branching stone fingers of quays and wharves extended. They were laid out with typical dwarfish precision, evenly spaced and perfectly positioned, to make manoeuvring in and out of the slips as easy as possible for the ships that docked there. There were thirty ships berthed there now, and room for at least fifty more.

A city of stone rose beyond the harbour. It was strange for Felix, who had visited more dwarf holds than most humans, to see such human structures as houses and mercantile buildings arranged along broad avenues under the shadow-hidden roof of the cave, but the dwarfs had made these surface-world forms their own. Never had Felix seen squatter, more massively built houses, all steel grey granite and decorated to the roof peaks with intricate geometric dwarf ornamentation. Even the smallest looked as if it could withstand a cannon-blast.

As they approached the embankment, a tiny dwarf steam ship, little more than a dinghy with a furnace, puffed out to them, and then guided them to an empty slip. A cheer erupted from the dock as the crew threw out their lines and extended the gangplank. There was a crowd of nearly a hundred on hand to welcome Captain Doucette and his crew as they stepped off the ship. Most were dwarfs, but there were a fair number of men as well.

The harbourmaster, a fat dwarf in slashed doublet and breeches, stumped forwards amid the general hubbub of congratulation and greeting. 'Welcome, captain, and twice welcome. You are the first ship to dock here in three weeks, since the accursed orcs set their barricade. A great deed, sir.'

Doucette turned to Gotrek. 'This one do the deed, sir. He blow up the man-o'-war with the single hand, hien?'

'Then we are indebted to you, Slayer,' said the harbourmaster, bowing low. Then, without further ado, he took out his ledger and got to business. 'Now, sir, what do you carry?' He licked his lips eagerly.

'I bring cinnamon and other spices from Ind,' said Doucette grandly, 'and oil of palm, patterned rugs of Araby, and little lace caps for the ladies. Very pretty, yes?'

The harbourmaster's smile crumpled, and many in the crowd fell silent. 'Spices? All you have is spices?'

'And rugs and caps.'

'Spices,' grunted the harbourmaster. 'What good are spices when we have no meat? You can't make a meal of pepper and salt.'

'Monsieur, I...'

'The orcs have been blocking the harbour for three weeks?' interrupted Gotrek. 'What ails you? Why haven't you blasted them out of the water?'

A dwarf sailor with his beard and hair in tarred braids spoke up before the harbourmaster could reply. 'Grungni-cursed greenskins got lucky and sank one of our ironclads, and the other is transporting dwarfs to the war in the north.'

'It's true,' said the harbourmaster. 'With so many gone to aid the Empire, we've barely enough dwarfs and ships to keep the orcs from entering the harbour, let alone chase them away. They infest the landside entrance as well. We're besieged land and sea.'

Gotrek and Felix glanced at each other.

'War?' asked Gotrek. 'What war?'

'You don't know of the war?' asked the harbourmaster. 'Where have you been?'

'Ind and Araby,' spat Gotrek, 'chasing our tails.'

'You say this war is in the Empire?' asked Felix.

'Aye,' said the sailor. 'The Chaos hordes coming south again: usual madness. Some "chosen one" and his lads making a try for the world. A lot of holds sent dwarfs north to help turn them back. Our ships carried many of them.'

'Chaos,' said Gotrek, his one eye shining. 'Now there's a challenge.'

'It were better if we left men's troubles to men,' said the harbourmaster bitterly. 'The orcs have taken advantage of the clans being away and are rising all over the Badlands. Many small holds and human towns have been put to fire and sword. Even Karak Hirn is lost. The other holds have buttoned themselves up tight until they're at full strength again.'

'But how goes the war?' asked Felix. 'Does the Empire still stand? Have they reached... Nuln?'

'The harbourmaster shrugged. 'Who can say? The overland caravans stopped coming more than a month ago, and every ship that docked before the orcs strung their rafts across our mouth had a different story. One said Middenheim had fallen, another that Altdorf was in flames. The next said the hordes had been pushed back to the Wastes and never got further than Praag. It might already be over for all we know. Grimnir make it so. These orcs must be put down or we shall starve.'

Gotrek and Felix turned back to Captain Doucette.

'Take us out of here,' said Gotrek. 'We must get north.'

'Yes,' said Felix. 'I must get to Nuln. I must see if it still exists.'

Doucette blinked. 'But... but, my friends, it is impossible. We must make the repairs, no? And I must take on water and supplies, and cargo. It will take a week at least.' He gestured to the entrance of the harbour, glowing orange in the late afternoon sun. 'And what of the green ones? Will we make the escape the way we make the entrance? It may not be so easy, eh?'

'Damn your excuses,' said Gotrek. 'I've a doom waiting for me. Let's go.'

Doucette shrugged. 'My friend, I cannot. Not for a week. It is impossible.'

Gotrek glared at him, and Felix was afraid he was going to grab the captain by the scruff of the neck and drag him back on board, but at last the Slayer cursed and turned away.

'Where's Makaisson when you need him?' he growled.

'Forgive me, harbourmaster,' said Felix, bowing, 'but can you tell me where we can find lodgings for a week?'

The harbourmaster barked a laugh. 'Good luck. The city is filled to bursting with refugees from every hold and human town in the Badlands. There isn't a bed to let at any price, and not much food either, but you've cinnamon to dine on, so you'll make out all right.'

Gotrek balled his fists as the crowd laughed. For once Felix was in a like mood. He wanted to punch everyone within reach in the nose. This was maddening. He had to get north. He had to learn what had become of his family – his father, his brother Otto. He didn't want to stay in some out of the way port while his home, his country, was ravaged by bloodthirsty barbarians. He had seen what the hordes had done to the lands of Kislev. That the same thing might be happening in the Empire – in the Reikland and Averland

– while he was far away and powerless to stop it, was almost more than he could bear.

'Come, manling,' said Gotrek at last, turning towards the city and hefting his axe. 'Let's go make some empty beds.'

CHAPTER TWO

THE HARBOURMASTER'S prediction proved true. Gotrek
and Felix visited thirteen taverns and not one had a
bed to spare. Most had rented out their stables and
haylofts to desperate refugees as well. Others had been
taken over by the city as barracks and hospitals for the
dwarfs and men who defended the city against the orcs
in the harbour and on the walls of the dwarf fort that
protected the port's landside entrance. Even the bawdy
houses in the human quarter were taking in boarders,
and making their girls ply their trade in downstairs
parlours and alcoves.

Barak Varr's lantern-lit underground streets were
crowded with dwarfs and men of every description,
traders, sailors, merchants, gaunt farmers with their
families in tow and their belongings on their backs,
angry men-at-arms talking of retaking their castles or
exacting vengeance on the orcs, lost children crying for

their mothers, the sick and the maimed and the dying moaning and ignored in alleys and dark corners.

The long-time residents of Barak Varr – both dwarf and human – who had three weeks ago welcomed the refugees with open arms, were now glaring at them behind their backs, their patience stretched to breaking point. Supplies of food and ale were dwindling rapidly, and with the orc blockade in place, there was little possibility of more supplies coming soon. Felix heard voices raised in complaint and argument on every street they turned down.

By the fourteenth tavern, the Sea Chest, Gotrek gave up and ordered an ale.

'Enough drinks, it won't matter where I sleep,' he said with a shrug.

Felix was not so easy about accommodations, but he needed a drink too. It had been a long day. They shoved in at a circular table with a crowd of dwarfs and men in the uniform of the city guard and stared for a long moment at the foaming mugs of ale the barmaid set down before them. Beads of condensation ran down the sides, and a heady scent of hops wafted from them like a memory of summer.

Gotrek licked his lips, but didn't reach for the mug. 'Real dwarf ale,' he said.

Felix nodded. He too was mesmerised at the vision of liquid gold before him. 'Not that damned palm wine we had in Ind.'

'Or the Bretonnian slop Doucette served on the *Celeste*,' said Gotrek. He snorted dismissively. 'Human beer.'

'Or the sugar water they served in Araby,' said Felix with feeling.

Gotrek spat a fat gob of phlegm on the floor, disgusted. 'That rot was poison.'

At last they could stand it no longer. They snatched up the steins and downed them in long, greedy pulls. Gotrek finished first, banging down his mug and leaning back, his eyes glazed, licking foam from his moustache. Felix finished a moment later and sat back as well. He closed his eyes.

'It's good to be back,' he said at last.

Gotrek nodded, and signalled the barmaid for another round. 'Aye,' he said.

After they had drunk their second and third in silence, Gotrek's brow began to cloud, and his one eye stared off into nothingness. Felix knew the signs and was therefore not surprised when a few moments later Gotrek grunted and spoke.

'How many years were we gone?'

Felix shrugged. 'I can't remember. Too long, at any rate.'

'And still alive.' Gotrek wiped the foam from his moustache and traced distracted circles on the patinated planks of the table. 'My best dooms are behind me, manling. I've slain trolls, vampires, giants, dragons, daemons, and each was to be my death. If they couldn't kill me, what will? Am I to spend the next three hundred years killing skaven and grobi? A Slayer must die to be complete.' He raised his axe high into the air, holding the haft by the very end so that the razor sharp edge glinted in the light. 'The axe must fall.'

'Gotrek...' said Felix uneasily.

Gotrek blinked blankly at the gleaming blade, then let it drop.

'Gotrek!' Felix squawked.

Gotrek stopped the blade a hairsbreadth from his nose as he caught it again, and then lowered it to his side as if he had done nothing untoward. 'Imagine a Slayer who died of old age. Pathetic.' He sighed, then took another long draught.

Felix's heart was pounding with reaction. He wanted to scream at the dwarf for being a fool, but after years in his company, he knew that any protestations would only make Gotrek dig his heels in and do something even more stupid.

'We must go north,' Gotrek continued after a moment. 'That daemon was the beast that came closest to killing me. I want another go at–'

'Pardon, Slayer,' said a voice behind them. 'You are Gotrek, son of Gurni?'

Gotrek and Felix turned, hands moving to their weapons. Two young dwarfs in travel-stained doublets and worn boots stood at a respectful distance.

Gotrek eyed them levelly. 'Who wants to know?'

The nearer of the two, whose sandy hair was pulled up in a clubbed topknot, ducked his head. 'I am Thorgig Helmgard, son of Thane Kirhaz Helmgard, of the Diamondsmith clan of Karak Hirn, at your service and your clan's. This is my friend and clan brother Kagrin Deepmountain.' The second dwarf, a round-faced youth with a brown beard even shorter than Thorgig's, ducked his head, but said nothing. His eyes remained fixed on the floor.

'We… We recognised your axe when you raised it,' continued Thorgig, 'though we have only heard it described.'

Gotrek frowned at the name of the hold. 'And that's excuse enough to interrupt a dwarf in his drinking, shortbeard?'

Felix glanced at Gotrek. That was unusually brusque, even for him.

Thorgig coloured a little, but kept himself in check. 'Forgive me, master Slayer. I only wanted to ask if you had come to Barak Varr to help your old friend, my liege, Prince Hamnir Ranulfsson, recover Karak Hirn, which was lost to the grobi not three weeks ago. He is organising an army among the refugees.'

'Old friend, is it?' said Gotrek. 'I wouldn't help Hamnir Ranulfsson finish a keg. If he's lost his father's hold it's no more than I'd expect.' He turned back to his mug. 'Off with you.'

Thorgig's fists clenched. 'You border close to insult, Slayer.'

'Only close?' said Gotrek. 'Then I've missed my mark. Hamnir Ranulfsson is an oathbreaking dog, not fit to shape tin or dig middens.'

Felix edged back.

'Stand, Slayer,' said Thorgig, his voice trembling. 'I would not hit a sitting dwarf.'

'Then I'll stay sitting. I don't want your death on my hands.'

Thorgig's face was as red and mottled as Felix's cloak. 'You won't stand? Are you a coward as well as a liar?'

Gotrek's hands froze on his mug and the muscles in his massive arms flexed, but then he relaxed. 'Go back to Hamnir, lad. I've no grudge against you.'

'But I've one against you.' The young dwarf's posture was rigid with a mixture of fear and fury.

'Fair enough,' said Gotrek, looking into his mug. 'Come back when your beard reaches your belt and I'll take your measure, but at the moment, I'm drinking.'

'More cowardice,' said Thorgig. 'You are a Slayer. You will be long dead by then.'

Gotrek sighed morosely. 'I'm beginning to doubt it.'

Thorgig and his companion continued to stare at Gotrek while the Slayer downed his ale, lost in moody reflection, and Felix eyed the scene anxiously, every muscle ready to jump away at the first sign of a fight. He had watched Gotrek's back in battles with daemons, dragons and trolls, but only a madman got in the middle of brawling dwarfs.

After a long moment, the awkwardness of his position at last became too much for the young dwarf and he turned to his companion. 'Come, Kagrin, we are fools to expect a Slayer to defend his honour. Do they not take the crest because they lost it long ago?'

Gotrek tensed again as the two dwarfs pushed through the crowd to the door, but he successfully stopped himself from going after them.

'What was all that about?' asked Felix when they were gone.

'Not your concern, manling.' Gotrek drained his mug and stood. 'Let's find another place.'

Felix sighed and rose. 'Another place will be better?'

'It won't be this place,' came the reply.

LODGINGS SUDDENLY BECAME available at the next tavern, a filthy dive called the Blind Alley, when two Tilean traders who had been staying there got in a fight with three Estalian sailors over the favours of a tavern girl, and all five of them were thrown out. There was a fierce bidding war for the room among the tavern's customers, but Gotrek showed the landlord a diamond the size of his thumbnail and the auction came to an abrupt end. He ordered a half keg of the tavern's best brew sent up and retired immediately.

Felix shook his head when he looked around the cramped, grimy room. There were mould stains on the walls, and the sheets on the two narrow cots tucked under the eaves were blotched and grey. 'That diamond was the gift of the Caliph of Ras Karim,' he said. 'It might have bought a townhouse in Altdorf, and you used it to pay for this?'

'I want some peace,' rumbled Gotrek, 'and if you go on about it, you can sleep in the hall.'

'Not I,' said Felix, pulling back his cot's patched blanket dubiously. 'I'll be too busy wrestling bed-bugs to speak.'

'Just be quiet about it.'

There was a deferential tap on the door, and two of the landlord's barmen waddled in with a half-keg. The mark of a Barak Varr dwarf brewery was branded on the side. They set it on the floor between the cots, then tapped it, left two mugs, and withdrew.

Gotrek turned the tap and let a few inches of ale slide down the side of the mug. He took a sip, then nodded, satisfied. 'Not Bugman's, but not bad. Ten or twelve of these and I could sleep in a pig sty.' He filled the mug to the brim and sat in the room's only chair.

'A pig sty might have been cleaner,' said Felix. He filled his mug too, and took a swallow. The rich amber liquid flowed, cool and pleasingly sharp, down to his stomach, and sent a warm tingle through his limbs. At once, a mellow glow spread over the whole room, a golden patina that blinded one to the dirt and disrepair. 'On the other hand, a pig sty wouldn't have this,' he said, lifting the mug. He took a longer drink and sat down on his cot. A slat creaked ominously, and he slid toward the centre. He sighed. 'So, is this what you mean to do while we wait out the week for the *Celeste*? Sit in this room and drink?'

'You have a better plan?'

Felix shrugged. 'It just seems a waste of time.'

'That's the trouble with men,' said Gotrek, 'no patience.' He took a drink. Felix tried to think of a better plan, but couldn't, so he had another drink too.

Four or five mugs later another knock came on the door. Felix thought it was the landlord again, bringing up another half keg, and levered himself out of the sway-backed bed, but when he opened the door, a prosperous-looking dwarf stood in it, four more behind him in the shadows of the hall. Felix recognised young Thorgig and his silent friend Kagrin among them.

The dwarf in the door looked of an age with Gotrek – though it was hard to tell with dwarfs – but considerably less weathered. His chestnut brown beard flowed down his green and gold doublet, bulged over a comfortable paunch, and was tucked neatly under his belt. A pair of gold spectacles dangled from a gold chain clipped to his collar. He had square, broad features and clear brown eyes, currently flashing with suppressed anger. 'Where is he?' he asked.

Gotrek looked up at the voice and glared balefully at the speaker from across the room. 'Found me, did you?'

'There aren't many one-eyed Slayers in town.'

Gotrek burped. 'Well, now you can go again. I already told your boot-boy I wouldn't help.'

The dwarf – Felix assumed it must be the aforementioned Hamnir Ranulfsson – stepped forwards, ignoring Felix entirely. 'Gotrek–'

'You set foot in this room,' said Gotrek, interrupting him. 'I'll kill you. After what has passed between us, you've no reason to expect anything from me except a cleft skull.'

Hamnir hesitated for a second, and then stepped deliberately into the room. It was an act of courage for, compared to Gotrek, he looked small and soft and fat. 'Then kill me. I've swallowed a lot of pride coming here. I'll speak my piece.'

Gotrek looked him over coldly from his chair. He shook his head. 'You've become a shopkeep.'

'And you've become a tavern bully by all accounts,' said Hamnir.

'I told your boy my grudge was with you. I didn't fight him.'

'I know our grudge, Gurnisson,' said Hamnir, 'which is why I don't come asking for myself, but for Karak Hirn, and all its clans, and for all the dwarfs and men of the Badlands as well. With Karak Hirn fallen there is no bastion to stop the grobi from raiding the countryside. It burns. Trade twixt dwarf and man has ceased. No grain for ale. No human gold for dwarf swords. The holds are slowly starving.'

'And how did this tragedy come about?' asked Gotrek, sneering. 'No fault of yours, surely.'

Hamnir looked down, colouring. 'The fault is mine more than anyone else's, I suppose. My father and older brother went north to join the forces fighting the Chaos invasion and left me with the running of Karak Hirn. As second son, I have dealt primarily with trade, as you know, and it has been my custom to come to Barak Varr to negotiate with the Tilean grain merchants, as they are known for their sharp practices and slippery ways.'

'No sharper or slipperier than yours, I'm sure,' muttered Gotrek.

Hamnir ignored him. 'So I left the hold in the hands of Durin Torvaltsson, one of my father's advisors, too old to go to war, and–'

'The orcs took the hold while you were away arguing over wheat?' Gotrek's disgust was palpable.

Hamnir clenched his jaw. 'We had no reason to expect an attack. The orcs were running wild in the Badlands, but they hadn't attacked the holds. Why would they when there were so many easier targets among the human settlements? But... but they did attack. We had been here three days when Thorgig and Kagrin slipped through the siege by night and found me. They said the orcs had come up from our mines, in overwhelming force. We were taken entirely unawares. Our alarms, our traps, all failed. Durin is dead, as are many others: Ferga, my betrothed, Thorgig's sister, may be one of them. I–'

'So you *are* to blame,' said Gotrek.

'And if I am,' said Hamnir, hotly, 'does it change what has been lost and what more will be lost because of it? Can a true dwarf turn away?'

'I am a true *Slayer*, Ranulfsson,' growled Gotrek, 'sworn to seek a great death, and I won't find that fighting grobi in Karak Hirn. I'm going north. There are daemons in the north.'

Hamnir spat. 'That for Slayers: vain and selfish. They seek great deaths, not great deeds.'

Gotrek stood, taking up his axe. 'Get out.'

The dwarfs in the hall put their hands on their axes and hammers, and stepped forwards, but Hamnir waved them back.

He glared at Gotrek. 'I hoped it wouldn't come to this. I hoped you would do the right thing and come to the aid of Karak Hirn out of loyalty to your race, but I see that you are still the same old Gotrek Gurnisson, still more concerned with your own glory than the common good. Very well.' He raised his chin, pushing his beard out like an auburn waterfall. 'Before the oath was made that birthed the grudge between us, there was another, spoken when we first became friends.'

'You dirty–' said Gotrek.

'We vowed,' continued Hamnir, talking over him, 'with blood passed between us, that come what may on life's bitter road, if called upon, we would aid and defend each other as long as there was still blood in our veins and life in our limbs to do so. I call on that vow now.'

Gotrek's single eye blazed and he advanced on Hamnir, axe raised. Hamnir paled, but stood firm. Gotrek stopped before him, trembling, and then whipped the axe down, so close to Hamnir's side that it shaved some stray threads from his sleeve, then bit into the floorboards.

Hamnir let out a relieved breath.

Gotrek punched him in the nose so hard that he landed on his neck at the feet of his dwarfs. They stepped forwards to cover him, but Gotrek stayed where he was.

'You've some gall calling on an oath, after what you've done,' Gotrek said as Hamnir tried to raise his bleeding head, 'but, unlike some, I have never broken a vow. I'll join your army, but this foolishness better be finished before the war is over in the north.' He turned his back on the dwarfs in the door and picked up his mug. 'Now, get out. I'm drinking.'

CHAPTER THREE

A WIDE BOULEVARD, the Rising Road, ran straight
through Barak Varr from the docks to the back wall of
the enormous cavern where the holds of the port's
founding clans were built into the solid rock in the
more traditional dwarf manner, each with a fortified
front door topped with the clan sigil. The boulevard
pierced the back wall and continued on, rising,
straight and broad and gradual, through the earth to
the surface, where it opened within a sturdy dwarf
fortress, built to defend the landside entrance.

On this road, three days later, Hamnir Ranulfsson,
Prince of Karak Hirn, mustered his army of refugee
dwarfs – five hundred doughty warriors from a score of
clans, along with dwarf smiths and surgeons, and
bustling dwarf wives, overseeing wagons full of food,
camp gear and supplies, all headed for Rodenheim
Castle, a human keep near Karak Hirn where,

according to Thorgig, the survivors of the orc invasion had taken refuge. The castle too had been ravaged by orcs, Baron Rodenheim slaughtered with all his vassals, but the green horde had soon abandoned it for fresh pillage, and the dwarfs had moved in.

Banners waved proudly at the head of Hamnir's column. The force was well kitted out with armour, shields, axes, crossbows, handguns and cannon – as well as provisions and fodder – for Barak Varr had helped outfit the army. Felix didn't doubt that this was because the dwarfs of the port wished Hamnir every success in regaining Karak Hirn and assuring the security of the dwarf race, but no doubt the fact that, with his force gone, they would have six hundred less mouths to feed probably had something to do with it as well.

Felix was the only man in the long column. This was not yet an army of general liberation. The dwarfs were going to take back Karak Hirn, and men were not invited freely into a dwarf hold, no matter how desperate the situation. Only Felix's status as 'Dwarf Friend' and Gotrek's 'rememberer' allowed him to join the dwarfs' solemn ranks. He stood with Gotrek near the front of the force while they waited for all the clans to form up.

There was a fair amount of argument about the order of march, with each clan claiming some ancient honour or precedent that would put them closer to the front, and Felix could see Hamnir standing in the centre of a crowd of clan leaders doing his best to keep his temper while he arbitrated amongst them.

Gleaming gromril armour covered Hamnir head-to-toe – if a little snug about the waist – and over this was belted a dark green surcoat stitched with Karak Hirn's sigil of a horn over a stone gate. A shield over his back had the same design, and he wore on his head an elaborate winged helm, the cheek and nose guards of which did not quite hide his lumpy broken nose and his two purple-tinged black eyes.

Gotrek swayed beside Felix, moaning, and propping himself up with his axe. True to his original intention, he had spent the last three days in their filthy room, blind drunk for the few hours he was awake each day. Yet it had been him – with a dwarf's uncanny ability to know the time under or above ground, in light or dark – that had woken Felix two hours ago and told him to get ready. Now, however, with nothing to do but wait and, eventually, march, the effects of the previous night's binge had caught up with him.

'Would you mind very much not breathing so loudly?' he growled.

'I could stop breathing entirely, if you like,' Felix said, snappily, for he too had been less than sparing with the ale the night before.

Gotrek pinched his temples. 'Yes, do. And don't shout.'

At last, after another hour of argument and re-forming, an order of march was settled upon, and the dwarf army got underway. They were accompanied by Odgin Stormwall, commander of the landside fortress, a stout, white-bearded old veteran, and a company of Barak Varr's city guard – fifty dwarfs in ring-mail and blue and grey surcoats accompanied them. Odgin explained the situation above as they marched.

'The grobi filth besiege the fort,' Odgin explained as they marched, 'though they're not trying very hard to take it. Mostly, they're eating and drinking every bit of forage to be had within fifty leagues, and slaughtering every caravan that comes to trade with us. When they get restless, they make a run at the walls and we turn them back. Usually they just lob rocks and gobbos at us.'

'Why don't you just march out and destroy them?' asked Thorgig, who walked at Hamnir's side with his silent friend Kagrin.

Odgin exchanged an amused smile with Hamnir, and then nodded at Thorgig. 'Oh, we'd like to, lad, but there's more than a few of them. Why should we put ourselves at risk when we're nice and safe behind our walls?'

'But you're starving in here,' said Thorgig.

'Aye, and they'll starve out there sooner,' said Odgin. 'When they've killed all the livestock and looted all the towns within a day's march, their hunger will win out over their patience and they'll move on. They always do.'

'What if you starve before they do?'

Odgin chuckled. 'Your orc isn't much on rationing. Our lads may complain about tightening their belts and running out of beer, but we can feed the hold for another two months or so on biscuit and spring water.' He turned to Hamnir. 'Now, Prince Hamnir, here's how we'll get you away. If you were to march out of the main gate, you'd have every orc in the camp after you, but there's a hidden sally port round the back. It goes underground for a bit and comes up in one of our old barns.' He grinned. 'Orcs smashed it up a bit, and burnt the roof off it, but they never found the door.'

'And the greenskins won't see us when we march out?' asked Gotrek. 'There are six hundred of us.'

'That's what these lads are for,' said Odgin, jerking a thumb over his shoulder at the company of Barak Varr city guard. 'It's them who'll march out the front gate, and when the greenskins come running to get stuck in, you will slip out of the sally port and away.'

Hamnir blinked and looked back at the dwarf guards. 'They mean to sacrifice themselves for us? That is more than we wished. I–'

'Oh, it won't be any sacrifice. They're like that short-beard there,' he said, nodding at Thorgig. 'They've been wanting to come to grips with the greenskins since this business started. We'll pull them out of the fire once you're away. They'll go no further than the gate.'

'Nonetheless,' said Hamnir, 'they put themselves in danger in order to help us, and I thank them for it.'

'There isn't a dwarf in Barak Varr that doesn't want to see Karak Hirn restored, Prince Hamnir,' said Odgin. 'The Hirn holds the Black Mountains together. It protects the Badlands. We'd not survive long without it.'

WHEN HAMNIR'S COLUMN reached the top of the Rising Road, great granite doors swung out and they marched into the wide central courtyard of Kazad Varr, a massively built dwarf fortress with thick walls and square towers at each corner. Felix looked behind him, momentarily disoriented. He had expected the doors to the long tunnel to be built into a cliff-face or mountainside, as was usual with the entrances of dwarf holds, but here there was no mountain. The doors were built into a squat, arrow-slotted stone structure that occupied the space where, in a castle, the central keep would have stood.

Within the fort all was calm. Dwarf quarrellers in blue and grey surcoats patrolled the walls, and cannon crews watched from the towers. They hardly raised their heads when, after a distant thud, an oddly shaped missile arced high over the wall and slammed, screaming, into the flagstones, not thirty feet to Hamnir's left.

Felix looked at it. It was a scrawny goblin with a spiked helmet and poorly made leather wings tied to its arms. Its neck was broken and its body burst. Blood spread out from it in black rivulets.

'Idiots,' said Gotrek.

Felix blinked at him. 'But you… on the ship, you did the same… '

'I made it.'

As the dwarfs of the Barak Varr city guard continued on towards the main gate, Odgin led Hamnir and his army towards the back of the fort to a stone stables, built out from the back wall. At the rear of the stables, Odgin unlocked and opened a pair of big ironbound doors. Behind them, a broad ramp descended into a tunnel that passed under the fortress wall.

'Hold here until the guard is fully engaged and the signal is given,' said Odgin. 'When you leave the barn, march straight ahead. The west gate of the old pasture wall is only a hundred yards beyond, and once through it, your force will be shielded from the eyes of the orcs.'

Gotrek spat, a disgusted sneer twisting his face. Felix smirked. Even when it made tactical sense, Gotrek didn't care to hide from an enemy.

There was a short wait. Then, from across the fortress came the clatter of chains and gears, and Felix could see the huge doors of the main gate swinging out and the portcullis rising. With a fierce shout, the Barak Varr guard marched forwards into the mouth of the gate, helms and axe blades flashing in the morning sun.

A rising roar from beyond the wall echoed their shout. It grew louder and more savage with each second.

'They've seen the bait,' said Thorgig, chewing his lip. It looked to Felix as if the young dwarf would rather be at the main gate than here.

Soon after came the unmistakable sound of two armies slamming together shield to shield and axe to axe. Thorgig's eyes glowed, and the other dwarfs shifted restlessly, gripping their weapons and muttering to themselves.

Gotrek groaned and massaged his temples. 'Don't suppose they could fight quietly?' he grumbled.

The sound of battle intensified. Felix could see violent movement in the open arch of the main gate – flashes of steel, falling bodies, surging lines of green and grey.

Finally, a flutter of red came from the wall above the gate – a banner waving back and forth.

'That's it,' said Odgin. 'The whole horde's coming now. Off you go.'

Hamnir saluted Odgin, fist over his heart. 'You have my thanks, Odgin Stormwall. Karak Hirn will not forget this.'

Odgin returned the salute, grinning. 'Remember it next time we come to trade sea pearls for sword steel, prince.'

Hamnir motioned his troops forward and marched down the ramp into the tunnel. It was a cramped space

compared to the Rising Road, with only room enough
for four dwarfs to march abreast. After less than two
hundred paces it ended in another ramp, rising, it
seemed, to a blank ceiling.

Hamnir called a halt as Thorgig stepped to a lever in
the left wall.

'Companies ready!' called Hamnir.

The dwarfs drew their axes and hammers. Quarrellers
set bolts on strings. Gotrek took a drink from his canteen.
Felix hefted his sword, nervous.

'Open!' called Hamnir.

Thorgig pulled the lever. With a rumble of hidden
gears, the ceiling rose and split, and bright morning sunlight poured into the darkness.

Hamnir raised his axe. 'Forward, sons of Grungni!
March!'

The column started up the ramp, Hamnir in the lead,
Gotrek and Felix in the first rank with Thorgig and
Kagrin. They came up in a ruined barn. The building was
roofless – the walls mere heaps of rubble. Skeletons of
sheep and cattle were littered everywhere, bits of rotting
meat still stuck to them.

As the dwarfs stepped from the barn and began marching towards the pasture gate directly ahead of them, Felix
looked around at the orc camp to their right – an endless
clutter of ragged skin tents, gutted and toppled outbuildings, make-shift boar pens and refuse, that spread out in
all directions from the front gate of the dwarf fortress.
Crude, leering faces were painted on the tents in blood
and dung. Flies buzzed over heaps of rotting garbage on
which human bodies and bones had been tossed. Prim-
itive totems hung above the bigger tents, proclaiming the
dominance of this or that chieftain.

From all over this shambles, orcs ran towards the main gate. The entire camp seethed with movement. Warbosses and their lieutenants chivvied their fractious troops towards the open gate with curses, kicks and slaps. Hulking green warriors snatched up their weapons and beat their chests. Tiny goblins unleashed fang-toothed, four-legged beasts that looked like deformed pigs. Blood-daubed war banners, decorated with severed human and dwarf heads, waved above swarms of enraged orcs, all roaring challenges.

There was a mob mustering directly behind a stand of tents just to the right of the dwarf column – so close that Felix could have seen the yellows of their eyes if they had been facing towards them.

The bulk of the fort was between Hamnir's force and the main gate, so it was impossible to see how well the Barak Varr guards were faring, but the sound of steel on steel still rang in Felix's ears, so he knew they weren't dead yet.

Thorgig ground his teeth. 'Not fair,' he said, under his breath.

Felix shook his head. Imagine wanting to be in the way of that savage green avalanche. He, for one, was happy to be slipping out of the back door. He looked around. They were almost halfway to the pasture wall gate, but the tail of the column had not yet emerged from the tunnel in the barn.

Suddenly, from the right, came a belligerent shriek, very close. The entire dwarf column looked right. A goblin that had been trying to corral one of its unruly pets had seen them. It turned tail and ran, bug-eyed. The dwarf quarrellers fired, and a score of crossbow bolts flashed after it. They were too late. The little greenskin dodged around a tent and ran towards the mustering orcs, screaming at the top of his lungs.

'That's done it,' said a dwarf behind Felix.

'Good,' said Thorgig.

Orcs were turning and pointing and calling to their mates. Warbosses were screaming orders.

Hamnir cursed. 'Double time!' he shouted. 'Double time! Hurry it up!'

'You running, shopkeep?' asked Gotrek as the dwarf column picked up its pace. 'Can't stomach a good set-to any more?'

'If I lose half my troops here for the sake of "a good set-to",' snarled Hamnir, his face tight, 'what am I to do at Karak Hirn, when the battle means something?'

Gotrek glared at Hamnir's logic, but continued trotting along with the others, much to Felix's relief.

The orcs were coming. A mob of massive greenskinned warriors poured around the shattered houses, roaring for dwarf blood, bone and skin totems bobbing like grisly marionettes overhead. Goblins scampered in their wake, long knifes glinting.

Hamnir's head swivelled from them to the gate and back. 'We're not going to make it,' he muttered. 'We're not going to make it.'

'Then turn and fight, Grimnir curse you!' said Gotrek.

Thorgig looked uneasily at Hamnir. 'Your orders, prince?'

'Orders,' said Hamnir, as if he didn't know what the word meant. 'Yes, of course. I...' He looked around again, eyes showing white. The orcs were fifty feet away and closing fast. 'Grungni take it. Quarrellers, right! Fire! Fire! Column, dress right!' His voice was thin with tension.

The quarrellers fired, and twenty greenskins went down. There was no time for a second volley. The orcs were on them, slamming into the right side of the column in a piecemeal charge as the dwarfs belatedly turned out to face them.

Axe and cleaver met blade-to-blade and haft-to-haft in an impact that Felix could feel through his feet. Notched black iron smashed through shining dwarf mail and sturdy dwarf shields, biting deep into dwarf flesh. Gleaming dwarf axes chopped through leather and scrap armour, cleaving green orc-flesh and shattering white orc-bone.

Gotrek pushed to the front line and laid about him like a thresher, separating orcs from their sinewy limbs and their ugly, thick-skulled heads. Felix drew his dragon sword, Karaghul, and joined him, keeping just out of the sweep of the Slayer's great axe. He stabbed a goblin in the mouth and ducked a club like a tree stump, swung by an orc with brass hoops piercing his up-jutting tusks.

Dwarfs fell right and left under the orc onslaught, but the line never wavered. They took the orcs' savage blows on their shields with stoic determination, and fought back with grim, glowering calm. There were no wild attacks, no desperate lunges, only a steady, relentless butchery that dropped orcs one after another. Even Hamnir was calming, as if the physical work of swinging his axe was steadying him.

A mob of orcs broke and ran, pin-cushioned with bolts and driven back by the dwarfs' implacable attack. The gang beside them caught their panic and retreated as well, bellowing savage curses.

'We're turning them,' said Hamnir, dodging back from a cleaver swipe and cutting its owner's wrist to the bone. 'We just might–'

A thunderous roar came from the cluster of tents. Felix kicked a goblin in the face and looked up. An enormous orc warboss was stomping towards the battle with a crowd of black orc lieutenants surrounding him. He bellowed at the fleeing orcs and pointed an angry finger at the dwarf column.

The orcs cringed from his displeasure and reluctantly turned back towards the dwarfs.

'Luck of the dwarfs,' growled Hamnir, bashing an orc in the knee with his shield.

'The big one's put the fear of Gork in them,' said Gotrek. He seemed almost pleased.

The warboss smashed into the centre of the dwarf column, his black orcs and the backsliders beside him. His huge cleaver cut a bloody trench through a company of Ironbreakers. It seemed to glow with a greenish light. Dead dwarfs flew back, severed limbs spinning away as the boss chopped and hewed. His black orc lieutenants ploughed in after him. Bolstered by his presence, the orcs attacked with renewed fury all along the dwarf line.

Hamnir cursed under his breath. 'You wanted a good set-to, Gurnisson,' he snapped over his shoulder. 'On your way, then.'

Gotrek was already out of earshot, charging down the column towards the rampaging orc chieftain. Felix hurried after him, as did Thorgig and Kagrin.

'Want to see the crested coward in action,' Thorgig grunted. 'Maybe he'll punch the orc in the nose when he isn't ready.'

Kagrin smirked, but said nothing.

The warboss was huge – twice the height of a dwarf, and nearly as wide as it was tall. Its armour was a patchwork of scrap metal and looted plate. Dwarf breastplates served it for shoulder pieces. A necklace of staring human heads hung around its tree-trunk neck, woven together by their hair. As Gotrek and Felix got closer, Felix heard an angry, high-pitched screaming, and realised it was the boss's green-glowing cleaver, keening for blood. The runes on Gotrek's axe glowed red as it neared the fell weapon.

All around the brute was chaos – dwarf warriors pushing forwards to get into the fight, quarrellers angling to get a clear shot, the warboss's hulking lieutenants hacking and chopping right and left, trying to win favour with feats of mad savagery.

The warboss cut a dwarf in two, the cleaver slicing through the warrior's heavy ring-mail as if it were butter. The metal literally melted and flowed at its touch.

Gotrek leapt up on a pile of dwarf bodies and swung his axe, its runes trailing red. The orc threw up his cleaver and the weapons came together in a shivering clash. Sparks flew. The cleaver shrieked like a wounded daemon. The warboss roared and lashed out, furious at being thwarted. Gotrek blocked and bashed back, and the axe and cleaver began weaving a whirling cage of steel and iron as he and the orc hacked and countered.

The boss's black orc lieutenants surged forwards, howling for blood. Felix, Thorgig and Kagrin closed with them to protect Gotrek's flanks. Felix dodged a serrated axe swung by a one-eyed orc, then stepped in and stabbed the monster in its remaining eye. It bellowed in rage and pain, striking out blindly in all directions. A wild swing gutted one of its comrades. Two more killed it and thrust it behind them.

Felix jumped back as the orcs slashed at him. There was no sense parrying. The massive axes would only shatter his blade and numb his arm. On Gotrek's left, Thorgig bashed an orc's club aside with his shield and chopped through its knee. It toppled like a tree. A cleaver caught the wings of Thorgig's helmet and knocked it flying. He blocked another attack with his axe. The force of the blow nearly flattened him. Kagrin, who had been hanging back, darted in and gashed the orc in the side with a beautifully made hand axe. Thorgig finished it off.

Gotrek parried another swing of the warboss's cleaver, then turned his axe so it screeched down the cleaver's haft and severed the orc's fingers. They dropped away like fat green grubs, and the glowing cleaver fell. The warboss roared and fumbled uselessly for it with its bloody stumps. Gotrek jumped up onto its knee and split its bony skull down to its sternum.

The black orcs stared as Gotrek rode the huge orc's collapsing body to the ground, and two died from dwarf axes before they recovered themselves. Three leapt at Gotrek, all trying to reach him first. He fanned them back with his axe and snatched up the warboss's cleaver. It crackled with angry green energy where it touched his skin. Gotrek didn't flinch.

'Who's the next boss?' he called. 'Who wants it?'

As the three black orcs advanced again, Gotrek tossed the humming cleaver behind them. They lifted their eyes, following its arc, then turned and dived, elbowing and punching each other to get at it. The other lieutenants looked back at the commotion and saw the first three fighting for the cleaver. They roared and joined the scuffle, their dwarf opponents forgotten.

The dwarfs pressed forwards, swinging for the orcs' backs, but Gotrek threw out a hand.

'Don't engage!' he shouted. 'Let them fight.'

The dwarfs stepped back. The orc brawl was turning deadly. One of the lieutenants buried his axe in the chest of another. Others were bellowing for their followers to come to their aid. Orcs began peeling away from their fights all along the dwarf column to rally to their leaders. Felix saw the glowing cleaver cut an orc's head off, but its wielder was stabbed in the back and another took it up.

Gotrek wiped his axe on the trampled grass. 'That's done it,' he said, satisfied, and started to the front of the column again. Felix joined him.

Thorgig glared at Gotrek's back as he retrieved his dented helmet and followed with Kagrin. He seemed disappointed that the Slayer had prevailed.

More and more orcs were deserting the dwarf line to join the scrum over the cleaver. Others were fighting amongst themselves. By the time Gotrek and Felix rejoined Hamnir, the dwarfs' line of march was clear.

Hamnir grunted, reluctantly impressed. 'Thought you'd take the Slayer's way, and try to fight them all while we died behind you.'

'I swore to protect you,' Gotrek said, coldly. 'I don't break my oaths.'

The column started forwards as the orcs fought on.

CHAPTER FOUR

THE DWARFS' MOOD, already grim because of the casualties the orcs had inflicted upon them during their exit from Barak Varr, grew grimmer still the deeper they travelled into the Badlands. Though they saw few orcs, signs of their rampage were everywhere.

The land had been plagued by the orc hordes for as long as dwarfs and men had settled there. Their invasions were as common as spring floods, and almost as predictable, and the hardy folk of the plains protected themselves from them as if from a storm. The few settlements huddled tightly around strong keeps, into which the farmers and their livestock could retreat when the greenskins came. There they would wait out the ravaging of their farms until the savage tide receded, then return to their land and rebuild.

This time, because so many men and dwarfs had gone north to fight, it had been much worse. There had been no one to stop them, and the orcs had followed their lust for slaughter wherever it took them. The devastation was entirely random. Hamnir's army came upon villages burned to the ground, everyone slain, and then, not five miles on, others absolutely untouched, the farmers harvesting their fields with nervous eyes straying to the horizon and look-outs posted on every hill.

They passed castles with banners waving, and others that were nothing but charred ruins. The farms and houses around these were razed to the ground, the picked bones of the peasants and their families strewn about the blackened circles of cooking fires. Nothing edible was left where the orcs had been. Livestock had been eaten, fruit trees and grain bins stripped, hogsheads of ale and wine drained and smashed.

The only men who hadn't been thrown into the stew pot were those who had been used for sport. Rotting corpses in ruined armour had been nailed, spread-eagled, to trees, crude targets painted on their chests. Dozens of black arrows stuck out of them. Most had missed the bulls-eye. Other corpses hung from the battlements of castles as warnings, savagely mutilated.

It was a grim march, and Gotrek was grim company, even more taciturn and dour than usual. He kept as far from Hamnir as he could, walking at the back near the baggage train, while Hamnir marched at the head. Only when the scouts reported orcs or other dangers in the vicinity did Gotrek return to the front and take up a guard position near his old companion.

The Slayer spoke to Felix hardly more than to Hamnir. He seemed entirely withdrawn, staring at the ground ahead of him as he marched, and muttering under his breath, ignoring Felix entirely. The other dwarfs ignored him too, eyeing him warily if they looked at him at all. Felix couldn't remember any other time in his travels with Gotrek when he felt more of an outsider, more alone. On all their other adventures, there had been at least a few other humans with them – Max, Ulrica – though she wasn't human any more, was she? Here, he seemed the only member of his species for a hundred leagues. It was a strange, lonely feeling.

At every stop, while the other dwarfs smoked pipes or cooked up sausages and mushrooms, or took their ease, and Felix penned the day's events in his journal, Thorgig's silent friend Kagrin took out a gold-trimmed dagger and a set of tiny files, chisels and gouges, and worked impossibly intricate designs into the pommel and crosspiece. He did these entirely freehand, and yet the work was perfectly symmetrical and precise, the epitome of the angular geometric style the dwarfs favoured. Even the other dwarfs were impressed, stopping in the middle of setting up their tents to watch him work and give him praise or advice. He took both without a word, only nodding curtly and bending even more intently over his work.

Felix watched him too, as much for his oddity as his workmanship. He had never seen a quieter dwarf. The race as a whole seemed born to bluster and brag, but Kagrin hardly ever raised his eyes, let alone his voice. On one or two occasions, however, Felix caught Kagrin frowning at him, only to look away as soon as Felix met his eyes. Other dwarfs in the camp stared at Felix as well, belligerent, challenging glares as if they were offended by his mere presence and asking him to defend the existence of his whole race. Kagrin's gaze was different – more curious than angry.

Then, on the evening of the forth day, after they had made camp and eaten dinner, Kagrin sat down near Felix and began to work on the dagger as usual. It took him an hour of filing and tooling before, at last, he looked up at Felix and cleared his throat.

'Aye, goldsmith?' said Felix, when Kagrin failed to speak.

Kagrin looked around, as if fearful of being overheard. 'Er, I… I wished to ask, as you are human…' He trailed off. Felix was about to prompt him again when he finally found his voice, rumbling almost inaudibly. 'Are… are dwarfs well thought of in the lands of men?'

Felix paused. He didn't know what question he had been expecting, but that wasn't it. He scratched his head. 'Er, well, yes, generally. Their craftsmanship is highly praised, as is their honour and steadfastness. There are some among the less learned who look upon dwarfs with suspicion and jealousy, but most treat them with great respect.'

Kagrin seemed heartened by this answer. 'And… and there are places where dwarfs live peacefully beside men?'

Felix looked at him surprised. 'There have been dwarf enclaves in the cities of the Empire for a thousand years. You haven't heard of them?'

Kagrin's shoulders tightened and he looked around again. 'Shhh! Aye, I have, but I've heard… I've heard it said that dwarfs must lock themselves in at night, for fear of men out to murder and rob them. They say dwarfs have been burnt at the stake as enemies of man.'

'Who says this?' asked Felix, frowning.

'Dwarfs of my clan.'

'Ah.' Felix nodded. 'Forgive me if I impugn the motives of your clan brothers, but perhaps they are reluctant to lose a goldsmith of your calibre, and tell you tall tales of the barbarity of man to dissuade you from leaving.'

'I haven't spoken of leaving!' hissed Kagrin angrily. His fists clenched.

'Of course not, of course not,' said Felix holding up his palms. 'I can see that you are only curious. So, er, to satisfy that curiosity: I have never heard of dwarfs being burnt at the stake or called enemies of men. It is true that there have been accounts of mobs – instigated usually by jealous and desperate smiths – attacking dwarf houses, but it is rare. I haven't heard of it happening in this century at all. Dwarfs are long established in the Empire. Most of these passions cooled long ago. A dwarf who did contemplate setting up shop in the Empire would have little fear of trouble, and great prospects for success, particularly if he was as skilled a goldsmith as... well, as some I could name.'

Kagrin nodded brusquely, and then shot a guilty look towards Thorgig, who sat with a handful of other dwarfs, playing a game with stone pawns and dice.

He turned back to Felix and bowed his head. 'Thank you, human. You... you have, er, satisfied my curiosity.'

Felix nodded. 'My pleasure.'

He watched after Kagrin as he gathered up his tools and retired to his tent. It was strange to think of someone who no doubt had thirty years on him, as a 'poor lad', but Felix couldn't help it. It was clear that Kagrin felt torn between the lure of the wide world and the bonds of friendship and family. He had a hard road ahead of him, whatever road he chose. Felix wished him well.

AFTER SIX DAYS marching at the slow but steady dwarf pace, the Black Mountains, which had been a low saw-toothed line on the horizon when the dwarfs had left Barak Varr, filled the northern sky, an endless line of giants that stood shoulder to shoulder for as far as the eye could see to the east and west. Dark green skirts of thick pine forest swept up to the towering black gran-ite crags that gave the range its name. Their snowy peaks shone blood red in a blazing sunset.

'Home,' said Thorgig, inhaling happily as he gazed up at the splendid peaks.

For mountain goats, thought Felix, groaning at the thought of all the climbing to which he would soon be subjected. A cold wind blew down off the slopes. He pulled his old red cloak tighter around him and shiv-ered.

And perhaps he shivered for reasons other than the cold, for, although the dwarfs thought fondly of the place as home, it stirred in Felix less pleasant feelings. It had been not far from here that Gotrek and Felix had helped the ill-fated Baron von Diehl try to found a set-tlement, only to have it razed to the ground by wolf-riding greenskins. At Fort von Diehl Gotrek had lost his eye, and Felix had lost his first love. He shook his head, trying to keep her ghost at bay. Kirsten. He wished he hadn't been able to remember her name.

'There is Rodenheim Castle,' said Hamnir, a little fur-ther on, pointing to a stern, squat-towered castle perched on one of the forest-covered foothills that splayed out from the mountains like claws. 'It is a great shame that Baron Rodenheim won't be among those who muster here to help us. He was a true Dwarf Friend. May his gods receive him.'

The army started up the weedy cart track that wound up the hill to the castle, and soon began to see signs of its demise. The little village that clung to the slopes below it was shattered and burned, the stone houses roofless and toppled, the shrines desecrated. Cracked bones were heaped in corners like snowdrifts. A horrible stench came from the town well. Flies hovered above it. The red twilight painted the scene with a bloody brush. Felix had seen a lot of slaughter and ruin in his years with Gotrek, so it no longer turned his stomach, but it never failed to depress him.

The castle too was the worse for wear. Though its walls still stood, they were scorched and black in places, and great chunks had been knocked off the battlements. Flags with the insignia of Karak Hirn flew over the roofs of burned towers.

As the dwarf army approached, a horn echoed from the walls, and Felix could see stout figures carrying long-guns marching to their positions behind the crenellations. Torches flared to life above them, revealing dwarf crews readying catapults and trebuchets and kettles of boiling lead. The horn was answered by another, followed by cries and commands from within.

A white-bearded Thunderer in well worn chainmail climbed onto the battlements above the gate, his finger on the trigger of his gun. 'No closer, by Grimnir!' he bellowed, when the head of Hamnir's column had come in range. 'Not until you announce yourself and your purpose!'

'Hail, Lodrim!' called Hamnir. 'It is Prince Hamnir Ranulfson, and I've brought six hundred brave dwarf volunteers. Have we leave to enter?'

The Thunderer leaned forwards, blinking myopically. 'Prince Hamnir? Is it you? Valaya be praised!' He turned and shouted over his shoulder. 'Open the gates! Open the gates! It's Prince Hamnir, come with reinforcements!'

With a creaking of winches, the portcullis went up and the drawbridge came down. Both showed signs of recent battle, but also fresh repair.

Even before the bridge had thudded to rest, a dwarf was running across it, arms outstretched. 'Hamnir!' he cried. 'Prince!'

He was tall for a dwarf – almost four and a half feet, and powerfully built. His receding brown hair was pulled back in a club, and bright white teeth flashed through a thick beard that spilled down his barrel chest to his belt.

'Gorril! Well met!' said Hamnir, as the two dwarfs embraced and slapped each other's backs.

'I am relieved to see you alive,' said Gorril.

'And I, you,' replied Hamnir.

Gorril stepped back and bowed, grinning. 'Come, prince, enter your hold, meagre human surface hut though it may be.' He turned to the cluster of dwarf warriors who stood in the castle door. 'Away with you! Prepare Prince Hamnir's quarters! And see if you can find beds for six hundred more!'

Hamnir turned and signalled the column forwards, then strode with Gorril through the gates and into the castle's courtyard, as Gotrek and Felix, Thorgig and the rest marched in after. The yard was crowded with cheering dwarfs, and more were pouring from every door, all hailing Hamnir and the new troops.

'You made it unscathed?' asked Gorril as they pushed through the crowd of wellwishers.

'Some trouble with orcs as we left Barak Varr,' said Hamnir. 'Nothing since.' He looked at Gorril hopefully. 'Any word of Ferga?'

'Or my father?' asked Thorgig, urgently.

Gorril's brow clouded. 'None. I'm sorry.' He gave Thorgig a sympathetic look. 'You and Kagrin are the only dwarfs of the Diamondsmith clan to have escaped. Many died in the defence, and your father is believed to have locked the others in his hold. They may still live, though food will be growing short.'

Thorgig clenched his fists. 'I should be with them. If they are hurt...'

'You can't blame yourself,' said Gorril. 'You held your position as ordered, and then there was no going back.'

'Then I should have died.'

Hamnir laid a hand on the young dwarf's shoulder. 'Easy now. If the worst has happened, at least we will have opportunity to avenge them.' He looked around at the cheering crowd and nodded approvingly at Gorril. 'Thorgig told me you were sending for aid. It seems you were successful.'

Gorril made a face. 'Not so many as we could have wished. The other holds hadn't many dwarfs to spare. Too many gone north.' He shrugged. 'But let's leave that for tomorrow, aye? Tonight's for feasting!'

He turned to the crowd. 'Set the board, you layabouts. Your prince has come home!'

There was a great cheer and axes and fists were thrust in the air. But as Gorril led Hamnir toward the keep, two dwarfs pushed forward.

'Prince Hamnir,' said the first, a hammerer with a braided red beard. 'As leader of this throng, we ask you to dismiss the dwarfs of the Goldhammer Clan, who have dishonoured the good name of the Deephold Clan by denying my great-great-great-grandfather the rightful command of his Ironbeards in the battle of Bloodwater Grotto, fifteen hundred years ago!'

'Don't listen to him, prince,' said the other dwarf, a broadshouldered miner with jutting blond eyebrows. 'We are guilty of nothing but common sense. A troll had his great-great-great-grandfather's arm off at the shoulder before that battle. What was my great-great-great-grandfather to do? A general must think of what is best for the battle. We–'

Two other dwarfs pushed in front of the first two. 'Prince, you must hear us first!' cried one, a burly, black-bearded ironbreaker. 'Their paltry dispute is nothing compared to the feud that exists between we of the–'

'Enough!' roared Gorril, waving them all away. 'Will you badger the prince before he has his helmet off? Hamnir will hold council tomorrow and hear grievances then. Surely grudges that have stood for a thousand years can wait one more day.'

The dwarfs grumbled their displeasure, but stepped aside.

Gorril rolled his eyes at Hamnir. 'It has been like this since the others began to arrive. All want to help. None want to work with anyone else.'

'It never changes,' said Hamnir.

Gotrek grunted, disgusted.

'TELL ME WHAT happened,' said Hamnir. 'Thorgig and Kagrin told us what they knew when they came to Barak Varr, but their stories were a bit… confused.'

The feast was over, and Hamnir, Gorril, Gotrek and Felix, and a handful of the survivors from Karak Hirn were gathered in Baron Rodenheim's private apartments, which had been set aside for Hamnir, to discuss the coming action.

Despite Gorril's words, it hadn't been much of a feast, as supplies were low, but the dwarfs had done their best, and none at the head table had wanted for food or ale. Felix had had an uncomfortable time of it, for the dwarfs, being handy with their tools, and unwilling to suffer the indignity of trying to use human-scale furniture, had sawn down the legs of all the tables and chairs in the keep's great hall so that they better fit their short, broad frames. Felix had eaten his dinner with his knees up around his ears, and his back ached abominably.

Now, tired from the long days of marching, and a bit drunk from the many toasts that had been drunk to Hamnir and Karak Hirn and the success of the mission, he nodded drowsily in an unscathed high-backed chair, while the others talked and smoked by the fire in chairs edited for dwarf use.

Gorril sighed. 'It was a bad business, and very strange… very strange.' He sucked at his pipe. 'The orcs came up from our mines, but not like any time before: not in a great screaming rush that we could hear coming from the highest gallery, not fighting amongst themselves, and not stopping to eat the fallen and raid the ale cellar. They came silent and organised. They knew every defence we had: all our alarms, all our traps, and all our locks. They knew them all. It's almost as if they had tortured the secrets out of one of us, or there was a traitor in the hold, but that's impossible. No dwarf would give secrets to the grobi, not even under torture. It was… it was…'

'Eerie, is what it was,' said a white-bearded dwarf, an ancient veteran named Ruen, with fading blue tattoos at his wrists and neck. 'In seven hundred years, I've never seen grobi act so. It's not natural.'

Felix noted that, like Ruen, most of the survivors were white-haired Longbeards, too crippled or enfeebled to follow King Alrik north to the war. Younger dwarfs had stayed behind as well, for someone had to guard the hold while the king was away, but most of those had died defending it when the orcs came.

'They came when we slept, and destroyed two clanholds outright – slaughtered everyone, dwarf, woman and child,' said Gorril, his jaw tight. 'The Forgefire and Proudhelm clans are no more. There were no survivors.'

Hamnir's hands clenched.

'As I said,' continued Gorril, 'Thane Helmgard was seen to order the Diamondsmith clan to lock themselves in. We don't know if they were successful.'

'Then there is at least a chance,' said Hamnir, more to himself than the others. He sat lost in his thoughts for a moment, and then looked up. 'How does it stand now? What do we face?'

'The orcs defend the hold as well as we did,' Gorril laughed bitterly, 'perhaps better. Our scouts report that the main doors are whole and locked, and they were shot at from the arrow slits. Orc patrols circle the mountain, and there are permanent guards watching all approaches.' He shook his head. 'As Ruen said, they don't behave like orcs. No fighting amongst themselves. No getting bored and wandering from their posts. It's uncanny.'

Gotrek snorted. 'So they have some strong boss or shaman who's scared them into toeing the line, but they're still grobi. They'll crack if we press them hard enough.'

Gorril shook his head. 'It's more than that. You haven't seen.'

'Well, I better see quick,' Gotrek growled. 'I want to be done with this scuffle and heading north before I lose my chance at another daemon.'

'We'll try not to inconvenience you, Slayer,' said Hamnir dryly. He turned to Gorril. 'Have we a map?'

'Aye.'

Gorril took a large roll of velum and spread it on a shortened table between the dwarfs. They leaned forwards. Felix didn't bother to look. He had seen dwarf maps before. They were incomprehensible patterns of intersecting lines in different colours that looked nothing like any plan Felix had ever seen. The dwarfs pored over it as if it was as clear as a painting.

'So, they guard the main door,' said Hamnir, his fingers moving over the velum, 'and the high pasture gate?'

'Aye. They ate our sheep and rams,' said a hunched old dwarf. 'We'll need to buy new breeding stock.'

'And the midden gate? That lets out into the river?'

'Three miners went up it five days ago, to have a look. They came back down in pieces.'

'What of Duk Grung mine?' asked an old Thunderer with an iron-grey beard. 'The undgrin connects it to our mines. The grobi came up at us from below. We could do the same to them.'

Hamnir shook his head. 'Its three days to the mine, Lodrim, and then two days back underground, *if* the undgrin is clear. The Diamondsmith clan may starve by then, and the grobi might guard the way from the mines as strongly as they guard the front door.' He tapped the map with a stubby finger. 'Do they patrol the Zhufgrim Scarp side?'

'Why should they?' asked Gorril. 'It's a sheer face from Cauldron Lake to Gam's Spire, and there's no entrance to the hold.'

'Yes there is,' said Hamnir, with a sly smile. 'There's the passage to old Birrisson's gyrocopter landing. You remember? Near the forges.'

'You're out of date, lad,' said old Ruen. 'That hole was closed up when your father took the throne. Doesn't hold no truck with such modern nonsense, your da. He burnt all those noisemakers to the ground.'

'Aye,' said Hamnir, nodding. 'He told Birri to wall it up, but Birri is an engineer, and you know engineers. He wanted to keep one of the gyrocopters, and to have a place to work on all the toys my father frowned upon. So, he walled up the passage at both ends, but set secret doors in them, and made a workshop of it.'

'What's this?' cried Gorril. 'The old fool built an unprotected door into the hold?'

The other dwarfs were muttering angrily under their breath.

'It's protected,' said Hamnir, 'engineer fashion.'

'What does that mean, pray tell,' asked Lodrim dryly.

Hamnir shrugged. 'That secret door has been by the forges for a hundred years, and none of you have found it. The one on the mountain face is as cunningly concealed. If dwarfs can't find it, could grobi? And Birri set every trick and trap an engineer can conceive of inside. If they found the outer door, they'd be chopped meat before they got the inner.'

'It isn't enough,' said Lodrim.

'How do you know of this, young Hamnir,' asked old Ruen, 'and why did you keep such a grave crime from your father's knowledge?'

Hamnir coloured a bit and looked at his hands. 'Well, as you know, I'm not so much my father's son – not the way my older brother is. Perhaps it's because he is crown prince, and I am only a second son, but I am not so hidebound when it comes to tradition. I was only a boy then. I liked the gyrocopters, and all of Birrisson's contraptions. One night I caught him sneaking through the secret door. He begged me not to tell my father. I agreed, as long as he agreed to teach me how to fly the gyrocopter, and to give me use of the secret workshop.'

'But, lad, the danger,' said Lodrim, 'to you, and to the hold.'

Hamnir spread his hands. 'I make no excuses. I know I was wrong in this, as was Birri, but I... well, I liked having a secret from my father. I liked having a place to go that no one else knew of. I took Ferga there a few times.' He smiled wistfully, his eyes far away, and then roused himself. 'The point is, no matter how the grobi learned our hold's secrets, this is one secret that only I and old Birri and a few of his apprentices know, and no one can make an engineer talk. They are the keepers of the secrets of a hold's defence. Grimnir would deny them a place in the halls of our ancestors.' Hamnir tapped the map again. 'The grobi won't be defending this door. If a small force can enter there, and then sneak through the hold and open the front door for the main force, they will not stand against us.'

Gorril nodded. 'Aye. It is our own defences that defeat us, not the grobi. If we can breach our walls, they are finished.'

The dwarfs stared at the map, thinking.

'It'll be certain death for those that open the door,' said Ruen.

'Aye,' said Hamnir. 'Likely.'

Gotrek looked up. Felix thought he had been asleep. 'Certain death? I'm in.'

Felix groaned. Wonderful. Gotrek never seemed to consider how his rememberer was going to live to tell his tale when he made these decisions.

'You are willing to die to aid me?' asked Hamnir.

'Are you insulting me again, oathbreaker?' snarled Gotrek. 'I'm a Slayer. I'd be fulfilling two vows with one deed.' He sighed and lowered his chin to his chest again. 'Not that I'll die, of course, Grimnir curse it. Not at the hands of grobi. But at least I won't have to endure your presence.'

The dwarfs in the room glared and grumbled to hear their prince so abused, but Hamnir just sighed. 'And I won't have to endure yours,' he said, 'so it's all for the best. Good.'

'It'll take more than one dwarf to do the deed,' said Gorril, 'no matter how strong. Two levers in two separate rooms must be pulled simultaneously to open the Horn Gate, and others will need to hold off the orcs while they're pulled.'

Hamnir nodded. 'We'll ask for volunteers at the council tomorrow. That is if we are agreed here?'

The other dwarfs still seemed uncertain.

At last, old Ruen shrugged. 'It's a plan, which is more than we had before. I suppose it'll have to do.'

'I don't care to put the fate of the hold in the hands of a dwarf who seems to care so little for its survival,' said the Thunderer, Lodrim, glaring at Gotrek, 'but I haven't a better idea, so I'll second it.'

The others nodded, but with little enthusiasm.

Hamnir sat back, weary. 'It's settled, then. We'll work out the details before council. Now... now I'm to bed.' He rubbed his face with a hand and smoothed his beard. 'I've a dozen grudges to try to sort out tomorrow, Valaya save me.'

CHAPTER FIVE

GOTREK'S JAW CLENCHED and unclenched over and over. His leg bounced restlessly as he tipped back in his sawn-off chair. Felix had his journal open, and was reading through his Araby entries. Rodenheim's dining hall was again full of dwarfs, but not for a meal. The representatives of the dwarf companies sent from the various holds sat before the head table where Hamnir, Gorril and other leaders of Karak Hirn's refugees presided. All were waiting to hear the plan of battle for the retaking of the hold, but before they could proceed to strategy, there were grudges to be resolved that determined who would fight alongside whom, and if some warriors would return home before the battle started.

So far, Hamnir had proved an admirable negotiator, and each of the nine grudges he had heard had been resolved, or at least postponed until after Karak Hirn had been retaken or the battle lost. It was a long process, however. They had been at it since just after breakfast, and lunch was a distant memory. The heat of the hall's enormous fireplace was making Felix drowsy. He was having trouble keeping his eyes open.

'You say the ale delivered was not of the quality you were led to believe?' asked Hamnir. He rested his cheek on his fist, looking bored and frustrated.

'It was undrinkable!' said a sandy-bearded dwarf with a belly that suggested he knew quite a bit about ale. 'The double-dealing Hardstone clan promised us we would be paid in Bugman's Best. They sent us Bugman's worst, if it was Bugman's at all.'

'If the ale was undrinkable,' said a fierce-looking, black-haired dwarf in a yellow doublet, 'then it was damaged in transit, for it was in prime condition when we sampled a barrel before sending it off. The Wide-belt clan should take up this dispute with the traders that we commissioned to transport it.'

'This is fools' work,' growled Gotrek under his breath. 'We should be marching, not talking. If Ranulfsson were the leader his father was, these hair-splitters wouldn't remember their grudges. They'd be rallying around his banner and howling for orc blood.'

It took another ten minutes for Hamnir to resolve the dispute, and required all his cunning and diplomacy to shame the two dwarfs into setting aside the matter of the ruined ale. Gotrek growled under his breath the whole time, shooting dangerous looks at all the participants.

When at last an accord had been reached, Hamnir sighed and looked around the hall. 'Now, are there any other clans who are at issue, or may we proceed with the order of battle?'

'Have you forgotten us, prince?' said a white-haired dwarf with blue eyes, jumping up. His beard was a magnificent snow-white field.

Another dwarf with his hair in long grey braids that hung before his ears was on his feet only a second later, glaring at the first. 'Aye, prince. You have not yet taken up the issue of the Shield of Drutti.'

Hamnir groaned, as did the entire room. Gotrek growled, but although the assembled dwarfs were impatient, they had too much respect for the institution of the grudge, and for the sacred duty of every dwarf to resolve every grudge recorded in his clan's book, to complain, so they did nothing but grumble and fold their arms and settle back in their seats.

'I crave your pardon, Kirgi Narinsson,' said Hamnir to the white-bearded dwarf, 'and yours, Ufgart Haginskarl,' he said to the other. 'Remind me of the grudge. It has been a long day.'

The dwarf with the grey braids bowed. 'Thank you, prince. We of the Stonemonger clan bear grudge against the Ironskin clan for stealing from us the Shield of Drutti, which had been a gift from Gadrid Ironskin, the father of their clan, to Hulgir Stonemonger, the father of ours, two thousand years ago, as a token of thanks when Hulgir rescued Gadrid's daughter from trolls.'

'It was not a gift!' barked Kirgi. 'There were no trolls! It was an affair of business, pure and simple. Our clanfather traded the shield to the treacherous Hulgir for mining rights in the Rufgrung deeps. Rights which were never given.'

Gotrek's leg was bouncing like a steam hammer. Felix could hear the Slayer's teeth grinding.

'Is that the shield in question?' asked Hamnir, pointing behind Kirgi to an Ironskin dwarf who held a massive, rune-carved shield at his side.

'Aye!' cried Ulfgart, angrily. 'They dare to flaunt their stolen goods before us and expect us to–'

'We did not steal it! We merely took back what was rightfully ours. When you pay us what is owed, we will gladly return it to you. It was our clanfather's honest, trusting nature that–'

'Right! That's it!' said Gotrek, standing suddenly and taking up his axe. He crossed to the Ironskin table and snatched the Shield of Drutti from its surprised keeper as if it weighed as much as a pot lid.

'I'll solve this grudge!' he said, and threw the shield on the floor and chopped it in half with his axe, hewing wood and iron with equal ease. He then split the halves, hacking madly as splinters flew.

There was a collective gasp from the assembled dwarfs, but they all seemed too stunned to move.

Gotrek scooped up the mangled fragments of the shield, crossed to the great hearth and threw them in. The fire roared. He turned, grinning savagely at the Ironskin and Stonemonger leaders. 'There. Now you have nothing to fight over. Let's march!'

Ulfgart of the Stonemongers was the first to regain the capacity for speech. He turned solemnly to Hamnir, whose face was buried in his hands. 'Prince Hamnir, the Stonemonger clan formally renounces our grudge against the Ironskin clan, and records instead one against the Slayer Gotrek Gurnisson, and let it be known that this grudge can only be resolved in blood.'

'Aye,' agreed Kirgi Narinsson, his blue eyes blazing. 'The Ironskin clan also declares its grudge against the Stonemonger clan cancelled, and claims a new grudge against Gotrek Gurnisson.' He drew his hammer from his back and stepped towards Gotrek, 'And I ask the prince's permission to resolve this grudge here and now.'

Hamnir raised his head and glared at Gotrek. 'Curse you, Gurnisson! Now we've two grudges where there was only one!'

Gotrek spat on the floor. 'Fah! I thought they were honourable dwarfs, so concerned with the right of things that they would let a karak fall to the grobi over a shield. Will such dwarfs have me break a vow in order to fight them?'

'What vow is this?' sneered Kirgi. 'A vow of cowardice?'

'My vow to Hamnir,' said Gotrek, staring down the old dwarf, 'to aid and protect him until Karak Hirn is recovered. Killing you won't aid him, will it? You'll have to wait to die.'

Kirgi gripped his hammer and glared death at Gotrek, but at last stepped back. 'Let none say that a warrior of the Ironskin clan ever caused a dwarf to break an oath. We will settle this in the feast hall of Karak Hirn, after we have drunk to its liberation.'

'It'll be your last drink,' said Gotrek.

Ulfgart turned to Hamnir. 'Neither will the Stonemongers endanger this enterprise by killing a proven Slayer.' Gotrek barked a laugh at this. Ulfgart scowled and continued. 'We too will wait until Karak Hirn is won.'

Hamnir gave a sigh of relief. 'I thank you both for your forbearance.' He looked around the assembly. 'Are there any other grudges to be brought forward?' When no one spoke, he continued. 'Very well, then

listen.' He stood. 'This is the plan we have decided
upon. As you know, our own defences protect the
grobi, and since they are good dwarf work, they are
almost impossible to breach. We are less than fifteen
hundred strong. We would lose more than half that
before we were inside, were we to attack head on.
Fortunately, there is a way into the hold that the
greenskins will not have discovered. A small company,
led by the Slayer Gurnisson, will enter through this
door and make their way through the hold to the main
gate. When they have opened it, the throng will enter
and split up. The bulk of the force will hold the main
concourse, while smaller forces sweep through the rest
of the hold, pushing the grobi before them. We will
work from top to bottom, and force them out through
the mine-head doors.'

'What?' asked a young dwarf. 'Will we leave them
the mines?'

'Of course not,' said Hamnir, 'but we must secure
the hold before we can retake the mines, or we are in
danger of becoming over-extended.' When there were
no other complaints, he continued. 'What is yet to be
determined, is what companies will do what, and
who will volunteer to open the doors. I hope,' he
said, his face hardening as a growing murmur rose
from the dwarfs, 'that we can reach an agreement on
an order of march and a division of duty quickly,
without argument or recrimination, for time is of the
essence.'

Dwarfs all over the hall began standing and raising
their voices, demanding this or that position.

Gotrek grunted and turned to Felix. 'Come, manling, they'll be at it all night.'

'You don't care to learn who you will be leading?' asked Felix.

'Not as much as I care to find a drink.' Gotrek walked out of the room, chuckling darkly as he passed the great hearth, where the Shield of Drutti was burning merrily.

CHAPTER SIX

EARLY THE NEXT morning, while the sounds of the clans forming up in the courtyard came through the open door, Gotrek and Felix looked blearily around the stables of Rodenheim Castle at the dwarfs who sat waiting for them in the dim interior, their packs and weapons, armour and coils of rope at their feet. Hamnir stood in the entrance, dressed in gleaming battle armour, and looking ill at ease. He held an ancient brass horn, filigreed with silver.

'These are your volunteers, Gurnisson,' he said, 'all sworn to follow you unto death, if need be, and to obey your commands.' He gestured to a befuddled looking old whitebeard with rheumy eyes and a wooden leg. 'Old Matrak here helped Birrisson wall up the hangar passage and build his secret doors. He will get you through the locks and traps.'

The engineer broke off chewing his long, white moustache and nodded blankly at Gotrek. Felix noticed that his hands trembled. All that and a wooden leg, he thought. Going to be interesting getting the old fellow up a cliff face.

Hamnir turned to Thorgig and Kagrin, who stood nearest him. 'Thorgig will...' He glared at the young dwarf. 'Thorgig will carry the war-horn of Karak Hirn, and blow it from the Horn Gate watch tower once you are ready to open the doors. We will not advance until we hear it.' He held out the horn to Thorgig, who stepped forwards to take it.

Before he could, Hamnir drew it back, his brow furrowing. 'Thorgig, are you certain of this? There is little hope of survival. There are others who might–'

'Who?' said Thorgig, his lips tight. 'I served as a guard of the Horn Gate for ten years. Who among the survivors knows better than I the mechanism of the gate, the placement of the rooms? It must be me.'

'Gotrek can read a map.'

'Can he blow a horn? Does he know the calls?'

Hamnir growled. Felix had the feeling that he and Thorgig had had this argument many times before.

The prince turned to Kagrin. 'You too, Kagrin? Your skill is in shaping axes, not swinging them. Will you throw your life away and rob us of your art?'

Kagrin shrugged and looked at his feet. 'Where Thorgig goes, I go,' he mumbled.

'I tried to tell him the same,' said Thorgig, angry, 'but he won't listen.'

'Try telling yourself,' snapped Hamnir. 'You have a long life ahead of you.'

'My life is already forfeit,' said Thorgig stiffly. 'I left my clan and my family trapped in a hold full of grobi, and escaped to safety. Only freeing them will expunge my shame.'

'You have no reason for shame. There was an army of orcs in the way,' Hamnir said. 'You would never have gotten through.'

'Then I should have died trying.'

Hamnir's fist tightened around the horn until his knuckles were white. It looked as if he might crush it. Finally, he shoved it at Thorgig, punching him in the chest with it, and turned away.

'You should start at once if you hope to enter the keep before we are in position,' he said as he passed Gotrek. At the stable door, he paused and looked back, his face solemn. 'Luck to you all. You are our success… or our failure.'

He walked out.

A chill settled on Felix's heart. 'Inspiring, isn't he?' he said to Gotrek out of the side of his mouth.

Gotrek shrugged. 'What do you want from an oath-breaker?'

Felix had no idea what that had to do with anything.

'Prince Hamnir is no oathbreaker!' said Thorgig. 'Take it back.'

'What do you know of it, shortbeard?' asked Gotrek. 'You weren't born then.' He turned away from Thorgig and scowled at the others. 'A Stonemonger and an Ironskin,' he said looking from a cold-visaged, black-bearded dwarf wearing the clan rune of the Stonemongers, to a blond-maned, blue-eyed Ironskin who was the spitting image of Kirgi Narinsson, save for being at least a century younger and having a scar that ran down the left side of his face. He had a sliver of charred wood knotted into his huge blond beard like a charm. 'Ranulfsson has a mean streak in him,' said Gotrek, shaking his head. 'He hides it well, but it's there.'

'We are not here at the prince's bidding,' said the blond dwarf, smiling mischievously as he toyed with the blackened wood. 'We volunteered, as he said.'

The black-bearded dwarf nodded. 'The Ironskins and Stonemongers both have an interest in keeping you alive in this venture.' His voice was a soft and cold as snow. 'We do not wish to be cheated of our opportunity to resolve our grudges with you.'

'You don't have to worry about me,' said Gotrek, sighing, 'not against grobi.'

'Do we bring the manling into the hold?' asked a grizzled Ironbreaker with a broken nose and braided white hair and beard. He eyed Felix as if he expected him to grow fangs and horns. 'He'll spy out our secrets.'

'He is a Dwarf Friend,' said Gotrek. 'I vouch for him.'

'Dwarf Friend?' snorted the old Ironbreaker. 'The dwarfs have no friends but the dwarfs,'

'No wonder our glory is behind us,' said Gotrek dryly. 'What's your name, doomsayer?'

'Sketti Hammerhand, I am,' said the dwarf, puffing out his chest, 'of the Hammerhand clan. Ironbreaker and Deep Warden of Karak Izor.' And true to his name, the haft of a warhammer stuck up over his right shoulder.

Gotrek turned away from him, unimpressed. 'And you?' he asked, looking at the black-bearded Stonemonger. 'The one who means to protect me so he can fight me later.'

'Druric Brodigsson,' said the dwarf in his mild voice. 'A ranger of the Black Fire Pass, yours to command, for now.' He bowed his head, which was covered in close cropped, bristly black hair. 'Though it may not be me who fights you; he who will have the honour of facing you is still being discussed. I pray I am chosen. I have always wanted to take the measure of a Slayer.'

'Take the measure of your coffin first,' said Gotrek. He turned to the others, his gaze passing over old Matrak, the engineer, who had gone back to chewing his moustache and staring into space, and came to rest upon the blond dwarf with the piercing blue eyes. 'And you're the son of the old blowhard who challenged me last night.'

The dwarf smirked and leaned back, hooking his thumbs in his wide belt. 'Aye, that's me, Narin Blowhardsson. At your service, and your clan's.'

The other dwarfs chuckled.

'What's the kindling in your beard for?'

Narin closed his hand around the sliver of wood, suddenly embarrassed. 'My father's idea, he bid me wear a piece of the Shield of Drutti so that you would always see it and remember our grudge against you.' He scowled down at himself. 'I don't care for it. It's dirtying my beard.'

Gotrek raised an eyebrow. 'You want to fight me too, I suppose?'

'No no,' said Narin. 'My father will not give up the honour. I'm only to make sure you keep your head until he has the pleasure of removing it himself!' He grinned, his blue eyes sparkling. 'You really got the old badger's dander up. Wish I'd been there, but there was a lass from Karak Drazh, and well, it took some time for us to get properly acquainted.' He shrugged. 'About time the old dinner plate was turned to tinder anyway. No use to anybody, save as beard jewellery.'

Druric's head came up. His eyes flashed. 'The shield of Drutti was a great and noble heirloom. The theft of it by the Ironskin clan...'

'Oh come, cousin,' said Narin scowling. 'It has never been taken into battle. It was mounted on the wall of your feast hall for a thousand years before my great-grandfather took it, and then it was mounted on the wall of our feast hall for a thousand years. It was a dinner plate.'

Druric glared at Narin for a long moment, and then sighed. 'Very well, it was a dinner plate, but that is entirely beside the point,' he said, raising his voice as the others laughed. 'Theft is theft. It matters not if it is a bar of gold or a loaf of bread, the dwarf who took it is without honour.'

Narin held up his hands. 'Take it up with my father. It isn't my fight. The dwarfs will have no future if we keep fighting battles two thousand years in the past.'

'And what sort of future will we have if it is achieved at the price of honour?' asked Druric.

'Enough,' said Gotrek, growling. 'Save it for the beer hall.' He passed over Thorgig and Kagrin, who he knew, and looked at the last dwarf, who sat on an overturned bucket with the hood of his cloak pulled so far forwards that his face was entirely in shadow. 'You at the back, what's your name? Let's have a look at you.'

The dwarf didn't speak, only reached up and pulled back his hood. The others swore and laughed. Even Gotrek blinked. Felix didn't blame him, for this dwarf was the strangest of that strange breed he had ever seen.

'What are you?' asked Gotrek, scowling.

The dwarf straightened his shoulders and looked directly at Gotrek, light green eyes glaring out of the eyeholes of the head-covering leather mask he wore. The mask was, in its way, a thing of exquisite craftsmanship, beautifully tooled and sculpted in the square fashion of old dwarf sculptures. Thick strips of orange tinted leather hung in tapering plaits from its cheeks and jaw-line to represent a beard, and a bristling horse-hair crest of flaming orange rose from a flap of leather that went up over the dwarf's scalp and buckled to straps that extended back from the face. 'I am a Slayer,' he said in a low rasp. 'Leatherbeard the Slayer.'

'A Slayer? With no crest?' Gotrek raised a shaggy eyebrow. 'What manner of...'

Leatherbeard put his hand on his axe. He was barechested, in Slayer fashion, and wore only the hooded cloak over his shoulders to keep off the morning chill. 'Do I ask of *your* shame, brother?' he growled. 'Do I ask *your* reason for seeking death?'

Gotrek's teeth clicked together. He sobered instantly, and nodded at Leatherbeard. 'Fair enough.' He turned abruptly from the masked dwarf and shouldered his pack. 'Come on, then. Up and out.' He started out of the stable without a backward glance.

Felix gaped at Gotrek as the dwarfs gathered up their gear and followed him out into the wet morning air. That had almost been an apology!

THEY TRAVELLED NORTH and east from Rodenheim Castle all morning, up and down thickly forested hills that rose one after the other like swells in a green sea. There was a road to Karak Hirn – the remains of one of the old dwarf roads – but they didn't take it. The road led to the hold's front door, and would be watched. Hamnir's army was marching up it, bold as brass. With luck, the orcs would keep their eyes fixed on the column, and miss the little company of nine that went the hard way.

They sloshed through rock-choked mountain streams and scrabbled up loose shale slopes, trekked through deep forests and across upland meadows. As they climbed higher, drifts of half-melted snow appeared in the shadows, though the sun was hot on their necks. Felix had thrown back his red cloak and was sweating though his shirt. His calves ached like fire, and they hadn't even reached the real climb yet. Too many months at sea. He'd become a tenderfoot again.

The dwarfs took it all in their stride, maintaining the same dogged pace on flat ground or steep hill. Even old peg-legged Matrak kept up, mumbling, as he limped along, in a monologue that no one else could hear.

Felix wished some of the others were as quiet. Sketti Hammerhand in particular would not shut up for more than two minutes at a time, and it was always the same subject.

'It's the elves behind it all. They want the dwarfs dead because we're what stands in the way of them ruling the world. You can be sure they're behind this grobi trouble.'

'How could they be behind this?' asked Thorgig.

The others groaned as Sketti's eyes lit up. He had only been waiting for someone to give him an opening.

'You don't know elves like I do, young one. I've met them, and a twistier set of shock-headed beanpoles you wouldn't want to find yourself dead in a ditch with. There are no depths to which they wouldn't sink. No plan is too devious.' He licked his lips. 'I'll tell you how it is, lad. You think the greenskins getting too big for their britches is because so many dwarfs and men have gone north, and there isn't anyone to keep them out of the Badlands. That's true as far as it goes, but that's only the surface. A true dwarf doesn't trust the surface of nothing. He looks beneath.'

Gotrek muttered something about true dwarfs knowing when to shut up, but Felix didn't quite catch it.

'What you need to ask yourself, lad,' continued Sketti, 'is why the northmen are invading in the first place. What stirred them up? Put aside the fact that it was the elves messing about with magic they couldn't control that opened the Chaos rift in the first place, making them the fathers of Chaos, you can be sure it was elves put the bee in this Archaon's bonnet as well. Now the "fair ones" like to make out that they have nothing to do with their dark cousins in Naggaroth, but everyone knows that's a trick to blame their evil deeds on someone else. I had it from a dwarf who trades with Bretonnian sailors who deal with Ulthuan that it was the dark elves who whispered in the ear of this "chosen one" and told him his "destiny" lay in the south.' Sketti spread his hands. 'So, he heeds their words and invades the Empire, and the dwarfs, who have pledged since Sigmar's time to protect mankind, no matter how often they steal from us and stab us in the back, go north to defend the ungrateful weaklings, and lo and behold, the grobi "coincidentally" choose that moment to rise and attack! You can't make me believe it isn't all some dark elf scheme.'

'You're saying it was the dark elves who convinced the northmen to attack the Empire just so the grobi could take over Karak Hirn?' said Narin, chuckling.

'And why not?' asked Sketti.

'So the elves give orders to the grobi now?' scoffed Thorgig.

'Not directly. Not directly,' said Sketti. 'But they're in league with the skaven, everyone knows that, and the skaven…'

Everyone groaned again. Felix shivered, recalling all the times that he and Gotrek had encountered the horrid, man-like vermin, and the single-minded grey seer who had dogged their steps so unflaggingly during their travels in the Old World. He couldn't imagine the great Teclis ever conspiring with the likes of them.

'Hammerhand!' said Narin, interrupting Sketti's rant. 'There's a manling among us. Do you truly want to reveal to him all this secret dwarf knowledge? Everyone knows that men are the lackeys of the elves. Do you want the elves to know how much you know?'

Sketti's mouth shut like a trap. He turned and glared at Felix with wild eyes. 'It's true,' he muttered. 'It's true. I have perhaps said too much.' He shot a last suspicious glance at Felix and marched on in silence.

Narin winked at Felix behind Sketti's back as the rest sighed with relief.

Felix nodded his thanks and stifled a grin. A good fellow, Narin. Not as stiff as the others.

JUST BEFORE NOON, the party stepped out of pine woods at the top of a shallow ravine to find the jutting peak of Karag Hirn towering above them, a long feathery scarf of blown snow trailing away from its white craggy peak across the bright blue sky. The rest of the mountain was as black and sober as a judge. Thorgig, Kagrin and old Matrak looked up at it reverently.

'To think the halls of our birth hold run with grobi,' Thorgig spat. 'To think that they defile our sacred places with their presence. We will avenge you, karaz. We will cleanse you of their taint.'

The others murmured answering oaths.

On the west side of the mountain, the gleaming switchback curve of a road could be seen, and above it, almost hidden by rocks and outcroppings, the regular planes of massive dwarf battlements.

'That is the front gate – the Horn Gate,' said old Matrak, pointing. 'Where we…' He choked on the words. 'Where we fled from the silent grobi. Hamnir and the others go there to wait for us. We…' He swung his hand to the right. 'We go there. The Zhufgrim Scarp.'

Felix's eyes followed the engineer's finger to the eastern face of the mountain. The base of it, where it rose from the trees, was notched, as if some dwarf god had hacked out a gigantic foothold with an axe. A vertical wall rose up from the notch, more than half way to the snow-peaked crown, and looked, at least from where Felix stood, as smooth and flat as a sheet of parchment. A thin line of silver glittered down the middle of it.

'At the base is the Cauldron,' said Thorgig, stepping up beside the old engineer. 'A deep lake fed by the falls that pour down the cliff. That is our road.'

Felix swallowed. 'Up the cliff? Do you have wings in your packs?'

Sketti snorted. 'Nothing to it, for dwarfs.'

'Hist,' said Druric. 'Orcs.'

The others went quiet instantly and turned to where he looked. A small company of orcs was pushing through the heavy undergrowth of berry bushes that covered the floor of the ravine below. The dwarfs stepped back from the edge, and squatted down so they could only just see over the lip.

'Twenty of them,' said Thorgig.

'And we are only eight,' said Sketti.

'Nine,' said Druric, 'with the man.'

'As I said, eight,' said Sketti. 'We'll still manage.'

Gotrek snorted at that.

'I'd manage alone!' said Leatherbeard, defensively.

'Forgive me for speaking out of turn,' said Felix, 'but isn't the aim of our mission to reach the secret door without being seen?'

'If they're all dead,' growled Narin, tugging on the charred sliver in his beard, 'how can they tell what they've seen?'

'If others find them chopped to pieces,' said Felix, 'they will know we were here. And if we are to open the Horn Gate in time to let Hamnir in, can we spare the time for a fight?'

The dwarfs hesitated, palpably angry at Felix's attempts at logic. They were tensed like wolves looking down on unsuspecting sheep. Every fibre in their squat, powerful bodies wanted to charge into the ravine and butcher the greenskins.

At last Gotrek sighed. 'The manling is right. This isn't the time for a fight.'

The others grunted their annoyance.

'How much time could it take?' asked Leatherbeard.

'We'll have plenty of fighting in the hold,' said Gotrek, 'enough to kill us. Or the rest of you, at any rate.'

'I have sworn to follow you,' said Thorgig, stiffly, 'but it pains me to let even a single orc live.'

'It isn't the dwarf way,' said Sketti.

'It's *my* way,' said Gotrek. 'Now wait until they pass.'

The dwarfs grumbled, but did as he ordered, watching in hiding as the orcs passed below them.

The greenskins walked in double file, their leader at their head, scanning the landscape. They did not talk or argue amongst themselves as orcs usually did. There was no shoving or fighting, no drinking or eating, or bored hacking at the underbrush with their weapons. They kept at their task with a sad dullness that looked almost comical on their hideous faces. Only occasionally would this listlessness break, when one of them shook its head and twitched, roaring like a bull stung by a wasp, and its eyes would blaze with the accustomed orcish fury. Then, as soon as it had begun, the outburst would end, and the orc would sink back into its stupor.

'What's come over them?' asked Thorgig.

Kagrin shook his head, baffled.

'What kind of orcs don't squabble?' muttered Narin, unnerved.

'It seems almost as if they are asleep,' said Sketti, frowning.

'Then they kill in their sleep,' said old Matrak, trembling, 'for this is how they came when the Karak fell: silent, but bloodthirsty. We didn't hear them until they were on us. We didn't...' He trailed off, his eyes wide and far away.

The other dwarfs looked away from him, uncomfortable.

'Elf work, no doubt,' said Sketti. 'White sorcery.'

Narin considered this. 'Could any sorcerer alive today command the wills of an entire hold full of orcs?'

'One could,' nodded Sketti sagely. 'Teclis of Ulthuan.'

'He could at that,' said Gotrek, stroking his beard thoughtfully.

'You see?' said Sketti. 'The Slayer agrees with me.'

'The Slayer thinks you have elves on the brain,' said Gotrek, sneering, and returned to watching the orcs.

When they had passed out of sight around a twist in the ravine, the dwarfs continued on. Gotrek frowned as they walked, deep in thought. It seemed that he had finally become interested in the task that Hamnir had set him.

CHAPTER SEVEN

AFTER TWO HOURS pushing up Karag Hirn's steep, forested flank, they reached the tree line and came out onto dark, quartz-veined rock, patched with green-grey lichen. The way got harder, the slope steeper and blocked by massive outcroppings, and they had to use their hands as often as their feet to climb. Felix found himself more winded than he expected. The air was thin, and the wind cold, but he was sweating through his clothes.

An hour later, with the flat wall of Zufgrim Scarp getting higher and wider above them all the time, they began to hear a low roaring. It grew louder and louder, until, as they crested a narrow pass between two looming fangs of rock, they came upon a steep-shored mountain lake, surrounded on three sides by low jagged peaks, and on the fourth by the scarp, which rose directly from its frothing waters. The cliff didn't appear to Felix to be any rougher, now that they were closer. It was still as flat as the wall of a fortress. The only break was the waterfall that dropped down its centre in a rushing white torrent and split it in two. The noise of the cataract smashing into the lake was deafening. It churned the water into a roiling boil that made the surface of the whole lake dance, flashing sunlight into their faces from a thousand, thousand ripples. The edges of the lake were crusted with a jagged rime of ice. Flurries drifted down from the snowcap, high above them.

Felix shielded his eyes and looked up. The scarp was even more intimidating from this angle than it had been when old Matrak first pointed it out. He found he had broken out in an icy sweat. 'It's… it's impossible.'

Narin snorted. 'Easy as falling out of bed.'

Felix swallowed. 'Falling is always easy.'

'Eat before we go up,' said Gotrek, 'and get your gear ready.'

The dwarfs fell out, sitting down on the black boulders to eat salted meat and oatcakes, and washing the dry stuff down with beer poured from little wooden kegs they had strapped to their packs. Kagrin as usual got out his dagger and his tools and got to work, ignoring everyone else. Felix found it hard to look away. One mistake, one slip of the tool, and it would be ruined, but Kagrin never slipped. His hands were steady and sure.

Narin munched his hard-tack and sighed as if a great weight had been lifted from him. 'This is the life,' he said. 'Grimnir and Grungni, but I miss it.'

'The life, he says?' said Sketti, cocking an eyebrow. 'Might be the death as well, like as not.'

'Then I'll take the death,' he said with feeling, 'and willingly.'

Leatherbeard looked up at that. 'You don't wear the Slayer's crest. Why would you seek death?'

Narin smirked at him. 'You haven't met my wife.'

Thorgig turned. 'Your wife? Didn't you say earlier you were wooing some maid from Karak Drazh yesterday when the rest of us were at council?'

'As I said,' Narin continued, 'you haven't met my wife.'

Most of the others chuckled at that, but Thorgig and Druric looked offended.

Narin chose to take no notice. He sighed, playing unconsciously with the burnt stick of wood tied into his beard. 'I had the wanderlust when I was a short-beard. I walked my axe from Kislev to Tilea as a mercenary and adventurer for fifty years, and loved every minute of it. Saw more of the world in that half century than most dwarfs see in five.' He trailed off, his eyes looking far away, and a faint smile on his bearded lips. Then he shook himself reluctantly. 'All that's gone, now that my older brother's dead.'

'Called back to the hold, were you?' asked Druric.

'Aye,' Narin said sadly. 'The second son of a thane has the best of it and no mistake – just ask Prince Hamnir – gold and opportunity, and no more responsibility than a cat. Only now, I'm the first son. The old badger probably has another century in him at least, but still I must come home and learn the running of the hold, and memorise our book of grudges from cover to cover, and make a favourable marriage, and...' He shivered. 'Produce sons with my... wife.'

'Every dwarf must do his duty,' said Leatherbeard, through his mask. 'We are a dwindling race. We must beget sons and daughters.'

'I know, I know,' said Narin, 'but I'd rather have your duty. Killing trolls is a more pleasant task than bedding one, and trolls don't talk as much.'

'Surely she can't be as bad as all that,' said Thorgig.

Narin fixed him with a sharp blue eye. 'Lad, we are all like to die on this little jaunt, are we not? Prince Hamnir said it was a suicide mission.'

'Aye, I suppose,' said Thorgig.

'Well, let me put it to you this way. I'll be disappointed if it isn't.'

'And I will be disappointed if it is,' said Druric.

'You're afraid to die?' asked Thorgig sharply.

'Not in the least,' said Druric. He turned his cold eyes towards Gotrek, who was wolfing down his food and paying the rest not the slightest attention, 'but if Slayer Gurnisson dies, the grudge the Stonemongers have against him will go unresolved. As long as I know he will live, I don't mind dying.'

Gotrek snorted derisively at that, but didn't bother to respond.

After the meal, there was much rummaging through packs and re-coiling of ropes. Each of the dwarfs hung a bandolier of ringed steel spikes over one shoulder and strapped a pair of cleats to his boots. Fortunately, though dwarfs and men were so dissimilar in size and proportion that they could rarely exchange clothes, dwarfs had big feet, so a pair of cleats had been found for Felix. Old Matrak unbuckled his wooden peg leg and replaced it with one that was a long, black-iron spike.

When all straps were tightened, the dwarfs tapped out their pipes and stood, slinging their packs over their shoulders. Kagrin was last to be ready, tucking his tools and the gold-pommelled dagger away reluctantly.

'Come on, lad,' said Narin. 'There'll be work for the other end of that elf-sticker presently.'

The dwarfs edged around the steep shores of the Cauldron, slippery with broken ice and loose shale, until they came to the cliff face, the falls booming to their right, and spraying them with a fine, freezing mist.

Right up against it, the cliff wasn't quite as smooth and featureless as it had appeared before, but it was still daunting – a long, nearly vertical stratum of grey granite, with few cracks or protrusions. The dwarfs didn't even slow down. They stepped to the wall, reached up to grab handholds that Felix couldn't see, jammed their cleats into the rock and pulled themselves up without ropes or pitons, as easily as if they were ascending a ladder.

By watching closely where Gotrek put his hands and feet, Felix was able to follow him up the face, but it was hard, finger-cramping work, and he was nowhere near as steady as the dwarfs. Even old Matrak was doing better than he was, his iron leg spike biting firmly into the granite.

It struck Felix as odd that dwarfs, with their short, thick bodies, would excel at climbing mountains. One would have thought that a climber with long, spidery limbs and a thin torso – an elf, for instance – would be better suited to the work, but although the dwarfs did have occasional trouble stretching for the next hand or foot hold, they made up for their lack of reach with incredible strength of grip and their uncanny dwarfish affinity for the rock itself. They seemed to find, more by instinct than sight or touch, ridges and cracks to slip their sturdy fingers into that Felix could not have found if he had been staring directly at them.

Unfortunately, this skill, and their vicelike grip, gave the dwarfs the ability to use, as handholds, tiny irregularities in the surface of the cliff that Felix couldn't get a grip on at all. Consequently, by the time the dwarfs were halfway up the cliff, Felix was far below them, his forearms on fire with cramp and sweat running into his eyes. He could no longer hear the others because of the sound of the waterfall roaring past thirty feet to his right.

He paused for a moment to flex his hands and try to shake the ache from his limbs, and made the mistake of looking down between his legs. He froze. He was so high up. One slip – one slip and... Suddenly, he wasn't sure he could hold on any more. A mad urge to just let go and relieve the tension as he fell to his death nearly overcame him.

He fought it off with difficulty, but found he still couldn't move. He groaned as he realised he was going to have to ask for help. Dwarfs hated weakness and incompetence. They had no respect for someone who couldn't fend for himself. Even when they were alone, Felix always felt a fool when he had to ask Gotrek for help. It would be worse here, with a pack of other dwarfs looking on. He would be mocked. On the other hand, better to live and be mocked than literally die of embarrassment, wasn't it?

'Your rememberer is lagging behind, Slayer,' came Narin's voice from above him.

Felix heard a grunt and a dwarf curse, and then, 'Hang on, manling.'

The echoes of dwarf chuckling reached his ears and turned them crimson. Then came a sound of hammering. Felix looked up, but it was difficult to see who was who, let alone what was going on. All he could see were the soles of dwarf boots and broad dwarf rumps.

'Take this,' called Gotrek.

A coil of rope dropped towards him, rushing at Felix's face like a striking snake. He ducked. A small iron hook cracked him on the top of his head. He yelped and nearly lost his grip.

'Mind your head,' laughed Thorgig.

The hook slithered down the cliff face between Felix's legs and stopped with a bounce below his feet at the end of the rope it was attached to.

'Can you get a hand free?' asked Gotrek.

'Aye,' said Felix. He was rubbing his head with it as he spoke.

'Then hook the rope to your belt.'

'Right.' Felix drew the rope up one-handed until he had the hook, then passed it under and around his belt twice and hooked it to the rope again. 'It's done,' he called.

The rope began to slide back up the cliff until it was taut.

'Come ahead,' said Gotrek.

Felix started up again. The rope slackened as he climbed, but then retightened every few feet. Felix looked up and saw Gotrek pulling it through the eyelet of a piton and holding it tight.

The other dwarfs were all watching him as he rose, amused smiles on their bearded faces.

'What's this fish you've caught, Slayer?' asked Sketti.

'Not much meat on it, is there?' said Narin.

'Aye,' said Thorgig. 'Throw it back.'

As he came level with them, Felix saw that Gotrek had tapped two pitons into the cliff, one about five feet above the other.

'Bide a bit, manling,' he said. 'Put your foot on this one, and hold onto this one.'

Felix stepped gratefully onto the lower piton and held onto the other. It wasn't much, but after clinging on with his fingertips for the last hour, it was a blessed relief.

'When you've got some strength back, follow on. We'll leave lines and pegs for you.'

'Lines and pegs,' snorted Sketti. 'Like a baby. No wonder men steal everything from the dwarfs. They can't do a thing for themselves.'

'That's enough, Hammerhand,' growled Gotrek.

'Pardon, Slayer,' Sketti sneered. 'I forgot. He is your "Dwarf Friend". He must be very friendly indeed to be worth the trouble.'

Gotrek fixed the Ironbreaker with his one glittering eye and the mirth died on the old dwarf's lips. His white beard moved as he swallowed.

'Right,' said Gotrek as he turned back to the rock face. 'Upward.'

The dwarfs started up the cliff again while Felix stood on the piton and flexed and stretched each of his arms in turn. When Gotrek had climbed another fifty feet or so, he jabbed another piton into the granite, making it stick with just the force of his hand, then seating it securely with a small hammer. He tied Felix's rope to it, and moved on. From then on, this was how they proceeded. Felix's humiliation at having to use a rope was tempered by the relative safety and ease of the arrangement. He was no longer falling behind, and he didn't freeze when he looked down.

Three-quarters of the way up the scarp, even the dwarfs had to use 'lines and pegs'. The cliff bulged out at the top, like melted wax at the top of a candle, and they had to climb up the underside of the bulge. Gotrek went first, reaching as high as he could to tap in a piton, and then hanging a loop of rope from it in which to sit so that he could tap in the next. Felix shivered at the sight. The Slayer was so heavy, his muscles as dense as oak wood, and the pitons so tiny, that he expected them to pull out of the rock and Gotrek to plummet earthward at any second.

The dwarfs talked, unconcerned, while they waited, as easy clinging to their ropes and resting on their pitons with the wind whistling around them as if they had been bellied up to a bar in a cosy tavern.

'Look there,' said Sketti Hammerhand, pointing and raising his voice to be heard over the falls. 'You can just see Karaz Izor from here: third mountain in, behind the split peak of Karaz Varnrik. You won't have grobi taking *our* hold. My line has been Ironbreakers and deep wardens since my great-grandfather's great-grandfather's time, and no greenskin has ever slipped past us. We've an unbroken record.'

'Do you imply that we lost Karak Hirn out of laxness?' asked Thorgig with a dangerous edge in his voice. 'Do you say we didn't fight hard enough?'

'No no, lad,' said Sketti, holding up his free hand. 'I meant no insult to the bravery of your hold or clan. I'm sure you all fought as true dwarfs should.' He shrugged. 'Of course, if any of your king's line had been there, things might have been different.'

'Now you insult King Alrik,' said Thorgig, his voice rising.

'I do not,' Sketti protested. 'He isn't the only dwarf to fall prey to this elf-birthed Chaos invasion. His heart was in the right place, I'm sure, wanting to help the men of the Empire in their time of need, but a dwarf's first duty is to his own. So–'

'If you dig yourself any deeper, Hammerhand,' said Thorgig, his fists balling, 'You'll strike fire.'

'Quiet!' came Gotrek's voice from above.

The dwarfs ceased their argument and looked up. Gotrek hung above them, craning his neck to see over the curve of the bulge. He had one hand on the haft of his axe.

A sound of movement came to them faintly from the top of the cliff, barely discernible over the roar of the falls. A spill of pebbles rattled past Gotrek to drop towards the lake.

Felix thought he heard a command given in a high, harsh voice, but couldn't make out the word. Whatever it was, the speaker hadn't sounded human or dwarfish.

The dwarfs stayed as motionless as statues, listening. The sounds of movement came again, fainter and to the west, and then were gone. After a moment, Gotrek resumed tapping in the next piton.

'Goblin patrol,' said Druric.

Narin nodded.

'Do they know we're here?' asked Sketti, looking up anxiously.

'We'd be dodging boulders if they knew we were here,' said Thorgig.

Leatherbeard grunted. 'Not a Slayer's death.'

'They know,' said old Matrak in a faraway voice. 'They know everything. They know where the keys are. They know where the doors are.'

The others looked at him. He was staring into the distance, his eyes seeing nothing.

'Poor old fellow,' said Narin under his breath.

Gotrek reached the top shortly thereafter, and threw down a rope. Old Matrak went up first, the line hooked to his belt for safety. As troubled as he was in his mind, he was still sure in his movements. He let go of his piton and swung out on the dangling rope without a qualm. Then he climbed up hand over hand until he reached the bulge and could gain purchase with his foot and iron leg-spike again.

Felix went up fourth, after Druric. He had shinned up many a rope in his travels with Gotrek, and faced many a danger, but swinging out over that drop was one of the hardest things he'd ever done. Only the sceptical scowls of the dwarfs waiting their turn kept him from hemming and hesitating endlessly before letting go. He would be damned if he would let them think him more of a buffoon than they already did.

Of course, this hope was dashed when one of his cleats slipped as he began climbing up the underside of the bulge. He lost his footing and slammed face first into the cliff, bloodying his nose. He caught himself and recovered almost instantly, but he could hear the guffaws of the dwarfs below and above him. His face burned with embarrassment as he topped the bulge and Gotrek held out a hand to haul him up.

'Well done, manling. You're the first to shed blood in the recovery of Karak Hirn,' said the Slayer, grinning.

'The first to shed his own,' said Thorgig, chuckling behind him.

'I'll be happy to shed somebody else's,' said Felix, glaring at Thorgig. The young dwarf was beginning to get on his nerves. He had reason to hate Gotrek, Felix supposed. The Slayer had been more than insulting, to him and to Hamnir, but Felix had given Thorgig no cause to be angry. No cause but his mere presence, he thought. Thorgig was no Sketti, but he had the dwarfish disdain for all things non-dwarf.

Felix looked around. The cliff top was a broad flat ledge, like a landing halfway up the mountain. The rest of the peak still loomed above him, its white snowcap silhouetted against the blinding sun. A deep black pool – a mirror-calm twin to the roiling cauldron below – was cut into the ledge by ages of erosion. To his right, the pool spilled over the edge of cliff to become the narrow silver thread of the falls. There wasn't much room twixt water and cliff edge. It felt as if he and the dwarfs stood on the rim of a giant stone pitcher that forever poured water into a stone cup far below. The top of the falls was thin enough to jump, but the prospect of slipping made Felix's skin crawl.

Druric was studying the ground at the cliff edge. 'It was goblins,' he said.

'So, they're looking for us?' asked Sketti, glancing around warily.

'Not necessarily,' Druric answered. 'There are regular patrols through here.' He pointed. 'New prints over the old.'

Gotrek turned to Matrak as he helped Leatherbeard up. 'Which way to the door?'

Matrak waved to the east, beyond the stream, where the cliff-top ledge rose gradually to a split between the main body of the mountain and a rugged smaller peak – a broad shoulder to the karaz's proud head. 'Up. Through there.'

'The grobi went that way,' Gotrek said. 'Get your armour on.'

The dwarfs took off their cleats and pulled mail shirts, pauldrons and gauntlets from their packs, replacing them with their climbing gear. Felix buckled on a scale-sewn leather jack, and fixed his old red cloak around his shoulders. None of them carried shields, which would have been too heavy and cumbersome while climbing.

Gotrek left the rope over the bulge in place and hopped the roaring falls. The dwarfs followed him across, apparently without a second thought. Felix held his breath as he took a running jump and tried not to imagine falling in the water and being dragged over the edge by the rushing current.

Safely on the other side, the company followed the ledge as it rose to the split between the mountain's head and shoulder. This was a narrow, shadowed cleft that wound crazily between the two peaks, and then opened out onto a sway-backed saddle of hard-packed snow that sloped up to the black flank of Karaz Hirn to their left, and down to a sheer cliff on their right. The last few yards before the cliff were black ice – frozen run-off from the slanting plain of snow, as glossy and smooth as the lip of a wine bottle.

As they were about to step out of the cleft onto the snow, a patch of red and green on the far side drew Felix's eye. A dozen goblins were hacking apart the carcass of a mountain goat, and its blood stained the snow all around them. Like the orcs they had seen before, the goblins were maintaining a very un-greenskin-like silence. They weren't fighting over the choice bits, or devouring their portions immediately, but instead stuffed the bloody legs and flank steaks into their packs for later.

'They're in the way,' quavered Matrak, pointing to a dark gap in the rock face on the far side of the slope of snow. 'The door's beyond that pass.'

'We'll have to take them, then,' said Narin.

'Thank Grimnir for that,' said Sketti. 'The day I hide from goblins is the day I shave my beard.'

Leatherbeard growled in his throat.

'Shut up and attack,' said Gotrek. He started forwards at a run.

The dwarfs charged after him as fast as they could, which, by Felix's standards wasn't very fast. He had to keep to a trot, so as not to get too far ahead.

The goblins saw them coming, but didn't shriek in alarm, or scatter in blind panic as goblins were wont to. Instead, they just dropped the bits of hacked-up goat they held and turned to face the dwarfs, as silent as monks.

Druric loosed a crossbow bolt that took one goblin high in the chest, then threw the crossbow aside and drew a hand axe. He and Felix and the dwarfs crashed into the runty greenskins like a battering ram, mowing them down with their sheer mass. Four goblins died immediately, axes buried deep in their scrawny chests and pointy skulls. Three more were bowled off their feet. Gotrek split one in two. Felix hacked at a second, a tiny, snaggle-toothed horror that rolled away from his blade. Old Matrak stomped on another with his iron leg-spike, impaling it.

The goblin leader chittered an order as he fought Thorgig, and two goblins peeled away from the fight to scamper up the rise. Leatherbeard sent one of his axes spinning after the runners, dropping one, but the other was nearing the opening at the top of the snowy slope.

'After him, manling!' called Gotrek. 'Make those long legs useful!'

Felix sprinted up the incline, his feet smashing holes in the hard crust of snow. The goblin darted through the dark gap and down into a dropping, rocky cleft. Felix charged in after him, gaining with every step. The goblin looked back once, emotionless as a fish, and then ran on.

The floor of the cleft was filled with rocks and loose gravel. Felix slipped and slid as he ran down it, twice nearly twisting his ankle. He came within a yard of the goblin and swiped at it with his sword, but it leapt ahead, ducking around a big boulder and out of sight. Felix swung wide around the boulder, and found himself suddenly on the lip of a wide crevasse that dropped away into blackness. He lurched left, heart thudding, his scrabbling feet kicking pebbles into the abyss, and twisted away from the edge barely in time.

The goblin scampered up a rocky rise before him. Felix surged after it, skin prickling at the closeness of his narrow escape. No one would ever have found him had he fallen into that chasm. No one would know what had become of him: a horrible end for a memoirist.

The goblin slipped on loose scree and fell on its face as it reached the crest of the rise. Felix closed on it rapidly. It picked itself up again and dived over the ridge. Felix leapt after it and tackled it to the ground. They rolled down the far side of the ridge in a tangle of limbs, and jarred to a stop at the base of the slope, the goblin on top. It raised its saw-bladed short sword to stab him, but Felix clubbed it off his chest with his free arm and rolled on top of it, slashing down with his sword. The steel bit through the goblin's skull. The little green monster spasmed and lay still.

Felix collapsed to the side and lay with his cheek on the cold rock, panting and wheezing, glaring at the dead goblin beside him. 'Got you at last, you filthy–'

An enormous fur-booted foot stepped into his circle of vision. He looked up. A huge orc in scrap armour loomed over him, staring down. Twenty more stood at its back.

CHAPTER EIGHT

THE ORC SLASHED down at Felix with a huge double-bladed axe. Felix yelped and rolled. He was deafened as the axe bit deep into the ground, an inch from his shoulder, pinning his cloak. Felix surged up, the cloak nearly strangling him before it ripped free. Another orc swung at him. He jerked aside and ran, stumbling and unsteady, back up the ridge.

The orcs raced after him, unnervingly silent. Felix pounded down the slope towards the black chasm, skidding within inches of the drop as he turned into the narrow confines of the rocky pass. He heard the orcs thundering behind him, and then a fading bellow as one of them missed its footing and tumbled into the depths. The rest came on, not sparing their lost comrade a backwards glance.

A stitch stabbed at Felix's side as he scrabbled up the tight, rising path, and his breath came in ragged gasps.

He'd already been winded when he caught the goblin. Now he felt as if he was going to die. He wanted to stop and vomit, but the orcs were so close at his heels that he could hear their breathing and smell their rank animal odour. The ground shook with their footsteps.

The light from the snowfield glowed at the top of the shadowed pass like a beacon of hope. It looked a hundred leagues away. He slipped on a loose rock and this time he did twist his ankle. It flared with sudden agony. He cried out, and nearly fell. Swift steel whistled behind him and an axe rang off the rock wall beside his head.

He scrabbled on, ankle screaming with each step. He didn't have the luxury of favouring it – just jammed his foot down and took the pain as best he could. At last, nearly fainting with agony, he gained the top of the pass, inches ahead of the orcs, and burst out onto the snowfield. A slashing cleaver grazed his scale-covered shoulder and sent him sprawling. He slid face-first down the snowy incline towards the cliff.

The dwarfs were marching up the slope with the dead goblins behind them. They readied their weapons as he sped toward them, looking beyond him with eager anticipation on their faces. Gotrek stepped out and Felix crashed into his knees. The Slayer hauled him up

'Er,' said Felix, probing his throbbing shoulder. The orc had cut through the leather and torn off some of his scales, but he was unbloodied. 'I got the goblin.'

'Good,' grunted Gotrek, and stepped past him, hefting his axe.

The orcs were spreading out in an even semi-circle and marching down in a dressed rank, weapons at the ready. Felix shivered at the sight.

'They aren't orcs,' said Sketti, uneasily, echoing Felix's unspoken thought. 'They can't be. They're something else, dressed up in green skin.'

'Elves, maybe?' said Narin, smirking.

Druric looked over his shoulder, down the slope. 'They mean to keep us in front of them. They want to push us off the cliff.'

'Let them try,' said Leatherbeard.

The orc leader jabbered an order and the orcs charged, uttering not a word. The dwarfs braced and met the attack with an unmoving wall of sharp steel. Gotrek blocked the leader's first strike, shattered its war axe with his return blow, and then cut its legs out from under it. Two more leapt in to take its place.

Narin and Druric fought back to back in a ring of three orcs. Leatherbeard was stepping over one dead orc to get to another, two dripping double-bladed axes in his massive hands. Sketti Hammerhand and old Matrak fought an orc that wielded an iron mace the size and shape of a butter churn. Thorgig and Kagrin butchered another with their axes and turned to face two more.

Felix fought a short, barrel-gutted brute with a head like a green pumpkin. Strange, he thought, as he slipped an axe stroke and missed with an attack of his own. Though their tactics were vastly improved, and though their fury seemed to be contained, the strange orcs still fought like orcs, slashing with great, clumsy swings that could flatten a building if they connected, but more often than not missed. Why had one aspect changed and not the other? And what had changed them in the first place? Then he stepped awkwardly on his twisted ankle and all thoughts went out of his head in a rush of pain.

The orc saw him stumble. It swung. Felix lurched aside and ran it through the ribs, jolting his ankle again. The orc collapsed. Felix nearly joined it. The world was fading in and out around him. Another orc attacked, this one stringy and tall. Felix groaned. He wasn't ready. He blocked and retreated, limping badly.

Half the orcs were dead, and not a single dwarf had yet fallen, but by sheer weight and numbers, the greenskins had forced the stout warriors back almost to the black ice that glazed the edge of the cliff. Gotrek killed another and it slid past him as it fell, spinning noiselessly into the void.

Felix stepped back again. His bad foot shot back on the ice. His knee hit the slick surface with a smack. His vision went black and red. He was sliding backwards. The tall orc pushed in, eager to finish him off, and instead sat down abruptly as its feet flew out from under it. Felix grabbed at the greenskin's belt, more to stop himself sliding than as an attack, and pulled the orc towards the edge. It scrabbled uselessly with thick yellow fingernails at the hard ice, then it was gone.

Felix shuddered, terrified, then crawled delicately back up onto the snow, hissing and groaning, as the battle raged around him.

To his right, Narin kicked an orc's leg out and it slammed down on its chin before sailing off the cliff. To his left, Thorgig jumped back from a cleaver slash and tripped over the corpse of a dead orc behind him. He fell flat on his back on the ice and started sliding headfirst for the precipice.

'Thorgig!' roared Kagrin, and stepped forwards, only to slip himself. He clutched at a boulder as he watched his friend spin towards the void.

Thorgig recovered at the last second, and slashed down with his long-axe. The hooked heel of the head bit into the ice and held. He swung to a stop, holding one-handed onto the very end of his axe-haft with his feet dangling off the edge.

Thorgig's orc swung at Kagrin, still clinging to the boulder. It swung. The young goldsmith pushed away, and the orc's axe struck sparks off the rock. Kagrin gashed it behind the knee with his handaxe and its leg buckled. It fell on its side, grunting, and slid, twisting and flailing, across the ice, coming perilously close to dislodging Thorgig as it flew off the edge.

'Hold fast, Thorgig!' called Kagrin, tearing into his pack and pulling out his climbing rope. He began lashing one end around the boulder, but another orc had noticed him and was coming around the fight towards him. Kagrin dropped the rope and stood.

Felix pulled himself to his feet and started for Kagrin, but his ankle gave out and he nearly fell again. He would never reach him in time. He looked around him desperately. Kagrin blocked a brutal blow with his hand-axe and was smashed to the ground, dazed.

A severed orc head lay behind Gotrek. Felix snatched it by its topknot and turned in a circle. The gruesome thing was amazingly heavy – all skull, no brain, no doubt. His ankle and knee blazed with pain as he spun.

'Hoy!' he shouted, letting go. 'Ugly!'

The orc looked up just in time to take the head of its comrade full in the face. It wasn't a hard blow, but it distracted it long enough for Kagrin to stagger up and bury his axe blade in the thing's gut. The orc stepped back, surprised, and its paunch ripped open, its entrails spilling out of the wound and slapping wetly on the ice. It slipped on them and crashed down into the snow. Kagrin stood and chopped it through the neck. It spasmed and died. Kagrin threw down the axe and turned back to his rope.

Felix limped forwards to defend Kagrin while he uncoiled the rope, but as he looked around he saw there was no need. The battle was over. The other dwarfs stood panting over their kills, the snow all around them stained with blood, both red and black. Gotrek climbed out of a circle of dead orcs and rubbed the blade of his axe with a handful of snow. Leather-beard had a long gash across his bare chest, but his was the gravest wound. The rest had only nicks and bruises.

Kagrin tossed the end of his rope towards Thorgig.

The other dwarfs turned.

'Careful, lad,' said Narin. 'No sudden moves.'

'That's why a dwarf always carries an axe, not a sword,' said Sketti, looking disapprovingly at Felix's longsword. 'A sword wouldn't have stopped you.'

Thorgig reached out gingerly with his free hand and felt for the rope beside him. He found it at last and gripped it tight.

'Don't try to climb,' said Gotrek. 'Just hold on.'

He took the rope from Kagrin and pulled it in gently, hand over hand. Thorgig slid up the ice in little jerks and starts, his axe dragging behind him, until Gotrek had pulled him to the snowline. Kagrin took his friend's hand and helped him to his feet. Thorgig's face was set and emotionless, but he was white, and his hands shook.

'Thank you Slayer,' he said. 'Thank you, cousin.' He turned to Felix and inclined his head, 'And thank you, human. I saw what you did. You saved my life and the life of my friend. I owe you a great debt.'

Felix shrugged, embarrassed. 'Forget it.'

'You can be sure that I will not.'

'Slayer,' said Druric. 'We should throw the bodies over the edge, and all the bloody snow with them. There may be another patrol, and it would be best if they didn't learn what became of the first.'

'Aye,' said Gotrek, nodding. 'Carry on.'

While the others pushed and rolled the orcs off the edge, and scooped the stained snow after them, Druric, who carried a field kit, dressed and bound Leatherbeard's wound, and wrapped Felix's swollen ankle in bandages.

'Not broken, I think,' he said.

'It may still kill me,' said Felix, thinking of the descent back down the mountain.

Sketti laughed as Felix forced his foot painfully back into his boot. 'Now maybe you'll slow down and walk at a proper dwarfish pace.'

'And maybe if I hung you by the neck you'd grow to a proper human height,' returned Felix.

Sketti blustered and reached for his axe.

Gotrek gave him a look. 'Never get into a war of words with a poet, Ironbreaker. You can't win.'

When all the evidence had been pitched off the cliff and the dwarfs had bandaged their wounds, they set off once again up the saddle-shaped slope of snow and down through the rocky pass.

'THERE,' SAID MATRAK, after another half hour of winding around the crags and cliffs of Karaz Hirn. 'There is Birrisson's door, that once led to the gyrocopter landing further up.' He pointed to an unremarkable stretch of black granite that looked to Felix no different from the rest of the mountainside.

Druric studied the ground as they paused before it. He shook his head, frustrated. 'The ground is too hard, and there is no snow here. I cannot tell if the grobi have used this door.' He sniffed. 'They have left no spoor nearby.'

'Where else would they have been going?' asked Narin.

'Circling back all the way to the entrance?' suggested Sketti.

'There isn't much of a path that way,' said old Matrak. 'No path at all.'

'If they do use this door,' said Thorgig, 'does it change our course? We must go in even if it is defended. Prince Hamnir depends on us.'

'It is likely not well defended even if it is used,' said Narin. 'They can't expect an attack from this quarter.'

'Open it and we will see,' said Gotrek.

Matrak stepped forwards, but then hesitated, staring blankly at the wall.

'Don't tell me we've come all this way to have you tell us you've forgotten how to get in,' said Narin. He took tinder from his pack and lit his tin lamp. The others followed his example.

'They know we come. They wait for us,' said Matrak. He was shivering. 'We will all die.'

'Enough of that, you old doomsayer,' said Sketti angrily. 'Open the door!'

As the dwarfs lit their lamps, Matrak nodded and did something at the cliff face that Felix couldn't see. He stepped back. The dwarfs went on guard. Felix drew his sword. At first it seemed that nothing happened. Then Felix frowned and shook his head, assaulted by vertigo. His eyes fought to focus. He felt as if he was sliding backwards, though his feet weren't moving. No, it was the cliff-face getting further away! A tall, square section of it was sinking into the surface of the mountain. Felix strained his ears, but could hear no sound of gears or grinding.

After a moment, the square of rock stopped, about fifteen paces into the mountain, revealing the edges of a dark, cut-stone chamber. When a horde of orcs didn't charge out of the door and attack them, the dwarfs started forwards.

'Hold!' said Matrak. 'There is a trap.' He squatted at the groove in the floor, which the sliding door travelled in, and reached down into it. After a moment of fumbling, there was a clunk that Felix felt more than heard, and Matrak stood.

'Now it is safe,' he said.

It didn't feel safe. Though Felix saw nothing particularly alarming, as he and Gotrek and the others stepped warily through the door, he could not shake the feeling that something wasn't right. His back tingled, and he kept looking over his shoulder, thinking he would find evil eyes glowing in the darkness, but there was nothing there.

Matrak closed the door behind them. On this side, a simple lever operated it. The chamber within was only of a moderate size, by the usual standards of dwarf architecture, with a low arched ceiling, criss-crossed with wooden beams that supported iron pulleys and winches hung with heavy chains. Workbenches, forges and writing desks cluttered the space, and old, half-built machines and contraptions were everywhere. Their shadows moved across the walls of the workshop like the skeletons of strange mechanical beasts as the dwarfs passed among them with their lanterns. A gyrocopter lay dismantled in a corner.

Sketti shook his head as he looked around. 'Engineers are mad,' he whispered. 'All of them.'

Matrak led them to a shadowed archway on the far side of the room. Beyond it was a short, narrow corridor that rose, in a series of long, shallow, slightly slanting steps, to a stone door at the far end.

'Be careful,' said Matrak, holding up his hand as he stopped before it. 'Here is where Birri set all his traps and–' He froze suddenly, and then whimpered softly.

'What is it, now?' asked Thorgig, annoyed.

Matrak stepped back, trembling. 'It isn't right. It isn't right,' said Matrak. 'Smells wrong. All wrong.'

The dwarfs lifted their bulbous noses and inhaled. Felix sniffed too, expecting the familiar animal reek of orcs, but could smell nothing. The dwarfs however were frowning.

'Fresh-cut stone,' said Kagrin.

'Aye,' said Druric. 'Not more than a week old.'

'The orcs have taken up masonry now?' asked Thorgig.

Kagrin thrust his lantern through the arch, illuminating the corridor, and examined it with a critical eye. 'Can't be,' he murmured. 'It's all straight and true.'

Felix scowled. 'You can tell how long ago stone has been cut by the smell?'

'Of course,' said Sketti. 'Men can't?'

Felix shook his head. 'None that I know of.'

'Yours is a sad, weak race, man,' said Sketti, pityingly.

'That rules the world,' Felix retorted.

'Only by theft and trickery,' said Sketti, his voice rising.

'Quiet!' barked Gotrek. He turned back to Matrak, who was staring into the corridor with wet, frightened eyes. 'What does it mean, engineer?'

'They've cut stone. Grobi who cut stone? It...' He moaned. 'It can only mean they've changed the traps.' He turned to Gotrek. 'Valaya protect us all. They knew we were coming! They set new traps!'

Gotrek grabbed him by the front of his chain shirt. 'Stop your snivelling, Grimnir curse you!' he rasped. 'If something's wrong, fix it!'

'He's lost his spine,' sneered Sketti, turning away. 'The greenskins stole it from him before he escaped the hold.'

'You didn't see!' wailed Matrak. 'You don't know! We are doomed!'

'Perhaps there's another explanation,' said Narin. 'It doesn't have to be cunning grobi. Perhaps the trapped clans have managed to retake some of the hold. Perhaps they have added new defences against the grobi.'

'Or maybe the greenskins just walled up the far side of the door, and that's what we smell,' said Leatherbeard.

'Whatever the case,' said Druric, 'we'd best go with caution. It would be a grisly joke to be cut to pieces by traps set by those we come to rescue.'

Gotrek released Matrak. 'Right. Get on, engineer.'

Matrak hesitated, staring unhappily into the tunnel. Gotrek glared at him, hefting his axe. The engineer swallowed and at last stepped reluctantly to the arch again, examining every inch of the surrounding floor and wall before finally touching in sequence three square protrusions in the decorative border. Felix heard nothing, but the dwarfs nodded, as if they sensed that the trap had been disarmed. They started forwards.

Matrak held up a hand. 'Just to be sure.' He took off his pack and dropped it heavily on the flagstones just inside the arch. The dwarfs stepped back, but nothing happened.

Matrak let out a long held breath. 'Right.' He took two steps into the corridor and froze, peg leg in the air. He backed away and waved to the others to retreat. 'There *is* a new trap.' He was sweating.

He squatted and examined the floor, running his fingers lightly along the hair-thin seam between two perfectly cut flags, and then looked around at the walls. Something along the moulding on the right side caught his eye and he shook his head.

'Is it dwarf work?' asked Narin.

Matrak chewed his beard. 'It can't be anything else, but it's… No dwarf would admit to work this bad.' He pointed to a section of the moulding. 'Look how poorly it's set.'

Felix could see no difference between it and the next, but the other dwarfs nodded.

'Maybe they were rushed,' said Thorgig. 'Maybe they tried to finish it before the grobi found the passage.'

'Even rushed, a dwarf would take more care,' Matrak said. 'Something's wrong. Something's wrong…' He bent and pressed the new piece of moulding, then let out a breath as he sensed something that Felix couldn't.

'Go on, engineer,' said Gotrek, more gently. 'Test it and move on. We're late as it is.'

Matrak nodded, and tested the new trap with his pack. Nothing happened. He picked it up and inched forwards again, lamp low to the ground. They proceeded in this slow, painstaking way all along the corridor, Matrak disarming traps he knew, finding new ones he didn't, and looking paler and shakier with each. The dwarfs watched his every move, tensing as he searched for the next trap, and relaxing as he disarmed it.

Felix looked around at the walls and ceiling as they progressed, trying to see signs in the stone work of where these traps would spring from, but he could make out nothing. There were no holes or suspicious ornamentation in the shape of axe or hammer. The stone blocks were so well set, and their patterns so regular, that he could not imagine any trap behind them.

While Matrak grew more and more petrified, the other dwarfs grew more at ease, becoming convinced that their brethren inside the hold still lived, and were putting up a spirited defence of reclaimed halls and chambers.

'They're keeping the grobi out,' said Sketti Hammerhand, as they neared the end of the corridor. 'It's as plain as the nose on your face. There'll be dwarfs on the other side of that door, I'll bet my beard on it. We should stop this pussyfooting and call them to let us in.'

'It will be my father,' said Thorgig. 'He wouldn't sit in his hold doing nothing, waiting for rescue. He would be fighting back, attacking the attackers.'

Matrak stopped before the last step. The door was only two strides away. 'The final step is the last of the old traps,' he said. He reached for a torch sconce in the right-hand wall and pushed on the side of the base with his thumb. It turned, and Matrak breathed a sigh of relief. 'There,' he said, turning to the others. 'Only new ones to find–'

Felix felt a deep thud under the floor and a click overhead.

CHAPTER NINE

THE DWARFS FROZE. There was a rolling sound in the ceiling.

Matrak looked up, blinking. 'The cunning villains,' he breathed, with something akin to admiration. 'They've trapped the disarming switch.'

'Run!' roared Gotrek.

The dwarfs turned, but before they had taken two steps, a huge square of the ceiling above the door swung down, its leading edge hitting the floor with a boom. Kagrin screamed, his foot trapped under it, his ankle crushed to paste. A rumbling came from the hole in the ceiling.

'Kagrin!' cried Thorgig, turning back.

'Fool!' Gotrek grabbed him by the collar and dragged him on.

Stone spheres the size of large pumpkins shot down from the hole and bounded down the hallway. The noise was deafening. One landed squarely on Kagrin's head, squashing it flat, and then sped on with the others, leaving red splotches with each bounce.

The dwarfs ran as fast as their short legs could carry them. It wasn't fast enough. Sketti was mowed down by three spheres. They mashed him to a pulp. Another sphere hit his battered body and vaulted up into the air. Gotrek jerked his head aside and the sphere only grazed his temple. He staggered and wove on, bloody. Thorgig recovered his feet and ran past him. A sphere took Matrak's peg leg out from under him and he landed flat on his back. Another dropped on his belly, bursting it.

Felix sprinted ahead of the dwarfs, ignoring the agony of his ankle, and threw himself left at the end of the corridor. A stone sphere flew past him, missing him by inches. He looked back and saw another sphere knock Druric sideways into the corridor wall. He fell. Leatherbeard scooped him up with brawny arms and dived out of the corridor to the right. Narin was right behind him. Thorgig dodged a careening sphere and landed face first beside Felix. Gotrek came out last, staggering and weaving inches ahead of two spheres, and crashed on top of Narin, clutching his bleeding head.

The spheres barrelled out of the corridor like charging bulls and smashed into Birri's contraptions and workbenches, turning them into scrap and kindling, before finally losing momentum and coming to rest. A tall copper reservoir tank toppled slowly, two of its metal legs bent, and collapsed to the floor with a metallic crash and a billowing eruption of dust.

Felix and the dwarfs lay where they had fallen, catching their breath and collecting their wits. Felix wasn't sure if he was hurt or whole, or how many of his companions were dead. His mind was still a whirl of running and dodging, and the nightmare grinding sound of the rolling spheres.

A groan from the corridor at last brought Thorgig up. 'Kagrin?' He stood.

'Don't get your hopes up, lad,' said Narin, sitting up and rolling his neck. He gingerly tested his left arm.

Thorgig stepped to the mouth of the corridor. Felix and Narin got to their feet and joined them.

Gotrek stood as well, but had to hold the wall. 'Who tilted the floor?' he mumbled.

Leatherbeard pushed himself up and stood behind the others, pulling his mask straight so he could see through the eyeholes. Only Druric stayed where he lay, curled into a tight ball, his eyes clamped shut in pain.

Another moan came from the hall. Felix and the dwarfs stepped forwards. Four yards in, they found old Matrak. He lay, half conscious, in a pool of his own blood, one of the spheres in the place where his stomach had been. He looked up at the dwarfs.

'Knew it wasn't right,' he murmured. 'Didn't I tell you?'

Thorgig took the old dwarf's hand. 'Grimnir welcome you, Matrak Marnisson.'

'Am I dying, then?'

He was dead before any could answer him. The dwarfs bowed their heads, and then Thorgig looked further up the hall. Sketti lay ten feet away, his body shattered, his sightless eyes staring accusingly at the ceiling. Beyond him was another broken lump. Thorgig started into the shadows.

'No lad,' said Narin. 'You don't want to see.'

'I must!' Thorgig cried.

But before he could take another step, the door at the end of the corridor swung slowly open, half hidden behind the granite ramp of the ceiling trap that had released the stone spheres. A crowd of hulking silhouettes filled it. One reached in and touched the decorative border that surrounded the door. There came a sound of gears and counterweights from the walls, and the trapdoor that had released the stone spheres tilted back up into the ceiling. There were clicks and thuds from behind the walls all along the corridor.

'These aren't the survivors,' said Narin, stepping back.

'But it's impossible,' insisted Thorgig. 'Grobi couldn't have set these traps!'

'Perhaps not,' said Leatherbeard, 'but they just disarmed them.'

The orcs pushed into the corridor, looking down at Kagrin's mashed corpse.

'Forget the traps,' slurred Gotrek. 'Get them.' He stepped ahead of the others, weaving drunkenly and slapping his axe haft into his palm.

'Aye,' said Leatherbeard, joining him. 'They've much to answer for.'

The orc leader spotted the dwarfs in the gloom, and barked an order. The orcs stepped over Kagrin and stalked ahead, silent and alert.

'Ah,' said Felix, back-pedalling. 'I hate to be the voice of reason again, but we won't make the front gate. Not with the whole hold roused. We'll leave Prince Hamnir high and dry.'

'The manling's right, Slayer,' said Narin, edging back. 'We must return to Hamnir and warn him off his attack.'

Gotrek spat and growled a vile oath, but stepped back. He plucked up the sphere that had crushed old Matrak as if it was made of wood rather than stone, and bowled it unsteadily, but forcefully, at the orcs. It caught the first two in the shins and knocked them back into the others, toppling them like ninepins and causing a jumbled pile-up. 'Right,' Gotrek said, turning. 'Out.'

As the other dwarfs started after the tottering Slayer, Leatherbeard stopped and squatted by Druric, who was still only semi-conscious.

'Get him on my back,' he called to Narin. 'Hurry.'

Narin turned back and lifted Druric under his arms. The ranger screamed in pain, spraying blood and spit. Narin ignored him. There was no time to be gentle. He draped him across Leatherbeard's broad back. The Slayer caught Druric's legs and stood. Then he went after the others. In the corridor, the orcs were picking themselves up and starting forwards again.

Thorgig pulled the lever and the dwarfs squeezed through the slowly opening door onto the mountainside, turning down the path that led to the Zhufgrim scarp. When they were all out, Thorgig flipped the lever down and ran through as the door began to reverse directions, but it was closing much too slowly.

They ran on.

The sun squatted on the horizon, a bleeding red ball gutted by the jagged peaks of the Black Mountains. All its warmth was gone. The thin mountain air was growing colder by the moment. It froze the sweat on the back of Felix's neck. The hour agreed upon for Hamnir's attack had arrived, if it was not already past, and there was nothing they could do to tell him that the horn blast would not be coming.

'I will repay the orcs ten-fold for the death of Kagrin Deepmountain,' said Thorgig, his face set. 'They have taken a great craftsman and a greater friend.'

Who had no business being there, thought Felix, as he looked over his shoulder. The door was sliding open again, and the orcs were pouring out of it like a green river. There seemed no end to them, and they were already gaining.

'Pointless to carry me,' gasped Druric from Leatherbeard's back. His face was white and slick with sweat. Each of the masked Slayer's jolting strides brought him fresh agony. 'Leg is broken. Hip as well. Won't make it down the mountain.'

'Bah!' said Leatherbeard. 'I'll strap you to my back. We'll get along.'

'We'll fall,' said Druric through his teeth. 'Pegs won't hold two. Leave me with my axe and crossbow. Let me buy you some time.'

'You want a great doom when I am denied one?' snarled Gotrek. 'Not likely.'

Felix observed that Gotrek was having a hard time running in a straight line.

'Aye,' said Leatherbeard. 'If there's anyone stays behind it'll be me. This is Slayer's work.'

'Ha!' Druric laughed. Blood flecked his lips. 'Do you really want to be remembered as a mere orcslayer? Leave me, and save yourself for a better death.'

No one replied, but only ran on in grim silence.

'Valaya curse you for fools!' cried Druric. 'I will not survive these injuries. Let me die as I wish!'

'Leave him,' said Gotrek, at last. 'A dwarf should have the right to choose the manner of his death.'

They carried Druric until the path became a narrow ledge between cliff and mountainside. The dwarfs could hardly walk it with their shoulders squared.

'Here,' said Gotrek.

Leatherbeard stopped and lowered Druric to the ground. Felix looked back. The orcs were hidden around the curve of the mountain, but he could hear them coming – heavy boots stomping, armour clanking.

The ranger slumped across the ledge, cringing in pain. He took off his pack and field kit. 'Pegs,' he said, teeth clenched against his pain. 'I cannot stand. Pin me to the wall.'

The dwarfs didn't question his order. Leatherbeard lifted him and propped him against the wall while Thorgig and Narin deftly tapped pitons through the back of his chain shirt at his neck and flanks.

Druric grinned. His teeth were filmed with blood. 'Good. This way I will block their way even when I am dead.'

Gotrek was still having trouble holding himself upright. He kept shaking his head and blinking his one eye, one hand on the mountain's flank.

'All right, Gotrek?' asked Felix, concerned.

Gotrek grunted, but made no answer.

'It's done,' said Narin, stepping back. He cocked and loaded Druric's crossbow and put it in the ranger's left hand as Thorgig put his axe in his right.

The orcs rounded into view fifty yards back, loping like patient wolves.

'I had hoped that I would be the one to fight you for the honour of my clan, Slayer,' said Druric. 'I regret that will not come to pass.'

Gotrek stood upright and looked Druric in the eye. 'I'm sorry too,' he said. 'Die well, ranger.' He turned and started down the path.

The other dwarfs saluted Druric in dwarfish fashion, fists over their hearts. They followed Gotrek without a word, Thorgig slinging Druric's field kit over his shoulder. Felix wanted to say something in parting, but all he could think of was 'good luck' and that somehow didn't seem appropriate. He turned, vaguely ashamed, and trotted after the others.

Fifty paces on, they heard sharp cries and the clash of steel on steel echoing from behind them. Gotrek and Leatherbeard cursed, almost in unison. Thorgig muttered a dwarf prayer.

Narin growled. 'He was a good dwarf,' he said. 'Stonemonger or no.'

For almost quarter of an hour it seemed that Druric might have stopped the orcs entirely, for the dwarfs heard no sounds of pursuit, but then, as they were climbing the narrow cleft to the treacherous snowfield, the heavy tread of boots found them again. Felix had fallen behind, his throbbing ankle slowing him, and he heard it first. He picked up his pace, hissing with each step, and caught up to the dwarfs.

'They gain again,' he said.

Gotrek nodded. He seemed to have recovered his balance, but the left side of his head was bruised and purple beneath the drying blood.

'We will have trouble at the top of the cliff,' said Narin. 'They will cut the first rope before we can all traverse the bulge to the pegs.'

'I will stay behind and protect the rope,' said Leatherbeard.

'*I* will stay behind,' growled Gotrek. He stopped as they reached the top of the pass. 'I'll hold here. When everyone gets below the bulge, peg the end of the first rope and blow the horn. I'll cut it myself and swing down. Keep them from following us down.'

'Swing down?' said Thorgig, alarmed. 'You'll pull the peg out.'

'Peg it twice then.'

The orcs appeared at the bottom of the pass and Gotrek turned to face them.

'Go,' he said. 'This is all mine.'

But as Felix and the dwarfs turned to step out onto the snowfield, Leatherbeard looked up. 'What's that?'

Felix listened. Boots were running above them. At first he thought it was a weird echo from the orcs in the pass, then he saw long, hulking shadows lurching across the mountainside above the pass. 'They've split up. Found another trail.'

Thorgig cursed. 'They mean to go around the pool and come at us from behind. They'll find the ropes and cut them.'

'Flanked,' Gotrek growled. 'To the cliff!'

He stormed out of the pass and led them down the saddle of snow. The orcs burst out not twenty paces behind them, flowing down the white slope after them like a green stain. The dwarfs ran as hard as they could, but they had been trekking and climbing and fighting all day, and were gasping and flushed. Felix hissed with each step. His ankle felt thick and spongy. By the time the dwarfs reached the mirror pool, the orcs were ten paces behind. As they raced around the shore towards the cliff-edge, they were only five paces distant, and Felix saw the other group coming down from the crags and circling around the opposite side of the pool. They would reach the ropes only seconds after the dwarfs did.

'Ironskin,' rasped Gotrek, as they hopped the rushing falls. 'You're down first.'

Narin grunted. 'Not much on sharing glory, are you?'

Gotrek skidded to a stop next to the rope and turned to face the orcs as they bounded the stream, a silent green avalanche of death. 'I'll hold the left,' he said. 'The rest of you hold the right. Then down on my call.'

With a roar, the Slayer sprang to meet the charging orcs, chopping down three with his first swing, and another two with his backhand. The orcs swarmed him, slashing at his naked torso with savage silence, but they could not penetrate the net of flashing steel he wove around himself. Orc limbs flew and orc axes shattered as Gotrek blocked and bashed, his orange crest bobbing wildly.

Felix shook his head. He had seen it a thousand times, but it never ceased to amaze him. The Slayer in his element was a terrible and awesome sight. He seemed not to have two arms, but six, and three axes, all moving at blurring speed.

The second group of orcs crashed into Felix and the others from the left, nearly driving them off the cliff. They held just at the brink, parrying and hacking furiously. Felix gored an orc and pulled another past him over the edge as it thrust with a crude spear. It bounced down the bulge and into empty air. Narin and Thorgig dispatched one each, and Leatherbeard hacked down two.

'Down, Ironskin!' came Gotrek's voice from the bloody scrum to their right.

Narin cursed as he gutted another orc, but backed from the combat as ordered, while Felix, Thorgig and Leatherbeard closed ranks. Narin snatched up the rope and started backwards down the cliff. 'You dare not die here, Gurnisson!' he shouted over the clash of weapons. 'You owe my father a fight.'

Felix and the others were pressed back to back with Gotrek as the orcs pushed in on them from all sides, a surging green wall, out of which lashed snapping tusks, massive fists and black-iron axes. Every swing and shift of weight made Felix's ankle scream. Gotrek fought the leader, a huge, milky-skinned orc whose beady black eyes glittered silently at the Slayer with cold intensity as they fought. Felix frowned. Didn't orcs have red eyes? Or yellow?

'Thorgig, down!' called Gotrek.

'What?' cried the young dwarf. 'Me before the human? I won't!'

'Down, or I throw you down,' growled Gotrek, swinging his rune axe up through the black-eyed orc's jaw and into his brain. 'The manling's fought by me for more than twenty years. He knows his business.'

The strangeness of the orc's eyes flew out of Felix's head and he felt a burst of pride as Thorgig started, snarling and reluctant, down the rope. He didn't think he'd ever heard Gotrek compliment his prowess as a fighter before. He fought with renewed vigour, inspired by the off-hand praise, protecting the Slayer's flank and rear as he'd always done, while Gotrek dealt brutal death left, right and centre.

On the other hand, he thought sheepishly, he wouldn't have minded entirely if Gotrek had thought less of him and let him go down first.

Dead orcs lay thick on the ground, but there didn't seem to be any less pressing them, and with Thorgig and Narin making their way down the cliff, Gotrek, Leatherbeard and Felix fought harder than ever. Felix wondered if even Gotrek could keep the orcs away from the rope alone. A cleaver grazed Felix's leg, opening up an angry red gash, and a dead orc, falling from Gotrek's axe, nearly knocked him backwards off the cliff. His ankle throbbed, one pain among many. He felt dazed and numb, the green horde blurred before him. He could hardly hold up his sword.

'Down, manling,' Gotrek shouted. 'It's Slayers' work now.'

Felix nodded and backed out of the fight, relieved, and took up the rope. He saw Leatherbeard puff up at Gotrek's words, just as Felix had a moment earlier, and lay into the orcs afresh, pleased to think that Gotrek counted him his equal. Strange how such a taciturn misanthrope could inspire with an unconsidered word.

As he let himself down, hand under hand, feeling gingerly for footholds with his damaged foot, Felix watched the two Slayers fight back to back, axes flashing crimson in the last rays of the sun, their deep-muscled chests and backs streaked with sweat and blood, their thick legs braced wide before the onslaught of the ravening green horde. And the mad thing was, they were laughing. Inches from the cliff-edge – where a single misstep could send them plummeting – battling scores of savage behemoths that lusted for their blood, and they laughed.

Felix understood this to a certain extent. He was not immune to the euphoria of battle, to the mad rush that came with putting one's life on the line, when pain and weariness and any thoughts of the future went away and one was lost entirely in the glorious violence of the moment. But, for him at least, this was a joy that always teetered on the edge of terror, the excitement always well mixed with fear. The Slayers seemed to have no such qualms. They looked entirely content.

As Felix edged below the bulge, he heard Gotrek shatter that contentment with three little words.

'Leatherbeard, go down!'

'Down? No!' shouted the second Slayer through his mask. 'The glory is here!'

'There's no glory in orcs,' said Gotrek. 'You heard what the ranger said. Down!'

'This is not the respect due to one Slayer from another Slayer!' said Leatherbeard angrily, but finally Felix felt the rope jerk above him as the masked dwarf began his descent.

Though Felix could no longer see the fight, the sounds of it rang down from the cliff like the clanging of a foundry, harsh cries and the clash of steel echoing through the thin mountain air. He looked down. Narin and Thorgig waited by the first peg, each hanging from his own pegged rope, looking up. The rope from the cliff top was, as Gotrek had requested, doubled pegged at its nether end.

'Hurry, human,' said Thorgig. 'The Slayer can't hold forever.'

'I begin to wonder,' said Narin thoughtfully. 'He will be a fearsome opponent. If my father dies fighting him, I will become Thane, Grungni save me...'

There was a thunder-crack bang from above. A body with a Slayer's crest hurtled past Felix, plunging down the cliff into the twilight shadows below. Felix gaped. Had it been Gotrek? Leatherbeard? He looked up.

The rope went slack in his hands.

He fell away from the cliff.

CHAPTER TEN

FELIX STARED AT the loose rope as he dropped, stupid with shock. Another body was falling with him, bellowing. He caught a glimpse of Thorgig gaping at him as he plummeted past him, and thought, 'I am going to die.' Then the rope jerked taut, and ripped out of his hands. He spun and slammed upside down into the cliff with teeth-jarring force, stopped short by something that grabbed his left ankle. His leg was nearly pulled out of its socket.

He sucked in a tremulous breath, heart pounding, and body ringing like a bell. His palms were wet with shock sweat. The world was upside down, and dim at the edges.

I'm alive, he thought, though he wasn't sure how. He should have been spinning down the cliff like a straw doll.

Someone groaned below him. He tipped his head back to look down. Leatherbeard held on woozily to the rope twenty feet further down the cliff, the right half of his mask scraped and scarred and his right shoulder bloody.

If Leatherbeard was hanging from the rope, then it was Gotrek who had fallen. Gotrek was…

A searing pain in his ankle drove the thought away. Well, he had twisted it, hadn't he? Then he realised it was the *other* ankle that hurt now. He fought gravity to look up at it. It was caught in a loop of rope – a loop that was being drawn tighter and tighter by the weight of the masked Slayer clinging to it below him. It was agony, a bright fire atop the dull throb of all his other aches and pains.

'Leatherbeard, get off the–'

Felix snapped his mouth closed, terrified by what he had almost done. The Slayer's weight was all that kept Felix from falling. If he let go of the rope and clung to the cliff instead, the loop would loosen and Felix would slip away.

'Hold fast, manling,' came Thorgig's voice, and the young dwarf rappelled down to stop beside him as Narin dropped down to Leatherbeard.

Thorgig held out his hand. 'Take it.'

Felix reached out and clasped it hard. Below him, Narin was helping Leatherbeard, swinging his rope towards him. The Slayer caught it and transferred easily. The pressure on Felix's ankle let up and he dropped again, scraping down the rough cliff face to swing free from Thorgig's hand.

'Now, take the rope,' said Thorgig.

Felix grabbed Thorgig's rope with his free hand, wrapped his legs around it, and let go of Thorgig's hand. He and the three dwarfs hung from the ropes and caught their breath. They could hear the orcs marching away above them, as voiceless as ever.

'The Slayer is dead?' Thorgig asked, looking down into the darkness below.

'We'll know when we get to the bottom,' said Narin.

'Surely even Gurnisson can't have survived a fall like that,' said Thorgig.

Narin shrugged. 'If anyone could it would be him.'

'But what knocked him off?' asked Thorgig. 'What was that bang?'

'Maybe they had a shaman with them,' said Narin.

'I saw no shaman,' said Leatherbeard wearily.

'Come on,' said Narin. 'Down we go. No point in speculating. We're late for Hamnir.'

Their descent was much quicker than their ascent had been. The dwarfs used lines and pegs the whole way, and rappelled down in grasshopper-like leaps.

Felix took it slower. His ankle would not allow him their long hops, and he went down in silence, his mind struggling to take in the thought that Gotrek, at whose side he had walked for more than two decades, might be dead.

It was too early to grieve – he couldn't yet believe the Slayer was gone. But the idea of a life without him made his head spin. What would he do? Following the Slayer had occupied almost all of Felix's adult life. His duty to record the Slayer's death had gone on for so long that he had a hard time remembering what it had replaced. What had he meant to do with himself before he met Gotrek? Write poetry, plays? Give up his bohemian ways and help his brother with the family business? Marry? Have children? Is that what he wanted now?

How old was he now? Forty? Forty-two? He had lost track of the years during his and Gotrek's travels in the east. Was it too late to pick up where he had left off? Was a forty-year-old student too ridiculous? Of course, even if Gotrek were dead, Felix still owed him some work before he got on with his life. His vow would not be fulfilled until he had written the epic of the Slayer's death.

His heart sank at the thought. Gotrek would be furious to have it recorded that he had died at the hands of 'mere orcs'. It wasn't a fitting death for a Slayer that had, in his time, killed daemons and giants, an anti-climax of the first order. Gotrek would never let Felix hear the end of it. Except... Felix choked back an unexpected sob as it finally hit him. Except Gotrek was...

'There he is,' said Narin, far below him, pointing down.

Felix stared down into the gloom of the cauldron vale, eyes searching, and at last made out a patch of bright red hair on the shore of the churning lake. The Slayer lay motionless on his stomach, half in, half out of the water. Had he fallen there from the cliff, or dragged himself to the shore? Felix almost lost his grip as he hurried to lower himself to the ground.

Narin, Thorgig and Leatherbeard were down before him, but out of some sense of fitness, waited until he had reached the ground before starting around the steep shore of the boiling lake to the broad, prostrate form. At Felix's limping pace, it seemed to take forever, but at last they stood over him. There was just enough light left in the vale to see that Gotrek's back and neck were a flaming, angry red, as if a giant hand had slapped him. His one eye was closed, and his crest was limp and bedraggled. Blood ran from his nose and mouth, and pooled on the black shale under his head. There was more trickling from under his shoulder. His axe lay beside him.

'Gotrek?' said Felix.

There was no answer.

Felix squatted down and reached out towards the Slayer, but then hesitated. If he touched him he would know, and he was afraid to know. 'Gotrek... Are you?'

Gotrek's eye fluttered open. He groaned, and then coughed violently. Water spilled onto the shale.

Felix and the three dwarfs breathed sighs of relief.

Gotrek's coughing subsided. 'Slow-pokes,' he said, barely audible. 'What took you... so long?'

Narin knelt beside him. 'Can you move, Slayer? Anything broken?'

Gotrek thought for a long moment, eyes closed, and then opened them again. 'No,' he mumbled. 'Just... stings a bit.' He tried to turn over and sit up, but his arms trembled and he sank back.

Thorgig and Leatherbeard helped him up and sat him on a rock. He hissed with every movement and touch. Felix saw that he had a deep, bloody wound in his left shoulder.

'What is that?' he asked, pointing.

Gotrek blinked down at the wound. 'That?' He lifted his hand towards it, but seemed too tired. He let it drop in his lap. 'That is the reason I left the orcs.'

'Don't tell me you made that leap on purpose,' snorted Leatherbeard.

'Of course he did,' said Narin. 'A sparrow insulted his great-great-grandfather, and he leapt off to challenge it.'

Thorgig laughed. They all seemed a bit giddy to find Gotrek alive. 'Sparrowslayer, they'll call him.'

'No,' Gotrek said, shaking his head heavily. 'They shot me. Knocked me clean off the cliff.'

'Shot you?' asked Thorgig, confused. 'With what? That's no arrow wound.'

'A long-gun,' said Gotrek.

'Orcs don't have guns,' scoffed Narin. 'They barely have fire.'

'A dwarf long-gun,' finished Gotrek.

The dwarfs fell silent.

'These are very strange orcs indeed,' said Thorgig at last.

Felix's memory flashed back to the orc lieutenant's glittering black eyes. He had to agree.

Thorgig opened Druric's field kit and brought out bandages. He bound Gotrek's shoulder as best he could as the others saw to their own hurts.

When he was all patched, Gotrek tried to stand. He swayed like a wheatstock in the wind and sat back down. 'Curse it. Leatherbeard, your shoulder. We can't wait.'

Leatherbeard helped Gotrek up and slipped his shoulder under his arm.

Gotrek cocked an eyebrow at Felix as they started around the pool. 'All right, manling? You look a little pale.'

Felix coughed. 'I... I'm just glad I didn't have to make "knocked off a cliff by orcs" sound heroic.'

'Didn't think I was dead, did you?'

'It… it crossed my mind.'

Gotrek snorted. 'You should have more faith.' He hissed and stumbled. Leatherbeard caught him and they continued. 'Good thing that pool was deep though.'

THEY HURRIED AS fast as they could around the base of Karaz Hirn. This wasn't very fast at first, but Gotrek recovered himself after about half an hour, and was able to walk on his own. They made better time after that, though it was still hard going, pushing through the rough terrain and dense undergrowth of the pine forests in almost utter darkness. The dwarfs, not wanting to draw the attention of any more grobi patrols, disdained the use of lanterns, and navigated the woods with the keen tunnel-born sight of their race. Felix, however, was constantly cracking his head on low branches, or re-twisting his ankle on protruding roots.

After a further hour of difficult travel, the five companions came to the valley through which ran the old dwarf road that led to Karak Hirn's front door. As they pushed through a thick wood towards the road, Leatherbeard stopped and held up a hand.

'Someone's on the road,' he whispered.

They listened. The clinking and rumbling of an army on the march reached their ears, and here and there torchlight winked through the tangle of branches.

'It can't be Hamnir,' said Thorgig. 'The forward position is a mile north at least. He can't still be getting into position.'

'Who else can it be?' asked Narin tugging on the burnt piece of the Shield of Drutti in his beard. 'Reinforcements from another hold?'

'Orcs coming up from behind?' asked Leatherbeard.

'We won't find out by talking,' said Gotrek. He pushed forwards and the others followed, more cautiously, unlimbering their weapons as they went.

Soon the wood thinned, and they looked out at the road from its shadows to see a dwarf army marching slowly south.

'It *is* Hamnir!' said Thorgig. 'What has happened? 'He's going the wrong way!'

Leatherbeard pointed to the tail of wounded and dead on stretchers and pony carts trailing behind the main column.

'Did the fool attack without our signal?' asked Narin.

'Prince Hamnir is not a fool!' said Thorgig angrily.

'He is if he attacked a buttoned-down hold,' said Gotrek. 'Come on.'

The dwarfs stepped out of the wood and walked up the weary column to its head. Along the way, various dwarfs glared at them, faces hard and angry. Some of them spat at the sight of them.

'Ah, the hero's welcome,' said Narin.

'What are we supposed to have done?' asked Thorgig.

When they reached the front, they found Hamnir marching grimly with Gorril and his other lieutenants. Hamnir had a cut on his forehead, and his chainmail was rent in two places. Gorril and the others were similarly battered. They looked utterly exhausted.

Hamnir gave Gotrek a flat glance as he fell in step with him. 'So, you live. I am sorry to hear it.'

'So am I,' said Gotrek. 'Wasn't through lack of trying.'

Hamnir ignored him. 'Dead, you would have been a hero – the brave Slayer who tried and failed to win his way into the hold to open the door for the army.

Alive... alive, you have a lot to answer for.' He looked at Thorgig sadly. 'As do you, Thorgig.'

'The grobi discovered us, prince,' said Thorgig, hurt. 'We would not have reached the front door to open it. We did our best to remain alive in order to return and warn you not to attack.'

'If you attacked without our signal,' said Gotrek, '*you* have a lot to answer for.'

'We did not attack!' cried Hamnir. 'We were attacked! The greenskins raided our position while we waited to hear the horn – archers in the hills that we could not engage, skirmishers who struck and ran, wolf riders. We dared not pursue, for fear of scattering our force, and so we sat, waiting, for a signal that never came, while they picked us off in ones and twos, and we killed one for every five they slew.'

'Prince,' said Thorgig, his young face pale behind his beard. 'Forgive us, we had no–'

'Indeed, I do have a lot to answer for,' continued Hamnir, hotly, interrupting him. 'For when Gorril and the others begged me to withdraw and give the day up for lost, I would not, for I had faith in my old companion, Gotrek Gurnisson. Surely the great Slayer would not fail. Surely it would only be a matter of a few more minutes before we heard the horn.' He hung his head. 'For my foolishness, I lost another fifty noble dwarfs.'

Gotrek sneered. 'You blame me because you're a bad general?'

Gorril and Thorgig bristled at that, but Hamnir waved them down with a tired hand. 'I am no general at all, as you well know. I am a trader, a seller of sharp steel, fine ale and precious gems. It is fate and duty that have brought me to this pass, not inclination. I can only do my best.' He turned hard eyes on Gotrek. 'Just as you vowed to do your best.'

'You think I have not?' Gotrek growled.

'You are alive and the door remains closed. Can you say you gave your all?'

'Our deaths would not have won the door, Prince Hamnir,' said Narin. 'The grobi were alerted to our presence when poor old Matrak tripped a new trap, which killed him and Kagrin, and Sketti Hammerhand. They came through the secret door and attacked us, and even had we defeated them–'

'New traps?' interrupted Gorril, his voice sharp. 'What do you mean, new traps?'

Hamnir moaned. 'Matrak and Kagrin dead?'

'There were traps in the passage that Matrak did not know of, my prince,' Thorgig explained. 'Dwarf work, he said, and built within the last week, by the smell of the new-cut stone. He found and disarmed all but the last.'

'The orcs opened the secret door and touched the secret levers that disarmed all the traps as if they had built them themselves,' said Narin.

'Impossible,' said Hamnir, ashen-faced.

'Aye,' continued Leatherbeard, 'but true none-the-less. We all saw it.'

'Even had we defeated the orcs who came through the secret door,' continued Narin, 'the alarm had already been raised. There would have been an entire hold of angry greenskins to fight through. Perhaps Slayer Gurnisson might have made it, but the rest of us would not have lived to help him open the doors.'

Hamnir's head drooped. He stared at the ground for a long while, and then, at last, looked up at Gotrek. 'If this tale is true, then I suppose I must believe that you have done what could be done.'

Gotrek sneered, unappeased.

'But how can these things be?' Hamnir continued, almost to himself. 'How can there have been traps that Matrak did not know of? How could the grobi know their use? It makes no sense.'

'I fear we may only learn the answers to these questions once we have retaken the hold, my prince,' said Gorril.

'Aye,' said Hamnir, his jaw tight with frustration. 'Aye, but how are we to do it? They seem to have counters for our every move! We thought this the only way possible. Can we find another?'

'Maybe you can convince them to trade the hold for some fine ale or precious gems,' Gotrek growled.

Hamnir's fists clenched. 'If there was a chance that it would work, I would do it,' he said. 'Would you, Slayer? Or would you leave the hold to the grobi because you found the winning of it lacking in glory?' He moved pointedly away from Gotrek, and began talking in low tones with Gorril.

Gotrek glared at Hamnir for a long moment, then grunted and looked away.

The Slayer and the prince remained silent and sullen for the rest of the march. Felix wondered again what it was that had made them hate each other so. Even among dwarfs, the grudge between them seemed particularly malignant. One usually only saw this sort of intense hatred between brothers who had fallen out. Gotrek had said it had been over a broken vow, but what had the vow been? Did it have something to do with Gotrek taking the Slayers' oath? An insult? A woman? As tight-lipped as the Slayer was, Felix might never know.

THE NEXT DAY, after a deep and well-deserved sleep, Felix joined Gotrek as he reconvened with Hamnir, Gorril, old Ruen, and the prince's other counsellors in Hamnir's quarters. It seemed that, however much enmity there was between Gotrek and the prince, Hamnir still wanted his advice.

Before the meeting, Felix was seen to by a dwarf physician, a white-haired long-beard with gold rimmed spectacles, who ignored all Felix's yelps, gasps and curses as he unmercifully prodded and twisted his swollen ankle. It felt as if the old mumbler was breaking what had only been a sprain, but to Felix's surprise, after the dwarf had smeared it with vile-smelling unguents and wrapped it in bandages, the swelling actually went down and he was able to walk on it almost without wincing.

Felix and the other members of the party who had attempted to penetrate Birri's secret passage were invited to attend so that they could relate everything that had occurred: every trap and every trigger they had found, every encounter with the strange orcs. As they finished, the assembled dwarfs shook their heads, bewildered.

'There are only two possibilities,' said Hamnir, 'and neither of them is possible. It can't be the greenskins, they haven't the skill, and it can't be the dwarf survivors, because they would never ally themselves with grobi.'

'Forgive me for speaking out of turn,' said Felix, 'but I can think of a few other possibilities.'

'Go on,' said Hamnir.

'Well,' said Felix, 'perhaps some covetous group of dwarfs has decided to overthrow your family, prince Hamnir, and take the hold for themselves, and are using enslaved orcs as a cover.'

The dwarfs laughed.

Hamnir made a face. 'This is a thing a dwarf would never do. Dwarfs do not war upon each other. We are too few to thin our ranks this way, and even if we did, no dwarf would send our most hated foes against his fellows, no matter what the provocation.'

'Are there not dwarfs that worship the Chaos gods?' asked Felix. 'From what I have seen of them, they would not scruple to use any weapon.'

'Aye,' said Hamnir, 'but their realm is far from here, beyond the Worlds Edge Mountains, and north. It would be extremely strange to find them so far south.'

'They have been known to enslave grobi,' added Gorril, 'but this is done with the whip and the club. Left alone, the greenskins rebel and do what they will. If the grobi we encountered had been slaves, there would have been Dawi Zharr overseers with them, driving them into battle.'

'Then what about sorcerous enslavement?' asked Felix. 'What if some wizard is bending them to his will?'

Hamnir frowned, thinking it over. 'A sorcerer might possibly enslave grobi this way, though so many, and at such great distances? I don't know. Dwarfs are resistant to magical influence, so it would take a very great sorcerer indeed to turn dwarf minds while at the same time maintaining a hold over all those grobi. I don't believe such a one exists in the world today.'

'Sketti Hammerhand suggested the elf mage, Teclis,' said Thorgig.

Gotrek snorted. 'Teclis may be as twisty as the next elf, but even he wouldn't stoop to using grobi.'

Hamnir sighed and looked off into the middle distance for a moment, lost in thought. 'Sorcery, treachery or enslavement, we must retake the hold regardless,' he said at last, 'and immediately! My worst fear was that the dwarfs of the Diamondsmith clan were murdered or starving to death, but Herr Jaeger has made me fear that even worse has befallen them. No dwarf would succumb to torture, but that does not mean the grobi wouldn't try it. If there is indeed sorcery involved, their fate may be more terrible even than that. I can't bear the thought that Ferga–' He broke off, embarrassed. 'I'm sorry, but we cannot allow them to suffer one more day than necessary.'

'Agreed,' said old Ruen. 'Their fate is a shame to us all.'

'The question remains,' said Narin, idly twisting the sliver of wood in his beard, 'how do we reach them? How do we retake the hold with all entrances watched and trapped?'

The dwarfs sat in silence, pondering the question morosely.

After a long interval, Hamnir put his head in his hands and groaned. 'There may be another way,' he said at last.

Gotrek snorted. 'Another "secret" door that the grobi know all about?'

Hamnir shook his head. 'They cannot know about this door, for it does not yet exist.'

The dwarfs looked up, frowning.

'What's this?' asked Lodrim, the Thunderer.

Hamnir hesitated for so long that Felix wondered if he had fallen asleep, but then he sighed and spoke. 'I did not mention this way before, for two reasons. One, it requires going overground to Duk Grung, and then returning on the deep road to our mines. I had feared our trapped brethren would die during the week this journey would take, but if the alternative is never getting in, then a week it must be. Second...' he paused again, and then continued. 'Second, this is a secret that I have sworn to my father never to reveal, under any circumstances, a secret that only three dwarfs in this world know about – myself, my older brother and my father. Even though I may save the hold by revealing it, I doubt my father will ever forgive me. I may never be allowed to live in Karak Hirn once it is recovered, but I can think of no other way.'

Gorril looked pale. He stroked his beard nervously. 'My prince, perhaps we can discover another way. I would not wish to see you banished from your home. Nor do I want to anger King Alrik.'

'I am open to suggestions,' said Hamnir. 'If there is another way, I would gladly take it. This is not a step I wish to make.'

The dwarfs thought, mumbling one to another.

'Perhaps...' said Gorril, after a while. Everyone looked up, but he trailed off, shaking his head.

'If there were only a way to...' said Thorgig a moment later, but he too left his sentence unfinished.

'We might...' said Narin, and then frowned. 'No, we mightn't either.'

At last Hamnir sighed. 'Very well,' he said. 'Then I must do what must be done.' He sat up and looked around the table, meeting the eyes of all his councillors. 'My father is a true dwarf, and takes a true dwarf's pride in keeping his personal wealth safe from all prying eyes and grasping hands. In pursuit of this goal, he built, with help from only myself and my brother, a vault of which no one else knows the existence.'

'Your father's vault is in the third deep of his clanhold,' said a long beard. 'All know…'

'That is the vault he shows the world,' said Hamnir, 'where he keeps the majority of his gold and his common treasures. But you will not find the Maul of Barrin there, or the Cup of Tears, or the War Standard of old King Ranulf, our clanfather, or the twenty ingots of blood-gold that could buy all the other treasures of the clan vault. They are not to be shown. They are for his eyes alone, as it should be.'

The dwarfs of Karak Hirn stared, amazed.

'Blood-gold,' murmured old Ruen.

'So,' asked Gorril, involuntarily licking his lips. 'So, where is it?'

Hamnir smiled slyly. 'That I will not tell more than those who need to know. Suffice to say that the entrance is hidden near my father's quarters, and from it, a small company might reach the front doors.'

'From it?' said Thorgig, confused, 'But, prince, how do we reach the vault to exit it? Does it have more than one door?'

'No, it does not,' said Hamnir, 'but there is still a way that we might enter. You see, the vault is an old exploratory shaft, from the first King Ranulf's time – sunk, then abandoned, when it struck no ore. My father found it in his youth, and kept the knowledge secret until he had sons to help him make a vault of it. He did everything in his power to erase any record of the shaft, destroying all the old maps and texts he could find.' His hands clasped each other nervously. 'While secret, the vault is not properly secure. We three were not able to reinforce its walls, nor inscribe them with protective runes. The treasures merely sit at the bottom of the shaft, reachable by the steps we cut into its walls, and surrounded by raw rock. The vault's strength was that no one knew its location, or that it existed at all.' He hung his head. 'With this admission, that strength has now vanished.'

'Er, you haven't yet told us how we are to enter it, my prince,' said Gorril gently.

Hamnir nodded. 'I am avoiding it. I apologise. Here it is. The shaft sinks to the level of the mines, near the diggings my great grandfather abandoned when they kruked out unexpectedly fifteen hundred years ago. One of the kruk's tunnels passes within ten feet of the vault shaft.'

The dwarfs looked at him silently.

'So we dig from the tunnel to the vault? Is that it?' asked old Ruen finally.

'Then we climb the shaft and exit the vault within the hold. Aye,' said Hamnir.

'You're right,' said Gorril. 'You father would not approve. Not only do you lead a party to the location of the vault, you open a door to it that cannot quickly be shut. The king's treasures could be stolen from below while we are busy trying to retake the hold.'

'What about the grobi? Won't they hear you?' asked Gotrek. 'They hold the mines too. Or do you expect me to hold them off for you while you mess about with picks and shovels?'

'The kruk is far removed from the active mines,' said Hamnir. 'There are leagues of tunnels and a stone door between them. The grobi haven't dwarf senses. They won't hear us.'

Gotrek snorted, 'Wouldn't surprise me if they're waiting for us inside the vault once we dig through the walls.'

'That is impossible,' said Hamnir, angry. 'Only three dwarfs knew of the vault before tonight, my father, my older brother, and myself, and none of us were in the hold when the grobi took it. They cannot know!'

'A lot of impossible things've been happening lately,' said old Ruen, thoughtfully.

The dwarfs considered Hamnir's plan in silence, puffing on their pipes and glowering. It was clear they didn't like it. A dwarf hold that lost its treasure lost its honour. They would be seen as weak: poor builders who couldn't protect their possessions. If Hamnir won the hold, but lost his father's treasure, many dwarfs would consider his victory a loss.

At last Gorril sighed. 'It seems it is our only option.'

'We could wait for King Alrik to return with his seven hundred warriors,' said the Thunderer. 'He would know what to do.'

Felix heard Hamnir's knuckles crack. His face was rigid. 'That… will not do. In the first place, our cousins who are trapped in the hold cannot wait that long. In the second, to allow the grobi to occupy our home for a day longer than is necessary is intolerable. Third, I will not have my father return to find such a tragedy unresolved. It would break his proud heart.'

Not to mention making you look a worthless fool in his eyes, thought Felix. It looked like the rest were thinking the same thing, but no one said anything.

'Right then,' said Gorril. 'Who will go?'

'I will,' said Thorgig immediately.

'As will I,' said Gorril, 'and we'll need some skilled diggers.' He laughed. 'The trouble will be stopping every dwarf in the castle from volunteering.'

'You will not go, Gorril,' said Hamnir.

Gorril looked stricken. 'But, my prince...'

'No,' said Hamnir. 'You proved yesterday that you are a more able general than I. Had you been in command, many dwarfs would be alive today. You will stay and lead the assault on the main door. I will lead the party to the mine. I can burden no one else with the knowledge of the vault's location. Its opening must be on my head alone. No other will suffer my father's wrath.' He turned to Gotrek. 'You, Slayer, may stay here, or go north to fight Chaos if you wish. You have already come perilously close to dying while honouring your vow to me. I free you from further obligation. I have no wish to force my unwelcome company upon you for the duration of our journey.'

Gotrek glared at Hamnir for a long moment. 'You must not think much of my honour, Ranulfsson,' he said finally, 'I swore to help you retake Karak Hirn. Unlike some I could name, I don't break my vows. I'll leave once you're sitting in your father's chair in the feasthall. Then, we'll talk about another vow we made once. Until then, I'm sticking by your side. If you're going to Duk Grung and back, I'm coming with you.'

CHAPTER ELEVEN

'THIS ISN'T RIGHT,' muttered Thorgig.

Felix, Gotrek, Hamnir and the others lay flat in a ditch, watching as the vague silhouettes of an orc patrol passed by not twenty paces away in a thick predawn fog. The party had left Rodenheim Castle not half an hour before, slipping quietly through the postern gate without lantern or torch, heading down out of the foothills towards the green plains of the Badlands. In addition to Hamnir, four had been added to those who had survived the journey to Birri's door and back – three brothers from Karak Hirn who had mined Duk Grung in their youth, and another dwarf of the Stonemonger clan, who was a skilled mine engineer.

'Woe if any other Slayer ever learns that I twice hid from orcs,' agreed Leatherbeard.

'And ran from them as well,' whispered Narin, helpfully.

'Quiet, curse you!' said Hamnir.

The orcs had been watching Rodenheim Castle ever since Hamnir's army had returned to it. They patrolled around it endlessly, watching every road and goat path. This was more proof of their strangeness. They should have been pouring out of the captured dwarf hold in a frenzied, futile attempt to come to grips with their ancestral enemies. The dwarfs could have wished for nothing more. If the orcs had thrown themselves against the walls of the castle, they could have gunned them down at their leisure, thinning their ranks and making their eventual raid on Karak Hirn all the easier. But the orcs came in skulking squads, observing, not attacking, and staying well away from the walls. It was eerie.

At last, as the dark forms moved off, melting once again into the mist, Hamnir stood. 'Right,' he said. 'On we go, but keep your eyes and ears open. We can't be seen.'

The fog was their friend in this. The party walked down the last ridge and onto the rough plain without hearing or seeing another patrol. Hamnir turned them east and slightly south, and they marched in damp, chilly silence.

After another hour, the fog began to lift, revealing the sparse pines and rocky ground of the barren, hilly land, and then later, the jagged line of the Black Mountains under low, iron-grey clouds. The air remained cold and wet around them, like a clammy embrace. Felix shivered in his old red cloak, and expected at any moment to be drenched with rain, but it never came.

Hamnir walked at the front of the party, Thorgig at his side, eyes moving alertly around the landscape.

Gotrek stayed at the back, his brow as clouded as the sky. The Slayer and the prince seemed disinclined to speak, either to each other, or to anyone else.

After a time, the mining engineer, a wide-shouldered, sway-gutted veteran with a red face, a redder nose, and a bushy ginger beard shot with grey, dropped back to Gotrek, sticking his chin out so his beard bristled. 'You know why I volunteered for this company, Slayer?' he asked, loudly.

Gotrek didn't acknowledge him, only stared ahead.

'My name is Galin Olifsson,' said the engineer, slapping his chest with a meaty palm, 'a Stonemonger of the Stonemonger clan, same as Druric Brodigsson. You remember him, Slayer?'

Gotrek spat. A wiser dwarf than Galin might have noticed the balling of his fists.

'Word is, you left him behind to die, Slayer,' snarled Galin, 'while you ran like a coward from mere orcs.'

Felix barely saw Gotrek move, but suddenly Galin was flat on his back with blood streaming from his nose into his moustache and mouth. He blinked up at the sky. Gotrek kept walking, but the rest of the party was turning.

'Curse you, Gurnisson!' cried Hamnir. 'Will every dwarf who marches with me have a broken nose before you're through? We must all be whole and ready if we are to succeed.'

'He asked for it,' said Gotrek, shrugging.

'I wasn't ready, you damned cheat,' said Galin, sitting up woozily and pinching his misshapen nose.

'You call a Slayer a coward and aren't ready to be hit?' asked Leatherbeard, laughing. 'Then you're a fool.'

'Druric asked to stay behind,' said Narin, offering Galin his hand. 'And if you've a fight to pick with the Slayer you'll wait until this business is finished like the rest of us.'

Galin batted aside Narin's hand, sneering, and stood by himself. 'The word of an Ironskin is to be trusted? They who stole the Shield of Drutti from us? You likely told the Slayer to leave my cousin behind.'

'No one tells the Slayer anything,' snorted Narin, then held out the sliver of wood twisted in his beard, his eyes bright with mischief. 'And I have the Shield of Drutti here, what's left out of it, if you care to carry it.'

'You mock me, Ironskin?' said Galin, puffing up his chest. 'You're next after the Slayer if you think–'

'Olifsson!' barked Hamnir. 'If you joined us only to fight us, you can return to the castle. Now stand down!'

Galin glared daggers at Narin and Gotrek, but at last turned away, straightening his armour and dabbing at his still bleeding nose with a voluminous kerchief. 'I can wait,' he grumbled. 'A dwarf is nothing if not patient.'

The other three dwarfs who had joined the party grinned behind Galin's back. They were the Rassmusson brothers, Karl, Ragar and Arn, who looked so alike that Felix had trouble telling them apart – a trio of bald, black-bearded miners whose skin had been permanently begrimed with the dirt and ore they dug. The seams of their faces and their cracked knuckles were grey with it.

'Nice one,' said one – Arn, perhaps, Felix thought.

'Don't see a punch like that every day,' said a second, nodding – Karl, possibly.

'I'll show you one,' snarled Galin, turning and raising his fist.

The third brother, who by process of elimination, Felix decided must be Ragar, raised his hands. 'No disrespect, cousin,' he said. 'We don't say you deserved it.'

'You took it well, too,' said the one that Felix had decided was Arn. 'No weeping or moaning.'

'No calling quits,' agreed the one who therefore had to be Karl. 'On your feet and ready for another right quick.'

Galin eyed them suspiciously for a moment, trying to see if they were laughing at him. 'All right then,' he said finally, and turned back around.

The brothers exchanged sly glances.

'Really was quite a punch, though,' said Ragar.

'Aye,' said Arn. 'Once in a lifetime, that punch.'

'Ha!' said Karl. 'Punch like that could *end* a lifetime.'

Galin's shoulders tensed, but he didn't turn around. The brothers grinned as if they'd won a victory.

FELIX FOUND HIMSELF falling behind the others because of his ankle. The dwarf physician had done a remarkable job, and there was no longer much pain, but it was still stiff, and his stride was stilted. Gotrek, apparently as much to keep at a distance from Hamnir as to keep Felix company, hung back with him.

'What is your grudge against Hamnir, anyway?' Felix asked at last. 'You two were obviously friends at one time. What came between you? A girl? An insult? Gold?'

Gotrek snorted. 'Men can't understand dwarf honour, since they have none of their own. He broke an oath. That's all you have to know.'

'What oath?' pressed Felix. 'What could he have done that was so bad? He seems a decent enough fellow, very even tempered, very reasonable.'

'Ha!' said Gotrek. 'You like him because he acts like a man, with a man's manners and smooth talk, but he's got a man's tricky nature too. He doesn't stick to his word. To a dwarf, an oath's an oath, big or small, but not to that one.' He scowled towards the front of the line. 'A pair of pretty eyes or a better offer and he'll turn his back on a brother. He'll squirm and twist and quote law to get out of his bond.'

'Ah, so it was a girl,' said Felix.

'I'll say no more.'

'Very well,' said Felix.

They walked on in silence for a while, but Felix's curiosity was aroused. 'When did all this happen? Were you already a Slayer?'

Gotrek shot him a sharp glance. 'You trying to pry it out of me, manling?'

'No, no,' said Felix. 'Only, if you die here, I'll need to include Hamnir and the others in the epic of your death: "The brave party the Slayer led", and all that. I'll need to know something about how you met and what you did, to give it some body, some breadth, aye?'

Gotrek thought for a moment, and then nodded. 'I suppose you've a right to some history. Every epic I ever heard told in the feasthall started in the cradle, and it's best you hear it from me and not that silk-tongued oathbreaker.' He shot a sharp look up at Felix again. 'Not that I'll tell you everything, mind. Just enough.'

'Enough will suffice, I'm sure,' said Felix, trying not to sound too eager. It was rare for Gotrek to share anything of his past. 'Go on.'

Gotrek walked on, frowning, as if gathering his thoughts. 'I met Hamnir when he came to the clan of my fathers,' he said at last. 'This was long before I took the crest, when I was still a shortbeard. There was peace in the hold then. Too calm for me. I wanted a fight.' He ran his hand absently through his beard. 'Hamnir was restless too. Wandered all the way from Karak Hirn to the Worlds Edge because of it.' He snorted. 'Read too many books. Wanted to see the world. Wanted to see the wonders he'd read about.' Gotrek shrugged. 'There was fighting in most of the places he talked about – the Sea of Claws, the Empire, Bretonnia – so I said I'd go with him.'

'It was just a travel arrangement?' asked Felix. 'You weren't friends?'

'Me? Friends with that treacherous...' Gotrek paused, and then sighed. 'Eh. Suppose I was. He seemed a good dwarf then. Kept me out of trouble when I was looking to get in it, and got me out of it if I was already in. Talked an elector count out of hanging me once. Whatever army we signed on with, he got us a good deal, and if our commander tried to cheat us, Hamnir always got the money anyway.'

Gotrek smirked and shot another glance towards Hamnir, then grunted and looked away. 'Wasn't much of a mercenary though. Handy enough in a fight, and a good tactician on paper, but he'd get muddled when things went wrong.' Gotrek snorted. 'Didn't have the mercenary spirit either. We'd loot castles and all he took was books. He once punched a captain of ours who smashed a statue. Didn't mind killing man, dwarf or elf, but you couldn't burn a painting around him.'

'How long did you travel with him?' asked Felix.

Gotrek shrugged. 'Ten years? Twenty? Can't remember. Might have been fifty. We fought through the Empire, Bretonnia, down the coast hunting pirates, the border princes, Estalia, Tilea...' He trailed off.

'Tilea?' prodded Felix.

Gotrek came back to himself and scowled at Felix. 'No, manling, I said I'd tell you enough. You'll get no more.'

'But how can you tell a tale and not the finish?'

'He broke his oath,' Gotrek snarled, 'that's the finish. Now leave me be.'

The Slayer strode forwards, catching up with the last of the dwarfs, leaving Felix to limp along behind by himself.

Felix cursed himself for a fool. He'd almost had it. If he hadn't pushed so hard at the end, Gotrek might have told him on his own. Still, he knew now about a stretch of Gotrek's life that even he hadn't known existed before. That was something at least.

ON THE MORNING of the third day, the dwarfs turned north again, winding their way up through narrowing valleys and canyons into the foothills of the Black Mountains until the Badlands disappeared behind a screen of pine-furred hills.

As they pushed on, Hamnir let the Rassmusson brothers lead the way, for in their youth they had worked the Duk Grung and had made the trip many times. The three dwarfs tramped confidently up slopes choked with mountain laurel and clinging nettles, along swift streams and deer tracks, and dirt roads long overgrown with weeds and wildflowers, commenting all the while.

'Isn't this the place where old Enrik dropped an ingot and made us search the bushes for six hours?' asked Arn, as they passed a fallen tree.

'Aye,' said Ragar, 'and he had it in his pack the whole time.'

'I remember,' said Karl, laughing. 'Found it when he bit into his pasty. Chipped his tooth.'

'Always thought Dorn had something to do with that,' said Arn, 'but he never owned up.'

A little further on Karl pointed to a granite ledge overlooking a small, fern-skirted pool. 'The rock of the full moon!' he cried.

His brothers laughed uproariously, but wouldn't explain what he meant.

As the sun reached its zenith, they saw ahead of them the mouth of a canyon that was walled off with thick stone battlements, in the centre of which stood an open gateway guarded by two squat towers.

'There we are,' said Arn, pointing. 'Duk Grung.'

Looking at the old walls peeking through the trees, Felix was struck again by just how long dwarfs lived. For though the walls were sturdy dwarf work and had stood the test of time with barely any weathering, they were thickly overgrown with vines, moss and bushes and the gates had long ago rusted away. The place looked like some ruin of antiquity, and yet Arn, Karl and Ragar had worked here when it was a going concern.

'Grown up a bit, hasn't it?' said Ragar. 'Had a human gardener in our time who did for the pruning.'

'I remember him,' said Arn. 'Wolfenkarg, or something. Ludenholt? Some mannish gibberish. Couldn't hold his liquor.'

'Wonder what's become of him,' said Karl.

'Well, he was a man,' snorted Arn, 'so he's long dead, isn't he?'

'Like may-flies they are,' said Ragar. He shot a guilty glance at Felix. 'No offence, human.'

Felix shrugged. 'None taken.' It was only the truth.

Approaching the rusted remains of the gate, the dwarfs saw a wide, deeply worn track running along the wall and through the gate. They stopped, growing quiet, their hands dropping to their weapons. The two Slayers studied the track intently while the others shot wary glances into the trees around them.

'A troll,' said Leatherbeard, 'and the tracks are fresh.'

'Two trolls,' Gotrek said. 'At least two.'

'One for each of us,' said Leatherbeard jauntily, but his voice was tight.

'Have they made their home in the mine?' asked Hamnir.

'Let's find out,' said Gotrek.

The dwarfs unslung axes and crossbows and followed him through the open gate, on guard. Felix drew his sword. Inside the wall, the canyon rose and narrowed, pinched between two steep, rocky hills. The crumbled remains of old outbuildings peeked out from thickets of young trees on either side of the troll track, which wound up through the centre.

'Cart mule stables,' whispered Karl, waving to the left.

'And Lungmolder's shack,' said Arn, motioning to the right. 'Trouble with wood. Doesn't last.'

'Was it Lungmolder?' asked Ragar. 'Thought it was Bergenhoffer, or Baldenhelder, or–'

'Hush, curse you,' said Galin. His eyes were bulging, and his red face was sweating.

They crept up the troll track to the end of the canyon, a tight funnel between the converging hillsides. In the western slope, there was a black opening, nearly hidden by a thick screen of raspberry bushes. The dwarfs approached it cautiously. As they got closer, Felix saw that the opening was a rough hole, broken through what appeared to be a large, walled-up door, its outlines only barely discernible under the dense cloak of vegetation.

'It's been breached,' said Karl.

'That's bad, that is,' said Ragar.

Arn shrugged. 'Kruked out anyway.'

'Might not have been iron they were after,' said Narin.

'Might have been trying to reach Karak Hirn,' said Thorgig, grimly.

Galin snorted. 'If they tried, lad, it was a hundred years ago, and Karak Hirn survived.' He pointed at the edges of the breach. 'Any dwarf with the eyes Grungni gave him can see that that hole was bashed in long ago. All the breaks are weathered.'

'Call me "lad" again, and I'll feed you the tongue Grungni gave you,' said Thorgig, glaring at the engineer.

'Until you can tuck your beard in your belt, I'll call you what I like,' said Galin.

'I'll tuck your beard up your–'

'Enough!' hissed Hamnir. 'Both of you.'

Leatherbeard pointed to the deep-worn troll track. It wound through the raspberry bushes and right to the hole. 'The hole may be old, but the place is occupied still.'

'Saves us looking for the hidden latch at least,' said Ragar.

'Right,' said Hamnir, taking a deep breath. 'Light your lamps and in we go, Slayers first.'

The dwarfs unhooked sturdy horn lanterns from their packs, lit them from tinder jars, and hung them from their belts so they would have both hands free. Gotrek lit a torch, which he held like a weapon in his off hand. When all were ready, they pushed through the undergrowth to the hole. Though it was small compared with the walled-up door, the break was still twice as tall as Felix, and twice as wide as Gotrek. They peered in. It was utterly black inside.

Gotrek stepped forwards, holding his torch back and to the side, so as not to blind himself. Leather-beard followed, with the others edging in behind him. A cold wind blew an astounding stench out at them – a rich mix of offal, rotting meat, mildew, and an acrid animal musk even more pungent than that of orcs.

Narin wrinkled his nose. 'Nothing smells worse than a troll.'

'Two trolls?' suggested Arn, or possibly Ragar.

'Quiet!' whispered Hamnir.

On the far side of the door, the hole opened out into a wide chamber. As Felix's eyes became accustomed to the dark, he could make out monumental doorways in each of the walls, and looming pillars holding up a high ceiling. Below this grand dwarf architecture, rubbish lay in swathes: heaped piles of bones, smashed furniture and machinery, rotting carcasses, burnt timber, as well as drifts of brown leaves and tree branches, blown or dragged in from outside.

In one corner, a fire pit had been dug into the stone floor, over which hung a dented iron pot, bigger than a nobleman's bath. Crude log stools and settles surrounded the fire, and two beds of bracken were laid nearby. Limp forms hung from spikes bashed into the walls – two men, an orc, a cow, and a wolf, all skinned and hung to drain. The bones and clothing of earlier feasts were piled within easy flinging distance from the fire pit. Skins were laid out on the floor and held flat with rocks.

'Seems lord and lady troll are not at home,' said Narin.

'Trolls in old Duk,' said Ragar, shaking his head. 'A damned shame.'

'Aye,' said Karl. 'To see the old place mucked up like this, it breaks your heart.'

'Not the tidiest housekeepers, are they?' said Arn, sniffing.

Hamnir looked around uneasily. 'I'd almost rather have found them in their lair,' he said. 'Worse not knowing where they are.'

'Another doom missed,' said Gotrek, morose.

'Which way to the deeps?' asked Hamnir, turning to the Rassmusson brothers.

They looked around, stroking their beards. Then Arn spoke up. 'Barracks that way.' He pointed right. 'Smelters that way.' He pointed straight ahead. 'Workface that way.' He pointed to the left.

'Left then,' said Hamnir.

Gotrek and Leatherbeard led the way across the chamber towards the left-hand arch. Their path took them past the pile of bones, boots and breeches near the cook pot, and as they walked by it, things glinted from it in the lamplight.

Galin stopped, followed by Ragar, and then Hamnir. The others turned to see what they were looking at.

'Is that…?' said Galin.

'Look at that now,' said Ragar.

'It is,' said Hamnir.

'Gold!' said Arn, and stepped to the pile of bones, tossing aside a ribcage and squatting down. The others were right behind him. Even Gotrek was pushing forwards.

Felix looked over their shoulders. The ground amidst the bones and torn clothes was littered with rings, neck chains, unset gems, armbands, gold ingots and the coins of a dozen different nations. The dwarfs snatched them up in handfuls. Narin snapped a finger from a skeleton hand to get at a silver ring. Karl was prying a gold tooth from a grinning skull.

'Stupid trolls,' chuckled Ragar, scooping greedily. 'Throwing away a fortune for stew meat.'

'They're animals,' said Narin. 'The lower orders don't understand the ecstasy of gold.'

'Do we have time for this?' asked Felix, looking anxiously behind him. 'The trolls could come back at any moment.'

The dwarfs ignored him.

Thorgig batted at Galin's hand. 'That was mine, Olifsson,' he snapped. 'I touched it first.'

'And you dropped it,' said Galin. 'It's mine now.'

'Mind your reach!' snarled Leatherbeard to Narin. 'This is my bit.'

'Can I help it if I have longer arms than some,' said Narin, his eyes glowing.

'And stickier fingers.' Leatherbeard shoved Narin, who fell back on his haunches.

'Shove me, will you?' growled Narin, reaching for his dagger.

'Cousins! Cousins!' cried Hamnir. 'Stop this! Stop this! What are we doing?'

Felix breathed a sigh of relief. The prince was going to talk some sense into the others. He at least realised the dangers of their position.

'This is not the dwarf way,' said Hamnir, 'scrabbling like men for scraps of bread. We are a military company on a military mission. This treasure is therefore spoils, and subject to strict division. Now come, take it all out of your pockets and pile it in the centre here. We will see what we have and make our split accordingly. Ten equal shares.'

Gotrek's snort interrupted him. 'Equal shares? That's rich broth coming from you, oathbreaker.' He turned to the others. 'I'd watch him if I were you. He's apt to put a little extra aside for himself.'

Thorgig sprang up, fists bunched. 'Do you call Prince Hamnir dishonest? You go too far at last, Slayer.'

'That's our chief you're speaking of,' said Ragar stepping up beside Thorgig.

'Have a care,' said Arn.

'A red crest don't scare us,' said Karl.

'Come, Slayer,' said Narin. 'Can you truly think that a prince known throughout the holds as a plain dealer would cheat on shares?'

'This from a dwarf who destroyed the property of my clan and won't make recompense,' sneered Galin.

'I don't think,' said Gotrek. 'I know. He's done it before.'

'Gurnisson,' said Hamnir, brow lowered.

'Oh, he'll have a reason,' said Gotrek, 'some excuse why this piece or that piece shouldn't be shared out with the rest. He's good with words. It all sounds reasonable, but whatever it is, in the end, you don't get all that's coming to you with Prince Hamnir the Honest around.'

'You don't get any understanding with Gotrek Gurnisson around, either,' said Hamnir hotly. 'The head and the heart don't matter to him, only the purse. Sometimes I think he's more of a merchant than I am. A dwarf who knows the price of everything and the value of nothing.'

'So, you admit these things he speaks of?' asked Narin, his eyebrows raising.

'Not as he says them,' said Hamnir. 'I cheated no one. In each case, I asked all parties if something could be held out. Put it to a vote. Only Gotrek voted no. The others had some compassion, some belief that the spirit of justice is more important than the letter of the law.'

'Not in every case, oathbreaker,' said Gotrek. 'In one case you just took what you wanted.'

'Because you wouldn't listen to reason!' shouted Hamnir.

His voice echoed through the hall, seeming to come back to them louder than it had left his mouth. The dwarfs looked around warily as the echoes faded to nothing.

'Gotrek, Prince Hamnir,' said Felix, into the silence. 'Perhaps you should return to this debate, and the division of the spoils, at a later date. We are not safe here, and we still have a long way to go.'

'I second that,' said Narin. 'We should move on.'

After a moment, Gotrek shrugged. 'Fair enough. Might be less of us to divide amongst at the end anyway.'

Hamnir nodded. 'Very well,' he said, 'and as my honesty has been questioned, I will not hold it. Nor will any of my hold.'

The dwarfs looked around. Thorgig, Arn, Karl and Ragar, were all of Karak Hirn; that left Galin, Narin, Leatherbeard, Gotrek and Felix.

Gotrek shook his head. 'I'm not carrying all that. It'll get in the way.'

'Aye,' said Leatherbeard. 'No thanks.'

'Nor I,' said Narin. 'I know my weaknesses. I'll not be put in the way of temptation.'

'Er,' said Galin. 'I would be honoured to hold the plunder. The honesty of the Stonemonger clan is known from Worlds Edge Mountains to–'

'And the dwarf who asks for the honour is the dwarf to keep your eye on,' interrupted Thorgig. 'You're not holding my share, Stonemonger.'

'You question my honesty!' said Galin, standing. 'Dwarfs have died for less!'

'Quiet!' snapped Hamnir. He looked at Felix. 'The man will hold it.'

'The man?' Galin gaped. 'But all dwarfs know men are greedy, grasping little–'

Gotrek growled menacingly.

Narin laughed. 'They say the same of us, but you'll note that he was the only one who didn't dive into the pile with both hands grasping. And anyone who's thrown in their lot with a Slayer for twenty years can't be accused of being a man who puts his holdings first.

'But, prince,' said Thorgig, 'he is the Slayer's companion. He will favour Gurnisson over the rest of us.'

'If he does, I'll kill him,' said Gotrek.

Hamnir nodded. 'Gurnisson may be a stiff, unbending berserker with the disposition of a dyspeptic cave bear, but he is as honourable as an ancestor. It isn't honesty he's wanting, but heart. He will not let Herr Jaeger cozen us.'

Arn shrugged. 'Fair enough.'

'Suits me,' said Karl.

'If the prince says aye, who are we to say nay,' said Ragar.

'If that's the way of it,' said Galin with a stiff shrug, 'that's the way of it.'

The dwarfs quickly emptied their pockets and pouches into Felix's pack and made ready to march again. Felix groaned as he stood and shouldered the pack. The greedy little grubbers had added a stone's weight to his load – they who could lift twice their own weight with ease.

The party took the left-hand arch and started down a corridor lined with long-unused dining halls and common rooms, the outlines of their sturdy furniture softened by centuries of dust. This had not been a true hold, only an outpost, a satellite mine, meant to feed the furnaces and anvils of Karak Hirn. Still, it was built with all the usual dwarf care and quality. There had been no cave-ins in the intervening centuries since the dwarfs had abandoned it. No water stains marred the walls. The flagstones that lined the floor had not cracked. The decorative borders looked as if they had been cut only yesterday.

After a few hundred feet, they came to the rusty rails of a mine cart track, which connected the deeps of the mine with the smelting rooms. The rails branched and turned down crossing corridors, glinting in the darkness. Here and there, they had been pulled up, the wooden ties beneath them too, but most were undisturbed. The dwarfs stuck to the main trunk, which soon led them to the shaft of an ancient dwarf steam lift, meant to raise and lower crowds of dwarfs, carts, mules and tonnes of ore at a time.

Galin, the only engineer among them, had a look at the steam engine that had once powered the thing, built into a room behind it. He came out shaking his head, his beard and eyebrows trailing dust and cobwebs. 'Not a chance,' he said. 'Half the gears have rusted into place, and someone's been at the boiler with a pickaxe. Take a week to make it go. Maybe more.'

'Don't know if the ropes would hold us anyway,' said Narin, holding his lantern out into the shaft. The huge hawser cables were frayed and black with mould.

Felix looked down the shaft. He couldn't see the carriage in the darkness below, but the ropes were tight, so it was down there somewhere.

'Wasn't to be expected anyway,' said Hamnir. 'We'll take the ladder.'

A narrow ledge led out to a square notch in the left side of the shaft, cut just deep enough for a dwarf to climb down into the depths on the ladder that was bolted to its wall without being knocked off by the passing of the lift carriage. Leatherbeard went first. The others lined up behind him.

'Are there any other ways to get down?' asked Felix, waiting his turn. 'I've had my fill of climbing recently.'

'Oh, aye,' said Karl. 'You can walk down through all the deeps by ramp and stair.' He grabbed an iron rung and started down into darkness.

'A lot of walking though,' said Arn, following him.

'This way's faster,' said Ragar.

'I wouldn't mind the walk,' said Felix, sighing, but he stepped onto the ladder behind Ragar and began lowering himself down rung by rusty rung.

Gotrek came last, for the dwarfs were concerned that the trolls might return home and follow them down. He exchanged his torch for a belt-hung lamp, so that he could have both hands free to climb.

For all Felix's grumbling, he found the descent easy. The ladder was dwarf work, and though over two hundred years old, it was still strong and firmly fixed to the wall. At regular intervals, they passed further deeps – wide, rough tunnels, laid with cart rails. Sometimes there would be abandoned mine carts at the lip. In one, something larger than a rat scrabbled away in the darkness. In another, picks and shovels were scattered about.

'Those aren't dwarf tools,' said Ragar.

'No,' said Arn. 'We took everything with us when we closed up shop. Dwarfs don't waste.'

'Someone else looking for scraps,' said Karl, snorting. 'Fool humans, most like. Should know better. Dwarfs don't leave untapped veins.' He looked up the ladder at Felix. 'No offence, human.'

Felix sighed. 'None taken.'

Halfway between the fifth and sixth level down, they found the elevator carriage, an open steel and wood cage hanging straight and true in the shaft as if it had only paused for a moment. Felix looked at it longingly as they passed it. It would have been luxury to step onto it and ride the rest of the way down, but closer inspection suggested that might be a very speedy trip. Near the steel rings that the ropes were fastened to, the hawsers were frayed and thin, as if rats had been chewing on them. It looked as if the merest feather landing upon the carriage would be enough to snap the rope and send the whole thing crashing into the nether depths.

'I am suddenly glad the engine wasn't working,' he said to no one in particular.

Another level down and Leatherbeard held up a hand. 'Something moving below,' he said.

CHAPTER TWELVE

FELIX AND THE dwarfs stopped, listening. At first, Felix heard nothing, but then he caught it – a faint scratching and skittering, echoing up the shaft. It was getting louder.

'What is it?' asked Thorgig. 'Rats?'

'Isn't trolls,' said Arn. 'That's certain.'

'Whatever it might be,' said Hamnir, 'it's coming this way.'

Narin pulled a torch from his pack, lit it from the lamp at his belt, and dropped it down the shaft. The dwarfs watched its ball of illumination fall swiftly away from them. Felix's heart lurched as, two levels down, the torch flashed past a churning mass of hairless, dog-sized monstrosities, briefly glinting off their jagged fangs and bulging black eyes, and the razor claws with which they were climbing the shaft's rough-hewn walls. Then the torch dropped below the things, returning them to darkness. There had been dozens of them.

'What are those?' choked Felix.

'Cave squigs,' spat Karl. 'Grobi rats.'

'Thought we'd killed them all off,' said Ragar.

'We did,' said Arn, 'two hundred years ago.'

'Difficult fighting them here,' said Thorgig, frowning. 'They'll tear us off.'

Felix shuddered. After all his years with Gotrek, he didn't mind a stand-up fight. He would have faced down this pack of horrors undaunted on level ground, but hanging off a ladder over a bottomless pit, with only one arm free to defend himself? No, thank you. He could already feel their teeth and claws tearing into him, ripping him savagely from the rungs.

'Wait here,' said Gotrek. He started climbing rapidly back up the ladder.

'Wait here?' asked Felix.

'Where's he off to?' growled Galin.

Felix shrugged. He had no idea.

The squigs were closing swiftly, much quicker than the dwarfs could have climbed back up the ladder. Felix could hear their hungry mewlings, and make out the movement of their limbs in the darkness. Most were in the shaft, but a few climbed the ladder. They reminded Felix of cockroaches scurrying up a storm drain.

The dwarfs drew their weapons and hung, one-handed, from the ladder, grimly awaiting their doom. Felix gripped his sword and prayed to Sigmar that whatever Gotrek was up to, he would hurry up about it. Leatherbeard had undone his belt, and was slipping it through a rung of the ladder to re-buckle it around his waist so he could hang from it and have both hands free.

Scores of glistening eyes reflected their lamplight, and the things' forms were becoming visible – lumpy, misshapen blobs of hairless flesh, all mouth and teeth, with spindly, taloned legs stuck on as if as an after-thought. They were possibly the most hideous things Felix had ever seen, and he had seen his share of horrors.

'Brace yourselves,' said Hamnir, unnecessarily.

'Guess we'll die in the Duk after all,' said Ragar.

'Always thought I would,' said Karl.

'See you in Grimnir's halls, brothers,' said Arn.

'Look out below!' roared Gotrek from above them.

There was a low *tung*, as if someone had plucked the string of a bass viol, and then suddenly the shaft was filled with a deafening, screaming, scraping cacophony.

Felix looked up, and then hugged the ladder as tightly as he could. The dwarfs did the same. With a rush of wind and a screeching of steel on stone, the lift carriage plummeted down towards them, then past them, tilting and disintegrating as it went, its tumbling struts and timbers carving deep white gouges in the walls of the shaft.

Felix looked down, following its passage, and caught just a glimpse of the squigs, eyes wide with fright, bull-frog mouths agape, before it smashed down on them and dropped into darkness, roaring as it went.

After what seemed an interminable wait, they heard a thunderous, wall-shaking boom as the carriage at last hit bottom.

'All clear?' came Gotrek's voice from above.

'Nearly,' called Leatherbeard.

Some squigs still scrabbled up the ladder, undaunted by the fate of their fellows, their teeth gnashing for a taste of dwarf flesh. Held in place by his belt, the masked Slayer waited for them, his two axes ready. They leapt up at him, howling with hunger. He chopped down furiously, catching one between the eyes, severing another's foreleg. They tumbled away, knocking others off as they fell, but not all. Leatherbeard slashed into the next wave. Thorgig and Narin fired crossbows over his shoulders. The other dwarfs grunted, frustrated that the narrowness of the ladder wouldn't allow them to get into the fight. Felix was content to watch.

At last, just as Gotrek reappeared above them, the fight was over. The last of the squigs spun squealing down into darkness, trailing a swash of black blood, and Leatherbeard hung, breathing heavily, from his belt.

'Well done, Leatherbeard,' said Hamnir.

'Bravely fought,' agreed Narin.

'Aye,' said Gotrek. 'Good work, squigslayer.'

Leatherbeard growled as he cleaned his axes and freed himself from the ladder. 'Not all of us have been fortunate enough to meet a daemon. I'll get my chance.'

'Not if you travel with Gurnisson,' said Hamnir. 'He may insist on a strict division of spoils, but he takes all the glory for himself.' He looked up. 'Isn't that right, Jaeger.'

Felix opened his mouth, and closed it again. He wanted to deny Hamnir's words, but couldn't quite. Gotrek was certainly always the one out in front when there was trouble, and it wasn't Felix that was called upon to retake holds or venture into uncharted lands. Of course, that was because Gotrek *could* do these things. He wasn't taking any opportunities from Felix. Felix would have died in seconds up against that daemon.

'Leave the manling out of this!' said Gotrek. 'Now let's get on!'

The dwarfs sheathed their weapons and continued down the ladder. They passed another seven levels before they saw the wreckage of the lift carriage glinting below them at the bottom of the shaft – a shattered pile of splintered wood and twisted metal, mixed in with mashed squigs and bleached bones that proved the hideous beasts were not the first living things to fall down the pit.

The party picked their way over the mess and stepped out of the shaft into a low mine tunnel, much rougher hewn than those in the highest levels, but still neatly cut and well braced, if a bit short.

'Is this the deep road?' asked Felix, stooping. He could not stand upright.

The dwarfs laughed.

'No, Herr Jaeger,' said Hamnir. 'This is still the mines. You will know the deep road when you see it.'

'He thinks this is the deep road,' chuckled Karl.

'Still down a few levels,' said Arn.

'Follow us,' said Ragar.

The dwarfs tramped along the dark tunnel, their lanterns making a travelling pool of light around them. Felix limped along behind, bent over like an old man. He hoped the passage would open up before long. He was already getting a crick in his neck. If they had to fight anything in here, he'd have to do it on his knees.

Gotrek walked beside him for a while, muttering under his breath and shooting sharp glances at Hamnir. Then, after the party had descended three more levels in silence, he stepped ahead and fell in with Leatherbeard.

'You did well there, Slayer,' he said. 'You'll find a good doom. I don't doubt it.' He looked forwards and raised his voice, loud enough to carry to the front of the line. 'And it won't matter who you travel with, for glory isn't something you share, it's something you win.'

Felix frowned. This sort of camaraderie wasn't Gotrek's way. What was the matter with him?

'You shouldn't worry about fighting unworthy foes on this journey,' he said, louder still. 'Even a Slayer may put aside his doom to honour his oaths, if, that is, he's an *honourable* dwarf.'

Now it made sense. Gotrek might be talking with Leatherbeard, but he was speaking to Hamnir. Felix was stunned. This level of indirectness was unheard-of for the Slayer. Gotrek was normally as blunt and forthright as, well, as a punch on the nose. Again, he wondered what it was about Hamnir that got under Gotrek's skin.

'Who is the one without honour?' said Hamnir, rising to the bait. He turned his head as they marched. 'You insult me. You strike me, and you know I cannot strike back for I need you in this enterprise. Is that honourable?'

'More honourable than a dwarf calling on an another's oath when he doesn't keep his own,' shot back Gotrek.

The party stepped out into an enormous room – the junction of many rail lines, all coming to a platform in the centre where the mine carts could be dumped into large ore trains. Battered old carts sat where they had been left on the rusty tracks, and neat stacks of rails and wooden ties hugged the near wall. The ceiling soared above the reach of the dwarfs' lamps.

'Only you say I am an oathbreaker,' shouted Hamnir. 'Only you say I am dishonourable. All others know me as a dwarf of my word.' His words rang back from the dark reaches of the room.

'That's because only I know you as you truly are,' growled Gotrek. 'Only I know your tricks. You wear a thicker mask than Leatherbeard.'

'It wasn't a trick,' said Hamnir, stopping and facing Gotrek. The party halted around them, looking warily into the darkness. 'It was a disagreement. You said it should be included in the spoils. I said it shouldn't. It was worthless anyway.'

'Ha!' Gotrek turned to the others. 'You see. He always has an excuse. Worthless, he says.'

'The others agreed with me,' said Hamnir.

'Only because your tongue is tricksier than an elf ambassador's!' Gotrek snorted. 'Hah! Maybe that's it. Maybe your mother had a night with some elf lord come to parlay.'

There was an intake of breath from the dwarfs, and Hamnir froze, staring at the Slayer. Finally, he broke, dropped his axe, and began struggling to shuck his pack.

'Right,' he said. 'That's it. We'll have this out here and now, as it seems that's what you want. I will waive your obligation to help me take Karak Hirn and we will fight dwarf to dwarf.'

'I don't want to fight you,' sneered Gotrek. 'I want you to pay me what you owe me. I want you to give me my share of what you held out from the split.'

'I owe you nothing but a thrashing,' said Hamnir. 'Perhaps that will finally penetrate your thick skull.' He threw down his pack and put up his fists. 'Now fight.'

'You're not worth fighting,' said Gotrek. 'Just pay me and you can end this grudge painlessly, as you could have a hundred years ago in Tilea.'

'Coward,' spat Hamnir. 'It's as I have long suspected. You won't fight without your axe in your hands. Without it you are nothing.'

'What do you say?' said Gotrek, bristling.

'I say that it is your axe that deserves your fame,' said Hamnir contemptuously, 'that any dwarf who picked up such an axe would have become great. Without it you are just another dwarf, and perhaps less than most.'

'You think so?' bellowed Gotrek, throwing aside his axe and his pack. He raised his ham-sized fists. 'Come ahead, elf spawn. I'll introduce you to the floor.'

Hamnir started for the Slayer, but Narin and Galin stepped in his way.

'Prince Hamnir,' said Galin. 'This isn't the time for this.'

'Aye,' agreed Narin. 'You must be whole and hale to lead us. Not battered–'

Hamnir pulled himself up, indignant. 'Who says I will be battered?'

Galin and Narin cast sidelong glances at Gotrek, eyeing his massive physique and comparing it sceptically to Hamnir's soft, merchant's body. Felix had to agree with their unspoken assessment. Hamnir didn't stand a chance. Gotrek was wider and more heavily muscled than any dwarf Felix had ever seen, and uncannily resilient, recovering from wounds and blows that would have crippled or killed another dwarf. Not five days ago, he had been shot and fallen the gods knew how many feet, and all he had to show for it was a bandage on his shoulder that seemed to trouble him not at all.

Narin coughed. 'This is all very brave, Prince Hamnir, but there's no need to prove–'

'I do not fight to prove my bravery,' said Hamnir, interrupting, 'but to defend my honour and that of my late mother.' He started forwards.

'But, prince,' said Galin, stepping before him again, 'you can't win. It's obvious. He–'

'Then I will die. At least I will die in the right.' He pushed past them and punched Gotrek as hard as he could in the ribs.

Gotrek didn't even grunt. He buried a fist in Hamnir's belly and the prince collapsed like an empty sack, dropping to his knees and retching.

Gotrek glared down at him. 'There. Had your fill?'

Hamnir shook his head, dazed, and tried to push himself back to his feet. He lost his balance and fell again. There was a harsh chuckle from the darkness. It sounded like someone grinding gravel between millstones.

The dwarfs looked up, grabbing for their weapons. Felix looked towards the edges of the room. Two massive trolls stood in the doorway that the dwarfs had only recently come through, watching the fight with moronic grins on their ugly, mottled faces.

CHAPTER THIRTEEN

THE TROLL ON the left roared something unintelligible and smacked his fists together, as if indicating that Gotrek and Hamnir should continue. The one on the right, a she-troll, even uglier than her mate, clapped her hands and hooted.

'Our hosts have come home,' said Narin.

'Isn't their home,' growled Arn.

'A worthy doom at last,' said Leatherbeard, drawing his two axes.

Hamnir lifted his head, mumbling, but couldn't get up. Thorgig stood over him protectively, glaring savagely at Gotrek. He looked like a hero in a painting.

Gotrek crossed to his axe and snatched it up. The runes upon it were glowing. No one had noticed. 'Start a fire, manling,' he said, and stalked forwards, his thumb stroking the axe's keen edge. It drew blood.

The trolls bawled, disappointed, and motioned again for Gotrek and Hamnir to keep fighting.

'A fire,' said Galin, backing from the trolls uneasily. 'Good idea. The man will need help.'

The others shot sly looks at him as they spread out and readied their weapons and shields.

'Knees shaking a bit, engineer?' sneered Narin.

'It takes more than axes to kill a troll,' Galin said defensively. 'You should thank me for allowing you the glory.' He started across the huge room. 'Come on, man. These ties should do.'

As Felix followed him to the stacked wooden rail ties, memories of the catacombs under Karak Eight Peaks flooded his mind – the hideous mutated troll that guarded the treasure vault, its wounds closing up almost as soon as Gotrek had opened them with his axe, Felix's desperate attempts to light the thing on fire. He was glad that Narin and the others seemed to know what they were about. They were unhooking their lanterns from their belts and holding them in their shield hands, ready to throw.

The trolls roared at the approaching dwarfs and banged clubs the size of tree trunks on the floor. Even twenty strides away, the impacts stung Felix's feet.

'Easy now,' Felix heard Narin say. 'No one get too far ahead.'

'For glory and death!' bellowed Leatherbeard, and sprinted at the male troll, swinging his two axes wildly.

'You mad idiot!' shouted Narin.

He and the others charged after him, Gotrek at the fore.

The troll roared and swung at Leatherbeard's head. The masked Slayer dived right and rolled up in front of the she-troll, gutting her with a swift upswing. She screeched and smashed down at him with her club as her intestines spilled from the bloody gash. Leatherbeard dodged the blow, but was jarred off his feet as the club shattered the flagstones next to him. The she-troll fell back, stuffing the ropes of her viscera back into the cut. It was already healing.

The rest of the dwarfs closed in, swinging axes and hammers, and then leapt back again almost instantly as a backhand from the male nearly decapitated them all.

'Force them this way!' called Galin, kneeling down next to the rail ties and digging in his pack. He pulled out a handful of shiny black coal lumps and placed them around the stacked wood.

Felix looked back at the fight. The dwarfs were dodging back as the troll spewed corrosive vomit at them. Smoking holes appeared in the floor where it had spattered. Arn threw away his shield as it began to disintegrate. The troll's mate was bashing at Leatherbeard again, the rip in her belly now little more than a thin slit. If there was going to be any forcing done, it looked like the trolls would be the ones doing it. It would be a lot easier of if they could take the fire to...

Felix stopped. The cart rails. The dwarfs and the trolls were fighting right on top of them, and they ran past the pile of ties.

Felix hurried to a nearby cart and started pushing at it. 'Olifsson, in here. Put the ties in here!' The rusty wheels complained bitterly, but at last began to move.

Galin looked up, saw the cart, followed the rails to the fight with his eyes, and grinned. 'Good thinking. You must have picked up some dwarf common sense, travelling with Gurnisson all these years.'

Felix nearly choked. Gotrek had many virtues, but he wouldn't have said that common sense was one of them. He stopped the cart at the stack, and he and Galin began hefting the heavy ties into it while keeping an eye on the fight.

The she-troll was taking another swing at Leatherbeard. He ducked and lashed out with a wild backhand, cutting her hand off at the wrist. Hand and club spun away and knocked Ragar and Karl's legs out from under them.

Narin hurled his lit lantern. The he-troll batted it aside with his club, but Arn threw his a second later and it smashed on the brute's shoulder, dousing it.

'That's done it!' cried Karl, getting up.

The flame didn't catch.

Ragar groaned. 'No it hasn't.'

Gotrek charged in under the thing's club and chopped into its left leg at the hip, nearly severing it. It howled in agony and swung at him. The Slayer blocked, and axe and club connected with a crack that hurt Felix's ears. Gotrek tried to pull back for another swing but couldn't. His blade was stuck in the wood of the club.

The troll swung the club up with both hands and lifted Gotrek with it, his hands still clamped tight around his trapped axe. The Slayer lost his grip as he flew over the troll's shoulder and spun through the air to crash to the floor neck-first, ten yards behind it, leaving his axe behind in the club.

The other dwarfs lunged in, smashing and chopping into the troll in half a dozen places, and then darting back as it screamed and fanned them back with the axe-stuck club. The haft of the axe chimed off Arn's pick and knocked him flat.

Leatherbeard continued to slash at the she-troll, trying to cut off her other hand. She vomited at him, but he danced back and the deadly bile missed its mark.

Gotrek staggered up, blinking and shaking his head like a bull, and aimed himself unsteadily at the he-troll's back. 'Give me my axe,' he growled.

'That's enough, Herr Jaeger,' said Narin, as they heaved a last tie into the cart. He lit the lumps of shiny coal from the wick of his lantern and tossed them in, and then smashed the lantern down on the wood. Oil splashed everywhere and the flames spread rapidly.

Felix made to push the cart, but Galin stopped him. 'Wait for it to catch properly.'

'Wait?' Felix looked anxiously back at the fight. Could they afford to wait?

Gotrek shoulder-tackled the troll behind the knees as the others danced and dodged before it. It slammed down on its back, roaring in surprise, and flailed its club at Gotrek, who had ended up half under it. He jerked aside and the troll mashed its own foot. It screeched in agony. Gotrek scrabbled on top of it and ripped the club out of its hand with sheer brute force.

The she-troll clubbed Leatherbeard to the ground with her stump and leapt on top of him, trying to bite his head off. At least her hand hadn't grown back, Felix thought, though there was already new flesh and bone forming at the cut. She didn't renew herself as quickly as the mutated troll had, Sigmar be praised.

The he-troll was up and grabbing for Gotrek. The Slayer dodged back, trying to free his axe from the club. The brute came after him, but without its club, it could no longer keep the dwarfs at bay. They slashed and bashed at it from all sides, cutting gaping wounds

in its legs, sides and back, and breaking its bones faster
than they could mend. It was giving ground.

'Now, man! Now!' cried Galin, pushing at the cart.

Felix and Galin pushed the flaming cart along the
rails towards the fight. The fire and smoke blew
directly in Felix's face and he coughed and cursed.

The troll heard the rumble and turned. Its eyes
widened at the sight of the flames and it jumped
aside. They were going to miss it!

Gotrek freed his axe at last and leapt at the troll,
roaring.

'Die, Grimnir curse you!'

He chopped through both of its knees with one
mighty blow. It shrieked horribly, and toppled off its
severed lower legs to crash into the blaze, knocking
the mine cart off the rails and scattering the flaming
rail ties.

Gotrek hacked its head off as it tried to crawl from
the flames, then tossed its legs on top of it. He
grunted with satisfaction. 'Trolls never smell better
than when they're burning.'

The others started for Leatherbeard, still thrashing
under the she-troll. His right arm was caught in her
remaining claw, the other held down with the bony
elbow of her handless arm while she tried to bite his
head off. He had lost one of his axes.

He glared at the dwarfs through the tangle of her
arms and her empty, swinging breasts. 'Leave me be!'
he shouted.

The dwarfs reluctantly did as he asked, watching
anxiously as he struggled. He had one leg free and
was kicking her as hard as he could in the stomach.
His neck, below his mask, was crimson and corded

with strain. Veins writhed across his trembling muscles.

Gotrek edged forwards.

'You're not going to interfere?' asked Felix.

Gotrek glared at him. 'Of course not, but if she wins...' He hefted his axe.

The she-troll's neck bulged and she made a horrid 'mumphing' sound. She was going to vomit! Leatherbeard would be reduced to a bubbling paste! With a desperate wrench, the masked Slayer ripped his right arm out from under her elbow and swung his remaining axe at her head. She jerked away and took it in the shoulder, spewing her vile puke on the flags beside him. A few spatters burned into his mask and neck.

He swung again. The she-troll let go of his off hand to grab the axe. He thumbed her in the eye. She reeled to her knees, howling and clutching at her face. He surged up and leapt at her, burying his axe in her skull and knocking her back into the flames with his weight. She screeched and lashed him with her claw. There was a ripping sound as he flew back and crashed to the floor on his face.

The she-troll tried to clamber out of the fire, but the split in her head was not healing, and her limbs only twitched weakly before she sank back dead, blackening in the blaze.

'Well done, Slayer,' said Narin, turning to Leatherbeard.

Gotrek nodded in agreement.

Leatherbeard pushed himself up, groggy and groaning. Felix and the dwarfs stared at him, shocked.

He blinked back at them. 'What?'

No one answered.

He reached up and touched his face. It was naked. 'My mask!' he cried, and looked back at the dead she-troll burning in the fire. The leather face hung from her claws, its straps snapped, its edges smouldering.

'No!' Leatherbeard leapt up and grabbed it out of the flames. He hurried to put it back on, but it was too late. They had all seen.

The Slayer had no beard. His chin was cleaner than Felix's. In fact, he was entirely without hair – his scalp was bald, and he was lacking both eyebrows and eyelashes. He looked like a pink, angry baby.

'Now you know,' he choked as he tried vainly to buckle the broken straps. 'Now you know my shame. Now you know why I took the Slayer's oath.'

'Aye, we see, lad,' said Narin, kindly.

'But,' Galin sputtered, aghast, 'what's wrong with you? Are you truly a dwarf? Were you born this way?'

'Grimnir forbid!' The mask wouldn't stay on. Leatherbeard snatched it off again, frustrated. Pain and rage burned in his eyes. 'Last year I fought the skaven in the undgrin with my clan brothers. They had strange weapons. One exploded in my face when I struck it. The next morning I woke up like this. I ran from my hold before any could see. The priests at the Slayer's hall helped me fashion this mask, and now… now it's ruined. How can I be a Slayer without a crest? How can I continue when all can see my shame?'

'I have needle and thread in my medic kit,' said Hamnir from behind them. 'You are welcome to them.'

Everyone turned. The prince was sitting up unsteadily, rubbing his stomach gingerly. He motioned vaguely towards his pack.

'Thank you, Prince Hamnir,' said Leatherbeard, and stepped to the pack, turning his back as he opened it and dug through it. The others began to tend to their wounds.

Thorgig helped Hamnir to his feet. The prince could barely stand. He glared at Gotrek. 'Just let me gather my strength, Gurnisson, and we will go again.'

'You want some more?' Gotrek shrugged.

'No, prince,' said Narin, looking up from patching a gash on his arm. 'Enough is enough. This cannot continue.'

'Aye,' chorused the brothers Rassmusson.

'Please, my prince,' said Thorgig, 'at least wait until after we win the karak.'

'You will stop a dwarf from fighting for his honour?' asked Hamnir, affronted.

'Never, prince,' said Narin, 'but I will *suggest* that you stop. This is madness.'

'When Gurnisson admits that he was wrong,' said Hamnir, 'I will stop.'

'When Ranulffsson pays me what he stole from me, I'll call it quits,' said Gotrek.

'If it's a matter of gold,' said Felix, 'I'll pay Gotrek what he thinks he's owed. Only let's move on.'

'Don't be a fool, manling,' snarled Gotrek. 'It means nothing for you to pay me. It's him or no one.'

'But what is it all about?' cried Felix, losing patience. 'What's so difficult about a division of spoils? I don't understand.'

'Of course you don't,' said Gotrek. 'You're not a dwarf.'

'The difficulty,' said Hamnir, 'is in the *definition* of spoils.'

'The difficulty,' Gotrek interrupted, 'is that you and I made a blood oath that we would split all spoils evenly! *All* spoils! There would be nothing held back or hidden on either side. We made the oath on the first day we set out, and you broke it.'

Hamnir sighed and sat wearily on the wheel of an old mine cart. 'Here is what happened. Gurnisson and I had hired on with the army of a Tilean nobleman who was in a war with another Tilean nobleman. The usual petty human squabbling.'

Felix snorted at this, but Hamnir didn't see the irony. He continued.

'We fought across the disputed country, retaking villages that our employer's rival had plundered and occupied. In one of them, there was a dwarf tavern keep, with a comely daughter, who showed me her appreciation for our liberation of the town by...' Hamnir coloured. 'Well, she was a very sweet lass, and we developed a fondness for each other in the week I was there, and she gave me a goodbye gift,' he glared at Gotrek. 'A *love* gift – a small book of old dwarf love poems.' He looked at Felix. 'When we came to divide the spoils of the battle, Gurnisson wanted to include it in the tally. I did not. It was not taken in war, it was given in love, and therefore not plunder.'

'It *was* taken in war,' growled Gotrek. 'She gave it to you for winning the battle and freeing the town. I got a gold coin and a new helmet from the blacksmith, because I stopped Intero's men from burning down his forge. I put that in. There is no difference.'

'There is, unless you kissed that blacksmith on the lips and spent the night in his arms,' said Hamnir dryly.

Narin chuckled at that.

'Was it valuable, this book?' asked Felix, flatly.

Hamnir shrugged. 'It was a copy of a copy, worth a few Empire pfennigs at most.' He looked towards his pack. 'If not for the sentimental value, I would have thrown it out long ago.'

'A few pfennigs?' Felix's voice rose of its own volition. 'A few pfennigs! You two lunatics haven't spoken to each other for a hundred years because of a few pfennigs?' He smacked his forehead and turned to Hamnir. 'Why didn't you just pay Gotrek half the cost of the book and have done?' He swung his head to Gotrek. 'And why didn't you tell Hamnir that a few pfennigs don't matter between friends, and forget about it?'

'It's the principle of the thing,' both dwarfs said in unison.

'He puts milk-sop sentiment before law,' said Gotrek.

'He puts law before common decency,' said Hamnir.

'You both put stubbornness before common sense,' said Felix. He turned to the other dwarfs. 'Do none of you find this to be madness?'

The dwarfs shrugged.

'Haven't spoken to my cousin Riggi for nigh on fifty years, because he didn't ask me if I wanted a drink when it was his turn to buy,' said Karl.

'My clan ceased all trade with another clan over a handkerchief,' said Leatherbeard.

Felix groaned. He'd forgotten who he was talking to, but he had to do something. They would be at this stupidity until the end of the world if he didn't. 'Can I see it?' he asked Hamnir. 'I would like to gaze upon the book that kept two friends apart for a hundred years. It must be wondrous to behold.'

Hamnir opened his pack, dug through it, and pulled out a small volume from the very bottom. 'It isn't much to look at,' he said, handing it carefully to Felix. 'Keepsakes rarely are.'

Felix looked at the little book. It was leather-bound parchment, so worn around the edges by its hundred years in the bottom of Hamnir's pack that it was nearly oval. He flipped it open to the centre. The words were in poorly formed Khazalid runes. 'What was her name?' he asked. 'The barkeep's daughter who gave you this?'

'Er…' said Hamnir. 'I… Morga? No… Margi? Drus? It will come to me…'

Felix snorted and ripped the book in two. He held out the halves to Hamnir and Gotrek. 'There,' he said, 'now it is divided equally. Your grudges are at an end.'

The dwarfs gasped. Even Gotrek gaped.

Hamnir started to his feet. 'What have you done, human?'

He grabbed for his axe. Thorgig was beside him, eyes blazing.

'Damned interfering fool!' shouted Gotrek, advancing on him. 'You've just given him an excuse not to pay me at all!'

Felix backed away, gulping and terrified. He hadn't considered what he would do after he destroyed the book. They were going to kill him.

Then Narin started laughing, great roaring belly laughs. After a second, Galin joined him. Gotrek and Hamnir turned on them, glaring.

'You find this humorous?' snapped Hamnir.

'Will you still laugh when I knock your teeth down your throat?' asked Gotrek, raising his fists.

Galin pointed from one half of the book to the other, trying to speak, but he was laughing too hard. Tears rolled down his cheeks and into his beard.

'The Shield of Drutti!' Narin gasped between spasms. He held up the charred wood in his beard and shook it at them. 'The human has smashed your Shield of Drutti!'

He and Galin broke into fresh gales of laughter.

'Not so funny when it happens to you is it, Slayer?' cried Galin.

Hamnir and Gotrek snatched the halves of the book from Felix's hands and turned on each other, eyes blazing with rage. They shook the pages at each other, stuttering and fighting for words. The ancient paper cracked and split. Bits of age-yellowed confetti fluttered to the ground like dirty snow.

Gotrek watched the falling flakes, and then glared at Hamnir. 'When was the last time you read this book?'

Hamnir looked at the pages crumbling in his hand. 'I...' He snorted. 'I...' He exploded in laughter, his whole body shaking.

'What, curse you?' Gotrek shouted, furious. 'What's so funny?'

'I never read it,' yelped Hamnir, his eyes running. 'It was awful!'

Gotrek stood, frozen, for a long moment, staring at Hamnir as if he was going to cut his head off. Then, with a sound like a steam engine exploding, he too began laughing, violent rasping gusts.

Narin and Galin burst into fresh laughter, but Thorgig and the brothers Rassmusson stared, unnerved and confused. Felix was just happy that they seemed to have forgotten about killing him.

'You stubborn, little–' Gotrek wheezed, pointing at Hamnir. 'Never read it. Can't remember her name. Kept it all this time just for...'

'For the principle of the thing!' wailed Hamnir, hysterical.

The Slayer and the prince collapsed upon each other, heads on each other's shoulders, shaking with laughter and slapping each other's backs.

'Maybe...' choked Gotrek, 'maybe you are a dwarf after all.'

'And maybe there's... more to you than an axe,' hiccupped Hamnir.

Their laughter continued for a long time while the others stood around awkwardly, but at last subsided.

Hamnir stepped back, wiping his eyes. 'It has been a quiet hundred years not having you to argue with, Gurnisson.'

'Aye,' said Gotrek, ruffling his crest and snorting noisily. 'And it's been a relief not having you yammering on about everything under the sun night and day. I forgot there was such a thing as silence when I travelled with you.' He shrugged. 'Even the best things have to end.'

They began to collect their packs and pull themselves together.

Thorgig frowned. 'So... so your grudges are cancelled?' he asked. 'You are no longer enemies.' He didn't seem to like this idea at all.

'Aye,' said Hamnir. 'The human ended it, and very neatly too.' He swung around to glare at Felix. 'Though you owe me a book of very bad poetry, man. Or I will have a new grudge.'

'And you owe me some very *good* poetry,' growled Gotrek. 'For this mischief, the epic of my death had better be the greatest poem ever written.'

Felix bowed, hiding a smile. That had gone better than expected. He had thought they would continue to hate each other, but they had put aside their grudge in favour of hating him more. 'I will do my best to oblige both of you.'

Hamnir nodded, and turned to the brothers Rassmusson. 'Come,' he said, 'we've wasted enough time here. Lead us to the Undgrin, miners.'

'Aye, prince,' said Ragar.

'It's just over there,' said Karl, pointing across the room.

'Nearly there,' said Arn.

The dwarfs finished binding their wounds and shouldered their packs, picks and axes, as the trolls continued to turn to black bones in the roaring fire. Leatherbeard pulled on his repaired mask. It was crudely sewn, and didn't fit as snugly as before, but it covered his shame, and he seemed content. When all were ready, they followed the Rassmussons across the vast room, in a more comradely mood than before. Even Galin and Narin seemed to have forgotten their grudges against Gotrek and each other's clans, and talked of this and that. Only Thorgig remained sullen, glaring at Gotrek's back with undisguised contempt.

CHAPTER FOURTEEN

THEY CAME TO the undgrin at the base of a long descending ramp, down the centre of which two large-gauge sets of cart rails were laid. The system of winches and pulleys that had lifted and lowered the carts up and down the slope still stood, dusty and rusted, but the carts themselves were gone.

When they stepped through the wide curved arch at the bottom of the ramp, Felix stared, gape-mouthed. The scale of the thing was staggering – a gargantuan tunnel at least forty feet wide and sixty high, its granite walls so polished that the dwarfs' lamps reflected in them as if they were mirrors. A double road of rails ran down the middle of the tunnel, glinting like sword blades until they disappeared in the darkness. On either side of these were raised walkways down which ten dwarfs could have walked side by side. The floor was covered in a thick layer of undisturbed dust.

No one had travelled the underground road in decades.

The Rassmusson brothers grinned at Felix.

'Told you you'd know it when you saw it,' said Ragar.

'Not bad, eh?' said Arn.

The idea that a tunnel this large had been built, not just between Duk Grung and Karak Hirn, but between almost every dwarf hold from the Worlds Edge Mountains to the Black Mountains was difficult for Felix to comprehend. 'It's… it's astounding,' he said at last.

'This is only a tributary road,' said Galin. 'The real undgrin is twice as big.'

'Too bad Duk Grung isn't running any more,' said Karl. 'The steam train ran then, taking ore up to the smelting room at Karak Hirn. We could have hopped it and been at the karak in a day.'

Ragar sighed. 'Those were the days. Ten days at the workface, a day up to Karak Hirn for a good bath and two days of slap and tickle with Iylda, a day down again on the undgrin and back to work.'

'Aye,' said Arn. 'Two days with a lass is about the right amount.'

'With a twelve day break in between,' agreed Karl.

'Mining at the karak, we see them every night,' said Ragar, glum.

'See them every night and they start talking about things,' said Arn.

'Weddings, for instance,' said Karl.

'And babies,' said Ragar, swallowing.

'Hope the chief finds a new mine soon,' said Arn.

The other brothers nodded fervently as the dwarfs started to the right at a brisk pace, lanterns swinging from their belts. The brothers began singing an old dwarf marching song, and the others soon joined in. After the sixteenth verse, Felix started to get a headache.

'Aren't they worried about drawing attention any more?' He asked Gotrek out of the side of his mouth.

'Nothing lives down here,' Gotrek said. 'Too deep, no water, and nothing to eat. Not even insects.'

Felix's wonder at the undgrin faded quickly as the party marched along its unchanging, unending length for mile upon mile. It was the safest, least difficult leg of their journey by far – a flat, dry, smooth roadway without bends or junctions – and consequently, the most boring, at least for Felix.

Gotrek and Hamnir had no difficulty passing the time. The walls of their century of silence having tumbled down at last, reminiscences and friendly insults poured out of them in a low rumbling flood. They walked side by side, heads together, with only the occasional 'remember...' or 'whatever happened to...' audible to the rest of the company, and now and then erupting in laughter that boomed down the tunnel and back again.

Felix found himself jealous of Hamnir's friendship with Gotrek. Gotrek and Felix had survived adventures a hundred times more desperate than those that Gotrek had shared with Hamnir, but had they ever laughed about them like this? Had they ever truly shared them? It seemed that, as much as they had argued and fought, Gotrek and Hamnir had been true friends. They had fought through the dangers they had faced side by side, not with Hamnir one step behind and to the right, as Felix did. They had caroused together, joked together and devised mad schemes together.

What had Gotrek and Felix done together? Travelled, yes, but had they conversed as they travelled? As little as Gotrek could get away with: 'This way, manling', 'Come on, manling', 'Leave it behind, manling', and more of the same. They had often drunk side by side, but there had hardly been more conversation there – no comradely sharing of troubles, no boisterous joking, no bantering insults. Even at his most inebriated, Gotrek kept himself at one remove from Felix. They were not friends. They were not equals. They were Slayer and rememberer, that was all.

Was it because they were of different races? Gotrek had little respect for men, it was true, but over the years he had come to count on Felix's resilience and prowess with a sword, as well as his opinion. No matter how grudgingly he listened, in the end he did listen – usually. Perhaps it was being Gotrek's rememberer that was the trouble? The Slayer was, in a way, his employer and one was rarely a true friend to one's employee.

But when he thought about it, Felix could think of no one in all their travels that Gotrek had ever treated as a true friend – no one until Hamnir. Not even the other Slayers they had known, Snorri Nosebiter and Bjorni and Ulli. Oh, they had drunk and roared in every tavern and every town they had ever visited, but Felix could not remember Gotrek ever once pouring out his troubles to any of them, or laughing with them over old times, or even hating them as much as he had hated Hamnir before they had buried their grudge.

Then Felix knew what it was. Gotrek had known Hamnir before he was a Slayer. Whatever had driven Gotrek to take the crest had not happened yet during the years he had travelled with Hamnir. Gotrek had been a different dwarf then, a dwarf who had yet to experience the tragedy that would cause him to turn his back on his family, his hold, and whatever plans he might have made for his life, and wander the world seeking a good death.

This was why Gotrek could joke and fight with Hamnir so freely. Hamnir brought him back to a time before his doom, whatever it may have been, and made him feel like the dwarf he had been then, the young adventurer who had fought his way up and down the coast of the Old World. Those were the years when Gotrek's heart had been open enough to allow him friends. Those days were past. Now the Slayer's heart was locked behind walls thicker than those around the vault of a dwarf king.

Felix suddenly felt sad for Gotrek. Perhaps he even understood a little of why the Slayer sought death. To be alone, even when surrounded by your closest companions, for the rest of a dwarf's long life, would be a misery hard to bear. If Hamnir was bringing back to Gotrek some of his lost happiness, why should Felix begrudge him? They were all likely to die at the end of this tunnel as it was. Let the Slayer live first.

The dwarfs made camp for the night around a fire of the same shiny lumps of coal that Galin had used to ignite the rail ties. Only a few of these tossed on the ground burned with the brightness and warmth of a normal wood fire, and for nearly as long. The dwarfs' shadows moved like giants across the soaring walls of the undgrin in the firelight, but as Felix looked left and right, down the endless underground road, he felt very small.

When they had all drunk a few cups of strong ale and finished their hard tack and biscuit, the evening turned into a dwarf boasting contest, each trying to top the others with the dangers and outlandish adventures they had experienced. Gotrek was remarkably restrained, considering that, having faced down a daemon, he could top them all. He told only stories from his time adventuring with Hamnir, long before he had found his rune axe or taken the Slayer's crest. Perhaps, thought Felix, that had nothing to do with restraint.

'Well, none of you has ever climbed as high as I have, I'll wager,' said Galin, taking a swig of ale.

'Ha!' said Narin. 'I climbed old Hammertop, just to have a look at the sunset. You climbed higher than that?'

Galin smiled smugly and wiped his lips. 'I was one of the young fools who joined Firriksson when he scaled the Maiden's Tresses.'

Thorgig gaped. 'You climbed the Tresses? With that belly?'

The others laughed.

Galin's eyes flashed, but then he relaxed and chuckled, patting his swelling midsection. 'I hadn't won my ale vault then. In fact, I was younger than you, shortbeard, and I thought Firriksson was the greatest adventurer that ever lived. Of course, we all found out later that he was as mad as a squig in heat, but then, well...' He puffed on his pipe for a moment, his eyes far away. 'You see, he'd heard the old wives' tale that the Maiden's Eye, that winks from the peak of the Maiden at sunrise and sunset, was a diamond as big as a mine cart, and he decided he wanted it. So up we went, a bunch of stripling shortbeards and Firriksson, a lunatic Thunderer who used to dance harvest jigs in his tent, by himself, for a half hour every morning before breaking camp. Said it kept him fit. Lost three of us on the way up. They fell down a crevasse in an ice field. Broke every bone they had. Bad business.' He frowned, and then shook off the memory and grinned. 'When we get to the top, after five of the coldest days of my life, Firriksson finds the Maiden's Eye, and it's everything that's promised, big as a mine cart, as clear and clean as spring water… and made entirely of salt.'

The dwarfs guffawed.

Galin shrugged. 'So, we carved our names in it, had a lick for luck, and went back down.'

'You think Kolin Firriksson was mad,' said Hamnir, 'try serving under a human. The sanest human is madder than any dwarf.' He looked over at Felix, suddenly remembering he was there. 'Er, no disrespect meant, Herr Jaeger.'

Felix ground his teeth. 'None taken.'

Gotrek snorted, 'And we once fought for one who was madder than a skaven with a warpstone helmet.'

Hamnir looked at him, laughing. 'You mean Chamnelac!'

'Aye,' said Gotrek. 'Duke Chamnelac of Cres, a pirate hunter out of Bretonnia, fierce as a badger…'

'And almost as intelligent,' said Hamnir, 'but if moustaches had been brains, he'd have been a mage. Had a pair of curling soup strainers you could have hung kettles on.'

Gotrek leaned forwards. 'We'd been chasing old Ice Eye, a Norse raider, who was the scourge of the Bretonnian coast at the time, and finally caught up with him south of Sartosa, on an island well known for being a refuge for pirates.'

'It had been a rough voyage,' said Hamnir, picking up the story. 'A bad storm three days out, a run-in with a Tilean corsair that had killed twenty dwarfs and men and wounded forty more; and Chamnelac had been in such a hurry to get after Ice Eye that he hadn't victualled or supplied himself properly. There was hardly any food or drinking water, and no surgeon. Chamnelac had left him behind by mistake.'

'His crew wasn't too pleased, needless to say,' continued Gotrek. 'We were under strength to be attacking Ice Eye in his hidey hole, and likely to die even if we won, for lack of bandages. There was talk of mutiny, and some of his officers went to him and begged him to turn back.'

'Chamnelac refused,' said Hamnir. 'He called them cowards. He didn't want to let Ice Eye get away. He anchored his ship on the far side of the island from Ice Eye's wooden fort, and ordered the men ashore, supposedly so they could take on fresh water and hunt for food.' He grinned. 'When they did...'

Gotrek laughed. 'When they did, he set fire to his ship! Burnt it to the waterline.'

'What?' said Arn, 'Humans are insane.'

'I see the sense of it,' said Thorgig. 'His men were wavering. He wanted to give them no choice but to attack. The only way to return home was to kill Ice Eye and take his ship. No retreat. No surrender.'

'Very brave, I'm sure,' said Narin, 'but even the boldest commander likes to leave himself an out, if he can.'

'Did it work?' asked Ragar. 'Did he win?'

Gotrek and Hamnir exchanged a sly look.

'Oh aye,' said Gotrek. 'Chamnelac won. Took the island without a fight.'

'Without a fight?' asked Galin. 'How is that possible?'

'Because...' said Hamnir, and then burst out laughing, 'because Ice Eye had seen the smoke from Chamnelac's burning ship and knew he was coming, and...' His laughter overwhelmed him.

Gotrek grinned savagely. 'He sailed away. Ice Eye took off with all his ships and left Chamnelac gaping on the shore!'

'Sailed away?' Thorgig goggled, 'But that means that Chamnelac...'

'Couldn't get off the island!' chuckled Narin, slapping his knee. 'He'd trapped himself! What a fool!'

Thorgig frowned. 'So, er, how did you get off, did you build a raft?'

Hamnir shook his head. 'Too far from shore. We were stuck well and proper. In the end, after three months went by and we were all thinner than human beer, another pirate, an Estalian, dropped anchor to take on water.'

'Did Chamnelac take his ship, then?' asked Ragar.

Gotrek grinned. 'Chamnelac was dead, murdered the first night we were marooned. Half his officers too. No, we signed the articles and joined up, the whole of Chamnelac's crew. Most of them stayed on the account too, as I recall.'

'The poor old duke birthed more pirates than he ever took,' said Hamnir, shaking his head.

Gotrek took a swallow of ale. 'Three months on an island with a bunch of filthy Bretonnians, and only berries and seagulls to eat, ruined my stomach for a year.'

'You had it easy,' said Narin. 'I was trapped in a hunter's shack in the Kislev oblast for two months in the middle of winter, with two ogres for company and nothing to eat but a cellar full of rotten turnips.'

'A dwarf can live on turnips,' said Galin. 'Don't sound such a hardship.'

'A dwarf can, aye,' said Narin. 'Unfortunately, ogres can't. Oh, they'll eat them. They'll eat anything, but it'll only leave them wanting something... meatier. Namely, me.'

The others laughed.

Felix saw Gotrek look over at Leatherbeard as Narin told his story. The young Slayer wasn't participating in the boasting. He sat a little way off from the others, staring into the fire through the eyes of his crudely patched mask. Gotrek glanced at him several more times during Narin's tale. Then, while the Rassmusson brothers were trying to top him by telling a very confused story about tricking a companion of theirs into eating troll dung, he got up and crossed to him.

'All right, Slayer?' Gotrek asked, squatting.

Leatherbeard shrugged.

'Not still troubled about us seeing your face?'

Leatherbeard shook his head. 'That isn't it. Not all of it.'

'Well then, what's the matter? It isn't every day that a dwarf graduates from squigslayer to trollslayer.'

Felix could just see the corners of the young Slayer's mouth turn up sadly through the mouth-slot of his mask.

'I am glad to have won the name, aye,' he said, 'but... but I didn't die. I didn't end my shame. Instead, I lost my mask and made it worse.'

Gotrek chuckled, a black, empty sound. 'Now you know the true pain of the Slayer, lad,' he said. 'Every victory is a defeat, for only if we die do we fulfil our destinies; but if we don't try to win, if we drop our axes and let the troll rip us apart, then Grungni won't accept us into the halls of our ancestors, for he doesn't care for suicides.' He sighed. 'I've been at it eighty years. The pain doesn't go away, but you get used to it.' He stood. 'Beer helps. Have another.'

He returned to the others and the tales continued.

THE NEXT MORNING – if there was such a thing as morning in the stygian underworld of the undgrin – a few hours after the dwarfs broke camp, they came to a place where it looked as if the tunnel had been crushed by a giant hand. The floor was buckled and broken, and the walls and ceiling had crumbled and fallen in. Boulders as big as houses littered the floor, crushing the twisted cart rails. Other boulders had fallen atop them, some precariously balanced, and the ceiling above the mess was mazed with cracks and missing blocks. It bulged down ominously in places.

'Did you know this was here?' asked Gotrek, his eyes travelling across the wreckage.

'I had heard there was some damage from an earthquake that occurred sixty years after the mine closed,' Hamnir said, 'but that it was passable.'

'I can see beyond it,' said Narin, twisting the sliver of wood in his beard, 'but it doesn't look to be a pleasant stroll.'

'Miner's nightmare,' said Galin, looking uneasily up at the ceiling. 'Those blocks could come down at any minute. Any one of us so much as raises his voice or stamps his feet and... boom.'

'My father meant to repair this,' said Hamnir, swallowing queasily, 'but there were always things closer to home that were more urgent.'

'I heard he left it this way on purpose,' said Karl.

'Aye,' said Ragar, 'so that no army could get through here without it all dropping on their heads.'

'A ready-made trap,' said Arn.

'A trap for us,' said Leatherbeard uneasily. 'A rock fall is no doom for a Slayer.'

'Olifsson,' said Hamnir. 'See if you can find us a way through.'

'Me?' said Galin, eyes bulging. 'Do you mean to get me killed?'

'You are an engineer,' said Hamnir. 'You came for this purpose. I want your advice on this.'

Galin swallowed. 'My advice,' he said, 'is to find another way around.'

Hamnir scowled. 'You know very well there is no other way. It's through, or back the way we came.'

'Are you a coward after all, Olifsson?' asked Thorgig. 'You look a little pale.'

It was true. Galin's normally florid face was mud grey.

'I'm a mine engineer,' he said. 'As the Slayer knows his axe and Prince Hamnir knows his markets, I know walls and ceilings and the weight they will bear. That ceiling is hanging by spider webs. We won't make it through.'

'But we must,' said Hamnir, 'and you're the dwarf to guide us.'

'It's death,' said Galin, his eyes never leaving the crumbling ceiling.

Hamnir stepped to him and looked him in the eye. 'Listen to me, engineer. I have a hold to save. I will not turn back. You are a volunteer. I have not ordered you to follow me. You are free to leave. The rest of us will try to cross through this death trap without you.'

Galin shook his head. 'You'll never make it.'

'Not without you,' said Hamnir, and he turned away to stand next to Gotrek, who was surveying the collapse.

The others turned away too. Galin stood behind them, lips tight, head down. Felix joined the others, as much to spare the engineer his scrutiny as to shun him like the rest.

'All right, curse you,' Galin choked after a long pause. 'All right, I'll have a look. I can't have you fools stomping in and killing yourselves.' He pushed through them, glaring furiously. He stopped at the edge of the mess, removed his pack and laid down his hammer.

Hamnir put a hand on his shoulder. 'Thank you, engineer.'

Galin shrugged him off, snarling, and then swallowed and took a deep breath. It seemed to Felix that he might have lost his courage once more, but at last he started forwards, one cautious inch at a time. Three paces in he looked back. 'Stay quiet.'

The other dwarfs waited as he picked his way cautiously through the boulders, placing every foot with care, testing the floor and the rubble with trembling toes and fingers. He soon disappeared around a fall of boulders, and Felix and the other dwarfs held their breath and craned their necks. After what seemed like forever, he reappeared, his legs trembling and his red face bathed in sweat. He inched back to them as slowly and methodically as he had left them, and at last let out a long breath when he stepped beyond the last bit of jumbled granite.

'Well, there is a way,' he said, mopping his brow, 'but you will all have to step exactly where I step and touch only what I touch. Kicking a pebble or slipping on a bit of scree in that mess will bury us. There're parts of that roof that…' he shivered. 'Well, I don't know what's holding it up.'

'Couldn't we make a big noise now and bring it down before we go on?' asked Felix.

The dwarfs gave him patronising looks.

'That would indeed be safest,' said Narin, smiling, 'but where's the guarantee that the road would still be passable after it fell?'

'I can guarantee it wouldn't be,' said Galin.

'Ah, yes. I see. Of course.' Felix blushed. He felt like a fool.

'Right,' said Hamnir, turning to the others, 'all in one line, close together. Take the exact step the dwarf in front of you took. Galin, you have the lead. Jaeger, you come last.'

Felix's heart thudded. 'Why am I last?'

'Because you have the longest legs to run with, if things begin to fall,' said Hamnir, 'and, forgive me if I'm blunt, you're more likely to put a foot wrong than a dwarf.'

Felix's fists balled. More insults.

'It's true, manling,' said Gotrek. 'We dwarfs were born to tunnels and cave-ins. We know our footing.'

'Aye aye, fine,' said Felix. He wanted to punch all the superior little know-it-alls in the nose, but he restrained himself. It would probably bring the roof down. He took off his red cloak and stuffed it in his pack so it wouldn't catch on anything.

'Follow close,' said Galin, 'and don't say a word.'

The dwarfs started ahead like a caterpillar on the march, walking in lockstep, each with one hand on the shoulder of the dwarf ahead of him. They seemed to have done it many times before. Felix put his hand on Gotrek's shoulder and did his best to follow along, staring intently at the Slayer's feet.

It was slow going. At the front of the line, Galin tested the way with the haft of his warhammer, making certain no rock or slab he put his foot on would shift or slip. Then he would step and test again, step, and test again. The next dwarf would then place his foot where Galin had placed his, and so on. At first, this wasn't difficult, but, as they began to weave through the maze of monolithic boulders and up through places where the floor had buckled and rose at a steep slant, the footing was trickier. The dwarfs braced each other as they went up and down, making sure they didn't slip backwards or tip forwards.

Felix's heart thudded so noisily as he followed Gotrek that he thought the vibrations would surely shake loose the ceiling. He was sweating like a fountain. Every trickle of dust, every clack of boot heel on rock made him cringe and hunch his shoulders. His neck ached with tension.

He watched Gotrek step over a jutting ridge of floor and carefully place his foot on the other side, exactly where the dwarf before him had placed his. Felix lifted his leg over the ridge and stepped down precisely, eyes on where Gotrek was stepping next, and…

Crack! He smacked his head on a low rock overhang. He clamped a hand over his mouth to stifle a yelp. The world was receding and turning yellow and black. His knees buckled. He had been so intent on Gotrek's feet that he hadn't seen the cantilevered slab of granite that Gotrek had simply walked under. He wanted to scream and jump up and down, but both would be suicide. He stood frozen. The tunnel spun around him. He was going to fall.

A grip like iron caught his upper arm. He opened his eyes. Gotrek was holding him steady, a stubby finger on his lips. Felix nodded, and then wished he hadn't. It almost toppled him. He looked past Gotrek. The other dwarfs had stopped, and were looking back at him with expressions that ranged from pity to contempt to amusement. Galin was staring wide-eyed up at the ceiling. His lips were moving as if he was praying.

After a moment, the tunnel steadied and the dizziness passed. Felix's head still ached abominably, and a thread of blood ran down to the tip of his nose, but he had recovered enough to walk. He motioned to Gotrek to go on. The Slayer turned back with the others and took another step. Felix ducked low under the projecting slab and followed.

Felix wasn't the only one who erred. Halfway through the wreckage, Galin's probing axe handle dislodged a skull-sized rock that rolled and bounced down a slanted section of floor as the dwarfs froze and looked up, their shoulders hunched. Dribbles of dust rained down from the ceiling, but it stayed in place. A little further on, Thorgig put his hand out to brace himself on a fallen block of stone and it began to tip. He gasped and stepped back, and the others looked around. The carriage-sized block was precariously balanced on a smaller rock below it, its balance point directly over the bottom rock's edge. The dwarfs froze as they watched it teeter slowly, and then settle back with the softest of thuds. Everyone breathed again.

At last, Galin led them beyond the ruptured floor and out from under the bulging ceiling, and they all let out great sighs of relief.

Felix dabbed at his bloodied forehead with his handkerchief and looked back. His limbs were shaking with reaction. 'I hope we don't have to retreat this way. I don't think I could take it again.'

'Retreat?' said Gotrek, frowning.

He and Hamnir looked at each other, and grinned. As one, they stooped and picked up heavy rocks.

'There is no retreat,' said Hamnir.

'For Chamnelac!' they cried, as they hurled their rocks back at the stretch of broken tunnel. 'Burn the boat!'

Both rocks bounced noisily off the top of the massive teetering block that Thorgig had nearly toppled with a touch.

The other dwarfs stared.

'You madmen!' breathed Felix as the block began to dip.

'Mad dwarfs,' corrected Gotrek.

The block's movement slowed and it looked as if it was going to rock back to its resting position like it had before, but just then the edge of the bottom rock crumbled under its enormous weight, and the top rock slipped forwards a foot, overbalanced and slammed to the floor with a booming crash that shook the whole tunnel.

A long ripping sound echoed from above, like the tearing of some enormous starched canvas, and a whole section of the ceiling tore away, breaking up as it fell towards the floor.

'Run!' shouted Galin.

The first blocks smashed into the rubble like cannonballs. The dwarfs were knocked off their feet. They bounced up again and sprinted away from the collapse in a mad scramble as the tunnel shook and boomed. Felix glanced back as he ran. More and more blocks fell, pulverising those that had fallen before. The walls were folding in and toppling. He was hit in the cheek by a pebble that stung like a bullet. A rock the size of a Marienberg cheese bounced past him, narrowly missing Ragar before rolling to a stop.

Another glance. A rising cloud of dust was obscuring the wreckage and billowing after the dwarfs faster than they could run. Felix choked as it enveloped him, silting his tongue, eyes and nostrils with powdered granite. The dwarfs' lamps were dull orange glows that bobbed around him in the grey murk, while the roar of falling rock continued to batter his ears.

Fifty paces on, they reached the edge of the dust cloud and slowed. The constant thunder was tapering off to individual smashes and booms. The dwarfs stopped.

Gotrek and Hamnir were cackling like naughty schoolboys, choking and laughing in equal measure as tears cut pink channels down their dust-caked cheeks. They and the rest of the dwarfs looked as if they had been dipped in a flour barrel. Felix was the same. They sneezed and hacked and spat, bent double from their sprint.

'Bit close there,' said Hamnir, giggling.

'Aye, a bit,' agreed Gotrek.

'You might have given us some warning!' said Narin.

'Not exactly tactically sound,' huffed Galin. 'It's all very well to say "no retreat", but…'

Gotrek looked up at him, glaring. 'There never was any retreat. This just makes it clear. The only way out is forwards.'

Hamnir sobered too. 'There is no other way into the hold. I will make it in this way or die trying. The same as you swore to do when you volunteered for this mission. If you are having second thoughts, well,' he laughed evilly, 'you're having them seconds too late.' He glared around at them all. 'Now, are you ready to go?'

The dwarfs nodded. They brushed the dust from themselves, squared their weapons and packs, and the party resumed its march. Felix put his red cloak on again. It was cold in the endless tunnel.

Hamnir looked back as they went, though the collapsed section was invisible in the dust and darkness behind them. He smiled grimly. 'Birrisson will be happy – if he still lives. Hasn't had a really big rebuilding project in centuries.'

CHAPTER FIFTEEN

THE PARTY REACHED the under entrance to the mines of Karak Hirn late in the afternoon of what the dwarfs assured Felix was the second day they had spent on the deep road. Felix had entirely lost track. It felt to him as if he had spent a month without seeing the sun. He was beginning to wonder if the overworld was only a dream he had once had. There were dwarfs who lived most of their lives without seeing the sun. It gave him the chills just thinking about it.

His companions hooded their lanterns and crept cautiously towards the entrance. They weren't about to underestimate the orcs again. A train of titanic ore carts, built to the scale of the undgrin, sat on the tracks near the entrance, and they padded along them, using them as cover. At the end of the train, they squatted down and peered under the last cart. In keeping with the rest of the undgrin, the opening that led into Karak

Hirn was immense – a three storey high archway in the wall of the tunnel, so wide that the eight side-by-side rail lines that emerged from it, bending right and left to connect to the undgrin lines, fitted in its mouth with room to spare. Giant stone figures of dwarfs stood guard on either side of it, thick stone hands resting on twenty-foot tall battleaxes.

A little ball of light bobbed slowly between the grim granite sentinels as a patrol of six orcs marched back and forth across the door's breadth, carrying torches.

Hamnir was staring beyond them. Inside the door, a broad ramp rose into the interior of the mine, the eight rail lines rising with it. The top of the ramp was illuminated by a flickering orange fire glow, and roaring and rushing came faintly to their ears.

'It appears they occupy the lower foundry,' said the prince. 'We will get past these six easily enough, but if the foundry hall is well lit...'

'No need for that, prince,' said Arn.

'Aye,' said Ragar. 'There's a stair just inside the door on the left, goes up direct to the eighth deep guard room.'

'So the lads at the door don't have to trek all the way around to the main shaft when they go off shift.'

'Excellent,' said Hamnir. 'Then that is how we will go. The old kruk is only five deeps above that.'

The dwarfs waited until the orc patrol was approaching the right side of the vast doorway, and then tip-toed from behind the train and hurried quietly across the tunnel to hide in the shadow of the left-hand statue. They waited again as the patrol marched slowly back towards them, made their turn, and started away again. Again, Felix and the others noted the orcs' strange behaviour – their blank, quiet demeanour, punctuated by short, howling outbursts that stopped almost as soon as they began. They reminded Felix of pitdogs being bitten by fleas.

As the orcs approached the far side of the door, Hamnir waved the others ahead. They slipped around the statue and through the archway. The Rassmusson brothers pointed to a small, black opening in the left wall. The dwarfs filed through it and up the stairs behind it, then waited once all were in, to hear if an alarm had been raised. All was quiet.

'Well done,' whispered Hamnir. 'On we go. To the east end of the third deep.'

The dwarfs carried on up the pitch-black stair, walking quietly and listening intently. Felix could hear nothing except their own breathing and footsteps, but a few flights up he began to notice a faint red light travelling with them.

'Gotrek,' he said. 'Your axe.'

The Slayer brought the axe up and looked at it. The runes on the head were glowing faintly. He frowned. 'Never shone for grobi before,' he grunted. 'Trolls, daemons, sorcery, aye. Not grobi.'

Hamnir's brow furrowed. 'Could it be the dark powers behind all this? They are strong in the north now.'

Gotrek shrugged. 'Whatever it is, we'll kill it when we come to it.'

But the glow of the rune grew fainter the higher they climbed, and when at last they reached the eighth deep it was entirely dark again.

Orange light shone through the bars of the gate at the top of the stair. Gotrek crept up to investigate while the others waited in the shadows, weapons at the ready. He flattened himself against the wall, peered through the opening, and then tried the gate. It was locked. He cursed under his breath and grabbed the bars, pulling with inexorable strength.

'Gotrek, leave off!' hissed Hamnir, starting up the stairs and pulling a silver key from his belt pouch. 'I am a prince of this hold, if you recall. I have a master key.'

Gotrek grunted and stepped back, letting Hamnir open the door, as Felix and the dwarfs came up behind them. The guardroom was still a guardroom. Orc weapons and bits of crude armour were strewn about, and the rancid remains of an orc meal sat on the table. Dwarf lanterns flickered on the walls.

'Filthy beasts,' said Thorgig, 'defiling our home.'

'Easy, lad,' said Hamnir.

Gotrek crossed the room and looked out into the passage beyond. 'All clear.'

Hamnir led the party into the passage and they crept through the halls and chambers of the vast mine. The sounds of the orc occupation echoed all around them: heavy marching feet, the roar of furnaces, the battering of hammers and picks. The dwarfs were horrified by these sounds, and when they came to a gallery that looked down into a deep excavation ringed with scaffolding, where hundreds of orcs and goblins dug at the walls in dreary silence, they stared, caught between wonder and fury.

'This is madness,' said Narin. 'Orcs don't mine. They don't smelt.'

'Aye, agreed Galin, 'the shiftless beasts haven't done an honest day's work in their whole history. They steal the iron they have from dwarfs.'

Hamnir nodded. 'I was afraid I was going to find shackled dwarfs under the whip of orc overseers, but this is...'

'Bizarre, is what it is,' said Leatherbeard in wonder.

'It isn't right,' said Thorgig, staring. 'The whole business is unnatural.'

'To think I'd live to see orcs walking around our mine like they owned the place,' said Karl.

'Aye,' said Ragar, 'a black day.'

'We'll chop them to pieces, brothers,' said Arn. 'Don't you worry. Once we open the front door we'll set all to rights.'

They moved on, avoiding lumbering orc patrols as they came to them, and keeping out of sight of the orc work parties that were busy digging and hauling ore and rock on every level. The dwarfs were sunk in a gloomy silence by the strangeness of the orcs and their mere presence in their ancestral mines.

Felix too was infected with gloom. Ever since they had entered the mine, a mood of dread and despair had come over him, and seemed to grow stronger with every step. His heart felt as if it were pumping ice water into his veins. He couldn't pinpoint the source of the anxiety. The party's infiltration had so far gone smoothly. Their mission was no more dangerous than it had always been, and yet he could hardly keep himself from sobbing. He had a sense that they were fated to fail: that some ancient doom had come upon them that there would be no avoiding. They hadn't a hope of succeeding. He should just give up and run straight into the first orc patrol he saw and end it all.

He shook himself. What was he thinking? He had never been prone to death wishes before. That was

Gotrek's burden, not his. What was the matter with him? Was the dwarfs' unease about the orcs' un-orcish behaviour rubbing off on him? Was it that Gotrek's axe had glowed? Whatever it was, he shoved the feeling away and forced himself to be calm. The last thing he needed was the dwarfs laughing at him for jumping at shadows. There were plenty of tangible dangers to worry about.

On the fourth level, they had to climb an airshaft to rise above an area crowded with orc work parties. Grated vents along its length glowed red from the rooms beyond, casting the dwarfs' features in grisly crimson. The dwarfs peered through these grates, cursing under their breath. One looked down upon a great forge room, where a hundred bellows roared, and a hundred anvils rang under the hammers of orc smiths.

'They are using our hammers! Our sacred anvils!' said Thorgig, his voice rising. 'We must slay them. They can't be allowed to–'

'Easy,' said Hamnir. But he was trembling too, hardly able to tear his eyes away from the sights beyond the grate.

Galin shook his head as he stared through. 'Axes, spears, armour, and of excusable quality too. Never seen orcs work like that.'

'And what designs are these?' asked Narin. 'Never seen the like. Look like spider parts.'

The red light glittered off Gotrek's one eye as he glared into the forge room. 'What do they make it for? That's the question. Looks like they're getting ready to make war on the whole world.'

The dwarfs looked at him, eyes wide.

'By Grimnir's beard,' said Thorgig. 'What *do* they mean to do? Is Karak Hirn the first hold of many that they mean to take?'

'No,' said Hamnir, grimly, 'it is their last.'

'It is their grave,' said Gotrek.

Felix shivered, the feeling of dread suddenly stronger. He shook it off with difficulty.

The dwarfs moved on, climbing the airshaft to exit into a dark chamber on the third level. Hamnir led them east, through a maze of sorting and smelting halls, forges and supply pantries. The further away from the main shaft they went the fewer orc patrols they passed, and the less populated the corridors and rooms became, until soon they seemed entirely alone. This was an old section of the mine, dug out when the hold was young, and long ago turned into storage rooms and workshops, all of which had been ransacked by the orcs and then abandoned.

Hamnir finally stopped at a large stone door in a dusty and disused corridor. 'The door to the kruk,' he said.

There were orc footprints in the dust before it.

Gotrek peered at the keyhole, holding a torch close. 'Been opened recently,' he said, 'with a key.'

Hamnir groaned. He took a key from his ring and inserted it in the lock. The dwarfs readied their weapons. The lock turned easily and Hamnir pulled it open. The dwarfs looked in. Orc footprints ran off into darkness down a dark old tunnel, smaller and rougher than the rest of the mine.

'Have they found *everything*?' asked Hamnir, angrily.

The dwarfs entered and Hamnir locked the door behind them. They moved quietly through the old

mine, glaring into the shadows as they followed the
orc trail. It wasn't too long, however, before the footprints stopped and doubled back, and the dwarfs
could find no more further on.

Hamnir breathed a sigh of relief. 'It appears that
they decided there was nothing to take. Good. Now,
this way.'

He led them swiftly, and with a dwarf's unerring
knowledge of where he was underground, through
the maze of crossing corridors, until he stopped at a
section of wall indistinguishable from any other in
the kruk.

'Here,' he said. 'My father's vault is ten feet behind
this wall.'

Galin stepped up and rapped on the wall with his
knuckles. 'May I take a sounding, prince?'

'By all means,' said Hamnir.

Galin turned to Narin, who carried a warhammer.
'Will you strike the wall, Ironskin?'

Narin nodded and readied his weapon. 'At your
command.'

Galin took off his helmet and pressed his ear to the
wall. 'Strike.'

Narin swung, and the hammer rang off the wall.

Galin listened to the rock intently, and then moved
a few yards down the wall and again pressed against
it. 'Once more.'

Narin smacked the wall again as Galin concen-
trated. As the echoes died, the engineer frowned and
stepped back, stroking his beard and shaking his
head. 'Afraid you've miscalculated, prince. There's a
cavity here right enough, but it's closer to twenty feet
in.'

Hamnir groaned. 'Twenty feet? Can we dig through that in time?' he asked, chewing his lip.

Galin rubbed a rough palm over the wall. 'Hmmm, sandstone, but there's a fold of gneiss that angles through it and we'll have to get through that first: denser stuff.' He shrugged. 'A seasoned miner should be able to clear a foot deep hole his own height and width through sandstone in an hour and a half, going all out, but he can't do it for more than three hours at the most without slowing considerably.'

He looked around at the dwarfs. 'I've done my share of digging, and I know these lads have,' he said, nodding at the Rassmusson brothers, 'but the Thunderers and Slayers and Hammerers might not have swung a pick in a century or so. If it's just the four of us, working in shifts...' He paused, doing calculations in his head. 'Thirty hours, probably more, to account for fatigue.'

'I can dig,' said Gotrek.

'As can I,' said Leatherbeard. 'It was as a miner that I fought the skaven.'

'It will still be thirty hours,' said Galin. 'Though, with six digging, we will be less weary when we break through.'

'We must be faster,' said Hamnir, his brow furrowed. 'It is the night of the fifth day, and we told Gorril that we would open the Horn Gate at sunset tomorrow. No more than twenty hours. His force cannot wait for ten hours. The grobi will pick them to pieces as they did before.'

'He will wait, prince,' said Thorgig. 'He would never abandon your cause.'

'I know,' said Hamnir. 'I know.'

'Then stop talking,' said Gotrek, 'and start digging.'

The Rassmusson brothers nodded, doffed their packs and their armour, took up their picks, and without any further preamble, began swinging at the wall with a practiced rhythm. It was deafening. Chunks of sandstone began to litter the floor.

'The first foot or two will go quicker,' said Galin to Hamnir, 'while three can work at once, but when the hole is deeper, only one dwarf will be able to reach the face.'

Hamnir nodded and turned to Thorgig, giving him his ring of keys. 'Cousin, go to the door and see if the digging can be heard from there.' He looked up at Felix. 'Go with him, Herr Jaeger. If we cannot be heard, go into the mine. We will need a barrow and beer or drinkable water, as much as you can carry.'

'And food,' said Galin. 'Digging is hungry work, and we've eaten nearly all we brought.'

'No food,' said Hamnir grimly, 'at least no meat. What grobi eat may be dwarf.'

Felix and the young dwarf set out as the others began setting up camp around the workface, laying out their bedrolls and knocking spikes in the walls from which to hang their lanterns.

When they had reached the door and closed it behind them, they stood still, listening for the clash of pick on rock.

Thorgig cursed under his breath. 'Faint but clear. This is bad.'

'I hear nothing,' said Felix.

Thorgig brightened. 'That is because you are a human. Good. The hearing of orcs is as inferior as that of men, so perhaps we are safe.'

Felix grunted, annoyed once again by the offhand insult.

Thorgig looked up, colouring. 'My apologies, Herr Jaeger. I know you don't like to hear about human shortcomings. You saved Kagrin's life, and mine. I owe you more respect. I will refrain from speaking of them in your presence.'

Felix tensed, choking back the urge to spit a few dwarf shortcomings in Thorgig's face, but what was the use? He wasn't trying to be insulting. In fact, he thought he was being polite. He didn't know any better, and now wasn't the time to educate him.

Felix bowed, hiding a smirk. 'I am humbled and honoured by your sense of tact, Thorgig Helmgard,' he said.

Thorgig nodded, pleased. 'Thank you, Herr Jaeger. The courtesy of the dwarfs seems to be rubbing off on you. This way.'

Felix followed him down the hall, shaking his head in wonder.

They skulked silently towards the more populated area of the mine, and were able to find and take almost all the things on Hamnir's list without arousing the attention of any orcs. The exception was beer. Every cask they found had been broached, smashed or drained. They did however find some stale dwarf flat bread that apparently hadn't appealed to the orc palate. They dumped it into the barrow along with two large skins of water, some shovels, and a jar of lamp oil, and hurried back to the kruk.

Felix was astounded by how much rock the brothers had dug in their absence. The hole in the wall was nearly a foot and a half deep already, and though too short for Felix to stand up in, wider than a dwarf. The three brothers did not appear to have slowed, keeping up their steady, machine-like rhythm without pause. The others had cleared away the rubble of their exertions as best they could, and Felix and Thorgig got to work shovelling it up and dumping it in the barrow. Then Felix wheeled it off down the corridor and dumped it out of the way.

For the next ten hours that was all he did. While the dwarfs chipped at the wall, and the hole got incrementally deeper, Felix shovelled the scrapings into the barrow and carried them away. It was all he could contribute. Asking him to swing a pick would only have slowed them down. He'd have been lucky to dig two inches in an hour.

At the two-hour mark, the brothers had dug as deep as three dwarfs standing side by side could dig, and fell back, exhausted. Galin took over alone, stripped to the waist, swinging at a steady unwavering pace that spoke of long experience. Hamnir and Narin worked behind him, widening the hole and scraping the tailings out to the passage where Felix picked them up.

The other dwarfs rested as best they could, and Hamnir sent Leatherbeard, and then, an hour later, Narin, to the kruk door to listen for orc patrols.

After two hours, Galin stumbled out of the shallow hole, having dug a further foot and a half. He was bathed in sweat and shaking. Leatherbeard took his place, removing his mask so that he might breathe better, but only after he was hidden in the hole. Two hours later and a foot deeper, he was replaced by Gotrek, who set at the rock as if it was a horde of orcs. Stone and dust flew.

'Easy, Slayer,' said Galin, lifting his head from where he lay. 'You won't last at that pace.'

'I know my limits,' said Gotrek, and continued at the same furious rate.

For a time, he was faster than the others had been, cutting through a foot of rock in an hour, but as he entered his second hour, his progress slowed, his bare back running with sweat. Even then, he maintained the pace that Leatherbeard had, and looked as if he could continue at that speed indefinitely. Although the others praised him and encouraged him, he seemed dissatisfied, growling and muttering.

Finally, he stepped out of the hole, wiping his brow and scowling.

'Ready to switch?' asked Ragar, sitting up. He had had six hours' rest and looked reasonably fresh.

Gotrek shook his head, picked up a second pick, and disappeared back into the hole without a word.

The other dwarfs crowded around the opening, watching gape-mouthed as Gotrek attacked the work-face with the two picks, swinging them as easily and skilfully as his companions had swung one. Sparks and chunks of sandstone flew everywhere.

His eyes glowed. 'Now we'll make some time,' he growled as he settled down into a rhythm. His massive muscles shone with sweat in the lamplight. The waste rock piled up around Gotrek's feet at an amazing rate.

'He's mad,' said Galin.

'He'll wear himself to a thread,' said Narin.

Hamnir stared hard at Gotrek's back, as if he meant to order the Slayer to pace himself, but instead, he backed into the tunnel and turned away.

Gotrek went three more hours and dug four more feet, an unheard-of feat that had the others, the Rassmusson brothers particularly, stiff with jealousy.

'Isn't proper form,' sniffed Karl, as he approached the workface for his second shift and swung his pick.

'Would never do for real mining,' agreed Arn, holding a lantern behind him.

'Real mining's for the long haul,' nodded Karl.

Felix was becoming unutterably weary, and felt guilty for it. While the dwarfs had laboured heroically, he hadn't done more than stoop and shovel and cart, but after twelve hours of it, he couldn't keep his head up, and shortly after Karl began his second turn, he handed off the barrow to Thorgig and lay down on his bedroll in the darkness beyond the lanterns, pillowing his head with his old cloak.

He fell asleep almost instantly, but it was a troubled slumber. The feelings of malignant dread that he had felt upon entering the mine, and which had never entirely gone away no matter how much he had tried to force them down, bloomed in his dreams like night flowers, pale and putrid. Amorphous fears loomed in his unconscious, pressing in on him from all sides and threatening to smother him. Insectile whispering, like the vibration of glassine wings, buzzed vile urgings in his ears. He felt as if he was being chased down the mine's cramped passages by an intangible evil that was everywhere and nowhere at once, but getting closer with every step. Whatever it was, it was going to kill him. He was going to die here. He would never leave these cursed tunnels. He would never see the sun again. Hands that were not hands were reaching out of the darkness to clutch at his throat. He could feel hard, cold claws slipping around his throat.

Felix snapped awake, panting. Sweat like ice prickled his brow. He sucked in a few deep breaths and looked around, his heart pounding. Flickering lamplight and the monotonous sound of pick striking rock came from the ragged hole in the wall. Around him, the dwarfs were asleep in their bedrolls, snoring like so many bullfrogs croaking.

He looked on them with a sudden loathing. Humans who had never met dwarfs often thought of them as just some breed of short men, but having spent so many years with Gotrek, Felix knew different. They were not men. They weren't even cousins to men. They were another species – a strange race of insular burrowing animals, with the hoarding instincts of pack-rats, and the stubborn intransigence of mules. He stared at Thorgig, snoring next to him. How had he ever thought of these monsters as people? Look at them, with their flat, furred faces, their blunt paws, their coarse, clay-textured hides, their fat, bulbous noses – more like pig snouts, really.

Strange how he had never noticed it before, but all at once he couldn't stand the sight of them – any of them. They repulsed him. Every aspect of them was revolting – and made all the worse by the fact that, unlike skaven or orcs or other monsters, they had somehow tricked men into accepting them as equals, superiors even! No! It was not to be countenanced. They were vile, stunted moles, grubbing in the earth, eating dirt and excreting gold, sacrificing his people to their rock-daemon gods, smashing the cities of his kind when they found them, and forcing him into his long hibernation.

He shuddered. He could no longer stomach their presence. Their stench made him gag. He could not allow them to live. If their wills could not be bent, then they must be destroyed. They stood in the way of his rightful domination of the world. He drew his dagger and stood, looking down at Thorgig. The foolish animal didn't know his doom was upon him. Felix bent and covered the dwarf's mouth as he plunged his blade into the artery under his jaw – hard to find through the beast's cursed fur.

The dwarf struggled briefly, but then sank back. Felix looked around. None of the others had awakened. Good. He stepped to Narin, curled on his side. Felix covered his mouth too, and drove his dagger under the blond dwarf's ear. He twitched and fought, but only for a second.

Beyond Narin was Gotrek. Felix's heart raced. He stood over the sleeping Slayer, glaring at him. He was even more alien than the others – a muscle-bound freak with skin like pink granite, a stiff strip of hair like the coxcomb of a rooster and, as he knew from experience, the strength of ten of his kind. He reached down slowly and quietly. The Slayer was too dangerous. He would have to kill him with the first blow, or he would be ripped to pieces. He cupped his free hand to cover Gotrek's mouth, and angled the tip of his blade towards the hinge of the jaw, as he had with the other two. One quick thrust and...

Gotrek's one eye snapped open and his hand clamped around Felix's wrist with blinding speed. Felix pulled back, trying to break free, but the dwarf's grip was like iron. He fought to get away, punching and kicking, but the dwarf held on, taking the blows as if they were snowflakes falling. Gotrek caught his other wrist.

'Manling,' he said. 'Manling, wake up.'

Felix tried to head butt the dwarf. He couldn't reach him. He thrashed in Gotrek's unshakeable grip. He...

Woke up.

CHAPTER SIXTEEN

FELIX BLINKED, CONFUSED. Gotrek was still in front of
him, holding his wrists, but disorientingly, it was
Felix who lay on his back and the dwarf who stood
over him, scowling. Felix's head spun with vertigo.

'Waving a dagger about in your sleep, manling,'
Gotrek said as he let go. 'You'll do yourself an
injury.'

Do *himself* an injury? He'd done more than that!
He'd... Felix sat up, heart pounding, mind racing.
By Sigmar, he'd murdered two of...

Thorgig and Narin were glaring at him from their
bedrolls, cross and bleary with sleep. The other
dwarfs were glaring at him from the shadows.

'Don't suppose you'd mind keeping your night-
mares to yourself?' said Narin sourly.

'We've little enough time for sleep as it is,' said
Thorgig, and lay back down.

A dream! Felix's heart flooded with relief. It had only been a dream!

'Sorry,' he muttered. 'I… I was fighting, er… daemons. I'll try to be quieter about it in the future.'

He lay back as Gotrek returned to his bedroll. He didn't want to try to explain to them what he had really been doing in his dream. He couldn't explain it to himself. Where had those thoughts come from? He had never had a dream so strange, or so real, in all his life. He certainly had plenty of reasons to be annoyed with dwarfs – a surly, unsympathetic lot if ever there was one, so convinced of their superiority over men that they insulted him unthinkingly every time they opened their mouths. But annoyed enough to try to kill them? No.

He tried to remember what it was that had fuelled his murderous anger, but already the dream was fading, becoming unclear. All that remained in focus – vivid focus – as he closed his eyes was the feeling of all-consuming fury, and the image of the tip of his dagger sinking to the hilt under Thorgig's ear.

He shivered and opened his eyes, then sat up and tied off his sword and dagger so it would be difficult to draw them in his sleep. Even with this precaution, he found it difficult to return to slumber, for fear of what he might do.

WHEN NEXT HE woke, his mind clouded and heart heavy from unremembered dreams, Karl was just finishing his second two hours at the rock face, having followed Arn and Ragar before him. Between the three of them, they had dug four feet while Felix had slept, and now there was an argument going on amongst the dwarfs about who should follow him.

'We're not going fast enough,' Hamnir was saying. 'It is now the middle of the afternoon of the seventh day. Gorril's army will have left Rodenheim two hours ago, and if all has gone as planned, they are almost halfway here. In three hours they will be waiting at the advance position to hear the blowing of the war horn, and if Galin reckons right, we still have four feet of rock to dig through. Another six hours of digging.'

'Let me dig again,' said Gotrek. 'I'm fastest.'

'Even you won't be fast enough,' said Galin. He sighed. 'I knew it was impossible when we started it, but...'

'Even if you do cut through in time,' said Hamnir to Gotrek. 'We need you fighting fit on the other side, not worn to a fare-thee-well.'

'Getting into the hold is more important,' said the Slayer. 'I'll do it.'

He took up two picks and stalked into the tunnel. The sharp clash of steel on stone started up immediately, sounding at an unheard-of pace. Gotrek was out-doing even his earlier stint at the workface.

Narin shook his head. 'He won't keep it up. It's impossible.'

Hamnir chuckled. 'He'll keep it up just to spite you for saying so.'

Then there was nothing to do but wait, while the ceaseless rapid-fire hammering of Gotrek's picks battered their ears. And waiting was something that the dwarfs, for all their talk of dwarf patience, didn't do very well. Perhaps the strange oppressive atmosphere, which was clouding Felix's mind, was also having an effect on the dwarfs' tempers. They were snappish and out of sorts, alternately slumping against the walls of the corridor or fidgeting restlessly. Narin and Galin paced moodily up and down the hall, snarling at each other as they bumped shoulders. Leatherbeard tried to sleep, but only tossed and turned. Even the brothers Rassmusson were arguing amongst themselves, fighting over the sharing out of the last of the flat bread.

Then, slightly more than an hour later, Galin jumped up, eyes wide.

'Did you hear?' he cried, pointing to the tunnel.

The others looked up at him listlessly.

'Hear what?' asked Hamnir.

'The boom!' said Galin, excitedly. 'The Slayer's picks are booming as they strike the rock. We are close. Very close. Within two feet.' He stepped into the tunnel.

Hamnir sprang up and followed him in. Felix and the dwarfs crowded around the entrance.

Galin was measuring the distance that Gotrek had cut in the last hour. 'A little more than a foot,' he muttered, scratching his head.

'You said there were six more feet, at least.'

'I, er, it appears I erred on the side of caution,' said Galin.

'Out,' said Gotrek. 'Give me room.'

The dwarfs stepped back. The Slayer was running with sweat. His one eye seemed glazed and unseeing, and the perfect control he usually had was slipping. His swings were wild and he was weaving on his feet, but his pace never slowed. It looked as if, were he to stop, he would fall, so he dared not stop.

'If he keeps up this pace,' said Galin, 'we'll be through in an hour.'

'Excellent news!' said Hamnir. 'We will have half an hour to make our way through the hold and reach the gate. Hardly enough time, but better than four hours late.'

After that, the waiting was even more difficult, for the dwarfs couldn't relax, knowing their goal was so close. They paced and fretted, drawing and then sheathing their weapons over and over again. They cursed each other for being impatient, and cursed Gotrek for being too slow.

Then, slightly less than an hour later, there was a clunk, and a pleased snort, and Gotrek called down the tunnel. 'I've holed it.'

The dwarfs pushed into the tunnel as Gotrek's hacking resumed. There was a fist-sized black hole halfway up the workface, which Gotrek was widening with every strike of his axe. The dwarfs cheered, and nothing Gotrek could say could keep them out of the tunnel, watching over his shoulder.

Fifteen minutes later, the hole was a more than a foot wide and they could see things shining in the darkness through it. Galin stepped forwards. 'Wait. The man will fit through that. Let him go through and work it from the other side.'

Gotrek nodded and stepped back. Galin waved Felix forwards and held up a lantern. Felix leaned through the hole and looked around. A clutter of half-seen golden treasures winked at him in the light of the flickering flame. The vault was a square shaft, about twelve feet to a side, which rose into darkness above as if it was the bottom of a well. With Galin and Hamnir's help, Felix wormed through the hole and lowered himself down until his feet touched. Then he took the lantern and pick that Hamnir passed through the hole and got to work.

With each swing, he had new respect for the strength and endurance of the dwarfs. He was weary after ten minutes, and they had gone for hours. But even Felix's inexpert hacking sped the work, and at last, after another fifteen minutes, the hole was wide enough for a dwarf to pass through. They cheered and then climbed one by one into the vault, Felix helping them to the floor.

Gotrek came through last and sat down wearily on a tapestry-covered casket, mopping his brow and staring blankly in front of him. Felix didn't know if he had ever seen the Slayer look so exhausted. His huge arms were shaking with fatigue.

The other dwarfs held up their lanterns and looked around in wonder at the treasures in the rough-hewn vault. Beautiful suits of gold and gromril armour were displayed on wooden stands, with horned helmets above them, making it appear that ghostly dwarf warriors guarded the vault. Intricately worked caskets of gold and silver were piled on top of each other, nearly as valuable as the treasures they contained. A chalice of gold and polished stone sat on a black marble shrine. A great stone-headed maul, inscribed with runes on its every face, was mounted on the wall. An ancient green battle standard, the horn of Karak Hirn stitched into it in gold thread, was propped against a Cathay vase twice the height of a dwarf. Dwarf books were stacked in the corners, and rolled vellum maps were tucked into gold and silver tubes.

But the thing that drew the dwarfs' attention like a fly to honey was a velvet-lined silver box that sat open on a table, the contents of which shone with a red orange glow in the lantern light.

'Blood gold,' whispered Narin, licking his lips.

'Look at it shine,' murmured Galin.

'Never seen so much in one place,' said Karl.

It didn't look like a lot to Felix. There were only twenty ingots in the box, and they looked about half-weight, but they had a hypnotic effect on the dwarfs. They couldn't take their eyes off them.

'Beautiful,' said Leatherbeard. 'Worth killing for.'

'Aye,' said Arn. 'Red as blood.'

'Up the stairs!' said Hamnir, slamming the box closed. 'You should not be looking upon any of this. We have less than half an hour. Gorril is already in position.'

The dwarfs blinked and came reluctantly back to themselves. Felix looked up the dark shaft. A rough staircase wound up it inside a dwarf-wide channel carved diagonally into the walls like the threads of a screw. More climbing. Wonderful.

As the others crossed to the stairs, Gotrek levered himself to his feet with the help of his axe and stumped after them. The sweat still boiled from his skin.

Hamnir paused, looking back at the hole in the wall with profound unhappiness. 'Leaving an unguarded door to my father's vault. Perhaps we could block it…' He cursed and forced himself up the stairs after the others. 'There is no time.'

Felix followed the dwarfs up, pressing as close to the wall of the narrow channel as he could. The steps were well cut and true, as was to be expected from any dwarf work, but there was no railing, and as they rose eight, and then ten flights, Felix's knees began to feel weak and his guts watery. There were no ropes and pitons here, and the dwarfs would have ribbed him unmercifully if he had decided to crawl up on his hands and knees, or asked for a rope 'in a stairwell of all places' so he kept his terror to himself.

Seven rotations later, the stair ended at a small landing with no apparent door, only a fat, polished marble pillar set incongruously in one rough wall. A brass lever and something that looked like the lens of a spyglass were placed at dwarf height beside it. Hamnir stepped to the lens and looked into it. He froze, and then stepped back, turning first pale, and then red with rage.

'There are grobi in my father's quarters. They have defiled… everything.'

'Can we get through the door without being seen?' asked Narin.

Hamnir nodded. 'They are not in the sleeping chamber, but I can see them moving in the receiving chamber beyond.' He put his hand on the lever. 'Thorgig, when I open this door, creep to the further door and spy out how many there are. We will have to take them silently.'

Thorgig cocked and loaded his crossbow. 'Ready,' he said.

The others drew daggers and hand-axes.

Hamnir pulled the lever and the fat column screwed down into the floor without a sound, revealing a dark bedchamber that reeked like a garbage heap built over a middens. The dwarfs winced and choked. Piles of rotting food and smashed furniture, broken weapons, squig carcasses, shattered crockery and empty hogsheads of beer were heaped waist deep – shoulder deep for the dwarfs – around the room. King Alrik's grand canopied bed was buried so deeply that only the four posts rose up out of the muck. All the other furnishings had been slashed and smashed.

The dwarfs trembled with rage when they saw the wreckage.

'Green savages!' muttered Galin.

'They will pay for this,' said Thorgig.

'Quiet,' said Hamnir, and motioned him into the room.

Thorgig picked his way through the heaps as silently as he could. Sounds of industry came from the further room, slappings and bangings and sloshings that Felix couldn't identify. And where was the reek of excrement coming from?

Thorgig edged to the side of the receiving chamber door and leaned out. Felix saw his eyes widen as he peered through it. He eased back and returned to Hamnir.

'They've made it into a tannery!' he whispered.

'A... a what?' asked Hamnir.

'A tannery!' Thorgig choked, overcome. 'There's a big vat of... of liquid waste where King Alrik's table was. Goblins are dunking skins and beating them, and stitching them together all over the room.'

'How many goblins?' asked Gotrek.

Thorgig frowned. 'Er, six, and two orcs are squatting over the vat, with one behind, waiting his turn.'

'The door to the corridor is closed?' asked Hamnir.

'Aye, but not locked.'

Hamnir thought. 'We'll wait until the orcs have left, and then kill the goblins, as quietly as possible.' He looked around at the others. 'Make sure we take them in one go, aye?'

They nodded.

Hamnir turned to Gotrek. 'You're not in this,' he said.

'Try and stop me,' said Gotrek. He was still slick with sweat and breathing heavily.

'I'm ordering you,' said Hamnir. 'Save yourself for the Horn Gate.'

Gotrek grumbled, but nodded.

The dwarfs stepped into the bedchamber and began to pick their way warily around the mounds of rubbish. Gotrek and Felix came last. When all were through the door, Hamnir turned to a decorative relief border by the column and pressed a bit of filigree. The fat column rose up again as silently as it had dropped. It looked as if it had never moved.

The dwarfs crossed the room and positioned themselves at the edges of the square of light that shone through the receiving chamber door. The scene was as Thorgig had described it. There was a four-foot high wooden vat in the centre of the room, filled with semi-liquid orc filth. A set of wooden steps led up to a two-holed outhouse bench that was built out over the vat. An orc was just pulling up his breeches and starting back down the steps.

A goblin stood on the rim, stirring the vile soup with a wooden paddle and pushing un-cured hides down into it. To one side of the vat, drying frames had been set up. Treated skins were being stretched in them. Some had dwarf tattoos. Goblins used wooden mauls to beat skins on square blocks of stone. Another cut them with a hooked knife. Two sat cross-legged on regal dwarf furniture, stitching the cut skins into what looked like leather cuirasses. The room was a shambles, littered with half-eaten ham hocks, and black with filth.

Hamnir trembled. 'This is a travesty,' he said under his breath. 'My father would…' He twitched and fell silent.

The orc exited through the door to the corridor. The goblins didn't look up from their tasks. They were as focused and unblinking as clerks at their ledgers.

Hamnir raised his hand. The others gripped their weapons, ready. He dropped his hand. The dwarfs charged through the door. Felix followed them. Only Gotrek waited behind.

Four goblins died on the instant, cut down before they could make a sound. The one with the hooked knife squawked as Leatherbeard ran towards it, and darted into what might once have been a dining chamber. Leatherbeard charged in after it. Felix cut at the goblin with the paddle, but it dived behind the vat. Aside from the first surprised squawk, the last two goblins uttered not a sound. They were as blank and emotionless as all the other grobi they had encountered.

'Get them!' hissed Hamnir.

Narin and Galin swung at the paddle goblin, but it dodged between them and they nearly decapitated each other. Karl, Ragar and Arn scrambled after it as it ducked behind the drying frames. Ragar slipped on a wet skin and fell on his posterior. The frames clattered down. A hollow smash came from the dining chamber.

'Grimnir's mother!' snapped Hamnir. 'Quietly!'

The paddle goblin leapt from the tangle of frames and climbed to the lip of the vat then sprang to the chandelier that hung above it, flailing its absurd weapon around at the dwarfs who tried to reach him.

'I have him,' said Felix, and ran up the wooden steps, swinging his sword. The goblin twisted out of the way and smacked Felix on the shoulder with the paddle. Felix overbalanced, nearly plunging into the vat. He caught himself, heart thumping. That would have been the crown to his regalia of indignities.

A crossbow bolt appeared in the goblin's chest. It squeaked and fell, half in, half out of the vat, drenching Felix's legs in a shower of vile liquid, as the chandelier pendulumed wildly back and forth.

'Little villain!' Felix barked, and slashed down at the thing as it flailed on the lip. He cut its head off and its body toppled down to the floor from the strength of the blow. Its head bobbed for a moment in the vat like a rotten apple, and then sank.

'Shhh!' said Galin. He stood at the corridor door. 'Someone's coming. Sounds like a patrol.'

The dwarfs froze, all but Leatherbeard, who was still chasing his goblin around the dining chamber table. The tramp of marching feet came clearly through the stone walls.

'Thorgig, help him!' whispered Hamnir. 'Karl, Ragar, Arn, hide the bodies, and then yourselves. Galin, Narin, cover the bloodstains. Jaeger…'

The last goblin ran out of the dining chamber as the dwarfs scrambled to obey Hamnir's orders. Leatherbeard dived after the fleeing runt and smashed it to the floor with his axe.

'Get it out!' hissed Hamnir, waving his hand. 'There are more coming.'

The marching feet stopped outside the door. Leatherbeard dragged his goblin back into the dining chamber as the Rassmusson brothers tossed the others to Gotrek, who stacked them up inside the bedroom door. Narin and Galin threw loose skins on top of the various bloodstains that spattered the floor. Felix hopped down the stairs and ran for the bedroom door, but Hamnir poked his head out of an alcove and pointed.

'Jaeger! The chandelier!'

Felix turned. The damned thing was still swinging. He cursed and jumped back up the vat steps. The dwarfs were disappearing through doors and ducking behind furniture. Felix reached up and steadied the chandelier. The handle of the corridor door was turning. He cursed. There was no time to reach any of the doorways. He was trapped in the open.

CHAPTER SEVENTEEN

THE CORRIDOR DOOR began to swing open. Felix jumped off the wooden steps and rolled under them, folding his lanky frame into the tight space. His back was against the vat. A crossbeam pressed painfully across his shins. His breeches clung to him wetly. They stank.

Through the open treads of the steps, Felix watched the knobby green knees of an enormous orc in a studded leather tunic and heavy boots enter the room and approach the vat. A company of orcs at parade rest stood outside the door behind it.

'Oh no,' he murmured.

The heavy boots creaked up the complaining steps and stopped directly over Felix's head. Felix held his breath. If he moved a muscle the orc would hear him.

There was a moment of rustling above him, and then a deep, contented sigh as something plopped wetly into the vat. Felix prayed it would all be over soon, but the orc must have eaten mightily, for the plopping and splashing seemed never-ending. After one particularly violent discharge, a splatter of drops rattled the boards over Felix's head. A bead of stinking brown liquid formed under one plank and hung there, directly over his face.

Felix looked up at it in horror. He daren't move. The slightest motion would alert the orc.

The orc grunted and shifted. The drop fell. Felix shut his eyes. It splashed on his right eye-lid, then slid slowly down. Felix tensed, fighting back a scream. The stuff burned like vinegar. He wanted to thrash and kick.

The orc stood, giving Felix a view of parts of its anatomy he could have done without seeing, then pulled up its breeches and started down the steps. Halfway down, it paused and jabbered a question. Its voice had a strange, chittering edge to it, not the usual orc grunt.

Felix groaned. It had finally noticed that the goblins weren't there. This was the end. They were going to have to fight the whole company, and then the whole hold. It was Birrisson's door all over again. Felix rolled his smarting eyes to the side and saw Gotrek and the Rassmusson brothers in the shadows of the sleeping chamber, readying their weapons.

The orc chattered its question again, and then stepped to the door and spoke to its captain. The captain stuck its head in, and the orc indicated the room with a sweep of its hand.

The captain frowned around for a long moment, then shrugged and told the orc to get back in line. Its voice too was sharp and staccato. The orc exited, shutting the door behind it.

A chorus of dwarf sighs came from all over the room. They stepped out from behind doorways and furniture, looking relieved.

Narin grinned as Felix squeezed out from under the steps. 'It's not often a man gets a view like that and lives.'

'It's not often a man gets a view like that and *wants* to live,' said Felix. He wiped his eyelid and looked around for something to dry his breeches with. 'And I got another sort of eyeful as well. Burns like fire.'

'Now that's a hero's brand if ever there was one,' laughed Galin.

'You find it funny?' asked Gotrek, stepping from the bedchamber. 'I wonder if you could have stood it.'

'Is it a hero's part to stand things?' asked Galin. 'I would have jumped up and killed it before the drop fell.'

'And doomed us all,' said Hamnir dryly. 'Very heroic.' He turned to the door. 'Now, hurry, before any more come to fill the vat.' He put his ear to the panels as the others gathered behind him. 'We go left,' he said, 'and then up. The Horn Gate is only three hundred yards due east, but this is the level of the great halls. It will be too populated. Two levels up are grain stores. We will traverse the length of the hold there, and return down a further stairwell nearer the gate. Ready?'

The dwarfs nodded, faces set and grim behind their beards.

Hamnir listened again, then slowly pulled open the door and peered out. The torch-lit corridor echoed with sounds of distant movement, but nothing nearby.

Hamnir turned left and slipped quietly down the hall. The dwarfs followed behind him in a single file, Felix looming at the back of the line, feeling clumsy and clammy in his moist breeches. Despite what Gotrek and Hamnir had said, it was hard to feel heroic when you were damp with orc-crap.

The stairwell to the upper levels wasn't more than twenty yards along the hall, but they had to pause and hide three times to let orc patrols and work details march past. Through every door they passed, they saw goblins and orcs busy at their labours, cutting and shaping wood, building torture devices and trebuchets, slaughtering and skinning animals, making food, weaving.

'Weaving?' whispered Galin, nonplussed. 'Grobi don't weave!'

'Place is more like a beehive than an orc nest,' muttered Gotrek.

'And what ails their voices?' said Narin. 'Chittering and gibbering like… like–'

'Monkeys?' suggested Thorgig.

'Mutants, I was going to say,' said Narin.

Hamnir paused at the stairwell and looked in warily, then waved them up. They climbed two levels and stepped out into a broad, unlit corridor. The dwarfs unshielded their lanterns and started down its length. The air was filled with the dusty, musty smell of rotting wheat.

Hamnir sniffed, frowning. 'Have they left a silo open to the damp? We haven't much wheat to spare this year.'

Huge doors lined both sides of the hallway for as far as they could see in the lamplight. They were all open.

Hamnir looked into the first one on the right. The room inside was small and stacked along its left wall with barrels and empty canvas sacks. An ironbound door, like a furnace door with a trough beneath it, was set in the back wall. The trough was barely visible, however, because the iron door was open, and pouring from it like a sand dune was a spill of golden grain. The sweet reek of mould grew stronger, and black shadows crawled over the mound – rats, dozens of them.

'Valaya curse them,' sneered Hamnir. 'For all their chittering and weaving, they are still careless savages.'

He looked in the door to the left. That silo was open as well, and the wheat spilled across the floor almost to the door. More rats crawled over the bounty.

Hamnir shivered. 'Two spoiled? It will be a lean winter. It…' He looked up the hall with slowly dawning horror, then hurried ahead.

The others followed quickly. Hamnir looked in the second pair of doors. Both rooms were the same as the first – the iron doors open and mounds of rotting grain alive with rats. Hamnir choked and sped to the next doors. Those silos too had been opened, as had the next set.

Hamnir slumped against the wall, covering his face with his hands. 'Grimnir,' he said, choking. 'They've killed us. Even if we retake the fort and drive them out, they have won. We will starve. No bread. No beer. The hold won't last the winter. Are they mad? Why have they done this? It's suicide for them too.'

'Something's coming,' said Leatherbeard.

The dwarfs covered their lanterns and stepped into the grain room. They peered through the door. A glow of torchlight and looming ugly shadows emerged from around a corner, far ahead. Then a strange procession appeared – two big orcs pushed a mine cart, while ahead of them scurried a dozen goblins, all armed with barbed spears and sacks. The goblins ran into the silo rooms, from which came sounds of struggling and squeaking. Then they reappeared, rats impaled on their spears. They stuffed these in their sacks, and carried on to the next rooms.

When they came out again, one goblin's sack was full. He emptied it in the mine cart, then followed his snaggle-fanged brethren further down the hall.

Hamnir stared open mouthed, but Narin stifled a snort. 'They use the grain to farm rats!' he whispered. 'Brilliant!'

'The fools!' said Hamnir shaking his head. 'The meat-brained idiots.'

'They'll be coming in here, prince,' said Thorgig looking at the rats swarming the grain at their feet.

'Right,' said Hamnir. He glanced around. Barrels were stacked along one wall. 'Behind those. Quick.'

The dwarfs waded through the spill of wheat and edged behind the barrels.

'Hiding from goblins again,' muttered Leatherbeard, disgusted, but he held his breath with the others when three goblins ran into the room, stabbing at the rats with their little spears. The rats squealed and ran for the corners. The goblins didn't bother to chase very far. There were so many vermin that they had each spitted three or four without much effort. They stuffed them in their sacks and ran out again.

The dwarfs remained where they were, listening as the rumble of cart wheels grew louder, and then diminished into the distance. When the rat harvesters were safely past, Hamnir stepped out. 'We must hurry. They may come back. Lamps closed.'

The dwarfs crossed to the door and looked out to the left. The orcs and goblins were fifty yards down the corridor. The dwarfs eased out and continued to the right, Hamnir cursing anew as they passed each new ruined silo.

The corridor turned right at its end, opening into a stairwell that went both up and down.

Hamnir turned to the others. 'We will be very close to the main corridor when we descend. Be careful.'

He led them cautiously down the stairs and they exited two levels down into a shadowy side passage. The glow of lamps from the main corridor, thirty feet to their right, glinted on the blades of their axes, and they heard harsh, gibbering voices. The tramp of heavy feet on the trot echoed to them as well. A large company of orcs armed with dwarf long-guns ran past from right to left.

When they had passed, Hamnir tapped Thorgig on the shoulder and motioned him forwards. The young dwarf padded to the main corridor and leaned out to look both ways. He ducked back suddenly and flattened himself against the wall as more boots echoed from the hall and a second orc company followed the first. They were armed with bows and axes. Thorgig looked after them as they continued down the hall, and then returned to Hamnir and the others.

'The first group went into the guardroom. The second into the passage to the sally port.'

Hamnir nodded. 'Gunners for the turrets and scouts to harass Gorril's line of march: he must be in position. Good.'

'Doesn't sound so good to me,' said Galin scowling. 'If the orcs are positioning gunners in the turrets, your army will be shot to pieces as they come in.'

Hamnir nodded. 'This is why Gorril must be able to run straight in when he arrives, so our brothers won't have to weather more than one salvo while waiting for us to open the gate. The difficulty is, if we are to open the doors, we will have to keep the orcs in the turrets from… Wait.' He frowned and looked around. There was an empty room just behind them. 'Come,' he said. 'I will lay it out for you. There is a lot to tell and not much time.'

He led the others into the bare, dust-thick room, and squatted down. The others hunkered around him.

'Here it is,' he said, sketching in the dust with a thick finger. 'The Horn Gate is approached through a narrow, steep-walled canyon. Our ancestors built eight turrets into those walls, four to a side, so that any force that tries to knock down the stone door can be riddled with crossfire as they come. Twenty feet behind the first door, there is a second, with murder rooms above and on both sides, so that our defenders can pour boiling oil upon, and shoot crossbows at, any attackers that get through the first door, while they are trying to break down the second.' The canyon, turrets and doors took shape with a few deft strokes of Hamnir's finger. Then he began drawing the rooms behind the gates. 'There are two guardrooms to the right and left of the main corridor, just behind the gate. A door in each guardroom leads to the turrets and murder rooms above. Once both of those doors are locked, the orcs in the turrets and murder rooms cannot get back into the guardroom.'

'Unless they bash down the doors,' said Narin.

'Er, yes,' said Hamnir, and continued. 'The two rooms that house the gate levers are also inside the guardrooms. The levers in the rooms must be pulled simultaneously in order for the gates to open. There are two such levers in each room: one for the outer gate, one for the inner. There is a speaking tube between the two rooms so those who pull the levers may act as one, as well as a cunning spyglass that shows the canyon outside the door. Am I clear?'

The dwarfs nodded. Felix would have liked to hear it all again, but didn't care to ask.

'Not as well thought-out as the gates of Karak Varn,' said Galin, sniffing, 'but stout nonetheless. A good system.'

'I'm glad it meets with your approval,' said Hamnir dryly. He turned back to the map. 'Here is what we must do. We must attack both guardrooms at once, subdue what guards we find there and lock the doors to the murder rooms and turrets without alerting the rest of the hold. When this is done, Thorgig...' He paused and looked at the young dwarf with a mixture of sadness and anger. 'Thorgig has volunteered to go up into the first turret and blow the battle horn to let Gorril know we are in position.'

'But... but the turrets are filled with orcs,' said Narin. 'He'll be killed.'

'Aye,' said Hamnir, eyes downcast, 'precisely.' He pounded his leg. 'Curse you, lad. Do you truly wish to throw your life away? Leatherbeard is a Slayer, as is Gotrek. They are looking for a noble death. He–'

'Must we argue this again?' asked Thorgig, interrupting. 'I have been a guard of the Horn Gate for ten years.

It was my duty to blow the horn then. It is my duty now.'

'But–'

'Prince, please,' said Thorgig. 'They don't know how to blow the horn.'

'Er,' said Leatherbeard. 'I… I could try.'

Thorgig glared at Hamnir defiantly. 'You see. It must be me. No other can be sure to be heard.'

Hamnir sighed. 'So it seems.'

'So,' said Gotrek. 'Thorgig blows the horn, we open the gates, Gorril runs in with the army, and the day is saved. Is that it?'

'Well, it will be a bit more difficult than that,' said Hamnir.

Felix sighed. Why weren't things ever easier than one expected?

'Go on,' said Gotrek.

'It is fifteen minutes' march from Gorril's advance position,' said Hamnir. 'We cannot open the gates until we see him enter the canyon, otherwise the orcs will form up in front of the gate and block their entrance. We will have to hold the guardrooms for those fifteen minutes to prevent the orcs from retaking them and stopping us from pulling the levers. This will be easy if the rest of the hold is not alerted, but the grobi will most likely hear Thorgig's horn and come running, in which case…'

Gotrek and Leatherbeard grinned.

'In which case we'll have a nice scrap on our hands,' said Gotrek.

'Aye,' said Hamnir. He looked much less eager at the prospect. He dug in his pouch and took out a key ring, which he opened with a twist, and then threaded off four keys. 'We will divide into two groups. One will take the guardroom on the left, the other, the one on the right. Three in each group will kill the occupants while the other two hold closed the doors to the murder room stairs until we can lock them.' He looked around at them. 'Gotrek, Jaeger, Narin, Karl and Ragar, you will take the left room. Who will be in charge of the keys?'

'I will,' said Narin.

'And which two will hold the door while the others fight?'

'I'll fight,' said Gotrek, 'and so will the manling.'

'We want to fight!' said Karl.

'Aye,' said Ragar. 'Let the Slayer be a doorstop! He's still tired from digging!'

'You want to try me?' growled Gotrek.

'Keep your voices down!' hissed Hamnir.

Gotrek gave Ragar and Karl a flat look. 'There'll be enough fighting for all of us when the day is done. You'll get more than you care for, I'll wager.'

The brothers glared back at him, and then shrugged.

Hamnir handed Narin two keys. 'The one with the square loop is for the door to the murder rooms and turrets. The one with the round loop is for the lever room.'

'Square, murder. Round, lever,' said Narin. 'Understood.' He tucked them in his pouch.

Hamnir turned to the remaining dwarfs. 'I will hold the keys for our side. Galin and Thorgig will hold the murder room door. Are we clear?'

The others nodded.

'Good.' Hamnir stood. 'Now, it is past time. Only remember that we must hold the two guardrooms against all comers until Gorril's force arrives, no matter what the cost.' He stepped to the door. 'Let's go.'

Felix followed the dwarfs as they crept down the side passage towards the main corridor. He swallowed, trying to keep his stomach where it belonged. It all sounded very noble and epic, but not particularly survivable.

Even if they managed to hold out until Gorril's force arrived, that was only the beginning of the fighting. They still had the whole fort to subdue after that. Felix had a vision of Gotrek alone in a sea of orcs, with all his companions dead around him, including Felix. It was hard to push it from his mind.

Ten feet from the main corridor, they stopped as they heard footsteps and jabbering voices approaching from the direction of the gate. They shrank back into the shadows, on guard. A massive orc, the biggest Felix had ever seen, strode past, chittering orders to a trailing wake of lieutenants and goblin hangers-on in a sharp, sibilant voice completely at odds with its size, but its voice was the least strange thing about it.

Its eyes were glittering black orbs, and its hide pale and waxy, as if it had been smeared in tallow. Irregular white lumps rose from its skull and forearms, as if tumours were growing under its skin and pushing their way out, and he stank, not like an orc, but sour and cloying, like week-old milk. It wore the strange, spider-shell armour that the dwarfs had seen the orcs forging in the mines, black and glossy and baroque with ridges and spines.

A curiously shaped golden torque twisted snugly around his massive, pale green neck, a faceted black gem glittering from it like a third eye. A hand the size of a prize pumpkin gripped an oddly shaped war axe, bigger than any orc cleaver, but made with almost dwarf skill. Most unsettling of all, though, was the fact that, despite his warlike appearance, his savage tusked face was as slack and dull as a sleepwalker's.

The dwarfs stared as this bizarre apparition continued down the hall, their noses wrinkling at his awful odour.

'What's that when it's at home?' whispered Ragar.

'He's the boss or I'm a halfling,' said Arn.

'But what's happened to it?' asked Karl. 'It looked… it smelled… unhealthy.'

'More proof that there's something amiss,' said Hamnir, hushed. 'The new traps in Birri's hangar, the mining, the weaving, the unorcish jabbering, this strange, ridged armour: it's not right, any of it.'

Gotrek nodded, staring at his axe. The runes upon its head were glowing again. 'Something's amiss all right.' He frowned after the huge orc as it disappeared into the depths of the hold, and then shrugged. 'Come on.'

Hamnir nodded. The corridor was clear to the gate. 'Right,' he said. 'Bolts on the strings and in at a run. Give them no time to react. Go.'

CHAPTER EIGHTEEN

THE DWARFS RAN out, splitting into their two groups, and raced for the guardrooms. The huge stone slab that was the Horn Gate's inner door loomed at the end of the wide hallway like a monolith, solid rock without crack or hinge. Two open doors were set into the corridor walls just inside it. Torchlight shone from them.

The dwarfs had traversed slightly more than half the distance when an orc stepped out of the right-hand guardroom on his way to the left. It turned as it saw motion in the corner of its eye. Thorgig and Narin fired their crossbows. The orc dropped with a thud, one quarrel in its throat, the other in its chest.

Questioning grunts came from the guardrooms. The dwarfs sprinted for them, Gotrek in the lead on the left, Leatherbeard on the right.

Orc heads popped out of the guardroom doors just as the dwarfs reached them. Gotrek buried his axe in the left orc's forehead and drove it backwards into the room with his shoulder. Leatherbeard did the same on the right, and the dwarfs piled in after them.

A single orc jumped up from a table in the centre of the left guardroom as Felix ran in, trying to draw its weapon as Gotrek leapt at it. The Slayer cut its head off before its cleaver cleared its scabbard. Karl and Ragar ran past and closed the door to the murder rooms and turrets. They put their shoulders to it.

Gotrek looked around in disgust. There was a rack of long-guns on one wall, an enormous brass alarm gong on another, and a second door on the same wall as the door the Rassmussons held, but no other orcs in the room. 'Where's my fight?' he asked.

A clash of arms rang from the other room.

'Ha!' Gotrek brightened and hurried for the door. 'Stay here and get the door locked.'

'Aye, Slayer,' said Karl, sneering. 'Go on.'

'We'll just stay here and let you have all the fun,' added Ragar as Narin stepped to them, fishing Hamnir's keys from his pouch.

Felix followed Gotrek across the hall. The right-hand guardroom was a mirror image of the other, complete with gun rack and gong. Four orcs lay dead on the floor, and Hamnir, Leatherbeard and Arn were busy with another six while Thorgig and Galin held the door to the murder rooms and turrets closed. They looked as if they'd rather be fighting.

'Much better,' said Gotrek. He waded in, killing two orcs instantly, as Leatherbeard and Hamnir dropped one each.

The orc facing Arn, seeing its brothers fall, leapt for the alarm gong.

Arn swung after it and missed. 'Watch him! He's–'

Felix dived at the orc and caught it by the ankle, tripping it onto its face, inches from the gong. Gotrek spun and buried his axe in its back.

'Ha!' Gotrek barked.

The last orc stumbled back from Leatherbeard, its guts spilling from its belly. Before any recognised the danger, it tripped over its fallen comrade and pitched, helmet-first, into the gong, dead.

A deafening musical crash rang out, shivering the room with its vibrations. Felix clapped his hands over his ears. Gotrek jumped to the gong and pinched it quiet.

'That's torn it,' said Arn.

Gibbering orcish voices rose in the murder room above, and boots thundered down the stairs. Thorgig and Galin braced their shoulders against the door.

'Quick!' said Hamnir, pointing.

The two dwarfs skidded back as orcs slammed into the door from the other side.

Hamnir pulled out his keys, hurrying towards them. 'Hold fast!'

Gotrek and Leatherbeard added their weight to the door and pushed it closed again. Hamnir stabbed the key with the square loop into the lock and twisted it. It didn't turn.

He paled. 'Have I got it backwards?'

'Hurry, blast you!' said Galin as the door bumped and jumped under his shoulder.

Hamnir stuck the other key in the lock, but just then Narin ran in holding a black iron key ring in one hand and two iron keys in the other.

'They've changed the locks,' he said, and threw the ring to Hamnir. 'Try these. I found mine.'

Hamnir caught the ring, groaning. There were at least a dozen keys on it. He stuck one in the lock. It didn't turn. He tried the next. That didn't turn either. The door bumped and slammed as the dwarfs fought to hold it closed.

'Orcs don't make keys,' muttered Galin.

Ragar stuck his head in from the hall. 'They've heard in the hold!' He shouted. 'They're coming!'

'How many?' called Hamnir.

'The whole damned horde, it looks like!' said Karl over his brother's shoulder.

'Hundred yards away!' called Ragar.

Hamnir turned to Thorgig as he tried another key. His eyes were grim and sad. 'It's now or never, lad. Up the other stairs before they think to try to come down behind us.'

'But they're alerted now,' said Narin. 'He'll be cut down before he has a chance to blow the horn.'

'No he won't,' said Leatherbeard, stepping back from the door. 'Rassmusson, take my place. I'll give him time.'

His eyes glowed through the holes in his mask, with the eager anticipation of battle against impossible odds Felix had seen so often before in the eyes of Gotrek, Snorri Nosebiter, Malakai Makaisson and the other Slayers he had known.

Hamnir clenched his jaw. His beard bristled. 'Right. Go.'

'Yes, my prince,' said Thorgig.

Arn put his shoulder to the door as Thorgig and Leatherbeard saluted Hamnir, fists over their hearts, and then ran across the hall with Narin to the other guardroom. Thorgig unhooked the war horn of Karak Hirn from his belt.

'Damn the world,' said Hamnir. He jabbed the next key into the lock. It too failed to turn.

'Seventy yards!' Ragar chimed from the door.

Felix could hear the orcs now – a rumble like a distant avalanche. He watched across the hall into the other guardroom as Narin unlocked the door to the left-hand murder rooms and turrets, and threw it open. Leatherbeard charged up instantly. Thorgig hesitated the merest fraction of a second, then ran after him, the war horn clenched in one hand. Narin slammed the door and locked it behind them.

There was a muted shout from the orcs in the room above, and then the crisp *tantara* of the horn, blowing a dwarf rally call. Felix heard a roar from Leatherbeard and the clash of axe on cleaver. The horn blew its rally again and again, accompanied by muffled grunts and clangs.

Hamnir found the right key at last and turned it, just as Thorgig's horn squawked abruptly and then cut off.

'Damn the world,' Hamnir said again. He lowered his head until his brow touched the door.

'I only hope they heard,' said Galin, stepping back with Gotrek and Arn.

'Forty yards!' Ragar shouted from the hall. The sound of boots was so loud that it almost drowned him out.

The orcs on the other side of the murder room door started battering it with their weapons. Hamnir continued to kneel before it, unmoving.

'Come on, Ranulfsson,' said Gotrek, gruff. 'Work to be done.'

Hamnir nodded and raised his head, face grim. 'Right.' He crossed to the lever room door. 'Rassmussons, hold the other guard room.' He started trying keys in the lock. 'And one of you, lock Narin into the lever room, in case… in case they get through you.'

'Aye, prince,' said Arn, saluting. He sprinted across to the left-hand guardroom with his brothers, as the thunder of running boots shook the room.

'Thirty!' screamed Ragar, as the brothers formed up in their door.

'Galin,' said Hamnir, not looking up from the lock. 'When I find the key, you will lock me in, and then help the Slayer.'

Galin nodded. 'Right.'

'You know what to do, Gurnisson?' Hamnir called.

Gotrek nodded. 'Keep your sorry hide whole, as usual.' He plodded to the hallway door. 'Manling, fall in.'

'Twenty!'

Felix took up a position to the left of the door and looked at Gotrek. The Slayer swayed slightly as he stood.

'All right, Gotrek?' he asked.

'Never better,' said Gotrek, and looked back at Hamnir. 'Fifteen minutes you said, Ranulfsson?'

'Aye,' said Hamnir.

Gotrek nodded and faced the door, raising his axe. 'I can stand anything for fifteen minutes.'

With a deafening clatter, the orc horde filled the end of the corridor like a green flood. Gotrek roared and swung as they pushed in at the guardroom doors, butchering them as they came. The press of the orcs behind shoved those at the front into Gotrek's axe ready or not. He cut them into flying green pieces.

Felix stabbed into them from the side, hamstringing and blinding them. Through the surging mass of sinewy green arms and armoured green torsos, he caught glimpses of the brothers Rassmusson swinging crimsoned picks in the door to the other guard room, digging into orc flesh with the same tireless swings they had used to cut through the wall to the vault.

At least a hundred orcs choked the end of the hall, and no doubt hundreds more packed the long hall behind them, trying to get to the fight. Fortunately, the doors to the guardrooms were only as wide as a single dwarf, and the orcs could only squeeze in one or two at a time. Gotrek stood a pace back, so he had an unobstructed swing, and split heads and chests, while Felix jabbed at feet, wrists and eyes, before they reached him.

There was a cry of triumph from Hamnir as he found the key to the lever room at last. Felix was too busy to look back, but he heard a door open and clang closed, and then Galin joined them, hewing from the right side of the door as Felix did from the left.

Fifteen minutes? Felix eyed Gotrek uneasily. Could the Slayer do it, weary as he was? Could the brothers Rassmusson? The Slayer's axe never slowed, but he was heavy on his feet, slipping in orc gore, and the savage, bared-teeth grin that usually spread across his face in battle was missing, replaced with a tight-jawed scowl of grim determination.

And would it be only fifteen minutes? What if Gorril encountered unexpected obstacles? What if his force was being ambushed by orcs? What if, Sigmar forbid, Gorril hadn't heard the horn at all? It might be that there was no help coming. Then, no matter how long Gotrek lasted, it wouldn't be long enough. The tide of orcs was never-ending. Eventually, they would force their way into the guardrooms and slaughter them all.

Felix chuckled bitterly. Orcs or no, here was the sort of death that Gotrek had longed for – a heroic fight against overwhelming odds, in pursuit of the noblest of causes. Of course, as always, Felix was as trapped in Gotrek's grand death as the Slayer was, and the chances of surviving in order to write the epic poem of his legendary doom were slim to none. One day, he would have to figure out how to chronicle Gotrek's death from afar – if there were any more days after today.

There was a bellow of pain and then a cry of 'Ragar!' from the corridor.

Felix looked through the crush of orcs to the opposite guardroom. Ragar was falling, his head half severed, blood matting his beard. His brothers butchered the orc who had killed him and fought on.

Felix did the same; there was no time to grieve. He moaned with weariness. It felt like hours had passed, not minutes. His arms ached from stabbing and hacking. The orcs crawled over the bodies of their slain comrades to attack Gotrek with stoic blankness, as if their own lives meant nothing – as if they knew they were the drops of water that wear down a rock. The bodies inside the door were up to Gotrek's shoulders.

Gotrek was weaving with each blow, and Felix and Galin had to do more and more of his blocking for him.

'How long?' the Slayer rasped a while later.

'Ten minutes gone, I think,' wheezed Galin, deflecting a mace, 'maybe more.' He looked over his shoulder to the lever room door, which had a grilled window in it. 'Any sign of them, prince?'

'No sign,' came Hamnir's voice, hollowly.

There was commotion in the hall – an orc voice chittering commands, and orcs shifting around.

Gotrek choked out a laugh. 'Grimnir, that's all we need.'

Felix risked a look around the doorframe and gaped. Ten orcs, armed with dwarf long-guns, were forming up back to back in the centre of the wide corridor, five facing each guardroom door, as other orcs got out of their way.

'Find a way to kill them, manling,' grunted Gotrek. 'If I go out there, the rest will come in here, and if I stay here…'

'I have it,' said Galin. He backed from the door and ran to the gun rack at the far wall. 'Wait there.'

'And where do you think I'd be going?' Gotrek asked through his teeth.

Felix looked back and saw Galin gathering up powder horns.

The orcs primed and loaded their guns like boys on their first day of gunnery drill – clumsy and slow, spilling powder all over the place, but at last they were ready. Their commander growled an order. They raised the long-guns to their shoulders and aimed.

'Olifsson!' shouted Gotrek.

'One moment!'

'Haven't got a damned–'

The orc captain dropped his hand and the orcs fired at Gotrek and the Rassmussons, utterly unconcerned about hitting their fellows who stood in the way.

Two of the guns exploded, their barrels ripping apart at the stock and blowing shrapnel and flame into the faces of the orcs around them. Four collapsed, skulls shattered. Three guns fizzled and failed to fire at all, but five got off shots. Two balls whizzed towards the Rassmussons, three towards Gotrek. One buried itself in the back of an orc. One whistled over his crest. Gotrek swung his axe up and the last spanged off it, and then bonged into the gong.

In the opposite door, Karl staggered back, clutching his arm. An orc cut him down before he could recover. Arn died a second later, alone and overwhelmed.

'The Rassmussons are down!' called Felix. 'The orcs have the other guardroom.'

Hamnir cursed from the lever room.

Having cleared the opposite doorway, all the remaining orc gunners turned to Gotrek's side and began to reload as, behind them, their comrades swarmed into the left hand guardroom and started hacking at the lever room door.

'Hurry, curse you, Olifsson!' called Gotrek.

'Just coming!' said Galin. He ran back to them holding a pair of powder horns with holes in their sides, stuffed with bits of paper wadding. He shook them. They rattled. 'Added some shot.'

He lit the wadding of one with his lamp and heaved it over the heads of the orcs in the door. It hit the floor near the orc gunners, and went off with a concussive crack and an eruption of smoke and flame. Orcs fell, howling and coughing, with holes in their legs and guts, but not as many as Felix could have wished. Five of the gunners were still up, though one of them was on fire and flailing. The captain chopped it down and shoved it aside, roaring at the others to fire.

An orc slashed at Galin as he tried to light the second grenade. He danced back and tried again.

'Throw it!' Gotrek shouted.

The wadding caught. Galin threw the horn just as three of the orcs finished loading, and raised their guns. The powder horn exploded, ripping into them.

It was a second too late. The orcs had got their shots off first.

Gotrek staggered and dropped to one knee, catching himself with his axe. There was a bloody trench along his outer thigh.

CHAPTER NINETEEN

FELIX BLOCKED DESPERATELY as an orc swung for the Slayer's unprotected skull. The cleaver screeched along his sword and missed Gotrek's face by a hair's breadth. Felix hooked Gotrek under his arm with his free hand and tried to haul him up. He was ridiculously heavy. More were coming in. Galin fought two.

Gotrek found his footing again and severed the arm of the orc with the cleaver, but the damage was done. There were five orcs in the room, and more pushing in behind them. The doorway was lost. Felix, Gotrek and Galin backed and fought in a line, trying to keep the orcs from encircling them. Gotrek's left leg was slick with blood.

Felix heard a tinny shout from inside the lever room – Narin yelling through the speaking tube from across the hall. 'They're nearly through to me! The door won't hold long!'

'Courage, Ironskin!' called Hamnir. 'Any minute now.'

There was a smash behind Felix. He glanced back. The blade of a cleaver stuck through the door to the murder rooms and turrets. The orcs from above were breaking through. They would soon be surrounded.

'Where in Grungni's name is Gorril?' grunted Galin, blocking an orc sword.

'Not here,' said Gotrek. He was weaving like a drunk, barely able to stand on his mangled leg. He swung at an orc and missed. Felix nearly dropped his sword in shock. Gotrek never missed. The orc pressed forwards. Felix stabbed it in the neck. Gotrek gutted it, but four more had got past. Gotrek, Felix and Galin had orcs on three sides of them. They were too tired. There were too many.

Then, over the clangour of the fight, very faint, they heard a horn, drowned out almost immediately by muted gunfire.

'A horn!' said Galin.

'They're in the canyon. They're running!' cried Hamnir from the lever room. 'Narin! At the ready!'

'Ready,' came the metallic reply.

'Oh Grimnir, the crossfire!' choked Hamnir. 'So many down. They're... Open the outer door. Pull! Pull!'

An enormous grating and rumbling shook the room as the outer door slowly began to lower, and then came a deafening boom as it sank home. The orcs in the guardroom looked behind them at the sound, and Gotrek, Felix and Galin cut down five of them. The battering stopped behind the door to the murder room, and they heard the orcs running back up the stairs to their stations in the turrets.

A second volley of cannon and small-arms fire resounded through the walls from the canyon.

'Now the inner! Pull, Narin!' came Hamnir's voice. 'Run lads, run!'

Another shuddering rumble and a roaring of wind, and the guardroom filled with cold air and the smell of gunsmoke. As the second door boomed to a stop, the wind rose and steadied to a deafening trumpet pitch that vibrated the whole corridor, as if blown through the throat of an enormous horn. The orcs twitched and cringed at the noise.

Hamnir roared from the lever room. 'The horn of Hirn! Now they will fear us!'

The orcs in the corridor were turning and backing away from the open door, their commanders shouting at them to form up. They were too late.

With horns blowing and banners waving, the dwarfs of Karak Hirn charged through the open doors eight abreast, Hammerers at the fore, and punched the disorganised orcs back like a gunner ramming a charge down a cannon's mouth.

Gotrek, Felix and Galin butchered the last five orcs in the guardroom as Gorril's force continued to pour in, rank after rank of sturdy warriors howling for orc blood.

As the last orc toppled, Gotrek staggered back and sank down onto a stool by the guardroom table. His axe head thudded on the stone floor. 'Grungni, I need a drink!' he said. His left leg, below the trench the bullet had cut, was red to his boot.

'Galin!' called Hamnir from the lever room. 'Open the door!'

Galin hurried to the lever room door and let Hamnir out. The prince surveyed the heaps of orc bodies in the room, and shook his head. He looked up at the three of them. 'Your deeds today will be recorded in the Book of Karak Hirn. I swear it.'

Gorril stepped out of the blur of dwarfs rushing past the guardroom, leading a company of his clan brothers. He saluted Hamnir, his fist over his heart. 'My prince,' he said gravely. 'I am glad to see you alive. Your army goes to gain a foothold in the grand concourse, and then awaits your orders.'

'And I am glad to see you, cousin,' said Hamnir, saluting in turn. 'We will need dwarfs here to open the murder room doors and take the orcs within. They must also close the gate when the column is in. There is not the glory to be had here that there will be in the concourse, but our rear must be protected.'

'Of course, prince,' said Gorril. He turned to his clan brothers. 'You heard him, Urlo. Divide up the lads and take the murder rooms.'

'Aye, Gorril.' Urlo saluted and began barking orders to his companions.

Hamnir glanced at Galin. 'Stonemonger, take the keys from Arn's body and let Narin out of the other lever room.'

'Aye, prince.' Galin saluted and stepped into the hall.

'And you, Gurnisson,' Hamnir continued, turning to Gotrek. 'I command you to have no more to do with this battle. The physicians will dress your wounds and you will take a well-deserved rest. You too, Herr Jaeger.'

'Humph!' said Gotrek.

'Now come, Gorril,' said Hamnir, stepping to the door with the tall dwarf. 'Have you sent Thunderers to the second-floor balconies? And are the Ironbreakers on their way through the secondary tunnels to come at the orc flanks? Have the miners gone to seal the doors to the mines?'

'All as you ordered, Prince Hamnir,' said Gorril. 'They are to secure each passage as they go, so the orcs may not get in behind us.'

Hamnir hailed a mule cart just coming through the front gate. 'Surgeons! Here! See to those within the guardrooms. The Slayer has been shot and is losing blood.'

'Aye, prince.'

The cart stopped and two dwarf surgeons bustled in, field kits in hand. One got busy patching up the minor cuts and scrapes that Felix had collected, while the other cleaned and dressed Gotrek's leg wound. As they worked, Urlo and Gorril's clan brothers unlocked the door to the murder rooms and turrets, and charged up the stairs within. The sounds of battle began to rage above them.

'You're lucky, Slayer,' Gotrek's surgeon said as he began wrapping his leg. 'Missed the bone entirely. Stay off it for a month or two, keep it clean, and it'll heal just fine.'

'A month?' growled Gotrek. 'I'll give you another *minute* before I use your guts to tie it off. Now hurry. There's a battle to fight.'

'Really, Slayer,' said the surgeon. 'I wouldn't advise it.' Nonetheless, he wrapped the wound in record time.

Gotrek surged up almost before he had tightened the last knot, and limped stoically towards the hall. 'Come, manling,' he said, 'I want to find that wax-skinned tusk-mouth in the black armour. An orc like that might almost be a challenge.'

'Not going to listen to Hamnir?' asked Felix, though he knew it would do no good. He followed the Slayer wearily.

'I swore I'd protect him,' said Gotrek, 'not follow his orders.'

Galin and Narin fell in with them as they left the other guardroom, their wounds also bound. All around them, surgeons and victuallers were unloading their carts and setting up cots and trestle tables in preparation for caring for the wounded and weary.

As Gotrek passed a cart piled with barrels and crates, he snatched up a small keg, wrenched the plug out with his fingers and upended it over his mouth, gulping down several pints of the golden brew as it splashed over his beard and crest. At last, he lowered it with a contented sigh and held it out to the others. 'Anyone else?'

Galin and Narin both took and lifted the keg in turn, though with more difficulty, and drank their fill. Felix took it up after them, glad that it was nearly empty, for he would never have been able to raise it full. Gotrek took it from him when he'd finished, had another guzzle, and then slammed it down on the cart and limped on, smacking his lips.

The corridor ended at a high, columned archway, beyond which wide, shallow steps descended into an enormous, marble-floored hall, the grand concourse of Karak Hirn, the central hall from which all the ceremonial and public chambers of the hold stemmed. It was three storeys tall, and pillars as big and round as castle turrets ran down either side of it, holding up an intricately carved, cross-vaulted ceiling.

It was swarming with orcs.

The dwarf army held the area around the steps, ranks of doughty warriors, Ironbreakers and miners lined up at their base, while Thunderers stood and knelt in two lines on the top step, firing over the heads of their brethren below. The dwarfs were already vastly outnumbered, and more orcs were pouring into the concourse through a dozen archways.

A tattoo of explosions came from beyond the battle. Felix looked up and saw that more Thunderers had taken up positions on two balconies, one on the huge room's right wall, one on the left, above and behind the main body of the orcs. Twenty orcs fell at this volley, and there was another right behind it as a second rank of dwarfs stepped up to the rail of the balcony and the first stepped back to reload. A third rank followed the second, and then the first was ready again. Orcs fell like cut wheat. The Thunderers' speed and marksmanship was awe-inspiring.

Directly below where Felix stood with Gotrek, Hamnir, and the others, the huge pale orc in the odd armour, and his similarly dressed and milk-skinned retinue, were smashing Karak Hirn's Longbeards to pieces. The rancid reek of them was almost blinding. The white-haired dwarfs fought them valiantly, eyes watering from the smell as they struck again and again, but the orcs were incredibly strong, and what was worse, disciplined. For every white orc that toppled, three Longbeards had their heads caved in. The Longbeards would never break, but neither, it appeared would the orcs. And none could touch the huge warboss. Three Longbeards bashed at him, landing blow after blow, but he took their worst and gave back murder. A white-haired dwarf staggered back, clutching his neck, his long beard a bright crimson tabard. It was old Ruen. He fell on his face before the steps.

'Stand aside,' said Gotrek, limping forwards.

'No, Gurnisson,' said Hamnir, stepping ahead of the Slayer. 'He is mine. He took my hold. I will take him. Besides, you're in no shape for a fight.'

'I'm always in shape for a fight,' Gotrek bristled, but then stopped, grunting. 'Bah! It's your hold. I suppose you have the right to challenge him, Valaya curse you.'

Hamnir and Gorril were already charging down the steps to join the Longbeards' line. Gotrek glared after them, angry, or perhaps concerned. Felix couldn't tell.

'Come on, manling,' the Slayer said, turning. 'We'll find some other place to get stuck in.'

'Why not take Hamnir's advice and sit this one out,' said Felix. 'You're not exactly at your best.'

'Why do you all say that?' growled Gotrek. 'All I needed was a drink.'

'Listen,' said Narin, trying to see through the gun-smoke that filled the hall like a fog. 'The Thunderers on the right balcony have stopped firing,'

'They're being attacked,' said Galin, craning his neck. 'Orcs have got around behind them.'

Gotrek turned to the corridor. 'Then we'll get around behind the orcs.'

'Just the four of us?' asked Felix.

Gotrek looked at the battle. The dwarfs were sorely pressed on every side. 'There's no one else to spare.'

He stumped back into the corridor. Felix, Narin and Galin exchanged a glance, and then shrugged and followed him.

A few strides down the hallway, they reached a rising stair held by a rank of Karak Hirn dwarfs.

'One of you lads, lead us to the right balcony over the concourse,' said Gotrek. 'Your Thunderers are in trouble.'

'One of us?' said a dwarf. 'We'll all come!'

'And desert your position?' snarled Gotrek. 'Your prince would like that. Just one.'

The dwarf who had spoken, a gruff veteran named Dolmir, came with them, leading them quickly up the stairs and through the passages of the floor above. Gotrek grunted with each limping step in an effort to keep up with the others.

Soon they entered a high, wide corridor that ringed the grand concourse. On the outer wall of the ring were a series of magnificent doors, each with the insignia of a clan carved above it in stone – the entrances to the holds of the clans who made Karak Hirn their home. Many of their doors hung open, or had been smashed off their hinges, and piles of stone and construction materials littered the corridor, as if the orcs had been attempting repairs. On its inner wall, the ring was pierced by numerous iron-latticed windows, balconies, and galleries that looked down into the grand concourse. The sounds of battle echoed up through them, but a nearer battle was louder. The companions turned.

Halfway down the corridor was the entrance to the balcony that the Thunderers had been firing from. A seething scrum of orcs surrounded it. The Thunderers had turned and fought them with hand axe and dagger. Both orc and dwarf bodies sprawled at the feet of the combatants, but the dwarfs were getting the worst of it. They were outnumbered two to one. They would be overwhelmed in moments.

'Grimnir take it,' cursed Gotrek as he hobbled forwards. 'I can't run.' He looked around angrily, and then pointed to the construction. 'Manling, that barrow!'

Felix ran to a pile of rubble and pulled out a wooden wheelbarrow. He rolled it to Gotrek. The Slayer climbed in, wounded leg first, and faced forwards, axe at the ready.

'Push!'

Felix tried, but the dwarf was impossibly heavy, much denser than anything made of flesh and blood had any right to be. 'Narin, help me.'

Narin took up one of the barrow's handles and together they ran it down the corridor, Galin and Dolmir pacing them. The orcs and the Thunderers were too occupied to notice them coming.

'Valaya's mercy, Gurnisson,' puffed Narin. 'Do you eat stone for breakfast?'

'Shut up. Push faster!'

Fifteen feet from the melee, the barrow's wheel struck a loose brick and bounced wildly. Gotrek catapulted forwards, grunting in surprise, but turned it into a bloodthirsty battle cry and raised his axe in mid-air.

The back rank of orcs turned at the noise and fell to the floor in pieces as Gotrek's axe passed through them, parting armour and bone as easily as it cut flesh. Felix and Narin ploughed the barrow into the orcs, then drew their weapons and charged in with Galin and Dolmir, slashing and chopping.

The Thunderers cheered and, heartened by the reinforcements, attacked with renewed fury. The orcs fought with the same blank silence that Felix had come to expect.

Dolmir, however, was unnerved. 'Why don't they cry out? Why don't they break?'

'I don't know, cousin,' said Narin, 'but they won't run. We'll have to kill every last one.'

And they did. Though Gotrek was nearly immobile because of his leg, it didn't matter. The orcs came to him, pushing forwards to swing at him, only to fall before his omnipresent blade. The swarm was quickly obliterated.

'Much obliged, Slayer,' said the captain of the Thunderers as his dwarfs recovered and took up their guns again. 'Tougher than we thought they'd be.'

They re-formed on the balcony and started firing down into the mass of orcs once again.

Gotrek, Felix and the others looked over the battle below. The dwarfs and orcs were fighting to a standstill along a curved line in front of the steps. It looked as if every orc in the hold was trying to get at the dwarfs, and in the centre...

'Grimnir curse him!' said Gotrek as he saw. 'Thinks he's a Slayer now?'

In the centre, Hamnir and the orc warboss still fought on, the tattered remains of their squads surrounding them. There were less than ten of the strange pale orcs left, and no more than a handful of Longbeards. Hamnir's helmet was dented and his gromril ringmail torn in a dozen places. His face was red with blood and exertion. The warboss's armour had similarly been smashed and ripped away, but strangely, its pale, green skin didn't have a mark on it.

As Felix and Gotrek watched, Hamnir swung his axe at the giant orc's exposed knee. At first it seemed he had hit it, for Felix could have sworn he saw Hamnir's shoulders jolt with the impact, but it must have been an illusion, for his axe sped on, unbloodied, and the orc took no wound. The orc hardly registered the attack, swinging its own shield-sized axe down at Hamnir so swiftly that the dwarf prince had to fling himself aside to avoid being chopped in two.

'Never was much good in a scrap,' grumbled Gotrek. He pulled himself up onto the balustrade. 'Hang on, scholar!' he roared, and without a second thought, leapt down to the floor, twenty-five feet below.

CHAPTER TWENTY

'GOTREK!' SHOUTED FELIX. He thrust his head over the rail. Narin and Galin did the same, eyes wide with alarm.

'It's all right,' said Narin wryly. 'His fall was broken by a dozen orcs.'

It was true. Gotrek was on his feet in the centre of a cluster of sprawling orcs, slashing around like a red-crested whirlwind as he forced his way towards Hamnir and the warboss. The bandage on his leg was crimson with fresh blood.

Felix's mouth opened and closed. 'Damn him! I... I... I'll break my legs. I...' With a curse he turned and bolted into the hallway towards the stairs. Narin and Galin ran after him, but quickly fell behind.

Felix pounded down the stairs, pushed through the dwarfs at the bottom and sprinted along the corridor to the grand concourse. He skidded to a stop behind the Thunderers on the steps and scanned the surging battle for Gotrek.

The Slayer was just reaching the warboss, a wide swath of broken and dismembered orcs behind him. He swung at the warboss's back. The blow ripped the shattered remains of the orc's black breastplate off and sent it spinning. As the brute turned to swing at Gotrek, Felix could see that its back was entirely unmarked. He groaned. Gotrek had missed for a second time today, though it wasn't any wonder: he should have been flat on his back in bed.

With its attention held by Gotrek, Hamnir and the Longbeards attacked the warboss from all sides. Their blows did nothing. Felix paled. Were they *all* missing? Or was something more sinister going on? The big orc made no attempt whatsoever to block them. Seven axes struck its back, legs and shoulders, and it shrugged them off as if it didn't feel them. It fought in leather rags and scraps of cloth, and still there was not a single wound on it.

It has some magic, thought Felix, some protective spell. No matter. Gotrek would make short work of that. He and his axe had cut down dragons and daemons. Magic siege engines had disintegrated at the merest touch of that fell blade.

Gotrek knocked the wax-fleshed monster's enormous battle-axe aside and lurched in with a clean unobstructed swing to its belly. The orc roared in pain and staggered back three steps, and Felix raised his fist. That's done it, he thought. But as the warboss straightened, Felix saw only a fading line on its belly, as one might see if one drew one's fingernail across the back of one's hand. The orc had taken a blow that should have come out through its spine, and was unmarked.

'Damned stinking beast!' Gotrek swore. 'What are you made of?'

The orc charged him, raining a storm of blows down on him as the Slayer blocked and swayed on his bad leg, cursing in pain and frustration.

Felix pushed through the Thunderers and charged the monstrous orc's back. A stupid thing to do, he knew, even as he did it. If Gotrek's axe could make no impression, what could he do? But he couldn't just stand aside and watch. He swung his long sword at the same time that Hamnir and the Longbeards swung their axes. Not one strike broke the skin. They all slid off the orc's pale green hide as if it were oiled marble.

The orc swept a lazy backhand at Felix, Hamnir and the others, splitting open a Longbeard's ribs and knocking him to the floor, dead. Felix leapt back, barely escaping the same fate.

Gotrek lunged in and swung with all his might at the orc's right shin – a blow like that would have severed the leg from an iron statue. The orc grunted and its leg buckled, but it recovered and spun back. Its huge axe shaved a tuft from Gotrek's orange crest.

Felix tossed aside his sword. Perhaps he couldn't wound the thing, but he might blind it. He leapt on its massive back, grabbing it around the neck, struggling to climb it. Its skin was slick with some foul mucus. The smell choked him, and he almost slid off.

The orc grunted, annoyed, and tried to shrug him off. Felix got his legs over its broad shoulders and clapped his hands over its eyes.

'Good, manling!' called Gotrek. 'Stay on him!' He struck the orc's chest with a blow that should have split its sternum.

The orc staggered back, bellowing in pain, but its skin remained whole. It lashed out blind and one-handed with its axe, and groped with its free hand for Felix.

Felix tried to squirm out of the way of the questing fingers, but they caught him by the arm.

Felix scrabbled desperately for purchase and caught at the gold torque wrapped around the orc's neck. The orc threw him crashing into Gotrek, sending them both sprawling.

'Curse you, manling!' grunted the Slayer from under Felix. 'I told you to stay on.'

A shadow of swift movement flashed in the corner of Felix's eye and he rolled instinctively aside. Gotrek rolled the opposite way. The orc's immense axe blade slammed down between them, burying itself deep in the marble floor.

Gotrek staggered up, lurching on his wounded leg, and swung with all his might at the orc's arm as it lifted the axe again. He chopped the massive green limb in half at the elbow.

Gotrek blinked as the orc howled and fell back, its stump spurting black blood. 'What in the name of Grungni?'

Hamnir and the Longbeards ran in as the orc staggered, clutching itself. Their axes bit deep, just as Gotrek's had. They chopped it to pieces.

'What happened?' asked Hamnir, as they looked down at its mangled body. 'Why did it suddenly become vulnerable?'

'Haven't a clue,' said Gotrek, ruffling his shortened crest and frowning.

'Er,' said Felix, and held up the thing he clutched in his hand – the orc's golden torque.

FELIX GAVE THE torque to Hamnir as the battle with the orcs continued. He was glad to be rid of it. Perhaps it would have made him invincible too, but it made his skin crawl just holding it. The glittering black jewel in its centre seemed to look at him, and dark whisperings seemed to fill his mind, urging him to put it on. Dwarfs were less susceptible to that sort of thing, he thought as he fought beside Gotrek, better for Hamnir to have it.

Felix's many battles against orcs had taught him that when one kills the warboss, the fight is over. The lieutenants start squabbling, and any cohesion the horde might have had dissipates in an explosion of infighting and panic. Although he and the dwarfs had ample evidence that the orcs they fought now were not like other orcs, it still came as a demoralising shock when they continued fighting just as resolutely after the invulnerable warboss had fallen as they had before.

So, for another weary, blood-soaked hour, the orcs threw themselves at the dwarf line with the dull mechanical ferocity of ants protecting their nest. Gotrek and Hamnir fought back to back in that swirling sea, roaring and joking, and exchanging reminiscences as if they were bellied up to a bar instead of butchering greenskins.

'That wasn't nine, scholar,' Gotrek growled, grinning. 'You only have eight. I finished off the one before last, so he's on my tally not yours. Is this how you count your manifests?'

'I dispatched the one you threw behind you,' retorted Hamnir, grinning. 'Do you think your every stroke is fatal? Someone has to clean up behind you, as it ever was.'

Felix was struck again by unexpected jealousy as he watched them. He had travelled with Gotrek for twenty years and could not recall one instance where Gotrek had been as comfortable and free in his presence as he was with Hamnir now.

Finally, the last orc fell, the echoes of steel on steel faded, and the grand concourse was silent, but for the moaning of the wounded and the dying. Felix could barely lift his sword, and Gotrek was the same, wearier than Felix had ever seen him, but happier too.

The dwarfs looked around in a daze at the piles of the dead and the lakes of blood that spread across the polished marble floor. Some of the survivors mourned over slain brothers and friends. Some clapped each other on the back and drank celebratory toasts from flasks. Some were so tired that they sat down where they were, unheeding of the corpses and the reek.

Hamnir limped unsteadily up the steps and turned to face his troops. He was a mass of cuts and bruises, his armour hanging off him like a gromril rag. 'Sons and friends of Karak Hirn, you have won a great victory here today.'

The dwarfs bellowed a deep-throated cheer.

'This enterprise may have started in my error, but it has ended in your victory. I thank you for your help and sacrifice. Bring our dead and wounded to the shrine of Grungni, but leave the grobi where they lay. We will begin to set the hold to rights tomorrow.

Tonight in the feast hall we will dine and drink and toast the valorous dead.'

There was another cheer, and then the dwarfs roused themselves to see to their maimed and murdered. As Hamnir stepped down to the floor again, dwarfs began to jog in from every archway, bearing news.

'Prince,' called the first, 'we have sealed the entrances to the mine. There are many grobi still below, but they will not get in tonight.'

'Prince Hamnir,' said another, 'we have cleared the upper galleries and the grain storage level, but several score of goblins have locked themselves in the third armoury.'

Urlo and the dwarfs of Gorril's clan returned from the guardrooms, bloody and battered, and missing half their number. Urlo knelt stiffly and held the Battle Horn of Karak Hirn out to Hamnir. The bell was split and crumpled.

Hamnir choked as he took it. 'Thorgig.'

'He died with it to his lips, prince,' said Urlo. 'He never drew his axe.'

'And Leatherbeard? The Slayer?'

'Ten dead orcs surrounded him,' said Urlo, 'and it took as many strikes to bring him down.'

Hamnir lowered his head. 'Their sacrifice won the day. They will be honoured.'

Gotrek nodded gravely. 'It was a good doom.'

More dwarfs approached as reports came from all over the hold. Pockets of grobi resistance here, a decisive victory there, ruined supplies, vandalised rooms, a storage room full of the rotting corpses of dwarfs who had barricaded themselves in and starved to death, looted treasure vaults.

Hamnir took it all, good news and bad, with a weary calm, dispatching orders and dispensing thanks and congratulations to those who merited it as he walked slowly towards the arch that led to the feast hall, but then came a piece of news that stopped him in his tracks.

'Prince,' called a Karak Hirn warrior, running up at the head of a dozen dwarfs, 'the Diamondsmith clan, their hold is unbreached! It looks as if the grobi tried to break down the door, but it is still whole. They may yet live!'

'Ferga!' whispered Hamnir. He looked around at Gorril and Gotrek, eyes bright. 'Come, we must see!' He strode across the hall, his exhaustion a thing of the past. The others hurried after him.

'Don't get your hopes up, prince,' said Gorril. 'It has been twenty days. There can't have been much food in the hall when they closed the doors.'

'Aye, scholar,' said Gotrek, gruff. 'Be prepared for the worst. It may be orcs behind that door.'

'I am prepared,' said Hamnir, but he still sounded eager.

They climbed broad stairs to the balconied corridor that ringed the grand concourse, and travelled past six breached clanholds until they came to a tall iron and stone door with the insignia of a diamond set above its lintel. The door was blackened with smoke, and chipped and dented as if from gunshots and hammer blows, but it was still intact.

Hamnir looked upon it with longing eyes. He stepped forwards, and then turned to the crowd of dwarfs who had followed him there. 'Are there any among you of the Diamondsmith clan? Do any of you have a key or know the clan secret to opening this door?'

None of the dwarfs spoke up.

'No Diamondsmiths save Thorgig and Kagrin escaped the hold, prince,' said Gorril. 'The rest locked themselves in, to the last dwarf.'

Hamnir nodded and turned back to the door, drawing his axe. He reversed it and rapped an odd, syncopated tattoo on the door with the square back of the head. From years in the company of dwarfs, Felix knew what this must be, though he had never heard it used – the mine code of the dwarfs, a system for communicating through miles of tunnels with nothing but a hammer. The code was more jealously guarded than the dwarf language, for with it they could talk though walls and across enemy lines.

Hamnir finished his short pattern and the assembled dwarfs waited for a response. None came. He rapped the door again, and again no response came. Gorril shifted, uncomfortable. Gotrek coughed. Hamnir set his jaw and raised his axe once more, but just as he was about to rap again, an uncertain tapping echoed through the door. It sounded as if the sender was just on the other side.

Hamnir gasped and beat an excited response on the door.

'Easy, scholar,' said Gotrek. 'You're stuttering.'

After a breathless silence, a slow reply came.

'Valaya be praised!' said Hamnir. He turned to the others. 'Stand back. They're opening the door.'

The crowd moved back, murmuring their amazement. Hamnir and Gorril were all smiles, slapping each other on the back and chuckling, but Felix saw that Gotrek kept his hand on the haft of his axe, and his face was wary. Felix understood his caution. If the orcs could learn how to build dwarf traps and shoot long-guns, they might have learned anything.

For a long moment nothing happened, and then there was a deep 'thunk' of stone bolts drawing back and the doors began to swing slowly out.

The dwarfs held their breath, and more than one followed Gotrek's example and lowered their hands to their axes, but when the doors boomed fully open, what faced Hamnir, Gotrek, Felix and the others through the huge arched door, was a handful of dwarfs so ragged and gaunt that it was hard to believe they still lived. Felix heard a horrified intake of breath behind him as the liberators gazed upon the liberated.

Felix had never seen dwarfs so thin. Even in the direst circumstances, dwarfs remained relatively robust, but these poor souls looked at death's door. The dwarf who stood to the fore, an axe hanging from his shaking hand, was practically a skeleton, his cheekbones jutting out above his grizzled and patchy beard like rock ledges. His doublet hung from his bony shoulders like a sack, loose and dirty. His hair and beard were brittle and dull.

Hamnir cried out and stepped forwards, taking the dwarf's bone-thin hand. 'Thane Kirhaz Helmgard! You live!'

'Prince Hamnir,' Kirhaz whispered, his voice as weak as a candle flame at noon, 'you have come.'

'And by Grimnir, Grungni and Valaya, I am thankful beyond all words that we are not too late. Unless,' he choked suddenly. 'Unless we *are* too late, and you few are all that survive!'

Kirhaz shook his head. 'Some have died, but most are spared. We have been allowed to live.'

Felix thought it was a funny way to put it, but Hamnir didn't appear to notice.

'And Ferga?' he asked eagerly. 'Does she live?'

'Aye, Ferga lives,' said Kirhaz.

'The ancestors be praised!' said Hamnir. He turned to the others. 'Summon the physics and surgeons! Bring food and drink! Our cousins are in need.'

More haggard dwarfs were appearing in the hall behind Kirhaz, shuffling forwards like slow-moving ghosts.

'By the ancestors,' said Hamnir, staring. 'What you have endured.'

He started forwards into the Diamondsmith hold. The others followed, calling out to old friends among the survivors and hurrying to them with glad cries and gentle embraces. The survivors met these greetings with wan smiles and blank stares. It seemed as if it hadn't yet sunk in that they had been saved. Their eyes remained haunted and far away.

Felix and Gotrek stepped with Hamnir and Kirhaz and the others into the central chamber of the clanhold. Frail dwarfs came out of arches and doors all around its perimeter, blinking like bears waking from hibernation.

All at once, Hamnir shouted and hurried across the room to a starved looking dwarf maiden, her long hair ratty and unbraided, and her dress like a tent around her bony frame.

'Ferga!' cried Hamnir, taking up her hands and kissing them. 'Ferga, beloved.'

She stared at him uncertainly for a moment, and then reached out and patted his face, frowning uncertainly. 'Hamnir. Prince. Have you come? Or is this yet another dream?'

'I have come, Ferga. You are free. Your ordeal is over.'

'Good. Good.' Her hand fell to her side.

Hamnir swallowed, his face a mixture of confusion and pain. This was obviously not the scene of tearful welcome he had constructed in his head. 'Beloved, you are weak. We must see to your recovery. I…' he paused and looked back at Kirhaz, who was crossing to them. 'I am afraid I must bring sadness to this joyous occasion.' He held up the war horn and looked at them both. He squared his shoulders. 'Your son and brother, Thorgig, is dead, slain by the orcs, but his sacrifice was not in vain. He won the day and freed you. He died summoning our troops.'

'Thorgig.' Ferga's brow furrowed, as if she were trying to remember what the word meant. 'Thorgig is dead?'

'My son,' said Kirhaz hollowly. 'Aye. That's bad. That's bad.'

Felix frowned. Even for dwarfs, Kirhaz and Ferga's response was stoic. They didn't seem to understand.

Hamnir was unnerved, but put the best face on it he could. 'Forgive me. I should not have burdened you with such news before you have had a chance to recover yourselves. I will trouble you no more until you have been fed and tended to.' He turned and addressed the dwarfs of the Diamondsmith hold, masking his pain with an effort. 'There will be a feast tonight in the feast hall. Your courage and steadfastness will be honoured there. If you are well enough, I beg all of you to attend. Let the drinking horns be filled and the trenchers heaped high! Tonight we celebrate a miracle!'

The rescuers cheered. The rescued took the news with dull indifference. The cheers faltered.

Hamnir bowed to Kirhaz and Ferga, and then turned away and whispered to Gotrek. 'It is enough to break my heart. Have you ever seen dwarfs so lost?'

'No,' said Gotrek, 'I haven't.' His hand was still on his axe.

CHAPTER TWENTY-ONE

FOR ALL HAMNIR's talk of piling the trenchers high, the feast was a lean affair. The dwarfs could not, or would not, trust any food touched by the orcs, nor use the great kitchens until they had been thoroughly scoured, so they had to make do with the provisions that Gorril's army had brought with them from Rodenheim Castle. Fortunately, Hamnir and Gorril had foreseen this situation, and the wagons had been packed to overflowing, though it was still hardly enough.

There was, however, plenty of beer. The dwarfs had been amazed to find two entire storerooms filled with untouched hogsheads – more proof, if any were needed, that the orcs who had held the hold were unusual indeed.

Toast after toast was drunk: to Hamnir, to Thorgig, the survivors, Gotrek, even Felix got a polite cheer. The Diamondsmith survivors – those few strong enough to attend – sat quietly among their roaring, guzzling cousins, sipping at their beer and mouthing their food, and raising feeble smiles at each toast. They seemed glaze-eyed and uncomfortable in the midst of all the uproar.

Hamnir sat between Thane Kirhaz and his old friend, the engineer Birri Birrisson, at the king's table at the head of the hall, trying his best to learn from them what had happened since the orcs had invaded. Whatever Birrisson had looked like before, now he seemed a skeleton with spectacles, his lank grey beard hanging from sunken parchment cheeks.

'But, Birri,' he said as the engineer forked ham mechanically into his mouth with a trembling hand, 'Gotrek reported that the passage from the gyrocopter hangar was laid with new traps, dwarf-built. Those traps killed Matrak, your old colleague, and two others. Are you certain no dwarf helped in their construction? Was perhaps one of your apprentices caught and tortured? Was anyone missing?'

Birri shook his bald head, not looking up. 'No apprentices lost. None that didn't die, at least. Not in our hold.' He frowned. His fork paused. 'Had a dream I set new traps in that hall, but…' He stopped, his eyes far away.

'A dream?' asked Hamnir, eyes wide. 'What sort of dream?'

Birri frowned again for a long moment, then shrugged. 'A dream. Only a dream.' He could not be induced to say more about it.

Hamnir sighed and shook his head as he filled his stein again. He leaned over to Gotrek and whispered in his ear. 'They are still too tired from their privations. I will wait until they have recovered.'

'They aren't just tired,' growled Gotrek, fixing his one eye on Birri, who was staring placidly into space, his food forgotten. 'Something's wrong with them. Dwarfs are made of sterner stuff.'

'Even a dwarf might grow weak after starving for twenty days,' said Hamnir.

Gotrek grumbled suspiciously but said nothing, only drank another stein dry.

Soon the Diamondsmith hold survivors began to nod in their chairs, the unaccustomed amounts of food and beer overwhelming them and making them drowsy. They excused themselves in ones and twos, and returned to their hold while their rescuers toasted each departure. With the last of them gone, the spirits of the remaining dwarfs rose again, and they began to get roaring drunk.

Strange, Felix thought as he watched Gotrek and Hamnir clash their steins together, that the feast's honoured guests had been a drag on the festivities. The listless misery of the survivors had made the victorious army uncomfortable and polite. They had kept their voices low, and courteously tried to keep the survivors engaged in their conversations, but now that they were gone, restraint went with them. Dwarf marching songs rocked the feast hall, and heated arm wrestling and boasting matches were being contested at every table.

Felix knew where it would all lead. He had seen it before. It was a dwarf tradition that they drink themselves into a stupor after a great victory, and it appeared this victory would be no exception. Already, there were dwarfs slumped in their chairs, snoring, steins still clutched in their fists, and those who had travelled with Hamnir were falling faster than the rest

– all the marching and digging and fighting of the past days catching up with when they were at last allowed to relax.

Gotrek was slurring his words and leaning heavily on his elbows as he spoke to Hamnir. Narin and Galin, sitting with their respective clans at the long tables below the dais, were both fast asleep, their heads back, snoring heavily. Felix too was drooping, his eyelids getting heavier and heavier until he too sprawled in his chair, unconscious.

FELIX'S HEAD JERKED up from the table. He blinked around blearily, so befuddled with sleep and ale that for a moment he had no idea where he was. The feast hall. Now he remembered. It was dark, the fire in the enormous hearth sunk to red embers, and the lamps and candles guttering. But what had awakened him? He could see no movement in the hall. The dwarfs around him snored softly, heads down on the tables, their beards soaking up puddles of beer and gravy and soup.

A strange feeling of dread came unbidden to his heart, and for a moment, he was afraid that he was having a reoccurrence of the nightmare he had in the mines – that at any moment he would begin stabbing Gotrek and Hamnir and the rest in their sleep. But no, he felt no homicidal urges, only fear.

Then he heard it again, a scream, echoing from the kitchens. That was what had woken him up. Someone had screamed. Around him, dwarfs were snoring and mumbling, their dreams disturbed. He looked towards the kitchen doors. The connecting corridor was bright with lamplight. There was nothing there, and then there was: a weaving shadow. A plump dwarf woman staggered through the door, wailing, and then fell between two long tables. Her back was split open like a melon. Felix could see her spine.

He nudged Gotrek roughly. 'Gotrek!'

The Slayer didn't move.

Around the chamber, dwarfs were waking, muttering and cursing in the darkness.

'What was that?'

'Who's screaming?'

'Ugh, my head.'

'Stop that cursed noise!'

Hamnir lifted his head, murmuring fretfully, and then sank back, his forehead thudding as it hit the table.

More shadows were moving beyond the kitchen doorway, hulking black shapes lurching across the floor, accompanied by harsh scraping sounds.

A dwarf near the door scrambled up out of his seat and backed unsteadily away, pointing. 'The orcsh!' he slurred. 'The orcsh!'

'Wuzzat, lad?' mumbled another, further from the door. 'Don't be daft. The orcs are dead.'

Felix saw Narin amongst his cousins, blinking and rubbing his face. On the opposite side of the hall, Galin was still fast asleep.

'Orcs?' murmured Hamnir. He sat up again, listing in his seat. His eyes blinked open. 'Where...' His chest heaved and he lunged to the side, vomiting over the arm of his chair.

'Gotrek!' Felix shouted, shaking the Slayer.

The shadows pushed into the feast hall, followed by the things that cast them. The dwarfs stared, most still half asleep and entirely drunk, as a dozen orcs shambled through the kitchen door, dragging their cleavers and axes behind them. The first orc was missing an arm. The next had three crossbow bolts sticking from its chest. Another dragged itself along the floor by its hands. It had no legs. The orcs' heads drooped at unnatural angles. Their eyes stared into the middle distance, vacant and dull. Their movements were slow and stiff. A side door crashed open and more jolted through, as ungainly as the first group.

A dwarf staggered up unsteadily from the table closest to the door and stood in the way of the orc procession. 'Grimnir,' he said, pointing. 'They're...'

The lead orc swung his axe around loosely, as if he meant to throw it, and the drunk dwarf went down, the top of his head opened like a hard-boiled egg. All over the room, dwarfs began roaring and fumbling clumsily for their weapons, as ungainly in their drunken stupor as the shambling orcs. More orcs pushed through the feast hall's main archway, a slow, spreading tide of herky-jerk monsters. The doors were choked with them.

Hamnir pushed himself upright, wiping his mouth and looking around. 'What... what is this? Do I still dream?'

'It's no dream, prince,' said Felix. 'Gotrek. Wake up!'

Gotrek's head snapped up, his beard grimy with crumbs. 'Wha?' he slurred. 'Who's that?'

'But the orcs are dead,' mumbled Gorril, blinking around on Hamnir's left. 'How can they...'

'Orcs?' Gotrek looked around, frowning and belching. 'Where? Where are they?'

Hamnir jumped to his feet. His chair crashed to the floor as he sprang unsteadily onto the table. 'Form up, brothers! Form up! Captains rally your men! Hurry!' His voice was lost in the chaos of confused shouting that echoed through the hall.

Gotrek lurched up and nearly fell over. 'What orcs? Light a torch. I can't see.'

A Longbeard charged an approaching orc and sunk his axe into its ribcage. The orc swayed under the force of the blow, but showed no pain. It raised its mace, and crushed the old dwarf's skull. The axe was still in its ribs.

The dwarfs bellowed at this horror and charged the orcs all around the room, hacking at them in drunken frenzy. Orc limbs spun away. Orc bones shattered. The orcs kept coming. With hands lopped off and intestines trailing behind them, with torsos pierced by axes and smashed by hammers, they kept coming. They flailed spasmodically with their weapons. Cutting off their legs only slowed them down. Then they clawed forwards, snatching and snapping at the dwarf's legs and feet.

Dwarfs fell with bashed heads and cleaved chests, with severed arms and split bellies. All around the room, they fought in ones and twos as the orcs pushed them towards the centre from all sides. Some were murdered before they woke. Felix saw Narin hack an orc's forearm off at the elbow, and then duck as the orc swung the stump. On the other side of the room, Galin was backing away from an orc with four bullet wounds in its chest and neck.

'Form up! Form up!' shouted Hamnir. 'Form up or we're lost!'

'Light the lights!' roared Gotrek. 'I can't find my axe!'

Felix glanced at the Slayer. 'Gotrek, your patch is over the wrong eye.'

Gotrek snarled and pawed at his face. 'Well, who played that fool trick?' He pulled the leather patch over his ruined socket and blinked around at the chaos in the hall. 'Grimnir's balls,' he breathed. 'What hell is this?'

'The orcs,' said Felix dully. 'They have come back from the dead.'

'It's madness,' said Gorril. 'Nothing stops them. They're unkillable!'

'We'll see about that,' said Gotrek and drew his axe from under the table.

Hamnir snatched up the battered war horn of Karak Hirn and blew a rally call. Its pure tone was lost. It sounded like a braying donkey, but it was loud. The dwarfs turned at its call.

'Form up!' he cried. 'Captains rally your companies! Thanes call your dwarfs! Form up and face out!'

The horn and the order had an almost magical effect on the dwarfs. As Hamnir and Gotrek, Felix and Gorril leapt down from the high table and hurried across the feast hall to where the orcs were the thickest, clans and companies rallied around their leaders and formed into ranks, facing out from the centre of the hall in a rough square. Companies overturned tables to make barricades, and attacked and defended as one. Hamnir, Gotrek and the others joined Gorril's clanbrothers in the thick of the fighting. Felix found himself beside Galin, still red-faced drunk and cursing like an entire ship of sailors. Narin joined them shortly. He had a cut over one eye, and a ragged gash across the back of his knuckles. The dwarfs slashed unsteadily but unceasingly at the blank-eyed orcs.

It wasn't enough.

Though they had fallen into formation with an organisation so practiced that it was almost instinct, the dwarfs were still too drunk and exhausted to stand against an enemy that felt no pain and was slowed only by the most grievous wound. Hamnir's order had slowed the massacre, but not halted it. Not one of the orcs had fallen, and the dwarfs were dying in droves.

Gotrek cut an orc off at the knees. It crawled forwards on the stumps. The Slayer cursed and jumped back, slashing at its arms.

'We must fall back,' said Hamnir, hacking ineffectually at an eyeless orc. His voice was tight with suppressed panic. 'We cannot hold here!'

'Fall back to where?' asked Gorril. 'We left dead orcs all over the hold. If they're all like this, we've nowhere to run!'

'We could abandon the hold,' said Galin.

'No!' said Hamnir. 'That I will not do. Not after all we went through to win it.'

'What then?' asked Narin.

'The Diamondsmith clanhold!' Hamnir cried at last. 'Their door is still whole. We will retreat there until we can recover and decide what to do.'

'Aye,' said Gorril. 'Good.'

Hamnir stepped back from the front line and blew the war horn again. 'Fall back! Fall back!' he called. 'Pass the word. Retreat to the Diamondsmith hold! Through the kitchens to the stairs and up!'

The dwarf companies began to retire in orderly fashion, forcing a path through the shuffling orcs towards the high table and the door to the kitchens.

The legless orc caught Gotrek's ankle as he tried to follow Hamnir. The Slayer stumbled and nearly fell. He booted it in the face. 'Damned thing! Die!'

The orc shrugged off Gotrek's kick and snapped at his knees with its tusks. Gotrek cursed and decapitated it. It flopped to the ground, its limbs still at last.

'It stopped,' Gotrek said, goggling at it drunkenly.

'Look out!' Felix dragged Gotrek back as an orc axe missed his neck by an inch. Gotrek jerked away from Felix's hand and decapitated that orc too. It collapsed like an empty sack.

Hamnir laughed, still drunk himself. 'You've done it, Gurnisson! You've found the way.'

'Ha!' said Gotrek, indistinctly. 'Knew it all along.'

'The head!' called Hamnir, up and down the line. 'Cut off the head and the body dies! Pass the word!'

'Prince,' said Gorril eagerly. 'Call off the retreat! We can finish them!'

'No,' said Hamnir. 'We are too tired – too drunk. We will die trying. We must recover ourselves first.'

The journey to the intact hold was a nightmare. Even knowing how to stop them, the orcs were hard to kill, and more attacked the dwarfs' flanks at every cross corridor and open chamber, stumbling out of the dark in a grey-green tide. At last, with orcs hemming them in on every side, the dwarfs reached the great doors of the Diamondsmith clanhold.

Once again, Hamnir rapped the mine code with the butt of his axe and, once again, they waited, while the dwarfs held off the press of orcs as best they could.

'Curse them,' said Gorril after five minutes had passed and many brave dwarfs had fallen. 'Where are they?'

'No doubt they sleep soundly,' said Hamnir, 'bellies full and free from fear at last.' He rapped on the door again.

At last there was an answering tap and the doors swung slowly open. Hamnir called the companies back one at a time and they made an orderly retreat into the hold, until only he, Felix, Gotrek and Gorril stood with Gorril's clan brothers, fighting off a wall of unblinking, unrelenting orcs.

'Now! Back as one!' Hamnir cried. Then, 'The doors! Close the doors!'

The dwarfs backstepped quickly, ranks still neatly dressed, as the doors swung in. The orcs pushed forwards, trying to follow them, but the doors closed inexorably, crushing a handful of orcs to paste between them. Gotrek, Felix and Gorril's lads decapitated the few that got in, the doors were locked tight, and all was quiet.

Hamnir leaned against the wall, catching his breath, and then pushed himself wearily upright and turned to the dwarfs ranked up at the ready in the dim corridor – all that remained of the force that had rallied to help Hamnir retake Karak Hirn not three weeks ago. They were much reduced. The battles with the living orcs and the orcs reborn had more than halved their number.

'Well fought, cousins,' Hamnir said, between breaths. 'Now come, let us impose on the hospitality of our recently rescued brothers. We must rest before we can fight again.'

The dwarfs parted and turned about, allowing Hamnir, Gorril, Felix and Gotrek to lead them down the corridor to the hold's central chamber. Galin and Narin came with them, having grown used to travelling with Hamnir.

Felix started as they entered the huge hall. Thane Kirhaz, Birri, Ferga and the other survivors were ranked up like an army in the middle of the hall, staring at them as they entered. All, even the women, were armed, if only with fire tongs and rolling pins.

Hamnir squared his shoulders and saluted them, overcome at this display. 'This is very brave, cousins,' he said, 'coming to our aid when you are in such straits yourselves, but there is no need. We are safe for now, and once we have slept and recovered ourselves, we will deal with the menace in the hold.'

The survivors said nothing. Nor did they move – they only stood and stared, unblinking.

'Kirhaz?' said Hamnir uncertainly. 'Birri? Are you well? Have you room for us to take our rest?'

Kirhaz raised his crossbow. It trembled in his shrivelled hands. He fired – a weak shot. The bolt struck Hamnir in the shin.

'You threaten the Sleeper,' said Birri. 'You must die.'

CHAPTER TWENTY-TWO

HAMNIR CRIED OUT, as much in surprise as in pain, and nearly fell.

'Prince Hamnir!' Gorril caught Hamnir and held him upright.

Everyone gaped at the Diamondsmith dwarfs, stunned. Kirhaz dropped his crossbow with a clatter and drew his axe. He and Birri motioned the other survivors forwards. They shuffled ahead listlessly, raising their weapons.

'Thane Kirhaz, Birri, I don't understand,' said Hamnir, wincing as he put weight on his punctured leg. 'Why do you attack us? Who is the Sleeper?'

Kirhaz and Birri didn't answer. Their gaunt troops came on, staring fixedly at Hamnir and his beleaguered army. Gotrek growled wordlessly.

'Grimnir, what's the matter with them?' cried Hamnir.

'They… they are just like the orcs,' said Gorril. 'How can this be? How did we not notice before?'

Hamnir took a step back. The others did the same. The entire army edged away from the strange, silent dwarfs.

'Is the Sleeper what we sensed in the mine?' asked Felix uncertainly. 'Has it turned their minds with sorcery?'

'Impossible!' said Hamnir, as if trying to convince himself. 'Dwarfs laugh at sorcery. It doesn't affect us.' He called to Kirhaz, who was raising his axe. 'Thane Helmgard, please! Come to your senses. Birri, have you forgotten our friendship? Ferga, make them listen.'

Ferga walked beside her father, as implacable as the rest, a carving knife in her hand. She didn't respond.

Gotrek stared at the approaching dwarfs, his one eye dull and miserable. He put a hand on Hamnir's shoulder. 'They're tainted, scholar,' he said sadly. 'I don't think they can be saved.'

'What? What do you mean?'

'I mean,' Gotrek paused, before going on, his voice rough. 'We will have to kill them.'

'No!' said Hamnir, wild-eyed. 'No! We rescued them! We can't turn around and kill them now! I won't do it!'

'They mean to kill us,' said Gotrek.

'There must be a way!' Hamnir looked around desperately.

A few Diamondsmith dwarfs had reached his lines and were swinging pathetically at their cousins. Their blows were slow and weak. Hamnir's dwarfs parried them easily, some crying out to their attackers by name, begging them to stop. It would have been the work of an instant to cut them all down, but none of the dwarfs had the heart to do it, and instead blocked and held them off.

'The gemcutters' guild hall!' said Hamnir suddenly, pointing to an ornate doorway open on the left wall. 'We will trap them inside, and then descend into the mine and find what has caused this horrible change, this "Sleeper", and kill it! Then they will recover!'

Gotrek shook his head. 'You're fooling yourself, scholar. They're too far gone. Look at them.'

'How can you say that?' Hamnir cried, furious. 'How can you condemn them when there might still be hope?'

'Experience.'

'Damn your experience! I refuse to believe it is too late! Stay your hand. I will not kill my own kin.'

Gotrek growled in his throat, but did not attack.

Hamnir whispered to Gorril. 'Pass the word. Retreat into the guildhall, rearguard first. When they follow us in, we will lock the door behind them, and then exit out the rear door and trap them within.'

Gorril saluted and hurried to each company, murmuring to their commanders, as more and more of the shambling dwarfs closed with Hamnir's army, and the strange, one-sided battle intensified. The dwarfs were relieved not to have to attack their cousins, and obeyed Hamnir's orders eagerly. The companies closest to the guildhall door backed through it while those before them protected their retreat.

Birri, Kirhaz and Ferga angled towards Hamnir and his companions.

Birri raised his hand and pointed. 'Kill the prince. Kill the Slayer. It is the will of the Sleeper.'

The mindless dwarfs obeyed, turning and joining Kirhaz, Birri and Ferga as they slashed at Hamnir and Gotrek, while all along the line the rest attacked Hamnir's troops.

Kirhaz raised his axe at Hamnir. Gotrek knocked it out of his hands. Felix blocked and parried as three dwarfs attacked him. Individually, they were nothing. Together, coming after his drunken slumbers and the mad, breathless retreat from the undead orcs, they were almost more than he could handle. If he could have fought back, the combat would have been over in a second, but he was as reluctant as the dwarfs to slay those he had come to rescue.

Birri aimed a smash at Gotrek with a hammer. Gotrek blocked it easily and kicked at him. The engineer barely seemed to feel it and struck again. Gotrek parried and kicked harder, frustrated. Birri staggered back and tripped over one of his companions, landing hard on his shoulder. He was up again almost instantly. Felix caught a glint of gold around his neck, under his beard.

'Gotrek!' Felix called, pointing at Birri. 'He wears a torque.'

'What?' cried Hamnir, and almost took Ferga's knife in the face as he turned to look.

Gotrek caught Birri's hammer in a bind, and twisted, disarming him. 'Get it, manling. Get it off him.'

Felix started forwards, blocking to both sides, but Birri stumbled back behind the other survivors.

'Stop them!' he murmured. 'Kill them!'

The blank-eyed dwarfs turned to do his bidding, getting in Gotrek and Felix's way as he retreated.

It would have been easy to follow him if they had wished to cut down the dwarfs in the way, but getting through them without harming them was more difficult.

'He's the leader,' rasped Gotrek as he prodded the dwarfs back. 'Not Kirhaz.'

'After him, Gotrek,' said Hamnir. 'Take him, but don't kill him. Perhaps this malaise will lessen if you remove his torque.'

'Aye, scholar,' said Gotrek, pushing forwards another foot. 'Come on, manling.'

They broke through at last, just as Birri was disappearing into a hallway on the far side of the room.

Gotrek stole a glance back at Hamnir as they limped after the engineer. 'Too soft-hearted for his own good. Always has been.'

They entered the corridor. Birri was nowhere in sight. Gotrek cursed. They hurried down it as fast as they could, which wasn't very fast. Their wounds, and all the drinking and fighting they had done had taken their toll. They hissed and grunted with every step.

Felix hobbled down a side corridor and looked in an open door. Birri was not within. He tried a closed door. It was locked.

'Manling,' came Gotrek's voice. 'Back here. I hear him.'

Felix returned to the main corridor. Gotrek was starting down a stairwell. Felix followed. At the bottom was another corridor. They looked left and right.

'There.' Gotrek pointed to the left.

Felix peered down the dim corridor. Far in the distance, he could see a dark form shuffling away from them.

'Got more strength than the others,' he said.

'It's the collar,' said Gotrek.

They started after him. It was a very sad race. Birri might have been fitter than the rest of the Diamondsmith defenders, but not by much. He lurched and staggered like a sleepwalker. Unfortunately, Gotrek and Felix were hardly better. They gained on him steadily, following him through corridors and chambers, and down winding stairs, but it was slow going. Gotrek grunted with each step, his damaged leg as stiff as a board. Felix was so dizzy with drink and weariness that he had to keep one hand on the wall to steady himself.

They had almost caught up with the engineer when he ducked into a side passage and put on a burst of speed. They hurried to the corner in time to see him scuttle through a wide door, through which glowed a steady orange light.

Gotrek and Felix limped through the door after him and stopped dead. They were in an engineer's workshop, its high ceilings lost above a web of girders and gantries, pulleys and heavy chains. The walls were crowded with workbenches, kilns, forges and machines the purpose of which Felix couldn't even begin to fathom. Along the far wall, copper water tanks, steam engines and open cisterns were grouped around a large, grated drain in the floor.

The thing that had taken them aback sat in the centre of the room on a length of steel track. It had once been an undgrin mine cart. Now, it looked like nothing more than an enormous iron scarab, crouching on six spoked wheels. Curved iron plates covered it like a carapace, and the muzzles of swivel guns stuck out through slotted openings. A huge cannon hung above it on chains, waiting to be lowered into a revolving housing on its roof.

'Sigmar,' breathed Felix, 'it's some kind of steam tank! Like we saw in Nuln!'

'This "Sleeper" means to mount attacks from the Undgrin,' muttered Gotrek. 'With that at the head of an orc army...'

He trailed off as Birri appeared on top of the armoured cart and clambered forwards to an open turret. He grabbed the crank of a strange, multiple-barrelled gun, and swung it towards them.

Gotrek and Felix dived for cover as Birri wound the crank and the gun began spitting a stream of bullets. Felix slid behind a forge as the rain of lead kicked dust off the flagstones where he had stood. Gotrek crouched behind a small smelting furnace. The noise of the gun was deafening.

'You only delay the inevitable,' called Birri over the clatter. 'The Sleeper will not be denied.'

'I'll deny him to my last breath, betrayer,' said Gotrek, looking around at the room's equipment. 'Dwarfs are dead because you set new traps in the hangar corridor.'

'Defended the hold, as I have always done,' said Birri, firing over their heads.

'How did this happen, engineer?' shouted Felix. 'Where did you get the torque?'

'I...' For a moment Birri's calm confidence seemed to falter. 'I wanted to get out. To get help. Too many grobi at the main gate. Used our secret door and made for the hidden hangar door. Caught. Fought. Foolish. None can fight the Sleeper. The others died. I fell and was taken below. Still I fought, but at last… at last I accepted the gift. Brought to my brothers in the hold.' He fired again and his voice strengthened. 'Now I am invincible.'

'We'll see about that,' said Gotrek. He motioned to Felix and pointed to winches bolted into the floor near their hiding places. Felix examined them. The chains that held the cannon above the tank cart wound around them. Gotrek made a hacking gesture.

Felix nodded, but eyed the heavy chains uncertainly. Gotrek would sever his in one blow, but could he?

'Join us,' called Birri. 'Join us and you will be invincible too.'

'Invincible?' said Gotrek, barking a harsh laugh. 'You try to tempt a Slayer with that?'

He held up three fingers, two, and then one. Felix surged up and rolled to his winch, raising his sword. The gatling gun chattered to life. Felix swung down with all his might and the sword bit deep into a steel link, but didn't sever it. He cursed as he heard Gotrek's chain snap behind him. The stream of lead was spewing his way. He hacked again.

The chain parted. Felix dived to the side as bullets smashed into the winch. He rolled behind a massive kiln and looked up.

The huge cannon was swinging down on its two remaining chains like the clapper of some gigantic bell, loose chains flailing, but because Felix's cut had been late, it didn't swing straight. It swerved around Birri like one magnet repulsed by another.

'Ha!' the engineer cried. 'You see? Invincible!'

The cannon swung to the limit of its arc. With a sound like twin pistol shots, the last two chains snapped, and the cannon crashed down behind the tank cart, its butt-end smashing through the iron grate that covered the huge drain. The cannon dropped out of sight like a crossbow bolt dropped down the neck of a bottle. Its chains followed it, rattling violently through their pulleys and lashing like furious snakes.

The end of a chain whipped around Birri's neck and jerked him off the tank cart so quickly that it almost seemed as if he disappeared. Felix stood just in time to see the chain whir into the drain after the cannon, dragging Birri with it.

'Well struck, manling,' said Gotrek.

They limped across the room to the broken grate and looked down the hole. They could see nothing in its pitch-black depths.

'Where does it go?' asked Felix.

'Underground stream, likely,' said Gotrek, spitting into it. 'Hope he rots before he dies.'

'It wasn't his fault, surely,' said Felix. 'The thing took over his mind.'

'Then he was weak. A true dwarf would never have been corrupted.'

Felix raised an eyebrow. 'So all of the Diamond-smith clan were weak?'

Gotrek grunted angrily, and turned towards the door. 'Let's get back.'

WHEN THEY RETURNED to the clanhold's central chamber, nearly all of Hamnir's army had retreated into the gemcutter guildhall. The last few companies backed slowly towards the big door, entirely surrounded by the lost dwarfs.

Gotrek shook his head. 'Pointless,' he said, but started forward nonetheless.

He and Felix pushed through the crowd of frail dwarfs, disarming and knocking down as many as they could as they went, and then joined Hamnir, Gorril and the others on the front line.

'Where is Birri?' asked Hamnir, between parries.

'He fell down a hole,' said Gotrek.

'You killed him, Valaya curse you!' said Hamnir. 'I told you–'

'His inventions killed him,' said Gotrek. 'I never touched him.'

Hamnir gave him a suspicious look, but they had reached the door of the guildhall.

'We hold here,' he said, and then turned to Gorril. 'Have the others fall back to the far door and wait beyond it. You circle back here with some of your clan. When our poor cousins have followed us in, close the doors behind them.'

Gorril saluted and hurried to the other companies, who waited in the middle of the guildhall. Gotrek and Felix joined Hamnir's company in holding the lost dwarfs at the door. It was easy work – in one way, the easiest battle Felix had ever fought – in another, the most unsettling. He fended off the feeble attacks almost without thinking, but looking into the faces of the attacking dwarfs was heartbreaking. Traces of their individuality remained in their clothing and ornament – the way a miner braided his beard, the brooch a dwarf maid wore pinned to her dress, the scars and tattoos of a hard-bitten warrior – but it was gone from their eyes. All had the same blank, dull expression he had seen on the orcs' faces. All fought with the same mindless, passionless ferocity, dampened only by their long starvation.

What made it worse was that, just as had been the case with the orcs, the lost dwarfs would sometimes come to themselves. A brief flash of intelligence would light up their eyes and they would start back in dismay at what they were doing, but then, almost as soon as it had appeared, while Gorril's dwarfs were calling out joyfully at their recovery, the awareness died, the dullness clouded their eyes once more, and they would attack anew. Several dwarfs fell to this phenomenon, as they lowered their weapons and took an axe in the neck from a friend they thought had returned to them.

At last, all of Hamnir's army passed through the far door of the guildhall. Hamnir and the others stepped back from the door and let the flood of lost dwarfs spill in after them. The swarm spread out, trying to encircle the defenders, but they were slow, and Hamnir's company easily outpaced them. Indeed, Hamnir slowed somewhat so as to remain almost within reach and keep their attackers' attention upon them. Felix felt like an Estalian bull-dancer waving a red cape at a herd of somnambulant bulls.

When they reached the far door, much narrower than the main entrance, Gotrek waved the others through. 'The manling and I will hold this.'

Hamnir hesitated, perhaps afraid that Gotrek would change his mind and start butchering the dead-eyed dwarfs. Then he nodded and led the others out the door.

Gotrek refrained from slaughter, though he looked miserable about it. 'Delaying the inevitable,' he muttered. 'Only be worse when the time comes.'

He and Felix held the door until the last of the Diamondsmith dwarfs wandered through the guildhall's main entrance and Gorril's dwarfs closed the big doors behind them.

As they heard the bars fall into place, Gotrek and Felix jumped back from the bizarre melee. Hamnir slammed the small door in the faces of the Diamondsmith dwarfs and locked it. Then he leaned his forehead against it as they beat listlessly at it from the other side.

'We fought so hard to free them,' he said miserably, 'only to lock them in again.' He raised his head and looked at Gotrek. 'My thanks for your mercy.'

'It isn't mercy,' said Gotrek, disgusted. 'It's torture, for them and for you, and it's needless. They won't recover.' He shrugged. 'But they are your kin.'

SAFE, AT LEAST for the moment, with the orcs locked out, and the lost dwarfs locked in, Hamnir's beleaguered army slept. Felix was asleep as soon as he lay down, exhausted by the ceaseless fighting of the past day, but he was again troubled by unsettling dreams. These were the opposite of the last. Instead of murdering the others in their sleep, he was running through Karak Hirn alone, looking for Gotrek. Every dwarf he asked turned blank eyes on him and tried to kill him. Hamnir, Gorril, Narin, Galin, all shambled after him, arms outstretched, as he backed away, his heart pounding.

At last, he found Gotrek, sitting in the guardroom near the Horn Gate, his back to the door. Felix opened his mouth to call out to him, but hesitated, overwhelmed by the fear that if Gotrek turned around he too would stare at him with one vacant eye. He took a step further, reaching out a nervous hand towards Gotrek's shoulder. Gotrek's head lifted as he sensed Felix behind him. He began to turn. Felix shrunk back. He didn't want to see. He didn't want to know. He...

He woke up, his sleep-thick eyes peeling open, and looking around in the dim light of Diamondsmith's central chamber, where he and Gotrek and most of Hamnir's force had laid down the night before. Shouted questions and running feet echoed all over the clanhold.

Gotrek rolled over and raised his head. 'What now?' he muttered.

Felix sat up, groaning. All his muscles ached. His wounds throbbed. He felt as stiff as a week-old corpse, and half as lively.

Gorril's lieutenant, Urlo, was picking his way through the rows of waking dwarfs looking around. When he spotted Gotrek, he hurried to him, going down on one knee to whisper in his ear.

'Gorril asks that you come see him, Slayer. It is urgent.'

'Gorril asks?' said Gotrek. 'Something wrong with Hamnir?'

'Er,' Urlo looked around uneasily at the other dwarfs. 'Gorril will tell you.'

Gotrek grunted, his jaw clenching. 'All right.' He pushed himself up, hissing as he bent his wounded leg. He collected his axe. 'Come, manling.'

Felix nodded and got painfully to his feet. He and Gotrek followed Urlo out of the room. They could hardly walk.

'HAMNIR'S MISSING,' SAID Gorril.

They were in Kirhaz's private quarters, which Hamnir had taken as his billet. Gorril paced back and forth beside a heavy dining table where an untouched breakfast had been set. Urlo stood by the door.

'Missing?' asked Gotrek. 'Since when?'

Gorril spread his hands. 'He was gone when I went to wake him this morning. I have my company searching the hold top to bottom, but so far, nothing.'

'Any signs of an attack?' asked Gotrek.

'None. I…'

One of Gorril's dwarfs pushed into the room behind them. He had another dwarf with him.

'Gorril. Some news.' Gorril's dwarf urged the other forwards. 'Tell him, miner.'

The miner ducked his head to Gorril. He had a nasty lump over his left ear. 'Aye,' he said. 'Well, last night I was posted to watch the secret door that goes from Diamondhold's third gallery to the main hold grain stores.' He shrugged, embarrassed. 'I must have dozed a bit, because someone got up behind me and gave me a knock over the head that put me on the floor. I opened my eyes just in time to see a dwarf go through the secret door and close it behind him.'

'Did you see who it was?' asked Gorril.

The dwarf shook his head, and then regretted it. 'Just legs and feet,' he said, massaging his brow, 'and all a bit blurred.'

Gorril punched the table. 'When did this happen? Why didn't you tell someone immediately.'

The dwarf flushed. 'I meant to, captain, I did, but somehow in the middle of getting up off the floor I, well, I guess I fell asleep again.' He swayed where he stood. 'Could do with a bit of a nap now, actually.'

Gorril crossed to the dwarf and looked in his eyes. He frowned. 'Take him to the physic. He may have cracked his skull.' He gripped the dwarf on the shoulder. 'Thank you, cousin.'

Gorril turned to Gotrek and Felix as Gorril's dwarf led the other out. 'What does this mean? Was it Hamnir? Why would he go out alone into a hold full of grobi? Could someone have taken him? The guard only saw one dwarf, but there could have been more. Did we miss some of the lost dwarfs?' He stopped, his face pale. 'Grimnir! Have they taken him below? Is he in the mines with their "Sleeper"?'

Gotrek was looking at the floor, his fists clenched. 'Aye. That's my guess.'

Gorril cursed. 'Then there is no time to waste! We must go look for him!'

Gotrek shook his head. 'No, lad.' He tapped himself on the chest. '*I* go after him. You won't be coming.'

'And you'll stop me?' asked Gorril, eyes flaring. 'Hamnir was my cousin, and my best friend. I can't stay here while I know he might be–'

'Do you want to leave Karak Hirn leaderless again?' asked Gotrek, cutting him off. 'You're all that's left.'

'There is you,' said Gorril. 'Why don't you lead them? I no longer...'

'I'm no leader,' Gotrek said. 'I'm a Slayer, and there is something in the mine that needs slaying. You are a leader, so lead. The hold must be cleared of the risen grobi and guarded until King Alrik returns.'

'You mean until Prince Hamnir is found,' corrected Urlo.

Gotrek's face tightened. 'Aye, or that.'

'You don't think you'll find him?' asked Gorril, his eyes troubled.

'I'll find him,' said Gotrek, 'or die trying, but alive? In his own mind?'

'Grimnir!' Gorril swore. 'What turned your heart so black, Slayer? Must you snuff out every spark of hope before it has a chance to kindle?'

'Hope lies,' said Gotrek, stepping to the door. 'Only a fool listens. Now go tell your troops that Hamnir is missing and ready your attack on the grobi. We'll go out when you do.'

Gorril glared at him, and then sighed. 'Very well, we will go in an hour.'

Gotrek nodded, and he and Felix stepped out of the door.

'Slayer,' called Gorril.

Gotrek stopped and looked back.

'If you have no hope, why do you go on?' Gorril asked. 'Why slay monsters at all?'

Gotrek's eye grew hard. 'Because there is one thing anyone may hope for that will eventually be granted them.'

'And what's that?' asked Gorril.

'Death.'

He turned and walked down the hall.

Felix followed. 'Especially if he follows a Slayer,' he muttered.

'What was that, manling?' asked Gotrek.

'Nothing. Nothing.'

CHAPTER TWENTY-THREE

HAMNIR'S ARMY WAS grim and silent as it waited inside the Diamondsmith hold's main door for Gorril to arrive and the sortie to begin. The news of Hamnir's disappearance, on top of the horror and pain of discovering the Diamondsmith clan's empty madness, had hit them hard. They were more determined than ever to take back the hold and rid it of the dread taint that infected it, but it would not be a joyous victory. There would be no repetition of the previous night's drunken celebration.

Gotrek and Felix waited at the front of the column. They were to help with the initial break out, and then split off on their quest to the mines once all the dwarfs had left. Gotrek was as dour as the rest. His eye was on the floor and he muttered angrily to himself. Felix wondered what, besides the obvious, was troubling him, but didn't like to intrude. It wasn't polite, and with Gotrek, it wasn't safe.

Narin and Galin pushed through the troops and stopped beside Gotrek. He didn't acknowledge them.

'I'm coming with you, Slayer,' said Narin at last.

'And I,' said Galin.

'No,' Gotrek grunted, apparently annoyed at being disturbed. 'This is Slayer's work.'

'And if you remember,' said Narin, touching the sliver of the Shield of Drutti in his beard, 'we both have a vested interest in making sure that you are not slain while doing it.'

Gotrek raised his head and turned a baleful eye upon him. 'You would rob me of my doom?'

'Will you use your doom to cheat us of our grudge fights?' puffed Galin. 'You cannot die until you face us. The honour of our clans demands it.'

Gotrek snorted. 'I put aside my Slayer's vow until now because of the oath I made to Hamnir long before I took the crest. Now, I might satisfy both oaths at once. A petty squabble over a shield comes a distant third.'

'A petty squabble!' cried Galin. 'He insults us anew!'

'You won't dissuade us, Gurnisson,' said Narin.

Gotrek glared at them, then shrugged and turned away. 'Do what you will. Just don't get in my way.'

The ranks of dwarfs parted and Gorril marched up the column with Urlo and his company to take their place at its head. Gorril turned and faced the dwarfs. 'I've no speech for you, cousins. Remember that they can only be stopped by taking their heads. Fight well. Die well. May Grimnir protect us.'

The companies muttered a short prayer in unison and Gorril signalled the wounded dwarfs who stood at either side of the door. 'Lock it behind us,' he told them, 'and be sure that we are still ourselves before you open it again.'

The dwarfs nodded and pulled the levers that unlocked and opened the doors. They swung slowly in. The undead orcs were still there, waiting, as patient as the grave, and as fragrant. They stumped silently forwards, their weapons raised, the stench of their decay rolling in before them like a fog.

The dwarfs were ready this time. They were rested. They knew what to do. They cut through the orcs outside the door like a hammer through sea foam. Teams of dwarfs worked in tandem, one knocking an undead orc to its knees, the other lopping its head off. The orcs did not bleed.

Gotrek and Felix blocked their ungainly attacks with ease, disarming them – sometimes literally – and separating heads from shoulders left and right. Narin and Galin did the same at their sides.

No matter how many the dwarfs cut down, the mob of walking corpses seemed not to shrink. They filled the broad corridor in both directions. The dwarfs pushed slowly but steadily into them, winning every inch with a decapitation, until all the companies were in the corridor, and the door to the Diamondsmith hold closed behind them.

'Right,' said Gotrek to Gorril. 'You're out. We're off.'

'Good luck to you, Slayer,' said Gorril. 'Bring Prince Hamnir back alive.'

'If I come back, he comes back,' said Gotrek. He looked to Felix. 'Which way, longshanks?'

Felix craned his neck to see over the horde of greenskins. 'Stairs to our left are closest.'

'Right.'

Without another word, Gotrek started hacking a path through the orcs. Felix, Narin and Galin followed in his wake, guarding his back and taking a few heads of their own as they went. After five minutes of the strange, bloodless slaughter, they reached the stairs and the edge of the orc mob. A few orcs followed them down to the grand concourse, but they were so slow that the four quickly left them behind.

Gotrek led them through the hold to King Alrik's chambers. The mineheads were locked tight, and the orcs inside were probably trying to break through them, but with luck, the hole from the vault to the kruk had not yet been discovered, 'with luck'. Felix laughed at that. Their luck had been terrible so far. Relying on it now seemed like madness. Still, it was the best of the bad choices available.

They met no resistance. The hold was deserted. The orcs had all converged on the Diamondsmith hall in order to fight the last of the dwarfs. King Alrik's quarters were as they had left them, minus the goblin bodies, which had apparently risen from the dead and left to fight. They passed through the makeshift tannery into Alrik's bedchamber, covering their noses against the reek of the piles of rotting garbage, and stepped across to the fat pillar on the far side.

'On your guard,' said Gotrek.

Felix, Narin and Galin readied their weapons as Gotrek felt around on the filigreed border beside the pillar. He found the catch at last, pressed it, and the column screwed down into the floor. There were no orcs behind it.

Felix let out a breath.

They descended down the winding, railless stair into King Alrik's vertical vault. At the bottom, Gotrek crossed resolutely to the ragged hole in the wall, but Narin and Galin had a hard time passing all the vault's treasures without slowing. Their eyes lingered longingly on the beautiful axes and suits of armour, and the casket full of blood gold.

'Surely we deserve some reward for our selfless service,' said Galin, licking his lips.

'Aye,' said Narin. 'What's an ounce of gold lost when we've won his hold back for him?'

'You want your reward before you've finished the job?' growled Gotrek.

Galin shrugged sheepishly. 'Only a joke, Slayer.'

'Aye,' said Narin, pulling his eyes reluctantly away. 'Only a joke.'

They followed Gotrek through the hole, and along the rough passage they had cut so laboriously only a day before, and so into the kruk. There was no sign in the abandoned mine that the orcs had yet discovered their diggings, and they hurried through them until they reached the door that led to the mines proper.

Gotrek turned to them. 'Pointless killing grobi until we find what's behind them, so keep quiet.'

'But how will we find it?' asked Galin. 'It could be anywhere.'

Gotrek held up his axe. The runes on its head glowed faintly. 'They burn brighter the deeper we descend. It'll lead us.'

He opened the door and they stepped into the Karak Hirn mines. They saw few greenskins as they trekked through corridors and down shafts, many fewer than they had seen on their way up from the Undgrin, but it surprised Felix that they saw any at all. He had expected that they would all be up battering at the minehead doors, trying to get back into the hold, but in every forge and foundry they passed, at every work-face and tailings pit, orcs and goblins still toiled, making weapons, machinery and armour.

It chilled Felix to think of it. How many orcs were employed here that some could still be spared from attacking the doors to continue working? And what supreme confidence must the mind behind this enter-prise have to carry on with the day-to-day work as if the retaking of Karak Hirn was a certainty? But then, any mind that could bend the will of a hold full of dwarfs and turn them against their brothers had every reason to be confident. Could such a thing, whatever it was, be defeated? If it could direct the actions of an army of orcs and dwarfs, what could it do if it turned all its power upon a single man or dwarf?

Felix's mind turned more and more often to this hopeless line of reasoning the deeper they went into the mine. Each level down, his mood got blacker and his conviction that there was no way they could win the coming battle got stronger. The knowledge that this gloom was undoubtedly artificial – an invasion of his consciousness by the thing they sought – did not ease his mind. In fact, it reinforced his fears that the thing was unbeatable. Its ability to twist his mind and make him feel hopeless was proof that there was indeed no hope of beating it. He chuckled bleakly to himself. If the rune axe wasn't already showing them the way, they could certainly have used his mood for a guide. The blacker it was, the closer they must be.

When he cut his own throat they would know they were at the source.

Though they said nothing aloud, Felix could tell that the dwarfs were affected by the thing's presence as well. They twitched and shook their heads as if beset by mosquitoes, and he could hear them muttering under their breath. Galin occasionally moaned and put his hand over his eyes. Even Gotrek was touched by the malaise, though he showed it by cursing in furious whispers and rolling his shoulders as if trying to shrug off a yoke.

Ten deeps down, three levels below the entrance to the Undgrin, the corridors grew narrower and the side passages fewer. This was the newest area of the mine, many of the tunnels were only tentative feelers pushed through the rock, looking for fresh seams of ore, and had not yet been heavily worked or expanded. The rune on Gotrek's axe glowed so brightly that they no longer needed lamps to see by, and the feeling of dread in Felix's heart pressed down on him like a giant hand, nearly paralysing him. He felt as if his bones had turned to lead. It was a supreme act of will just to put one foot in front of the other.

As they made their way down a cramped corridor, Gotrek paused. There was a light ahead – torch-glow coming from an opening in the left-hand wall. Sounds of movement came from it as well.

'Back and find another way?' whispered Narin.

'Hide until they're gone?' suggested Galin.

Felix blinked at the dwarfs. He had never seen such fear in their kind before. Of course, he felt the same, but he was only human.

Gotrek spat, disgusted. 'Go back if you want,' he said. 'There is no other way.' He held up his axe. 'What we seek is beyond here, and I saw no other branches.'

'Still,' said Galin, chewing his moustache, 'it might be wise to check. Look around a bit.'

Gotrek shrugged. 'It'll only be a few grobi.'

'But, they could kill us,' said Narin. He was shaking.

Gotrek looked around at him, disgusted. 'You're afraid of orcs now?'

'I... No,' said Narin. He shook his head violently. 'No. What's gotten into me? Of course not.'

'I know what's gotten into us,' said Galin, quavering. 'It's the Sleeper. It knows we're coming. It's making us afraid. It can read our minds. It's hopeless. It's–'

Gotrek flattened him with a left hook. 'Pull yourself together, Stonemonger. Whatever it is, if it lives and breathes, it can fall to an axe.'

Galin sat up slowly, rubbing his jaw through his beard. 'I'm sorry, Slayer. It's... it's hard to keep it out.'

'I told you not to come. Now fight it or go back and leave me be.' Gotrek turned and eased towards the torch-lit opening. The others inched along behind him, weapons at the ready. Felix's legs were shaking so much it was hard to walk. He knew it was the Sleeper making him afraid, but that didn't make the fear any easier to dispel, or his heart pound any less.

Gotrek pressed against the wall and leaned forwards to peek into the opening, the light of his rune axe hidden under his arm. He frowned, watching through the door for a long moment, before stepping silently past it and motioning the others to follow.

The other dwarfs were similarly transfixed as they passed the door. Felix came last, and he looked in with a mixture of curiosity and dread, his mind imagining all sorts of horror and filth. Instead, what he saw was a handful of orcs at the far end of a long, low chamber, assembling a wooden crate around a ridged, resinous sack the size of a hogshead of ale. Beneath a sheen of mucus, it had the texture and translucent lustre of insect wings. Through it, Felix could half see something pale and half-formed curled inside. There were at least twenty assembled crates set along the walls of the room, and enough unbuilt to hold twenty more of the glistening sacks.

The dwarfs whispered together a safe distance down the corridor.

'Dozens of them!' Narin was saying. 'Dozens!'

'But... but what are they?' asked Galin. 'And what birthed them?'

Gotrek turned down the dark corridor. 'We'll know in a minute.' He started forwards.

Only a hundred feet further along, they came to a crude side tunnel dug in the right wall. It slanted down at a sharp angle into the earth.

Gotrek's axe blazed like a torch as he stood on the tunnel's threshold. 'This is it,' he said.

He marched into it. Felix tried to follow, but found that he could not. A wave of fear and despair stronger than any that had previously washed over him turned his legs to lead. His little joke about cutting his throat was suddenly no joke. He was so frightened, and so certain that whatever was at the end of the tunnel would not only kill him but turn him into a mindless monster that would turn on his friends and spread the Sleeper's influence far and wide, that he wanted to push his dagger through his neck just to make an end of his misery and save the world. He wanted to tear his eyes out so that he wouldn't have to see it, but his hands were shaking too hard. Narin and Galin were similarly paralysed.

Gotrek looked back at them. 'What now?'

'Don't you feel it, Slayer?' asked Narin, his teeth chattering. 'Are you made of stone?'

'I feel it,' said Gotrek, 'but the worst that can happen is that we die, and that's been true since we left Rodenheim.'

'Death is not the worst,' choked Galin. 'It will take us. It will make us like the Diamondsmith clan. It will turn us against our own kind.'

'It will, if you just stand there and quake,' said Gotrek. 'Stop thinking and start walking. That's the only way.'

He turned and started down the tunnel again, and whether it was Gotrek's words, or the mere fact that listening had freed him momentarily from the bottomless spiral of his imaginings, Felix found that he was able to move again. Narin and Galin too started after the Slayer, following the tunnel deeper into the earth, straight as an arrow.

'This is orc work,' muttered Narin, 'but orcs never dug anything this straight.'

A hundred yards down, the tunnel stopped at a wall of polished basalt blocks, mirror smooth, and so well set that it was almost impossible to see the joins between them. A wide, low door, narrower at the top than the bottom, opened into a pitch-black chamber, a border of strange symbols all around it.

'This is old,' said Galin, caught between wonder and horror, 'older than dwarf-kind. What made this?'

'Not dwarf, nor man, nor elf,' said Narin. 'That's certain.' He pointed at the symbols. 'Are those wards meant to keep something out, or something in? Is this a temple, or a tomb?'

'Whatever it is,' said Gotrek, 'it should have stayed buried.' He stepped through the black door.

CHAPTER TWENTY-FOUR

FELIX, GALIN AND Narin followed Gotrek into the buried basalt structure. Felix had to duck under the low lintel. The red light of the rune axe reflected darkly from the glossy black walls, revealing a large octagonal room with more of the low trapezoidal doorways leading off into darkness. Felix shuddered. There was a feeling of unfathomable age about the place that reminded him of the tunnels of the Old Ones that he and Gotrek had almost lost themselves in during their travels with Teclis. It made him feel very young and small and insignificant.

Something about the scale of the doors made him realise that the place had not been built for anything that walked on two legs. For a moment, he tried to imagine what it might have been, but then he stopped himself. Following that line of speculation would send him screaming up the tunnel again.

It was almost comforting to see signs of orcish occupation in this alien place. Orcs might be horrible viscous monsters, but they were *familiar* horrible, viscous monsters. Long planks had been laid over a wide circular hole in the centre of the room to make a bridge, and a trail of dust, pebbles and orc footprints crossed from the door that Felix and the dwarfs had entered to another in the far wall. The place had the familiar stink of orc to it too – a harsh animal stench, mixed with the reek of death and rotting garbage.

'How did the orcs know this was here?' asked Felix, staring around. 'How did they find it?'

'They didn't,' said Gotrek. 'It called them.'

'Gurnisson,' said Narin. 'Hide your axe a moment. I think I see light.'

Gotrek tucked the head of his axe under his arm, blocking the glow of the rune and plunging the room into darkness. As his eyes got used to the dark, Felix saw a pale green phosphorescence coming from the far door, so dim that it was hard to be sure whether it was really there. Then something blocked it. Huge shadows hunched rapidly towards them along the hall.

'Something's coming!' said Galin.

Gotrek unshielded his axe as Felix, Narin and Galin went on guard. Out of the far door ducked six huge mutated orcs, each the size of the warboss they had faced in the grand concourse, their black faceted eyes glittering red in the rune-glow. A choking rotten egg smell wafted from them like a cloud.

Felix and the dwarfs gagged and covered their mouths as the orcs spread out, moving to encircle them and hefting their weapons.

'Grungni!' said Narin. 'These aren't orcs any more. They've become something else.'

'Mutants,' spat Galin. 'Tainted by Chaos.'

It was true. The mutations that had twisted the war-boss were fully realised in the hideous creatures that faced them now. Where the warboss had been pale, these were dead-fish white and glistened with a sticky sheen. Where he had been covered in lumps and tumors, these sported translucent barbs and horns growing from their skulls and shoulders like milky icicles. One had a ring of tiny tentacles sprouting from the centre of its chest around a suppurating stoma. Their arms were long and distorted, reaching almost to the ground, and their forearms were crusted over with spined glassine carapaces, like the shells of albino cave crabs. Gold and onyx glinted at their necks.

Gotrek ran his thumb along the blade of his axe, drawing blood. He grinned. 'Now *this* will be a fight.'

'It'll be a slaughter!' moaned Galin. 'They have torques. All of them have torques. They're all invincible. This is the end.'

'Shut up,' said Gotrek angrily. 'We take them off is all.'

'And cut their heads off,' said Narin, grimly, 'to make sure they don't attack again after they're dead.'

'Manling, with me,' said Gotrek. 'Take the collars and I'll kill them. Galin, do the same for Narin. Go!'

Gotrek and Felix ran at the orcs to their left, while Narin and Galin ran to the right, but it was impossible. The orcs seemed to know instantly what they intended, and when Felix tried to edge around the first, the others attacked him and not Gotrek. He had to skip like a schoolgirl to avoid getting gutted. Gotrek got in the orcs' way and held them off, but they were immensely strong as well as untouchable, and forced him back.

Galin and Narin were having the same trouble. They fell back before the other three orcs, dodging and parrying madly, then ducked aside and ran for the other side of the room. The orcs followed.

'Not working, Gurnisson!' called Narin.

Felix returned to Gotrek's side, slashing around him with all his might, though he knew it was pointless. His sword skimmed off the orcs' slimy white flesh as if it was stone.

'Try again,' grunted Gotrek as he bashed at the orcs.

Felix nodded and made to circle behind the orcs, but they were on him again in an instant. He fell back. On the far side of the covered hole, Galin and Narin were trying to avoid being cornered.

Felix looked at the hole again, and the boards that covered it. 'The hole!' he cried.

'What?' said Gotrek.

Felix broke away and ran to the hole. He dropped his sword and started heaving aside the planks. A wave of death reek rushed up at him like a punch in the nose. Under the planks, the hole dropped straight down for about ten feet. Sigmar only knew what its original purpose had been, but it was a grave now. Heaped at the bottom were a score of orc corpses, so old and rotten that their skeletons were showing through their putrefying flesh.

Felix cursed. He'd hoped it was some sort of well. The orcs would climb out of this in an instant.

'Watch out, manling!'

Felix rolled aside instinctively as an orc cleaver slashed down at him. It splintered the plank he had been about to lift. The orc swung at him again. Felix dived low and rolled past it, snatching up his sword as he came to his feet.

'Good thinking,' said Gotrek, backing away from the other two. 'Narinsson! Olifsson! Clear the boards!'

'No. Won't work,' gasped Felix, ducking another swipe. 'Not deep enough. They'll climb out. Unless...' An idea came to him. He leapt back to Gotrek and snatched the unlit lantern from his belt. Then he dodged around the orcs to the hole again and smashed it on the rim. The glass reservoir inside the tin case shattered and oil leaked out. Felix shook it along the edge of the hole until the orc lunged after him. He threw the lantern in its face and squirmed past it, barely deflecting an overhand bash.

The orc turned for another attack, slipped on the oil, recovered and came after him. Felix backed away from it, smashing his own lantern as he had Gotrek's, and sprinkled another stretch of the lip with oil. The orc's axe smashed black splinters out of the basalt floor an inch from his foot. He jumped away again.

As the orc lumbered after him, Felix marvelled at how clear his head was. The Slayer had been right. Once the fighting had started, his fear had fallen away. It wasn't gone, coils of dread still slithered in Felix's stomach, but it wasn't all-consuming now. He could think. He could act. He didn't want to give up. He didn't want to die.

On the far side, Narin and Galin were trying to obey Gotrek's order and pull up the planks, but with three orcs chasing them, they weren't having much luck. They were too busy dodging axes to grab the boards.

Gotrek backed towards the hole, luring his two orcs forwards. At the edge, he feinted left, sending one lurching to the side to try to block him, and then veered back and chopped at the other's midsection.

The orc took the blade of the rune axe on its exposed white flesh with no more than a grunt, and stepped in to swing its ponderous axe at Gotrek's head. The Slayer surged forwards under the slash, ramming his shoulder into the orc's gut and pressing up at it with the haft of his axe, held in both hands like a staff.

Propelled by Gotrek's lift and its own forward motion, the orc went up and over the Slayer's back, and came down with a smash on the remaining boards. They snapped like dry twigs under its enormous weight and it fell into the hole, landing on the mounds of its rotting kin.

Gotrek's second orc charged him, mace raised. Gotrek rolled left, out of the way. The mutated greenskin tried to stop and turn, but he slipped on the spilled oil and skidded into the hole, landing on top of the first.

Galin and Narin ran past Gotrek along the edge of the hole with their three hulking pursuers hot on their heels. The dwarfs deftly avoided the drips of oil, but the lead orc was not so nimble. It crashed down on its back, right arm and leg hanging over the edge of the hole. Felix, backing away from his orc, saw the opportunity. He ran and kicked the orc in the side. It slid into the hole, scrambling with its transparent claws at the slippery edge, before dropping over the side.

Felix spun and ducked a bash from his orc's cleaver and found himself back to back with Gotrek, Galin and Narin. The three remaining orcs surrounded them. Behind them, corpse-white hands were reaching up and pawing at the rim of the hole, trying to gain purchase on the slippery basalt.

'Evened the odds,' said Gotrek, approvingly. 'Now, you three kill one, while I hold the other two.'

'You can hold two?' asked Narin.

'Depends how quick you kill the one,' said Gotrek. 'Go!'

Suddenly the Slayer became a whirlwind of flashing steel, the red glow of the rune axe leaving curving comet trails inscribed on Felix's retina as he pushed two of the orcs back with simple brute ferocity.

Felix, Narin and Galin attacked the third orc, doing their best to emulate Gotrek's ceaseless assault. Felix dodged behind its back and reached for its torque. It jerked away and slashed at him. Felix danced back, a hair ahead of its axe, and Narin made a grab for the torque from the other side. It spun back as Narin ducked. The axe cut a horn off Narin's helmet. The fight reminded Felix suddenly of some children's game, a deadly version of tag or keep-away.

He lunged in again, and this time got his fingers around the gold circlet. He pulled, but it was tight, cutting deeply into the orc's slimy, cable-muscled neck. The brute twisted around and caught Felix on the side of the head with his carapaced forearm. White sparks exploded behind Felix's eyelids and he crashed to the ground, but the torque came with him as he fell.

He dimly saw the orc raise its cleaver over him for the death stroke. Then it grunted and dropped to its knees, thick, clear blood gushing from its mouth as galin chopped through its spine. Felix flinched and stuck his sword up as the orc pitched forwards on top of him. The point sank into its white gut up to the hilt.

Narin rolled the corpse off Felix, and Galin severed its neck. Felix stood unsteadily and tugged his sword free. The side of his head was running with blood. The world seemed tilted. He tossed the torque aside.

'Well done, manling,' said Narin.

'Only five more to go,' grinned Galin.

'Hurry, you jackdaws!' shouted Gotrek. The two orcs had the Slayer pressed against the wall, and he was blocking and dodging for all he was worth.

Narin, Galin and Felix ran to help. As they passed the hole, one of the fallen orcs hooked its axe over the lip of the hole and another started climbing its back.

'Grimnir!' cursed Galin. 'They're coming out!'

'Go on,' said Felix. 'I have this.'

He grinned. This was not to be missed. As Narin and Galin ran on, he stepped to the edge of the hole and reached out over the climbing orc's head for its torque. The brute snapped at him. Felix jerked his hand back, and tried again.

This time he got it, and ripped it from the orc's filthy neck. 'Ha!' he cried, tossing it aside and drawing back his sword to chop its head off.

The orc threw out its unnaturally long arm and caught Felix's ankle, yanking it. Felix slammed flat on his back, his sword bouncing away with a clang. The orc got its other hand up and tried to lever itself out of the hole, but its palm slipped on the oil and it started sliding slowly back, dragging Felix with it. Felix threw his free leg out and tried to dig in with his heel, but the oil was underfoot. He couldn't get purchase. The orc was pulling him inexorably towards the blade of the axe that the first orc had hooked in the lip of the hole. The blade was going to cut him in two from balls to brains.

Felix flailed for his sword. He couldn't reach it. 'Gotrek!'

The dwarfs were too busy with the other orcs. They didn't hear him.

'Gotrek!'

Gotrek looked around. His eye blazed. 'Curse you, manling! How do you get into...'

He broke away from the fight and ran to the hole. His two opponents charged after him, shouldering Narin and Galin to the floor as if they were children. They seemed to understand that the Slayer was their greatest threat.

The climbing orc was backsliding quickly, its transparent nails scraping across the oily stone like shards of glass. Felix slid with it, his crotch inches away from being bifurcated by the razor-sharp axe.

Gotrek slammed his blade down on the climbing orc's wrist, and then dodged aside, inches ahead of his pursuers. Felix's orc fell back into the hole, stump spurting clear blood, and Felix crabbed back from the axe blade, the severed white hand still gripping his ankle. Near the wall, Narin and Galin were getting to their feet.

Gotrek spun to face his attackers, batting aside one slash and dodging another. They hammered at him unceasingly, pushing him back towards the hole.

As Felix snatched up his sword, he saw the orc who had hooked its axe in the rim of the hole trying to climb its haft. Felix kicked the axe-head on the flat.

It screeched across the floor, cutting a white line in the basalt, and dropped off the edge. The orc tumbled back onto its mates.

Felix stood as Narin and Galin ran to help Gotrek. Narin bashed the left orc on the spine. Galin ran straight up the back of the one on the right and grabbed its torque with his thick fingers. The orc spun, hacking at him. Galin flew off and crashed to the floor, his head bouncing off the stone flagstones with a hollow thud. The gold band flew from his limp hand and skittered across the floor.

The orc clapped a hand to his bare neck, grunting. Gotrek swung for its face. It grabbed his arm, but not quickly enough. The axe blade imbedded itself between its eyes. With a gurgling sigh, it toppled backwards into the hole, still clutching Gotrek's arm. The Slayer and the orc crashed down on the mound of rotting bodies as the orcs in the pit leapt aside.

'Gotrek!' Felix cried.

But he had his own problems. The second orc was after him, swiping mightily with its maul. With its elongated arms, its reach was incredible. Narin harried it from the rear, but it still had its torque, and his blows did nothing. Galin lay behind them, blood streaming from the back of his head, struggling to regain control of his limbs. Sounds of furious fighting came from the hole.

'Get behind it, Jaeger,' said Narin. 'I can't reach its neck.'

'Easier said than done.' Felix ducked under a wild swing and tried to slip to the orc's rear, but it turned with him.

Narin joined him in front of the orc. 'I'll hold him. Move.'

Felix slipped left again. The orc turned, but Narin hooked its knee with his axe, slowing it. The orc turned back and swung at Narin to dislodge him, and Felix got behind it. Narin skipped back, laughing, as the maul ruffled his blond beard.

'Come on you unnatural brute!' he jeered. 'Can't you see with those eyes?'

Felix leapt on the orc's back, his sword arm around its throat, and grabbed the torque.

The orc bucked, trying to throw him off. Felix held on, his legs flopping and banging, and pulled again. The torque came free.

'Ha!' Narin ran in, axe high, and chopped into the orc's chest, shattering its ribs.

The orc roared and spasmed, as if it had regained its orcish fury in the moment of death. It swung its maul and hit Narin's chest with a sound like a melon popping. The dwarf and the orc collapsed to the floor as one, their blood mingling.

'Narin!' cried Galin. The engineer was sitting up, a lump like a bleeding plum on the back of his head.

Felix fought back nausea and sadness as he blinked at the red ruin of Narin's chest. There was no time to mourn. Gotrek was still in the hole. He ran to the lip, skidding to a stop just short of the spill of oil, and looked down.

The orc with the severed hand was dead. Gotrek fought the other two on the mound of rotting corpses, which moved and shifted with their every step. The Slayer was bleeding and battered. The orcs didn't have a scratch on them.

Galin joined Felix at the edge. He looked unsteadily back at Narin. 'Poor lad,' he said. 'Died well, for an Ironskin.'

Gotrek dodged behind an orc, putting it in the way of the other. They stumbled around on the uncertain footing, trying to close with him again. It looked as if they had been performing this dance for a while. Gotrek staggered and nearly caught an axe between the eyes. 'Get their torques!' he rasped over the din of steel.

Felix nodded. Yes, get the torques, but how? Jumping into the pit was not an option. There was barely enough room for Gotrek and the orcs, and if he tried to lean in over the oily edge and grab one, he'd fall in. He needed... 'The planks! Galin! A plank! Help me!'

Felix stepped to one of the planks he had heaved aside earlier and took up one end as Galin took the other. They laid it across the hole.

'Hold it steady,' said Felix as he stepped out over the hole.

Galin nodded and sat on one end. Felix carefully lowered himself to his chest on the narrow board, and slid out along it. The orcs fought right below him, but didn't look up. They were too intent on killing Gotrek. Felix reached down a hand towards one. His fingers brushed the torque, but he couldn't grasp it. He strained further. The orc lunged at Gotrek and circled away, taking the torque out of his reach. Felix cursed silently. It was like trying to pluck a brass ring off the horn of a rampaging bull.

The other orc moved under him, angling for Gotrek's flank. Felix strained down again. The orc dodged back and forth as it tried to corner the Slayer. Felix edged his chest off the board for a better reach. The orc backed up – right into Felix's hand. He grabbed the torque. The orc jerked forwards, turning to see who was behind it, and the torque came free.

Gotrek struck too fast to see. One moment the orc was looking blankly up at Felix; the next, its head was flying from its shoulders. It collapsed like a ruined tower.

The other orc also struck quickly, swinging at Gotrek's back in the same instant that the Slayer cut down its comrade. Gotrek dived to the side and the cleaver cut a ragged slice through the meat of his left shoulder. He slammed into the wall and fell among the corpses.

The orc spun to finish him off, raising his axe over his head, right at Felix! Felix yelped and pushed himself up. The axe missed his nose by inches, but smashed through the plank, splitting it in two. The two ends tipped into the hole and Felix went down with them, crashing on top of the orc. He clutched at its arm, as much to save himself from falling as to stop its swing.

The orc hardly wavered. Felix, dangling from the slimy bicep of its axe arm, stared in terror at the greenskin's white, horned face. It was like clinging to a greased statue.

Gotrek lurched up from the mound of corpses. His left arm was red to the wrist. He started unsteadily across the shifting, stinking ground. 'That's it, manling! Hold it.'

Felix laughed mirthlessly. Hold it?

The orc plucked him off like a man picking lint from his sleeve, and held him up by the throat. Felix kicked and fought, choking as the massive fingers tightened around his windpipe. He slashed with his sword at the orc's face. The blow glanced off harmlessly. The orc didn't even flinch. It drew back its axe to cut Felix in half. Gotrek fell as he put his foot through a rotten ribcage and slipped on putrid organs. He wasn't going to make it in time.

'Hoy! Arsebreath!' Galin launched himself from the rim of the hole and caught the orc's axe arm in a bear hug. The orc stumbled, its weapon drooping.

'Come on, Slayer!' roared Galin.

The orc shook its arm, trying to dislodge the dwarf. He held fast.

Gotrek was getting to his feet.

Felix slashed at the orc's head again, the world dimming around him, the torque winking tauntingly at him, only a sword's length away. A sword's length?

As the orc slammed Galin against the wall, Felix stabbed at its neck with his sword. Its point slid across the slick white skin as if it was marble, and wedged under the torque.

The orc bashed Galin into the wall again. Blood flew from the dwarf's mouth. Felix pushed his blade under the torque and twisted. Another bash and Galin dropped, stunned. The torque wasn't coming free. The orc swung its axe at Felix. There was no escape.

'No you don't!'

Sparks flew as a red and silver streak flashed in the way of the orc's strike. The cleaver skimmed an inch over Felix's head. Gotrek!

The orc grunted and raised Felix up as he swung at Gotrek. Through the roaring in his ears, Felix heard a jingle of metal rattling against metal.

Gotrek kicked the orc between the legs. Fool, thought Felix dimly. Axes can't hurt it. Why would a boot? But the orc groaned and let go of Felix's neck. Gotrek hacked its head off with a grunting backhand as Felix fell amongst the corpses. The orc sank to its knees and pitched forwards, its head rolling down its back.

Gotrek sat down heavily on the chest of another orc. The wound in his shoulder gushed red.

'But, how?' whistled Felix through his crushed throat. 'I didn't get the–'

'Didn't you?' Gotrek pointed at Felix's sword. The greenskin's torque dangled from his quillions.

Gotrek shook his head and wiped his brow. 'Grimnir's beard, what a scrap.' He raised his voice. 'Ironskin! Lower a rope.'

'Narin... Narin is dead,' said Galin, sitting up and clutching his head.

'Dead?' said Gotrek. His face hardened.

Felix stood, massaging his throat. He could hardly swallow, and his head throbbed abominably. 'Thank... thank you, Gotrek. I would be...'

Gotrek shrugged. 'Thank yourself. That kick wouldn't have done a thing if you hadn't got its cursed torque off.' He stood and picked up one of the broken planks. He grounded one end in the floor of corpses and leaned the other against the wall. 'Let's get out of this stink-hole.'

One by one they crawled up the narrow board and out of the pit.

When he reached the top, Gotrek looked at Narin, lying in his own blood under the orc he had slain, and shook his head. 'Stubborn fool. Told him not to come.'

'Gotrek…' came a weak voice.

'He's alive!' said Galin.

They crossed to the dying dwarf, their boots splashed in his blood. His ribs rose from his smashed chest like broken white fingers from a red stew.

He looked up at them, grinning glassily. 'Well I… I did it. Escaped being thane. Escaped my… wife. My conjugal bed.' It was an effort for him to get the words out. 'Tell my father I'm sorry I… I didn't give him an heir. But not… very.' He laughed wetly, blood spraying from his mouth.

Gotrek knelt. 'Aye, I'll tell him.'

'And… give him his splinter back.' His hand fumbled in the blood-matted mess of his beard and tugged out the charred sliver of the Shield of Drutti. 'Tell him I… wish him good luck fighting… you.'

'I'll tell him that too.' Gotrek tucked the piece of wood in his belt pouch and took Narin's hand. 'May your ancestors welcome you, Narin Narinsson.'

Narin was already dead. Gotrek and the others lowered their heads.

Felix cursed silently. He had liked the sharp-tongued dwarf. Certainly, he had teased and insulted Felix like all the rest, but it had been different coming from him somehow – the easy familiar ribbing of an old friend, not the sullen distrust of the outsider that he had felt from the others.

There was a footstep. Felix and the others looked up. The surfaces of the room were so hard that it was difficult to tell from what direction the sound had come.

'Who's there?' asked Galin, looking around. 'Show yourself!'

All the dread that fighting the orcs had pushed away closed around Felix's heart again. The hairs raised on the back of his neck. The orcs had only been servants of the thing they were here to destroy. They still had yet to face the master – a thing so powerful it could warp, not only the minds of its minions, but also their bodies.

Another step. A shadowy figure appeared in the far door. They turned to face it, weapons at the ready. It stepped into the red light of Gotrek's axe.

'Hamnir!' cried Galin. 'Hamnir, you live!'

'Welcome, friends,' said Hamnir slowly. 'Welcome to the realisation of our dreams.'

Through the parting of the dwarf prince's beard Felix could see a glint of gold.

CHAPTER TWENTY-FIVE

GALIN GROANED. GOTREK grunted like he'd been shot. Felix stared.

Hamnir drifted forwards in a somnambulant glide, spreading his hands. 'I am sorry your welcome has been so violent, but you have slain so many of us that the Sleeper was threatened and sought to protect itself.'

'Prince Hamnir,' said Galin, stepping forwards. 'What has it done to you? Take it off.'

Hamnir touched the torque around his neck. 'This is the greatest honour ever bestowed upon me. I wear it with pride.'

'Take it off, damn you!' Galin was red in the face. There were tears in his eyes. 'It's a thing of Chaos! Fight it!'

'Do not threaten me,' said Hamnir, calmly. 'The Sleeper...'

'A plague take the Sleeper! Take it off!' Galin launched himself at Hamnir, reaching for his neck.

Quicker than the eye could follow, Hamnir drew his axe off his back and lashed out at Galin. The blade cut through Galin's armour and his ribs as if they were so much paper and twigs. The engineer fell back, dead before he hit the floor.

'Do not threaten me,' said Hamnir, as calmly as before. Felix and Gotrek stared as he cleaned his axe on Galin's beard. He took another torque from his doublet and looked up. He held it out to Gotrek. 'The Sleeper does not wish to kill you, Gotrek. You are strong. You will be a great asset in the coming struggle. Take this and join us.'

Gotrek closed his eye. His head drooped. Felix had never seen him in such pain. 'Ranulfsson,' he said, his voice rough. 'Hamnir, take it off. Fight it. You are a dwarf: a prince, not a slave.'

'I am still a prince,' said Hamnir, 'a prince that follows a great god. Take the torque, Gotrek, and you will see.'

'No, scholar,' said Gotrek. 'I have no master, dwarf, god or daemon.' He raised his eyes and glared at Hamnir. 'Now take it off, or I'll take it off for you.'

'Listen to me Gotrek,' said Hamnir, his eyes shining with the fire of a zealot. 'For how long have the fortunes of the dwarfs been on the wane? For how long have we lost hold after hold? For how long have we ceded territory and power to elves and men, and even vile skaven? With the torque comes strength, invulnerability. Nothing will stand in our way. With the grobi as our slaves, to dig our ore and work our foundries, we will become mightier even than we were in the golden age!'

'Hamnir...' said Gotrek, but Hamnir wasn't to be interrupted.

'The Sleeper enlisted first the grobi, because their minds are simple and easily reached, but even with its enlightened leadership, an empire of grobi will not stand. They cannot be taught more than the most rudimentary skills.' He stepped closer. 'But the dwarfs, the dwarfs are a great race, a race who will not be slaves, but equal partners in a shared destiny. It will give us its strength and power and the wisdom of ages beyond reckoning, and all it asks in return is to share the torques with our kin and to bring its children to every hold we visit.'

'Its children?' growled Gotrek.

'Did you not see them as you came?' asked Hamnir. 'Even now the grobi ready them for travel. Soon the steam carts will carry them along the Undgrin to every hold in the world.' He held out the torque again. 'Take it, Gotrek. All your doubt, your black moods, your fear, will dissipate like a cloud, to be replaced with blissful peace. You will never be angry again. Take it. Join us.'

Gotrek slapped it out of his hand. It jangled across the floor. 'No.'

Hamnir looked genuinely sad. 'Then, old friend,' he said, sighing, 'I'm afraid you must die.' He licked out with his axe as quickly and casually as a man swats a fly, and nearly caught Gotrek in the throat.

The Slayer jumped back, cursing, wisps of beard fluttering to the floor. Felix dodged back too. Even after Hamnir's words the attack was unexpected. Attacks usually had a preamble – raised voices, threatening gestures, the glint of anger in the attacker's eye. Hamnir's swipe had had none of these.

The prince swung again, as blank as before, and Gotrek blocked the blow with the rune axe, backing up. 'Don't do this, Ranulfsson,' he said, brow furrowed. 'I don't want to hurt you.'

'And I don't want to hurt you,' said Hamnir calmly, slashing again, 'but if you will not take the torque, I have no choice. Those who are not with us are against us.'

Gotrek continued to back away, parrying every blow, but never returning one. Felix had never seen the Slayer so unhappy to be in a fight. It was a battle he couldn't win. Killing Hamnir was a tragedy, not a victory, and being killed by him was no grand doom, and would indeed very likely doom the dwarfs, and perhaps the whole world, to mindless slavery.

But if Gotrek didn't strike soon, he might never be able to. He was weakening with every step. The axe wound in his shoulder had lost him a lot of blood, and it was still bleeding. Felix saw him stagger as he parried a chop to the head. Hamnir wasn't tiring in the least.

Felix edged around Hamnir, angling for the torque.

'No!' snapped Gotrek. 'This is my fight!' He glared at Hamnir. 'And his. Stay back.'

So Felix stood by while Gotrek back-pedalled around the pit with Hamnir in calm, implacable pursuit.

'Fight it, scholar,' hissed Gotrek. 'Fight it! You're the smartest dwarf I know. Can't you see what it's doing? Can't you smell the reek of Chaos on it?'

Hamnir slashed at his belly. Gotrek barely blocked it in time.

'Don't you remember what it made of Ferga?' Gotrek asked. 'Do you want to be like that?'

Hamnir's brow creased momentarily, but then smoothed again. 'Had I known then what I know now, I would have joined her.'

'This god of yours took your hold by force, killing innocent dwarfs and using grobi to do it – the ancient enemies of our people. How can you side with it?'

'We refused to listen,' said Hamnir placidly. 'It did what it had to do. For those who listen there is only joy.'

Gotrek gritted his teeth as he slipped and jarred his leg. 'How long have we been friends, scholar? How many times have we fought side by side, and drunk ourselves blind, and split up a treasure, and argued over everything and nothing?' His voice was hoarse with emotion. Felix had never heard him like this. 'Is that less to you than the joys of being a slave?'

Hamnir was silent, his face troubled. His attacks faltered.

'Good, scholar,' called Gotrek. 'Fight it!'

Hamnir stopped, axe frozen and hands trembling, a war waging within him. 'Fighting it is useless,' he said, his voice strangled. 'We are but two, when it is thousands. We are children, when it is ageless. If I take off the torque a hundred others will pick it up. What I do doesn't matter. We have already lost.'

'We haven't!' roared Gotrek. 'Take off the torque and we'll kill it together.'

Hamnir shook his head sadly. 'Nothing can kill it. It is too strong. Too old.'

Gotrek snarled. 'What kind of dwarf are you? Will you doom your race because you gave up without a fight?'

It was the wrong thing to say.

Hamnir's face became calm again. He raised his axe. 'It is to save my race that I obey it, for if we oppose it we will be destroyed. Only by joining it will we live.'

'With torgues around our necks,' Gotrek spat.

'But we will live.' Hamnir swung at Gotrek again.

Gotrek parried and backed away, his face working grief and rage.

'Gotrek,' said Felix, distraught. 'Let me take it off him. Perhaps he'll come to himself.'

'*He* has to do it,' said Gotrek, glaring at Hamnir. 'He has to be strong and take it off himself.'

'Maybe no one is strong enough.'

'A dwarf should be strong enough!'

The pain in Gotrek's voice was almost too much for Felix to bear. 'There's a whole clanhold above that says otherwise,' he said.

Gotrek cursed.

Hamnir hacked again, but this time Gotrek returned the attack, battering at Hamnir's axe and trying to disarm him. Hamnir blocked and countered with blistering speed. He was twice the fighter he had been without the torque. They circled near Galin's corpse.

'You're running out of chances, scholar,' grated Gotrek. 'Take it off or die!'

But it wasn't clear who would die first. Gotrek was fighting one-handed now, his wounded arm useless. He was barely stopping Hamnir's blows from reaching him.

The Slayer backed up, stepping around Galin's body. Hamnir pressed forwards, swinging savagely, and slipped on Galin's blood.

Quicker than blinking, Gotrek caught Hamnir's axe in a bind, and ripped it from his grip with a savage twist of his wrist. It bounced into the hole.

Hamnir stepped back. Gotrek leapt at him like a wrestler, slammed him to the ground, and straddled his chest. He ripped the torque from Hamnir's neck and flung it away, staring into his face, his axe raised.

Hamnir blinked up at him, calmly. 'Will you kill me then, Gotrek? You swore to protect me until one of us should die.'

Gotrek's face collapsed. 'And I failed,' he choked. 'You're already dead.' He buried the axe in Hamnir's chest. Hamnir bucked and contorted, choking, and then lay still, eyes staring at nothing.

Felix gaped, stunned, as Gotrek slumped over his dead friend. Sigmar, he thought, what had the Slayer done?

'Don't look at me, manling,' Gotrek growled, his voice thick. He hid his face in one massive, blood-stained hand, 'or I will kill you where you stand!'

Felix stepped back, shaking, and turned away. He dug his field kit out of his pack, allowing Gotrek his grief while he patched his wounds and tried to make sense of what had happened. Gotrek had killed a dwarf! Hamnir! His friend: without waiting, without giving him time to recover. Felix couldn't stop replaying the scene over in his mind.

How could Gotrek have known if Hamnir had recovered or not? What Hamnir had said hadn't sounded 'wrong'. Had he made a mistake?

After a long interval, Gotrek stood, unsteady. His left arm was red from shoulder to wrist. 'Right,' he said, clearing his throat. 'Let's finish this.'

He pulled a length of bandages from Galin's pack and started winding them around his sliced-open shoulder as he crossed to the doorway from whence

Hamnir had come. The edges of the door were carved all over with the same ancient warding symbols that had marked the outer door. Felix was certain now that they had been placed to keep something in, and he was beginning to understand what that something was.

The Slayer's face was as dead and cold as Felix had ever seen it. He wanted to ask him about Hamnir, but he was afraid he would kill him if he did. He held his tongue and followed him.

As they reached the door, the oppressive dread and despair welled up in Felix again, stronger than before. If the Sleeper could turn the mind of a dwarf like Hamnir, what chance did a human like himself have? Worse, what if it turned Gotrek's mind? What if it already had! What if it had decided that Gotrek was a better pawn than Hamnir? Was that why the Slayer had killed his friend? Or perhaps Gotrek had gone entirely mad at last, and couldn't distinguish between friend or foe. Felix felt like running for his life, but he was more afraid of being separated from Gotrek than of being killed by him.

They walked down a short corridor, then ascended a shallow ramp to a wider hallway that curved away to the left and right. The sickly corpse-flesh glow grew brighter with every step, and the thick, sour-milk reek clogged their nostrils. A series of open arches on the inner wall of the curving corridor shone faintly from within. Felix looked in the nearest one, gagged and stepped back. Gotrek scowled into it behind him.

Three-quarters of the large room was filled, floor to ceiling, with what looked, to Felix's unsettled mind, like translucent white custard – custard that had been left out far too long. It was from this bulging, gelatinous

substance that the pale phosphorescence emanated, and
the smell too. Flickers like green heat lightning flashed
deep within its milky depths. Ropy white tentacles
protruded from it and lay, long and flaccid, across the
floor. They pulsed with sluggish life. Cancerous goiters
and weird growths blossomed from it like blackcurrants
in a pudding, and thick white cilia stood out like hairs
on its surface.

Through the cloudy substance, Felix could just see a
doorway on the far side of the chamber. The shattered
remains of a stone door lay in front of it, entirely buried
under the gelid flesh. It looked like the horrid mass had
burst the door and grown to fill the room.

Felix covered his mouth at the smell. 'What is it?' He
asked through his fingers, fighting the urge to vomit.

Gotrek stepped up to the bulging white mass. He
prodded it with a booted toe. It shivered like jelly. The
cilia around the point where Gotrek had touched waved
like a field of weeds in a wind.

They moved on. The next room too was overfilled with
the translucent stuff, pressed against the walls of the
chamber like a mattress full of snot shoved into a too
small closet. The white tentacles trailed across the floor
like dead snakes, and there was another burst door on
the far side of the room.

Gotrek and Felix continued along the curving corridor,
passing room after room, each filled with more of the
horrible tentacled jelly. Felix began to realise that the
corridor was a vast ring. Halfway around its circumfer-
ence, they came to a second ramp, this one angling
down under the centre of the circle.

The corpse glow was stronger here, and Gotrek
turned down the ramp immediately. Felix hesitated,

the irrational fear filling his veins with ice, then forced himself to go on. If he stopped, he would never be able to start forwards again.

There was another massive trapezoidal arch at the bottom of the ramp, its edges limned with the rancid green light. Gotrek and Felix stepped to it, and then stopped, retching. Felix covered his mouth again and forced his stomach to be still. The smell was overwhelming, but the smell was the least of it.

They looked into a low circular chamber. The floor was littered with black basalt rubble. The ceiling – Felix flinched away from it. It made him want to vomit, to run. The ceiling was of the same gelatinous grub-flesh that had filled the rooms above. The weight of it had caved in the original ceiling, and it bellied down from above like the underside of some filthy bed canopy, making the low room even lower.

And hanging limply from the centre of the mass, like the desiccated shell of some impossibly large praying mantis, was the Sleeper.

There was no question in Felix's mind that this was the thing they had come to kill. It could be nothing else. It was absolutely motionless, head slumped, limbs dangling – asleep. Felix might have thought it already dead, except for the aura of fear and madness that emanated from it like cold from a glacier.

It had once been some sort of insect, but time, imprisonment and some dark pact with the Ruinous Powers had warped it into something infinitely more foul. Its translucent shell was white and waxy, like tallow, and through it Felix could see white, striated muscle and the flow of viscous liquid through glassine veins. Eight long, sharp legs like glass sabres hung below a spined, carapaced head with ten black faceted eyes and a thicket of cruel mandibles. Thick, whip-like antennae curved up from its ridged brow.

Its thin thorax was attached somehow to the gelatinous ceiling, and at first Felix couldn't make out how. Did it cling to it like a bat? Was it somehow trapped in it? Then, with a fresh wave of revulsion, he understood. The jelly was the rest of it! The great fleshy mass, that had grown into every room along the circular corridor, and that had become so heavy that it had broken through the stone ceiling, was the thing's bloated abdomen! Gotrek and Felix had not explored every corner of the crypt. The gods only knew how many other rooms it had filled with its bulk. Felix swallowed convulsively as he realised that he might be looking at the largest living thing in the world.

Other things hung from the bulging ceiling as well – glistening translucent sacs, bulging at the end of twisted umbilical ropes. Felix recognised them as the chrysalises they had earlier seen the orcs putting into crates. There were pale, angular forms inside them, with long forelegs and ten faceted eyes. The Sleeper's children: the end of the world.

The Sleeper did not turn its head, or in any way acknowledge their presence as they stepped into the round room. And yet, Felix was more afraid to approach it than any thing of flesh and blood he had ever faced. Crippling terror paralysed him. He couldn't take another step.

Gotrek hadn't stopped, but he had slowed, leaning forwards and struggling to put one foot in front of the other like a man pushing into the teeth of a gale.

'Fight it, manling,' he said through gritted teeth. 'It's out of servants. It's using the only weapon it's got left.'

Felix couldn't move. If he got any closer, it would eat his brain. He knew this. It was already eating it. If he didn't run, he would end up like the others, a mindless slave, doing the bidding of some Chaos-corrupted insect. It would all be Gotrek's fault – dragging him into certain death time and time again. 'You fight it,' he spat. 'You're the Slayer! Must I always fight your battles?'

Gotrek glared back at him. 'You fight my battles? Ha! That's a joke. Half the battles I fight are to save your worthless hide! Grimnir, what a weakling! Why did I choose a human for a rememberer? A dwarf would have taken care of himself!'

Felix choked, outrage flaring in his heart. 'Weakling? You call me that after all I've been through with you – and all on the strength of a drunken vow I should never have made!'

Gotrek turned on him, the Sleeper forgotten. 'And I should never have held you to it. By my ancestors! Twenty-five years travelling with a snivelling wet blanket too weak to pull his own weight, having to turn back every second step to pull your scrawny arse out of the fire, having to listen to, "That isn't wise, Gotrek", and "Maybe we shouldn't do that, Gotrek", in my ear like a damned mosquito. Why I haven't cut your throat before now, just to shut you up, is beyond me!'

'You think it's been a joy travelling with you?' shouted Felix, his neck pulsing with rage, 'Insulted and ignored every day for a quarter century by a stunted, taciturn bully without a kind word for anybody. I can't think of a single instance when you thanked me or praised me for a job well done. It's always "Shut up, manling", and "Out of the way, manling", and "Get the bags, manling".' He clenched his fists. 'When I think of the life I could have had if I hadn't sworn to follow your ugly posterior around the world until you finally killed yourself! You haven't even had the decency to die quickly like most Slayers.'

'You've seen more of the world than any hundred men of the Empire, thanks to me,' bellowed Gotrek, 'and you complain about it? Grungni's axe! Why didn't I make my peace with Hamnir and ask him to be my rememberer? He at least was a dwarf, not a spindle-shanked weakling!'

'Weakling, again.' Felix put his hand on his hilt. 'You call me weak when I'm still here and your oh-so-sturdy dwarf friend Hamnir is dead? Who's the weakling?'

Gotrek's face went white. His one eye glittered with cold fury. 'You insult the dead? You'll die for that.'

'I insulted him,' Felix sneered. '*You* killed him.'

With an outraged roar, Gotrek lurched unsteadily towards Felix, slashing one-handed with his axe. Felix leapt back, gasping and drawing his sword. He felt the wind of the axe's passing on his cheek.

Terror stabbed through his heart like an icicle. Sigmar, what had he done? Gotrek was attacking him! The axe that had killed daemons and giants was swinging for his neck!

He scrambled backwards, parrying desperately. Gotrek limped after him, the rune axe a blur. Each strike nearly knocked the sword from Felix's hands. He was still alive only because Gotrek fought one-handed, and was weak from his wounds and loss of blood.

Felix cursed himself as the rune axe flashed past, an inch from his chin. What madness had inspired him to goad the Slayer like that? Had he been out of his mind? Then it came to him that the inspiration had indeed been from outside of his mind. It had come from the Sleeper. It was stirring them up like pit dogs. It was defending itself by making them fight each other instead of it.

'Gotrek!' he cried as they circled. 'Stop! It's the Sleeper. It's forcing us to fight! It's in our minds!'

'Trying to trick me into letting down my guard? Ha!' Gotrek hacked unrelentingly at Felix, pushing him further into the room.

Felix could feel the Sleeper's presence behind his left shoulder as he backed closer to it. His skin crawled. 'Gotrek, curse you, fight it!' he shouted. 'What's become of your unbendable dwarf will. Fight it!'

They slashed and hacked directly in front of it, circling slowly, as if they were gladiators, fighting for its amusement. Gods! Why wouldn't Gotrek listen? How dare he accuse Felix of weakness and then fall under the Sleeper's power himself? If he wouldn't listen, Felix would just have to beat it into him. He'd cut the Slayer's head off and shout it down his throat.

'Stubborn fool! I'll teach you!' Felix aimed a lunge at Gotrek's poorly bound shoulder wound.

The Slayer's axe blocked the strike, shivering his sword and stinging his hands.

'It's you who needs teaching, longshanks! Saying you're better than a dwarf!' He aimed a bash at Felix's head that would have sheared it in half if he hadn't leapt back. 'I'll gut you for insolence!'

Felix cursed. Even one-handed and near collapse, Gotrek was stronger and faster than any opponent

Felix had ever faced, but the Slayer was reeling, unsteady on his feet. If Felix could make him fall, he could finish him. He continued to circle right, trying to get on Gotrek's weak side.

Gotrek turned with him. 'I'll spit you like a rabbit!' he roared, raising his axe over his head. He tripped on a chunk of rubble. He staggered, off balance.

An opening! Felix darted in, stabbing for Gotrek's bad leg. Gotrek swung down with his axe, blindingly fast, smashing his sword out of his hands, then kicked him in the stomach.

Felix flew back, his sword bouncing away, and crashed into the Sleeper. His arms tangled in its spiny legs. The back of his head smacked it between its rows of eyes. It jerked, waking and hissing, mandibles clattering.

'I'll chop you in two!' Gotrek bellowed, and hurled his axe straight at Felix's head.

Felix yelped and dived to the ground in terror. The axe spun by over his head, ruffling his hair, and severed one of the Sleeper's antennae.

The Sleeper screeched, its legs lashing about, its claws clacking. One clubbed Felix across the shoulder and knocked him halfway across the room. He grunted in pain as he hit the floor, but also in relief. His mind was suddenly clear. All his unreasoning rage was gone. The Sleeper's wound had distracted it.

Felix pushed himself up. Gotrek was diving past the chittering, thrashing thing and snatching up his axe. Felix goggled at him as he turned.

'You... you...'

'Not now, manling,' Gotrek rasped, standing. 'Kill it.'

The Slayer limped towards the Sleeper from behind. The thing twisted and curled itself in every direction, trying to turn to face him, but it was held in place by its gargantuan abdomen. It couldn't move to defend itself.

Gotrek smiled savagely, prepared for the slaughter. Felix stood and recovered his sword. With its vile influence gone from his head, the Sleeper seemed no threat at all. It was pathetic, in fact, made helpless by its own mutations.

Something long and white dropped down beside him. He flinched away from it. It looked like a wrist-thick strand of snot dripping from a giant's nose. Another dropped in front of him. The drips curved towards him like blind snakes, their skins thickening and muddying. They were growing from the Sleeper's bloated abdomen!

The first split at its tip like a seedpod opening, and Felix saw teeth and a purple tongue inside the cavity. The other sprouted hooked barbs and squid-like suckers. They lunged.

He slashed at the one with the mouth, decapitating it. Thick rank liquid exploded from it, making his eyes water. Two more strands dripped down around him. 'Gotrek!'

Gotrek was beset with five of the things. He slashed three in half, and four more dropped down to grapple with him. One looped around his bad leg. Another caught him around the neck. They were trying to hold him away from the Sleeper.

'Chaos-cursed filth!' Gotrek roared.

Felix chopped through two more, but another had his waist and was lifting him off his feet. He swung his sword behind his head and crashed to the floor as he cut through it. He landed in a puddle of grey muck.

The cut tentacles were pouring thick streams of mucus from their wounds onto the floor. It smelled impossibly foul. Felix jumped up, trying to shake it from his hands, and nearly fell again. The basalt floor was slick with the stuff.

The circular chamber was suddenly a swaying forest of slimy white tentacles, all reaching for him and Gotrek. They weren't hard to cut, but there were too many of them. One, with a mouth like a lamprey, bit Felix on the back of the leg. He screamed and chopped it through, but another raked his face with ridges like broken glass.

He hacked at everything that came within reach, slipping and spinning in a mad frenzy. On the other side of the Sleeper, Gotrek did the same, but new tentacles grew out of the bulging ceiling every second, and more than forty truncated tentacles poured viscous goop onto the floor. The stinking mucus was ankle deep. As Felix backed away from three of the mutating pseudopods, he stepped under a shower of muck, and was drenched to the skin. He gagged as it got into his eyes and nose, and plastered his hair to his scalp.

Felix sobbed with frustration as he wiped his eyes. It was hopeless. No matter how many tentacles he cut there would always be more. They would never reach the Sleeper to kill it. The tentacles would tear them apart. He should just throw down his sword and…

He froze. It was back in his head, trying to reassert control. He forced it out savagely, cursing it with each slash of his sword. Then he turned and started slogging, one slippery step at a time, through the lake of snot towards it. He would not let it distract him. It would *not* take his mind from him again.

Gotrek had won free as well, at least momentarily, chopping through the tentacles faster than they could form. The severed heads of three of them hung by their teeth from his arms and legs as he waded towards the thing, and his slime-drenched crest hung in his face like a wet red mop.

The Sleeper chittered in distress and more tentacles writhed the Slayer's way, but he was not to be stopped. He backhanded through six, and then chopped at the thing's face. It lashed out with its glassine legs and the rune axe sheared through two of them at the joints.

The Sleeper shrieked, a deafening insect whine, and swung a pincered foreleg at Gotrek. He made to block, but a tentacle caught his wrist and he couldn't bring his axe in line. A crimson gash opened across his chest. The blood mixed with the slime, and painted his torso red.

Gotrek turned to cut the tentacle, and the Sleeper's other foreleg cracked him on the back of the head. He staggered and almost fell.

'Leave them!' cried Felix, as he finally reached the centre of the room. 'I'll get them!'

Gotrek said nothing, only turned his full attention on the Sleeper as Felix hacked through the tentacle that held his arm, and slashed at all the others that were questing forwards. There seemed to be hundreds of them. All with different mutations, all visions of an unhinged mind.

Gotrek laid into the Sleeper with all his might, but it still had six legs to his one axe, and it blocked every attack, chips and chunks of translucent chitin spinning away with each clash. He cut off another leg, and ducked as the Sleeper lashed out at his head.

Behind him, Felix spun like a dervish as he lopped tentacle after tentacle, but never enough. He laughed bitterly to himself. It was easy to say that he would keep the tentacles off Gotrek, but who would keep them off him? He was fading fast. The mucus was up to his knees – almost to Gotrek's hips – and it felt like he was fighting in quicksand. Worse, the bulging abdominal ceiling was drooping lower, as if it was deflating. Felix kept bumping it with his head. If they weren't torn apart or drowned, there was a good chance the Sleeper would smother them to death. He chopped through two sucker-covered tentacles that were looping around his legs. Then he slashed at three more that were reaching towards Gotrek. His sword arm was as heavy as lead. A tentacle grabbed his left ankle, another bit his right bicep, and more were coming.

Gotrek swung at the Sleeper's right foreleg. It blocked with another leg, and lost it as the axe smashed through it. The Slayer surged forwards, pressing the attack, but suddenly he jerked to a stop, grunting in pain. The Sleeper had him around the waist with its left pincer, lifting him off the ground and squeezing hard. Gotrek grabbed at it with his off hand, trying to keep it from scissoring him in two. He raised his axe to sever the arm, but its right pincer caught it by the haft and tried to pull it out of his hand. The Slayer bellowed in rage and pain.

'Hang on!' Felix cried.

He struggled forwards, hacking through three tentacles. Three more held him tight, and another two were grabbing for him. The Sleeper was lifting Gotrek towards its razor-sharp mandibles as he struggled. The Slayer couldn't let go of the Sleeper's claw to use both hands to free his axe, or it would cut him in two, and he couldn't let go of his axe to use both hands to force open the claw or he would lose the axe.

Felix roared and slashed all around him, chopping through half a dozen tentacles. Still more held him. He freed his arms and dove for the Sleeper, lashing out with the last of his strength as the tentacles around his ankles tried to yank him back.

He connected! The very tip of his blade caught the wrist of the pincer that held Gotrek's axe.

He splashed down face first into the slime and went under. Had he done it? Was it enough? Had the Sleeper let go?

He pushed desperately to the surface, coughing and shaking the muck from his eyes, just in time to see Gotrek, with a guttural howl of triumph, bury the rune axe between the Sleeper's two largest eyes.

The Sleeper shrieked and spasmed, its remaining legs flailing. Every tentacle in the room lashed and writhed like a pinned snake. Gotrek was thrown across the room and crashed into the wall. A dozen frenzied tentacles bludgeoned Felix. His brain was filled with a mad insectile chittering, a thousand crickets sawing violently inside his head, as horrific, shattered-mirror images of blood and dismemberment, and black chambers seething with a million haycart-sized insects crawling over one another, flashed behind his eyes. He thrashed and kicked in the swamp of mucus, screaming, hands clapped over his ears, heart pounding, gorge rising.

Gotrek was staggering to his feet, his arms over his head, grimacing and roaring.

The whole world seemed to be shaking. Was it all in his head? A chunk of basalt splashed down beside him, raising a thick fountain of muck. It was not in his head.

'Out, manling!' called Gotrek.

Felix struggled to his feet and sloshed drunkenly through the chaos of waving tentacles after Gotrek, as huge blocks of stone crashed down all around them, and the Sleeper's mental storm continued to batter his mind. Image piled on top of image, each more chaotic and confused than the last: cave-coffered insect cities; towering black basalt pyramids; slave armies – hairy, heavy browed troglodyte humans, digging and building and cleaning up after their chitinous masters; earthquakes; slave rebellions; cave-ins; assassinations; an insect emperor making a pact with entities more ancient even than itself, a pact that gives it new powers, brings it victories, treasure, godhood; then come jealousies; betrayals; invasion by pale overdwellers; battles; defeats; hiding itself in the temple where once the others had come to worship it; the overdwellers locking it in with spells and wards; waiting, growing, waiting.

Gotrek and Felix ran up the ramp and into the circular corridor, which was already half buried in falling rubble. White tentacles flailed from the open doorways as they sprinted and dodged around the ring. Walls crumbled as the vast gelatinous bulk juddered and shook. The Sleeper's psychic scream rose in pitch and volume, losing any semblance of cohesion until it was only a deafening, mind-blasting rush of rage, agony and ancient hate.

A huge slab of black stone crashed down in front of them, missing them by inches. Felix vaulted it. Gotrek dodged around it, and they dived into the ramp, bouncing and rolling down to the hall below as, with a roar like an earthquake, the Sleeper's chambers collapsed altogether.

The Sleeper's presence winked out as the rocks fell, leaving only gibbering echoes. Felix was too scared to care. He lay huddled at the base of the ramp, his head covered with his arms, expecting at any moment that the roof would cave in.

After a while, the rumbling and shaking subsided and all grew still. Felix slowly uncurled, blinking and shaking his head. Gotrek was sitting up too, clutching his temples and groaning.

After a few moments spent leaning against the wall and catching his breath, Felix looked dully over at the Slayer. 'You tried to kill me,' he said.

'What?' said Gotrek. 'Never. You tried to kill me.'

'Only because you wouldn't stop trying to kill me!' said Felix. 'Couldn't you understand? It was the Sleeper. It was forcing you to fight me.'

'Oh, I knew.'

'Then why didn't you stop?'

Gotrek frowned, and looked down, his fists clenching, chagrined. 'I couldn't. The thing was damned strong.' He rubbed his mucus-covered face with his hands and sighed. 'Guess I don't blame Hamnir so much now. Only broke its hold by giving in.'

'Broke its hold? You didn't break its hold.'

'It got out of our heads when I hit it, didn't it?'

'You hit it by accident.'

Gotrek shook his head and stood up on wobbly legs. 'Couldn't stop attacking you, much as I tried. Or turn my axe on it, either. It was too strong for that. But I could put you between me and it.' He shrugged. 'I knew you'd duck.'

Felix blinked, and surged unsteadily to his feet. His blood boiled. 'You knew I'd... You... But... but what if I hadn't?'

Gotrek grimaced and cleaned the mucus off his axe as best he could. 'What choice did I have?'

Felix opened his mouth to argue, but he didn't know what to say.

Gotrek slid the rune axe through his belt, and turned away. 'Come on.'

They walked down the corridor to the room with the pit in the centre and stopped at Hamnir's body.

Felix swallowed as he looked at Hamnir's face, calm in death, and then down at the ruin of his chest. 'How... how did you know?' he asked. 'How did you know he hadn't recovered? That he wouldn't recover?'

'I knew,' said Gotrek. 'It was in his eyes. He had spent too long with it. He wasn't coming back.'

'But...'

'He wasn't coming back!' Gotrek squatted abruptly, slid his arms under Hamnir's body, and lifted him. He stumped towards the exit.

Felix stared after him. Perhaps the Sleeper's death would have ended its dominion over him, he wanted to say. Its corrupting influence might have died with it. Perhaps Hamnir would have returned to himself once it was dead. He couldn't force himself to speak. He followed after Gotrek, his heart at war with itself.

Halfway up the tunnel that led to the mines, Gotrek
cleared his throat. 'You will tell Gorril that Hamnir
died well, fighting the torqued greenskins. It is best.'

'You don't want him to know you killed him?'

'I don't want him to know that he... lost himself.'

'Why don't you tell him?' asked Felix.

'I don't lie.'

'And I do?' Felix was insulted.

'You write plays, don't you?'

A sharp retort rose up in Felix's throat, but he let it
die unspoken. He didn't like it, but perhaps it *was* for
the best. The last thing the beleaguered dwarfs of Karak
Hirn needed to learn was that their prince had
betrayed his own race, and it had always been the job
of poets and playwrights to put the best face on the
deaths of heroes.

'All right, I'll tell him.'

CHAPTER TWENTY-SIX

GOTREK PUT HIS axe through each of the chrysalises in the room where the orcs had been packing them up, and set fire to the crates just to be sure. Once smoke began to fill the room, they turned and continued on up through the mine.

Felix looked with growing despair on the few orcs they passed. He had been afraid their return to the hold would be a nightmare – dodging rampaging orcs newly returned to their ferocity now that the yoke of the Sleeper's evil influence had been lifted from their necks. The reality was worse. The orcs they passed stood blank and lost, staring into space with their weapons and tools hanging limply from their hands. Even when Gotrek and Felix came upon four in a narrow corridor – walked right into them around a corner – the orcs did nothing, only pawed at them lazily, like sleepy bears. Gotrek pushed through them as if they were so much furniture, growling low in his throat. They didn't follow.

Finally, after retracing their steps up the winding stair of King Alrik's vault and through the empty halls of Karak Hirn, they came to the Diamondsmith clanhold. Gorril was just outside its doors, supervising details of dwarfs who were piling the beheaded bodies of the undead orcs onto carts and wheeling them away.

'Gurnisson!' he cried when he saw then. 'We had hope of your success. The last of the walking corpses dropped dead all at once about half an hour–' He stopped when he saw what Gotrek carried. 'Prince Hamnir!' He rushed to Gotrek. 'Is he... Did he...'

'He is dead,' said Gotrek.

'He died well,' said Felix, remembering his part. 'There were more torqued greenskins below, defending the Sleeper. He slew two. Another slew him. He died to stop Chaos and corruption from spreading to other holds.' Which was true enough after all.

'And did you slay the Sleeper?'

'Aye,' said Gotrek. 'It's dead.'

'Then he did not die in vain.' Gorril took Hamnir from Gotrek's arms, his face working, as the other dwarfs gathered around, baring their heads for their fallen prince. As he carried Hamnir into the clanhold, the dwarfs followed him, and more came out into the central chamber to watch in mournful silence as Gorril laid him upon the base of a statue of some ancient dwarf patriarch.

Gorril turned to the assembled dwarfs, tears in his eyes. 'Friends, our prince is dead. We will mourn him as befits a fallen hero, but in this tragedy is triumph, for with his death, he has freed us from the horror that held us in its clutches. The Sleeper is dead. The hold is ours. The worst is behind us.'

'It isn't,' said Gotrek under his breath.

'What?' asked Gorril, turning to him with a frown. 'What do you mean? You killed it. We are free.'

Gotrek sighed and pushed through the crowd of solemn dwarfs to the doors of the gemcutters' guild-hall. 'Open it,' he said.

A dwarf brought a key and turned the locks as Gorril and Felix and the other dwarfs filled in behind him. The door swung open.

The dwarfs of the Diamondsmith clan turned towards the door as the light from the hall fell upon them. They stared empty-eyed at the dwarfs who looked in on them, and then slowly started shuffling towards them, their weapons raised, their hands clutching.

Gotrek drew his axe from his belt. 'The worst is still before us.'

Gorril and the other dwarfs moaned in despair, and Felix's last faint hope died.

After a long, stunned moment, Gorril sighed and wiped his eyes. He straightened his shoulders, gripped his axe, and turned to the others.

'Fall in, sons of Karak Hirn,' he said. 'There is sad work to be done.'

EPILOGUE

'PLENTY MEAT ON norther man,' said the ogre. 'Taste funny though.'

The men gagged and edged away from him.

The dwarf grimaced. 'Grungni! Is there anything you ogres won't eat?'

The ogre ruminated for a moment, rubbing his several chins. 'Don't think so,' he said at last.

Felix listened with only half an ear. He and Gotrek were marching with a group of mercenaries who had banded together for safety while traversing the Black Fire Pass. All were heading north to sell their swords and axes to the Empire in its fight against the invasion of the Chaos hordes. Ahead of them was a company of Tilean Pike, outfitted in gaudy red and gold, and behind, thirty Estalian crossbowmen in brown leather. The dashing son of a border prince trotted past with twenty lances at his back, all on massive chargers, brave pennants fluttering from their lance tips. Ten dwarfs marched slowly beside two pony-drawn cannon, making sure the wheels didn't get stuck in the muddy, snow sprinkled ruts of the rough road.

Gotrek listened not at all. His one eye was turned inwards. He stomped along with his head down, taking no notice of the men, dwarfs or ogres around them. The Slayer had been in the blackest of moods since they had left Karak Hirn ten days before, and Felix didn't blame him. The events of the past weeks had been enough to depress even the most cheerful, and Gotrek was not known for his sunny disposition even in the best of times.

In a way, the fact that the Diamondsmith dwarfs had not come back to themselves had been a blessing, at least for Gotrek's sanity. It meant that he had been right to slay Hamnir – that the prince would not have returned to his right mind. And yet, what a bleak comfort that was. Cutting down the lost dwarfs had been the saddest battle of Felix's life. They had hardly fought back. They had blinked at the oncoming axes like cattle waiting for the maul. It had taken moments, and not a dwarf of Gorril's force had got a scratch, but Felix wondered if they would ever recover.

The thought of losing family made Felix think again about his own. Were they still alive? He had thought a lot recently about going home and settling down. Would he still have a home to return to? Was his brother Otto still running the family business? What of his old friends and companions? Did Max still live? Heinz, the innkeeper who had employed them in Nuln? Snorri? Ulrika?

A pang went through his heart as Felix thought of her. If she lived, what side did she fight for?

The news that came from the north was a hodge-podge of rumour, fear and hope. There were some who said the war was over, and the Chaos-crazed northmen driven back to the Wastes. Others said that Altdorf was aflame and Karl-Franz dead. No two stories were alike. None could be trusted.

'Yer wasting your time if ye think ye'll get in on the fighting,' said a swaggering gunner with a Nuln accent and the notched ear of a convicted thief. 'It'll all be over in a month. Archaon's smashing his head against the walls of Middenheim as we speak. Pretty soon his brains will fall out. No one's ever cracked the Fauschlag, no one.'

'So why you march?' asked the ogre.

The gunner shrugged. 'Lot of open positions after a war,' he said. 'Lot of crimes forgotten when the ranks get thin.'

Gotrek raised his head, glowering. 'Better not be over,' he muttered under his breath. 'I must wash the dwarf blood from my axe in a bath of Kurgan gore.' He held up the axe and gazed mournfully at its shining steel edge. 'Though it will never be enough.'

He and Felix trudged on in silence as, ahead, the setting sun painted the northern sky red as blood.

ABOUT THE AUTHOR

Nathan Long has worked as a screenwriter for fifteen years, during which time he has had three movies made and a handful of live-action and animated TV episodes produced. He has also written three Warhammer novels featuring the Blackhearts, and several award-winning short stories. He lives in Hollywood.

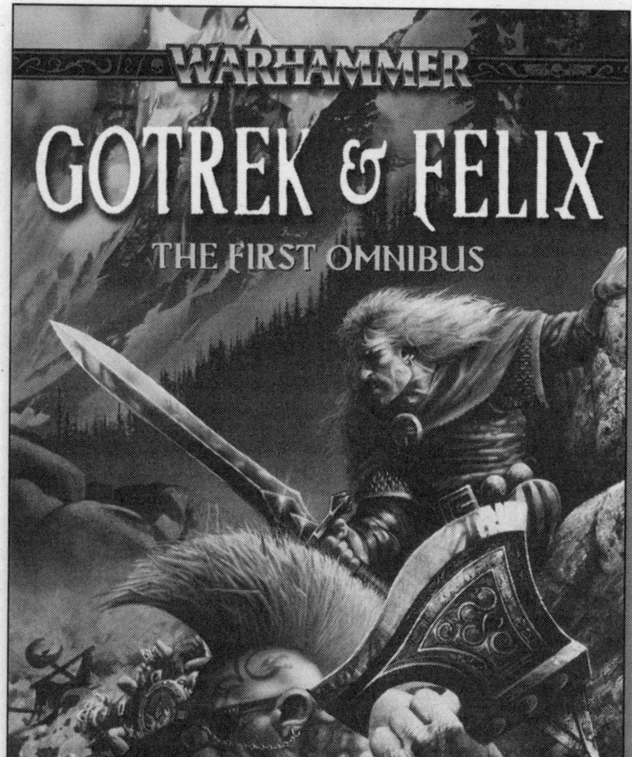
WARHAMMER
GOTREK & FELIX
THE FIRST OMNIBUS
TROLLSLAYER • SKAVENSLAYER • DAEMONSLAYER
WILLIAM KING

Check out Gotrek & Felix's early adventures in

GOTREK & FELIX
THE FIRST OMNIBUS

'DAMN ALL MANLING coach drivers and all manling women,' Gotrek Gurnisson muttered, adding a curse in dwarfish.

'You did have to insult the lady Isolde, didn't you?' Felix Jaeger said peevishly. 'As things are, we're lucky they didn't just shoot us. If you can call it "lucky" to be dumped in the Reikwald on Geheimnisnacht Eve.'

'We paid for our passage. We were just as entitled to sit inside as her. The drivers were unmanly cowards,' Gotrek grumbled. 'They refused to meet me hand to hand. I would not have minded being spitted on steel, but being blasted with buckshot is no death for a Trollslayer.'

Felix shook his head. He could see that one of his companion's black moods was coming on. There would be no arguing with him and Felix had plenty of other things to worry about. The sun was setting, giving the mist-covered forest a ruddy hue.

Long shadows danced eerily and brought to mind too many frightening tales of the horrors to be found under the canopy of trees.

He wiped his nose with the edge of his cloak, then pulled the Sudenland wool tight about him. He sniffed and looked at the sky where Morrslieb and Mannslieb, the lesser and greater moons, were already visible. Morrslieb seemed to be giving off a faint greenish glow. It wasn't a good sign.

'I think I have a fever coming on,' Felix said. The Trollslayer looked up at him and chuckled contemptuously. In the last rays of the dying sun, his nose-chain was a bloody arc running from nostril to earlobe.

'Yours is a weak race,' Gotrek said. 'The only fever I feel this eve is the battle-fever. It sings in my head.'

He turned and glared out into the darkness of the woods. 'Come out, little beastmen!' he bellowed. 'I have a gift for you.'

He laughed loudly and ran his thumb along the edge of the blade of his great two-handed axe. Felix saw that it drew blood. Gotrek began to suck his thumb.

'Sigmar preserve us, be quiet!' Felix hissed. 'Who knows what lurks out there on a night like this?'

Gotrek glared at him. Felix could see the glint of insane violence appear in his eyes. Instinctively Felix's hand strayed nearer to the pommel of his sword.

'Give me no orders, manling! I am of the Elder Race and am beholden only to the Kings Under the Mountain, exile though I be.'

Felix bowed formally. He was well schooled in the use of the sword. The scars on his face showed that he had fought several duels in his student days. He had once killed a man and so ended a promising academic career. But still he did not relish the thought of fighting the Trollslayer. The tip of Gotrek's crested hair came only to the level of Felix's chest, but the dwarf outweighed him and his bulk was all muscle. And Felix had seen Gotrek use that axe.

The dwarf took the bow as an apology and turned once more to the darkness. 'Come out!' he shouted. 'I care not if all the powers of evil walk the woods this night. I will face any challenger.'

The dwarf was working himself up to a pitch of fury. During the time of their acquaintance Felix had noticed that the Trollslayer's long periods of brooding were often followed by brief explosions of rage. It was one of the things about his companion that fascinated Felix. He knew that Gotrek had become a Trollslayer to atone for some crime. He was sworn to seek death in unequal combat with fearsome monsters. He seemed bitter to the point of madness – yet he kept to his oath.

Perhaps, thought Felix, I too would go mad if I had been driven into exile among strangers not even of my own race. He felt some sympathy for the crazed dwarf. Felix knew what it was like to be driven from home under a cloud. The duel with Wolfgang Krassner had caused quite a scandal.

At that moment, however, the dwarf seemed bent on getting them both killed, and he wanted no part of it. Felix continued to plod along the road, casting an occasional worried glance at the bright full moons. Behind him the ranting continued.

'Are there no warriors among you? Come feel my axe. She thirsts!'

Only a madman would so tempt fate and the dark powers on Geheimnisnacht, Night of Mystery, in the darkest reaches of the forest, Felix decided.

He could make out chanting in the flinty, guttural tongue of the Mountain Dwarfs, then once more in Reikspiel, he heard: 'Send me a champion!'

For a second there was silence. Condensation from the clammy mist ran down his brow. Then – from far,

far off – the sound of galloping horses rang out in the quiet night.

What has that maniac done, Felix thought, has he offended one of the Old Powers? Have they sent their daemon riders to carry us off?

Felix stepped off the road. He shuddered as wet leaves fondled his face. They felt like dead men's fingers. The thunder of hooves came closer, moving with hellish speed along the forest road. Surely only a supernatural being could keep such breakneck pace on the winding forest road? He felt his hand shake as he unsheathed his sword.

I was foolish to follow Gotrek, he thought. Now I'll never get the poem finished. He could hear the loud neighing of horses, the cracking of a whip and mighty wheels turning.

'Good!' Gotrek roared. His voice drifted from the trail behind. 'Good!'

There was a loud bellowing and four immense jet black horses drawing an equally black coach hurtled past. Felix saw the wheels bounce as they hit a rut in the road. He could just make out a black-cloaked driver. He shrank back into the bushes.

He heard the sound of feet coming closer. The bushes were pulled aside. Before him stood Gotrek, looking madder and wilder than ever. His crest was matted, brown mud was smeared over his tattooed body and his studded leather jerkin was ripped and torn.

'The snotling-fondlers tried to run me over!' he yelled. 'Let's get after them!'

He turned and headed up the muddy road at a fast trot. Felix noted that Gotrek was singing happily in Khazalid.

FURTHER DOWN THE Bogenhafen road the pair found the Standing Stones Inn. The windows were shuttered and no lights showed. They could hear a neighing from the stables but when they checked there was no coach, black or otherwise, only some skittish ponies and a peddler's cart.

'We've lost the coach. Might as well get a bed for the night,' Felix suggested. He looked warily at the smaller moon, Morrslieb. The sickly green glow was stronger. 'I do not like being abroad under this evil light.'

'You are feeble, manling. Cowardly too.'

'They'll have ale.'

'On the other hand, some of your suggestions are not without merit. Watery though human beer is, of course.'

'Of course,' Felix said. Gotrek failed to spot the note of irony in his voice.

The inn was not fortified but the walls were thick, and when they tried the door they found it was barred. Gotrek began to bang it with the butt of his axe-shaft. There was no response.

'I can smell humans within,' Gotrek said. Felix wondered how he could smell anything over his own stench. Gotrek never washed and his hair was matted with animal fat to keep his red-dyed crest in place.

'They'll have locked themselves in. Nobody goes abroad on Geheimnisnacht. Unless they're witches or daemon-lovers.'

'The black coach was abroad,' Gotrek said.

'Its occupants were up to no good. The windows were curtained and the coach bore no crest of arms.'

'My throat is too dry to discuss such details. Come on, open up in there or I'll take my axe to the door!'

Felix thought he heard movement within. He pressed an ear to the door. He could make out the mutter of voices and what sounded like weeping.

'Unless you want me to chop through your head, manling, I suggest you stand aside,' Gotrek said to Felix.

'Just a moment. I say: you inside! Open up! My friend has a very large axe and a very short temper. I suggest you do as he says or lose your door.'

'What was that about "short"?' Gotrek said touchily.

From behind the door came a thin, quavering cry. 'In the name of Sigmar, begone, you daemons of the pit!'

'Right, that's it,' Gotrek snapped. 'I've had enough.'

He drew his axe back in a huge arc. Felix saw the runes on its blade gleam in the Morrslieb light. He leapt aside.

'In the name of Sigmar!' Felix shouted. 'You cannot exorcise us. We are simple, weary travellers.'

The axe bit into the door with a chunking sound. Splinters of wood flew from it. Gotrek turned to Felix and grinned evilly up at him. Felix noted the missing teeth.

'Shoddily made, these manling doors,' Gotrek said.

'I suggest you open up while you still have a door,' Felix called.

'Wait,' the quavering voice said. 'That door cost me five crowns from Jurgen the carpenter.'

The door was unlatched. It opened. A tall, thin man with a sad face framed by lank, white hair stood there. He had a stout club in one hand. Behind him stood an old woman who held a saucer that contained a guttering candle.

'You will not need your weapon, sir. We require only a bed for the night,' Felix said.

'And ale,' the dwarf grunted.

'And ale,' Felix agreed.

'Lots of ale,' Gotrek said. Felix looked at the old man and shrugged helplessly.

Inside, the inn had a low common room. The bar was made of planks stretched across two barrels. From the corner, three armed men who looked like travelling peddlers watched them warily. They each had daggers drawn. The shadows hid their faces but they seemed worried.

The innkeeper hustled the pair inside and slid the bars back into place. 'Can you pay, Herr Doktor?' he asked nervously. Felix could see the man's Adam's apple moving.

'I am not a professor, I am a poet,' he said, producing his thin pouch and counting out his few remaining gold coins. 'But I can pay.'

'Food,' Gotrek said. 'And ale.'

At this the old woman burst into tears. Felix stared at her.

'The hag is discomfited,' Gotrek said.

The old man nodded. 'Our Gunter is missing, on this of all nights.'

'Get me some ale,' Gotrek said. The innkeeper backed off. Gotrek got up and stumped over to where the peddlers were sitting. They regarded him warily.

'Do any of you know about a black coach drawn by four black horses?' Gotrek asked.

'You have seen the black coach?' one of the peddlers asked. The fear was evident in his voice.

'Seen it? The bloody thing nearly ran me over.' A man gasped. Felix heard the sound of a ladle being dropped. He saw the innkeeper stoop to pick it up and begin refilling the tankard.

'You are lucky then,' the fattest and most prosperous-looking peddler said. 'Some say the coach is driven by daemons. I have heard it passes here on Geheimnisnacht every year. Some say it carries wee children from Altdorf who are sacrificed at the Darkstone Ring.'

Gotrek looked at him with interest. Felix did not like the way this was developing.

'Surely that is only a legend,' he said.

'No, sir,' the innkeeper shouted. 'Every year we hear the thunder of its passing. Two years ago Gunter looked out and saw it, a black coach just as you describe.'

At the mention of Gunter's name the old woman began to cry again. The innkeeper brought stew and two great steins of ale.

'Bring beer for my companion too,' Gotrek said. The landlord went off for another stein.

'Who is Gunter?' Felix asked when he returned. There was another wail from the old woman.

'More ale,' Gotrek said. The landlord looked in astonishment at the empty flagons.

'Take mine,' Felix said. 'Now, mein host, who is Gunter?'

'And why does the old hag howl at the very mention of his name?' Gotrek asked, wiping his mouth on his mud-encrusted arm.

'Gunter is our son. He went out to chop wood this afternoon. He has not returned.'

'Gunter is a good boy,' the old woman sniffled. 'How will we survive without him?'

'Perhaps he is simply lost in the woods?'

'Impossible,' the innkeeper said. 'Gunter knows the woods round here like I know the hairs on my hand. He should have been home hours ago. I fear the coven has taken him, as a sacrifice.'

'It's just like Lotte Hauptmann's daughter, Ingrid,' the fat peddler said. The innkeeper shot him a dirty look.

'I want no tales told of our son's betrothed,' he said.

'Let the man speak,' Gotrek said. The peddler looked at him gratefully.

'The same thing happened last year, in Hartzroch, just down the road. Goodwife Hauptmann looked in on her teenage daughter Ingrid just after sunset. She thought she heard banging coming from her daughter's room. The girl was gone, snatched by who-knows-what sorcerous power from her bed in a locked house. The next day the hue and cry went up. We found Ingrid. She was covered in bruises and in a terrible state.'

He looked at them to make sure he had their attention. 'You asked her what happened?' Felix said.

'Aye, sir. It seems she had been carried off by daemons, wild things of the wood, to Darkstone Ring. There the coven waited with evil creatures from the forests. They made to sacrifice her at the altar but she broke free from her captors and invoked the good name of blessed Sigmar. While they reeled she fled. They pursued her but could not overtake her.'

'That was lucky,' Felix said dryly.

'There is no need to mock, Herr Doktor. We made our way to the stones and we did find all sorts of tracks in the disturbed earth. Including those of humans and beasts and cloven-hoofed daemons. And a yearling infant gutted like a pig upon the altar.'

'Cloven-hoofed daemons?' Gotrek asked. Felix didn't like the look of interest in his eye. The peddler nodded.

'I would not venture up to Darkstone Ring tonight,' the peddler said. 'Not for all the gold in Altdorf.'

'It would be a task fit for a hero,' Gotrek said, looking meaningfully at Felix. Felix was shocked.

'Surely you cannot mean–'

'What better task for a Trollslayer than to face these daemons on their sacred night? It would be a mighty death.'

'It would be a stupid death,' Felix muttered.

'What was that?'

'Nothing.'

'You are coming, aren't you?' Gotrek said menacingly. He was rubbing his thumb along the blade of his axe. Felix noticed that it was bleeding again.

He nodded slowly. 'An oath is an oath.'

The dwarf slapped him upon the back with such force that he thought his ribs would break. 'Sometimes, manling, I think you must have dwarf blood in you. Not that any of the Elder race would stoop to such a mixed marriage, of course.'

He stomped back to his ale.

'Of course,' his companion said, glaring at his back.

FELIX FUMBLED IN his pack for his mail shirt. He noticed that the innkeeper and his wife and the peddlers were looking at him. Their eyes held something that looked close to awe. Gotrek sat near the fire drinking ale and grumbling in dwarfish.

'You're not really going with him?' the fat peddler whispered. Felix nodded.

'Why?'

'He saved my life. I owe him a debt.' Felix thought it best not to mention the circumstances under which Gotrek had saved him.

'I pulled the manling out from under the hooves of the Emperor's cavalry,' Gotrek shouted.

Felix cursed bitterly. The Trollslayer has the hearing of a wild beast as well as the brains of one, he thought to himself, continuing to pull on the mail shirt.

'Aye. The manling thought it clever to put his case to the Emperor with petitions and protest marches. Old Karl Franz chose to respond, quite sensibly, with cavalry charges.'

The peddlers were starting to back away.

'An insurrectionist,' Felix heard one mutter.

Felix felt his face flush. 'It was yet another cruel and unjust tax. A silver piece for every window, indeed. To make it worse, all the fat merchants bricked up their windows and the Altdorf militia went around knocking holes in the side of poor folks' hovels. We were right to speak out.'

'There's a reward for the capture of insurrectionists,' the peddler said. 'A big reward.'

Felix stared at him. 'Of course, the Imperial cavalry were no match for my companion's axe,' he said. 'Such carnage! Heads, legs, arms everywhere. He stood on a pile of bodies.'

'They called for archers,' Gotrek said. 'We departed down a back alley. Being spitted from afar would have been an unseemly death.'

The fat peddler looked at his companions then at Gotrek, then at Felix, then back at his companions. 'A sensible man keeps out of politics,' he said to the man who had talked of rewards. He looked at Felix. 'No offence, sir.'

'None taken,' Felix said. 'You are absolutely correct.'

'Insurrectionist or no,' the old woman said, 'may Sigmar bless you if you bring my little Gunter back.'

'He is not little, Lise,' the innkeeper said. 'He is a strapping young man. Still, I hope you bring my son back. I am old and I need him to chop the wood and shoe the horses and lift the kegs and–'

'I am touched by your paternal concern, sir,' Felix interrupted. He pulled his leather cap down on his head.

Gotrek got up and looked at him. He beat his chest with one meaty hand. 'Armour is for women and girly elves,' he said.

'Perhaps I had best wear it, Gotrek. If I am to return alive with the tale of your deeds – as I did, after all, swear to do.'

'You have a point, manling. And remember that is not all you swore to do.' He turned to the innkeeper. 'How will we find the Darkstone Ring?'

Felix felt his mouth go dry. He fought to keep his hands from shaking.

'There is a trail. It runs from the road. I will take you to its start.'

'Good,' Gotrek said. 'This is too good an opportunity to miss. Tonight I will atone my sins and stand among the Iron Halls of my fathers. Great Grungni willing.'

He made a peculiar sign over his chest with his clenched right hand. 'Come, manling, let us go.' He strode out the door.

Felix picked up his pack. At the doorway the old woman stopped him and pressed something into his hand. 'Please, sir,' she said. 'Take this. It is a charm to Sigmar. It will protect you. My little Gunter wears its twin.'

And much good it's done him, Felix was about to say, but the expression on her face stopped him. It held fear, concern and perhaps hope. He was touched.

'I'll do my best, frau.'

Outside, the sky was bright with the green witchlight of the moons. Felix opened his hand. In it was a small iron hammer on a fine-linked chain. He shrugged and hung it round his neck. Gotrek and the old man were already moving down the road. He had to run to catch up.

The story continues in

GOTREK & FELIX
THE FIRST OMNIBUS

by William King

Available from The Black Library
www.blacklibrary.com